BONES OF THE BURIED

Also by David Roberts:

Sweet Poison

BONES OF
THE BURIED

DAVID ROBERTS

CARROLL & GRAF PUBLISHERS
New York

MYS
R6437160

Carroll & Graf Publishers
An imprint of Avalon Publishing Group, Inc.
161 William Street
16th Floor
NY 10038-2607
www.carrollandgraf.com

First published in the UK by Constable,
an imprint of Constable & Robinson Ltd 2001

First Carroll & Graf edition 2001

ISBN 0-7867-0908-1

Printed and bound in the EU

For Olivia

Don Adriano de Armado: The sweet war-man is dead and rotten; sweet chucks, beat not the bones of the buried; when he breathed, he was a man.

William Shakespeare Love's Labour's Lost

Prologue – Eton, 1917

'Boy!' The call echoed round the house and a scurry of small black-garbed figures raced to answer it, slithering to a halt outside the library. Eight senior boys in the house constituted 'the library' and it was also the name given to the room they used as a common-room. It had almost no books in it – just a broken-backed sofa, several armchairs, all of which had seen better days, and a table with one leg amputated at the knee, supported uncertainly by a pile of textbooks. There was also a dartboard, a wind-up gramophone with a spectacular horn, a few records in brown paper sleeves and an ancient kettle. Next to the grate, beside a couple of toasting forks, a bunch of canes rested negligently against the wall, assuming an air of innocence which belied the very real threat that lay behind their willowy form.

The last in line was, as always, Featherstone, a small boy dressed in bum-freezers. This was the uniform reserved for first-year Etonians below a certain height. The short coat, cut off just above the posterior, contrasted with the tail coats worn by all the other boys and marked him out as the lowest form of school life. Oliver Featherstone was very miserable. He badly missed his father who, out of love, had inflicted upon him this particular torture. His father was the owner of several oil wells in Persia but, to Oliver's great grief, was also the proprietor of a famous department store on Oxford Street in London. His mother, whom he rarely saw, was a film actress whose photograph appeared in picture-papers on both sides of the Atlantic.

Unfortunately, he had discovered that neither his father's wealth nor his mother's celebrity was anything to be proud of at

1

Eton. What was worse, his father's name was not really Feather-stone but Federstein. There were several Jews at Eton, one of whom was a member of Pop, the select society of popular boys which ran the school, but the Jews whom Eton welcomed, as Oliver painfully discovered, were the sons of merchant bankers who had bankrolled the government and the monarchy for almost a century. None of these held out to him the hand of friendship. Despite his wealth, his father had himself been ostracised from polite society and, in a clumsy attempt to ease his son's passage through the school and protect him from bullying, had tried to conceal his origins by changing the spell-ing of his surname. It took only three weeks for it to become known that Featherstone was really Federstein and that his father was 'a grocer'. Oliver at once became the innocent victim of his father's subterfuge.

'Federstein!' All the other small boys ran away chirruping gratefully like a swoop of starlings.

'Yes, Hoden?' said Oliver, wearily.

Hoden scribbled on a piece of paper, folded it several times and thrust it at him. 'Take this to Stephen Thayer at Chandler's, and hurry.'

'But Hoden, please! I've got an essay for tomorrow and I've already had three rips. My tutor said it would be PS next time.'

'Well, you'd better run then,' said Hoden unsympathetically. When a boy's work was not up to scratch the master – or beak as he was called at Eton – would tear it at the top and the errant pupil would have to take it to show his housemaster. Too many rips would result in Penal Servitude – PS for short – which involved sacrificing already scarce free time on 'extra work'.

Highly disgruntled, Oliver set off at a run down Judy's Passage, the narrow pedestrian way which threaded the red-brick buildings, the last of which was Stephen Thayer's house. Half-way, he got a stitch in his side and slowed to a walk. There was a large stone, big enough for a small boy to sit on, where the path made a dog-leg and there, strictly against the rules, Oliver perched and unfolded the note Hoden had given him. It read: 'Stevie, can you meet me underneath the arches tomorrow after six. Send word by the oily Jewboy, love, M. PS But he is rather pretty isn't he?'

Oliver's eyes began to water. How dare this horrible man call him an oily Jewboy, and pretty. Neither his father nor his mother had told him anything about sex before he went to school. Had he but known it, his mother was an expert on the subject but, in his eyes, she was as pure as a garden rose and it would have embarrassed him horribly if she had said anything with a view to preparing him for life in an English public school. As for his father, he assumed that in some magical way his son was to be transformed into an English gentleman, in his view a creature second only to the gods themselves. He visualised Eton as holy water in which his son would be purified. It was odd that a man so generally shrewd in the affairs of the world should be so naive when it came to baptism.

Oliver looked at his hand with horror. In his anguish, and without being aware of what he was doing, he had scrumpled up Hoden's note. He couldn't deliver it now without Thayer knowing that he had opened it but he dared not go back without an answer. The tears began to trickle down his cheeks. Half-blinded by the savage grief of childhood, he did not notice that someone was walking down the passage towards him. It was the very boy to whom he was to deliver the note.

'What's up, Featherstone – that is your name, isn't it? Come now, why are you blubbing?'

He spoke not unkindly and Oliver was persuaded to hold up the crumpled piece of paper for his inspection. 'I'm . . . I'm truly sorry, Thayer. I didn't mean to open it. It just sort of came undone.'

Thayer took the note, read it and blushed deeply. He bit his lip and tried to decide what to say. He knew he could get into bad trouble if the substance of the message came to the attention of his housemaster, and Hoden would certainly be sacked. Homosexual feelings, though common enough in a single sex school, or indeed because they were so common, were anathema to the authorities and no housemaster would hesitate to have a boy removed from the school if anything of the kind was proved against him.

Damn Hoden, Thayer thought. He really would have to drop him. 'Stop all that noise, Featherstone. No one's going to punish you but really, you know, it was very wrong of you to open a private note.'

'Ye . . . s,' Oliver agreed. 'Should I say anything to Hoden? He may want to whack me.'

3

'No,' said Thayer hurriedly. 'Don't do that. I got the message and no one else saw it. We'll leave it at that. No harm done.'

'No . . .? Thank you, sir.'

'Don't call me "sir", you little idiot. You only call beaks "sir".'

'Yes, Thayer.'

'Oh, and don't get upset about people calling you . . . names. You can't help being . . . whatever it is he said you were . . . not oily I mean but the other. It's nothing to be ashamed of. Now off you go, and remember: say nothing of this to anyone or you will get into trouble.'

'Yes, Thayer. And thank you,' said the small boy, managing a smile. Could it be that this god figure, a member of Pop and therefore one of Eton's elect, was going to forgive him, to be compassionate? It never occurred to him for a moment that he, the most miserable of worms, had through an accident, through his own clumsiness, gained a measure of power over one so mighty. He looked at Thayer, noticing him for the first time as a person – his expensively cut hair, his coloured waistcoat, which only members of Pop could wear, gleaming like armour, his buttonhole freshly cut that morning in his tutor's garden. From his white 'stick-up' collar to his shoes shiny enough to reflect his face, Thayer was perfect and Oliver felt an overwhelming desire to fall on his knees and worship.

In his second 'half' at Eton, Oliver began to enjoy himself. In the way of small boys, he quickly forgot the misery of his first half, though he kept out of Hoden's way as much as possible. He even made a few friends and almost anything is bearable with a friend to commiserate with you. And Eton had a lot to offer. He took to the pleasures of the river and would take a 'whiff' upriver to Queen's Eyot, a little island where he could eat sausage and mash, drink the weakest of beer and read. Reading was his chief pleasure. With books he could escape to . . . to wherever he desired and he did still want to escape. He found too that he was musical and would spend hours in the music school trying to master the piano, with some success.

In fact, sex was the only thing which spoiled Oliver's life – not his own feelings, which had not yet begun to trouble him, but he was bewildered and distressed by the attention of some older boys. Hoden, in particular, would summon him to the library and maul him about until he wept, when he would be

4

contemptuously dismissed. One afternoon – this was in the summer half and the days were long and hot – he happened to be in the house instead of on the river. He had strained a muscle in his leg and had been told not to take out his whiff for a couple of days. The dreaded cry of 'boy' sounded round the virtually empty building and, with a groan, Oliver left his book and ran to answer it. It did not cross his mind that he might safely ignore the summons. When he arrived, he found he was the only boy to have answered the call and resigned himself to carrying some stupid message to another house or making some lazy senior a cup of tea.

He knocked on the door and opened it when a hoarse voice shouted, 'Come!'

He recognised the voice immediately as belonging to Hoden and his heart missed a beat. But, when he was in the room, he saw that Hoden's friend, Tilney, was also there and his spirits rose a little. Surely Hoden would not try anything on in this other boy's presence. But he was wrong.

'Ah, Federstein.' Hoden took pleasure in making the name sound as foreign as possible. 'You've come at last. My friend Tilney here doesn't believe that you can act but I heard you had a part in the school play – Shakespeare?'

'*Love's Labour's Lost*, but I've only a very small part, Hoden.'

'So I've always imagined,' Hoden sniggered. 'As a girl, I understand?'

'Yes,' said Oliver miserably.

'Well, Tilney and I want to "hear your lines". Isn't that what thespians say?'

'Oh, I . . . I don't know them yet.'

'Well, we'll assist you.'

'No, I can't remember . . .'

'I think it might help,' Hoden said, 'if you took off some of your clothes.' He pretended to appeal to Tilney who was smirking uneasily at his friend's teasing. 'He can't pretend to be a girl dressed in trousers, now can he, Tilney old man?'

'I should say not,' said the other boy as heartily as he could manage.

'Take off your clothes, Federstein. We want to see if you're a girl.'

'No, please, Hoden, let me go, won't you.'

Oliver was now very frightened. He was not physically brave and he was almost excessively modest. He hated undressing in the bathroom with other boys and one of the things he most appreciated about Eton was that even 'new boys' had separate rooms and did not sleep in dormitories.

'I won't, Hoden. Tilney, tell him to leave me alone.'

'Oh, let the little sod go,' Tilney said lazily, but Hoden now had the taste of blood.

'No, Tilney, this little Jewboy has to be taught a lesson. Here, help me take his trousers off so I can whack him.'

Reluctantly, Tilney got up from the sofa and seized hold of the wriggling boy as Hoden removed first his 'bum-freezer' jacket, and then his shirt. By this time Oliver was in tears and, as Hoden began to tug frantically at the boy's trousers, Tilney said, 'I say, I think we ought to let the little tyke go.'

'No fear,' said Hoden, picking up a cane from the pile in the corner and striking at Oliver's back. 'Stand still, you malodorous animal, if you don't want to get badly hurt,' he ordered, waving the cane over his head as if he were trying to swat a fly. Then he screamed. A lucky kick from Oliver's flying heels had caught him on the shin. 'That does it, Tilney, I'm going to show the little Jew what for.'

He raised the cane above his shoulder but, before he could strike, the library door opened and Stephen Thayer entered. He took in the scene at a glance. He strode over to Hoden and tore the cane from his grasp. Without a word he swung it hard against Hoden's cheek, raising a red weal as thick as the bamboo. Hoden screamed again and let go of Oliver who gathered up his clothes and fled.

Oliver's awe of Thayer was transformed in a moment to love. When several days later he met him as they were both taking boats off the racks, he tried to say something of what he felt.

'Oh, Thayer, I wanted to thank you . . . but why are you going on the river? I thought you were a drybob.'

'I am, but I like to scull when I have the time. And please – don't thank me. I've told Hoden and Tilney if they ever come near you again I will have them sacked. I don't think they will try anything like that again but if they do – tell me.'

'Oh, Thayer, thank you. I suppose there's nothing I can do for you, is there?'

'No, certainly not . . . though wait a minute.' He pretended an idea had just struck him. 'Isn't your mater the film star, Dora Pale?'

Oliver blushed. 'Oh yes, I'm sorry, Thayer. I keep it as quiet as I can.'

'No, you silly beggar, you misunderstand me. I would like to meet her if that were possible. Does she ever come down to see you?'

'No, I told her not to.'

'Well then, ask her . . . to please me.'

'Oh gosh . . . yes, Thayer, I will, but are you sure? You won't . . . you won't laugh?'

'Oh no,' Stephen said, 'I won't laugh.'

Her skin was almost translucent. 'Pale, pale Dora, adorable Dora Pale,' he murmured, turning over in bed to stroke her cheek. 'You're not asleep so why pretend you are? Do you know you have freckles? Would you like me to lick them off for you?'

'I do not have freckles,' Dora said, her eyes still shut.

'You do,' he said stroking her stomach in the way he knew she liked.

'You know, Stephen, you're almost as good-looking as you think you are, but you've got a pimple coming just here,' she pinched him quite hard on the cheek, 'and what does that tell us?'

'Ouch, that hurt. So what does it tell us, mistress mine?'

'It tells us, Master Thayer, that you are still a child and I don't sleep with children.'

'Oh but you do . . . frightfully well.' He turned his handsome head to look at her and she met his stare unblinkingly. His eyes were black and lustrous and his eyebrows met above his nose in a dramatic slash of black.

'I do it "frightfully well",' she mocked. 'Well, perhaps I do occasionally make exceptions. I like to think of myself as a teacher. Do you like me to teach you?'

'Extra-curricular coaching.' He mouthed each syllable lovingly. 'We call it extra work, you know.'

'Huh! Extra work, you young . . . ah!' He had touched her and she had responded as he knew she would. 'Again, touch me there again. That's . . . right. You're a good student and one day your wife will have cause to thank me. Wait!' There was a knock on the door. 'Be a good boy and open the door, Stephen. I ordered more champagne.'

He rolled out of bed, slung on a white bathrobe and went to the door and opened it.

'Over there by the window . . .' he began to say, and then stopped and wrapped the robe round him more tightly. 'Oh, it's you. What are you doing here? I thought you were on the river.'

Oliver looked past his friend and mentor to the rumpled bed.

'Who is it, darling?' Dora said, raising her head a little off the pillow. Her eyes met those of her son which opened wider than might have been thought possible.

'Oh Christ! Oliver, darling, it's not what you think. We were just . . . we were just talking.'

The boy had still not said a word but his mouth hung open and the pupils of his eyes were dilated. He looked from his mother to his friend and back again. Then he turned and ran down the corridor sobbing. Stephen, white-faced, turned to the woman in the bed who now seemed not the desirable sex siren he had just made love to so violently but a middle-aged woman with lines under her eyes and bleached hair showing dark at the roots. 'I'd better get dressed and go after him,' he mumbled.

'Oh Christ,' she said again. 'Oh Christ!' Wearily, she let her head fall back upon the lipstick-stained pillow.

Part One

1

It was good to be home. Lord Edward Corinth lay in his bath splashing himself contentedly with an enormous yellow sponge. Now and again he put it on his head and let the water dribble over his eyes and ears to lubricate his brain, which felt arid and infertile after the transatlantic crossing. He had disembarked from the *Normandie* at Southampton, along with the other English passengers, at seven o'clock the previous morning, and reached his rooms in Albany six hours later. His man, Fenton had grilled him a chop, which he washed down with half a bottle of Perrier-Jouet and then, overcome with lassitude, he had strolled round to the hammam in Jermyn Street. Steamed, scrubbed and massaged within an inch of his life, he had slept in his cubicle for an hour. Then, feeling a little restored but as weak as a newborn lamb, he had tottered round to his club in St James's. There, he hid himself away in a corner unable to face social intercourse and had Barney, the smoking-room waiter, bring him potted shrimps, scrambled eggs, angels on horseback, along with a weak whisky and soda. After which he had snoozed in his chair for half an hour and then crawled back home. He toyed with a pile of letters which lay on his desk but could not face opening any of them and was in bed not much after nine.

This morning he had awoken refreshed but still curiously reluctant to face the world, despite having looked forward for so long to seeing his old friends and revisiting old haunts. In the six months he had been away, an era had ended with the death of the King on January 20th. The new King, Edward VIII, with his film-star good looks and easy charm, was hugely popular, to judge from what he read in the papers, but he was mistrusted by the 'old guard' who suspected he lacked his father's sense of duty. They did not like his friends either. In New York, Edward had heard disquieting rumours concerning his lady friend, Mrs Simpson, a divorcée of dubious morals. It looked as though 1936 would prove to be an interesting year.

He submerged himself in the rapidly cooling water until only his aquiline nose showed above the surface like the periscope of a submarine. He suspected that Dr Freud, whose works he had been perusing on the boat coming over, might mutter something to the effect that his bath provided a womb into which he could retreat when in need of comfort and reassurance, and it was true that just the sight of this huge, ornate iron bath, standing four-square in the centre of the room on massive gilt claws, had always aroused in him a most profound sense of well-being. The United States – well, New York – seemed to assume its denizens preferred showering to lying in a soup of bath salts and soap, and the *Normandie* – beyond criticism in every other respect – boasted baths which, to be enjoyed, demanded amputation at the knees. Luxurious though that great ship was, the next time he crossed the Atlantic he promised himself a berth on the *Queen Mary*, which was about to set out on her maiden voyage. All the talk on the *Normandie* had been of this new Cunard liner whose launch demonstrated that the economic depression was at last raising its dead hand from British industry. Among the passengers wagers were given and taken on whether or not it would wrest the Blue Riband from the *Normandie* which, ever since it had made its first transatlantic crossing the previous year, had been hailed as a miracle of engineering and the acme of luxury.

Edward supposed the first-class passengers were, for the most part, good enough people but, to his jaundiced eye, they appeared a seedy set – American millionaires, their women decorated like Christmas trees, and every kind of mountebank and charlatan. He recognised one South American card-sharp he had punched in the face on a railway train out of Valparaíso three years before. Edward watched him playing poker with a Hollywood producer and his girlfriend and, as he was pondering whether or not to warn them that they were about to be fleeced, the man caught his eye and had the gall to give him a wink. Edward supposed he ought to advise the company that there were sharks on board even if there were none in the ocean, but how to distinguish the predators from their victims? He decided he did not care enough to work it out. One evening, at dinner in the art deco glory of the first-class Café Grill, a little actress, her hair unnaturally blonde and her lips coated in vermilion – attached, he thought, to a German businessman of quite staggering corpulence – offered herself to him for dessert and he had suddenly felt disgusted with himself and the company he was keeping.

Yes, it was good to be home. He loved New York. It invigorated him; the skyscrapers, the noise, the bustle, even the sight of the policemen, dressed up to look like postmen, gave him an electrical charge. Each evening, as he walked down Fifth Avenue in the direction of Broadway, he found himself whistling. He had made a host of friends there. He had been elected an honorary member of the Knickerbocker, the city's most exclusive club, which he privately thought was even duller and more hidebound than the Athenaeum, but it was in the night-clubs, long after working New Yorkers had taken to their beds, that he and Amy dined and danced till there was light in the sky. Amy Pageant, the girl on his arm, was Broadway's newest, brightest star, and the couple had been fêted in a manner which would have turned him into a conceited ass if he had not realised that their popularity, pleasant though it was, was so much hooey.

The dream could not last. Six months after Amy had flung herself into his arms in her dressing-room at the Alvin Theatre, they had regretfully come to the conclusion that they were not, after all, in love with one another. There had been nothing so tacky as his finding her *in flagrante delicto* with her leading man, but he was wise enough to see that she was indeed on the point of falling for a wealthy sprig of New York society. Better to bow out gracefully than be ejected from her apartment after some slanging match in which both parties said things they did not mean but which left genuine hurt. No, Edward had kissed her, told her she would always have a place in his heart – that they would share some very special memories. She, for her part, had wept, whispered tender regrets in his ear but, in the end, had not tried to shake him in his resolve to return to England and find something to do which might stretch him.

'I'm not cut out to be a lotus-eater, darling,' he had told Amy. 'I'm getting lazy and that turns me into a dull dog. You are

13

already a great star, but you still have a world to conquer and it wouldn't be right for me to hang on your coat-tails like some stage-door johnny until we hated the sight of each other.'

'Never that!' she exclaimed. 'You and I discovered each other before any of this . . .' She waved her arms vaguely at the bed with its pink silk sheets, the champagne bobbing in the silver ice bucket, the vases of flowers that bedecked every available surface – the evidence of a glorious 'first night' when she had glittered in a Gershwin musical which looked set to run as long as she was prepared to star in it. 'You and I will always be . . . a part of one another.'

But she had not begged him to stay and so they had parted, still a little in love with one another, basking in a relationship from which both had drawn strength. Though Amy would not have said it or even thought it out with cold, deliberate logic, it had helped her career to be seen with the wealthy, good-looking brother of an English duke. It had given her glamour and status – made her invulnerable to the sneers of society matrons and eased her passage into the centre of what Edward called 'Vanderbilt City'. She acknowledged in her heart that he gave her much more than status: he was older than she, for one thing – almost thirty-five – and absolutely at ease with his own place in society. She had been brought up by two elderly aunts on Canada's new frontier and seen nothing of the world until she had come to London to meet the father who had abandoned her almost at birth. A few months later, she had been whisked off to New York by a theatrical agent who had been taken to see her singing in a Soho night-club and had recognised star-quality when he saw it.

It could be lonely on the Great White Way, even frightening. So much was expected of her and, when she delivered, they expected more and, inevitably, success brought enemies. The society gossip columnists had interspersed adulation with little spiteful dagger-thrusts of speculation and rumour. She was the daughter of the Canadian press lord, Joseph Weaver, but there was something mysterious there. She had appeared from nowhere. Was she his illegitimate child by a mistress he had turned away when he was quite a young man? There was certainly no word of any mother. Amy was able to brush off the innuendoes and the spite but there were evenings when she

14

would read some lie about herself and run and bury her face in Edward's shoulder and sob as if she were still a lonely, abandoned child.

Now, back in London, lying in his bath in his spacious if rather spartan rooms, Edward hummed contentedly to himself one of his favourite songs from *Girl Crazy*: 'Boy! What Love Has Done To Me!' Amy had sung it in the show and it still sent shivers down his spine. He could hear Fenton in the little kitchen preparing his breakfast. Unexpectedly, Fenton had adored New York and had been reluctant to leave it. Edward had heard that he had been offered a position as butler to one of the city's 'royal families' and had been touched that he had in the end decided to stay as his gentleman's personal gentleman. Nothing was ever said between the two of them about the temptation which had been resisted but Edward noticed that Fenton would on occasion drop American phrases into his conversation and his breakfast eggs might be offered him 'easy-over' or 'sunny-side up'.

Edward resurfaced and made a determined effort not to think of Amy. He was content to be back in London. Or rather he was not content yet, but he was determined to find a cure for his restlessness. While he had been in New York, he had received a letter from an old Eton and Cambridge friend with a high, if ill-defined, position in the Foreign Office, offering him what sounded very much like a job. Basil Thoroughgood was too canny to commit to paper a form of words which might be construed as anything quite as definite but there was certainly the offer of lunch and 'a chat'. Edward had cabled that he expected to be in London on February 18th and had been surprised to receive a 'wireless' half-way across the Atlantic which set one o'clock at Brooks's – the club of which they were both members – on the 19th, only his second day back in the metropolis. It hinted at urgency on Thoroughgood's part but Edward could scarcely believe it. Unless Thoroughgood was a different young man from the slouching, half-asleep character he remembered from the university, he would have laid odds on 'urgent' not being a word in his vocabulary.

His musings were interrupted by the muffled sound of knocking and then the noise of Fenton opening the door to the apartment and exchanging some sort of greeting. Edward

15

stopped soaping himself and tried to make out who this unreasonably early visitor could possibly be. Confound it all, he thought irritably, couldn't he even get dressed and have his breakfast in peace? In any case, as far as he was aware, no one, except Thoroughgood, knew he was back in London, and none of his friends – if they had, in some magical way, discovered he was back in town – would have dreamed of calling on him before ten o'clock at the earliest and he knew for a fact that it was only a little after nine.

After a few more moments of puzzlement, he heard Fenton's respectful knock on the bathroom door.

'What is it? Did I hear someone at the door, Fenton?'

'Yes, my lord, there is a lady who wishes to speak with you.'

'A lady? But I am in my bath. Did you tell her I was in my bath, Fenton?'

'I did, my lord, and she said she would wait.'

Edward splashed angrily and yanked at the chain with the plug attached to it. All the pleasure of the bath leaked away with the water and, as he towelled himself, he called, 'You haven't told me who it is, Fenton, who breaks in upon my ablutions at this ridiculously early hour.'

There was something cold and wet in the pit of his stomach – not the sponge lying abandoned on the wooden bath mat – which warned that he knew perfectly well the identity of his unexpected guest. There was only one among his many female friends and acquaintances who would have the nerve to visit a young man in his rooms without prior appointment and before that young man had got outside eggs and bacon, and that was a girl who ought to be in Spain.

'It is Miss Browne, my lord.'

'Verity! I knew it!'

'Yes, my lord.'

Edward was almost sure he heard Fenton add under his breath, 'I am afraid to say.' Fenton did not approve of Verity. It wasn't just that she exhibited a contempt for the tried and tested conventions of good society which he held to be sacred. It wasn't even because she had a job – she was a journalist, a foreign correspondent no less, for Lord Weaver's *New Gazette* – when she should have been content with a husband, babies and a string of pearls. What shocked Fenton to the core of his being

16

was that Verity Browne was an avowed communist, communism being a political philosophy of which Fenton had the greatest suspicion. What right had girls – that is to say nicely brought-up young ladies and Verity Browne was certainly one of these – to have political opinions at all? In short, in Fenton's view, Verity Browne, though in many ways a charming young lady, was not someone whom he could ever esteem. She was pretty – he could admit that. She was plucky – he had direct evidence of her fighting spirit. She had money; she dressed and spoke like a lady, so it made it all the more inexcusable that she did not behave like one.

'Tell her I will be out in a jiffy,' Edward called as he stropped his razor and stirred up a storm in his soap tin with his badger-hair shaving brush.

'Very good, my lord,' said Fenton gloomily.

'Oh, and ply her with coffee and kippers, will you.'

When Edward burst into the dining-room ten minutes later – partially clothed, his tow-coloured hair not yet laid low by his ivory-backed hairbrushes – he was full of questions and complaints but these died on his lips unuttered. He was brought up short by Verity's appearance. The merry, plump-faced child he had sparred with six months earlier had become a woman. She had cut her hair short as a boy's. Her face, if not actually gaunt, was thin and spoke of poor food and too little of it. Her skin was pale and the smudges under her eyes indicated that she was under considerable strain and not sleeping properly. He hesitated – for only a moment – before going over and kissing her on the cheek but she had seen his surprise – no doubt had anticipated it – and said, with a wry smile, 'As bad as that?'

'No! I mean, of course not, Verity. It is splendid to see you after so long. I just thought ... I just thought you looked too thin. How long are you going to be in London? Have I got time and permission to fatten you up?'

Verity smiled and put her head on one side and was once again the light-hearted bird of a girl he had ... he had almost ... no, damn it! the girl he *had* loved the previous summer when they had joined forces to discover the killer of one of the Duke of Mersham's guests – the Duke being Edward's elder brother.

'No, I'm sorry,' she said. 'At least, not here. I have to be back in Madrid the day after tomorrow.'

17

'So I won't see you again?'

'Well, that was why I came here. I was hoping you would come with me.'

'To Spain!' he said in amazement. 'Why? What has happened?'

Verity laughed – a little guiltily, he thought. 'Maybe I just wanted your company . . . but no,' she said, her face clouding over. 'You're right. Something has happened.'

'To David?' inquired Edward with a flash of understanding.

'How did you guess?' said Verity rather bitterly. 'Yes, something has happened to David.'

Edward drew Verity down into a chair and watched her closely as Fenton provided her with black coffee. She waved away his offer of eggs and bacon but asked for a cigarette. Edward proffered his gold cigarette case and was concerned to see her hand was shaking so much that she had some difficulty in extracting one. He lit it for her and she inhaled gratefully. 'That's good. It's hard to get American cigarettes in Madrid.'

'I didn't even know you smoked.'

'I do now,' she said shortly.

'Tell me what has happened and how I can help,' he said calmly, studiously avoiding any hint of 'lean-on-my-shoulder-little-woman', which he knew she would detest.

'You've not seen anything in the papers then?'

'The English papers? No, what have I missed? You see, I only returned from New York yesterday and . . .'

'Oh, of course,' said Verity drily. 'And how is Amy? I gather she is quite a star now.'

There was something so sour about the way Verity said this that Edward gazed at her with surprise and hurt.

'I'm sorry,' said Verity, seeing the look on his face. She put out a hand and timidly laid it on his. 'I mean, I am delighted . . . really pleased . . . for you both.'

'Oh, as for that, there's no "both" about it. We're just chums, don't you know.' Edward got up and went over to the coffee tray on the table and refilled his cup, anxious that Verity should not see his face and guess at his real feelings. He felt something on his cheek and rubbed at it with his fingers. He was surprised to see it was a fleck of blood. He must have nicked himself shaving. He turned to Verity and showed her his hand. 'Love

18

lies bleeding.' If it was a joke, neither of them laughed. 'Tell me about David,' he said more firmly. 'Is he in danger or what?'

David Griffiths-Jones was the man Verity respected most in the world. He had been her lover – Edward knew that for a fact – and still was as far as he was aware, but he was a cold fish and Verity certainly did not have the look of a woman in the middle of a love affair. He and Griffiths-Jones were natural enemies; they had been at Cambridge together but while Griffiths-Jones had become a committed Communist Party worker, Edward had come to hate everything the Party stood for and not just because 'social justice' seemed to involve hanging people like him from lamp-posts or at least curtailing their personal liberty 'in the interests of the proletariat'.

Edward believed passionately in personal liberty, although he accepted it did not mean much if one were a slave to poverty. He regarded with suspicion any political party – on the right or the left – which claimed to be acting in the interests of the working class. Everything he had seen of Fascism disgusted him but he was convinced that one did not have to espouse communism to be anti-Fascist. He had listened to David Griffiths-Jones and Verity go on about 'the proletariat' and 'the working classes' as though working people were little better than sheep needing a shepherd. If the shepherds were going to be of Griffiths-Jones' persuasion, he foresaw they would 'fold' their charges into the abattoir.

He distinguished, however, between genuinely good-hearted idealists such as Verity, misguided though they might be, and cold, calculating ideologues, such as Griffiths-Jones, obsessed with 'the masses', a meaningless class definition in his view. But, if Edward were honest with himself, his political differences with David Griffiths-Jones were exacerbated by their locking of horns over Verity. No word of love had ever been spoken between Verity and himself, but there was some sort of understanding between them which probably neither of them would have been able or indeed willing to define. As far as Edward could see, Verity was completely in the other man's thrall. He had commanded her to go to Spain with him and she had obeyed. She was to promote the communist cause by writing for Lord Weaver's *New Gazette*, and for the *Daily Worker*, the official organ of the Communist Party, describing the political struggle

19

in Spain in terms of communism – good – against Fascism – evil – when even Edward knew it was something much more complicated. To be fair to Verity, the three or four reports of hers he had read in the *New Gazette* had seemed honest attempts to report the truth of the situation, so maybe she had too much integrity to toe the Party line as closely as Griffiths-Jones would like.

'He's in gaol,' she said bluntly.

Edward took a breath and said coolly, 'What is he supposed to have done?'

'He's done nothing!' She looked at him accusingly, as if he would automatically disbelieve her.

'Yes, I expect not, but what do they say he's done?' he said, rubbing his forehead, which he always did when he was surprised.

Verity stuck out her chin. 'Oh, it's all nonsense. He hasn't done anything, I tell you.'

'Yes,' said Edward patiently, 'but what's he accused of?'

'They say he killed a man,' she said reluctantly. 'They say he's a murderer.'

Verity blurted out the word 'murderer' as if she could still hardly credit it. Edward was not quite as shocked as perhaps he ought to have been. He had always considered David Griffiths-Jones to be one of the most dangerous men he knew and was reasonably certain that, if the Party required it of him, he could kill – might already have done so. Edward had the faintest suspicion that, deep down, Verity thought so too but this was clearly not a good moment to explore the idea.

'So tell me about it,' he said, leaning back in his chair. 'Who is he supposed to have killed, and when did it happen?'

'Over a month ago. He was arrested on January 10th.'

'And when is his trial?' He spoke with studied neutrality. He could sense that she wanted to hit out at someone and, if he gave any sign of pitying her, her carefully prepared defences might crumble. She would hate herself and him if she burst into tears. It must have taken some courage, or maybe sheer desperation, for her to come to him. She knew how he felt about David, the Party, and her rushing off to Spain, but she had trusted him enough to come to him at this moment of crisis. He tried not to feel pleased. At all costs he must not seem to be taking advantage of her.

'Oh, he has been tried,' she said airily. 'He's going to be shot next week unless you can think of something to make them change their mind.'

'Shot?'

'Or garrotted – no, shot. Spain has joined the twentieth century.'

Edward gulped. If what Verity said was true, there was absolutely nothing he or anyone else could do to save the man. If Griffiths-Jones had been tried by a Spanish court and convicted of murder, how could Verity possibly think he might be able to do anything about it? It was absurd.

'Oh gosh, Verity, that's awful but . . . but what can I do? I mean, I don't suppose even the Prime Minister could do anything,' he said weakly.

' "Oh gosh"!' Verity mimicked him scathingly. 'Is that all you can say? Has your brain been softened by champagne and canapés? Of course we can do something about it. We can find out who really did kill Tilney, for one thing.'

Edward's ears pricked. 'He was an Englishman – the man who . . . who got himself killed?' he said, leaving Griffiths-Jones out of it.

'Yes, didn't I say so? That's why I have come to you.'

'How do you mean?'

'For God's sake, Edward: wake up! Godfrey Tilney – he was at school with you, wasn't he? That's what he always said.'

'Godfrey Tilney!' Edward exclaimed. 'Well, I'm damned. Tilney dead? What happened, Verity?'

'No one really knows,' she said more calmly. 'He and David were out together – on some Party work I think, but that was never gone into at the trial and David's not saying anything. They were out the whole day – in the mountains – and David came back alone. He said that Tilney had left him to go back on his own. Apparently, he said to David that he wanted to go and see a friend on the way home.'

'Who was the friend?'

'No one knows and naturally the police thought David had invented it. I told them that if he had wanted to make up a story

21

about why he had parted from Tilney when he did, he would have come up with something much better, but they weren't interested.'

'And Tilney? When . . . when was his body . . .?'

'Tilney's body was discovered the next morning by a shepherd,' Verity said. 'He – Tilney – had a knife in his stomach.'

Edward, bewildered by what he was being told, could only come out with: 'But surely, someone else could have stabbed him?'

'That's right, they could have, and what's more they did,' said Verity animatedly. 'It is a wild area in the mountains. Lots of brigands and God knows what.'

'So why were they so certain David had killed Tilney?'

'Oh well, mainly because it was David's knife.'

'What! You mean whoever it was who found the body discovered David's knife in him?'

'Yes, in him or beside him, I'm not sure which, but there are many ways the knife could have . . .' Before Edward could say, name three, Verity changed tack. 'He would hardly have left his knife in Tilney if he really had done the killing.'

'That's true,' said Edward grudgingly. 'How does David say the knife got . . . there? Did he lose it?'

'He says he either lost it or it was stolen.'

'What sort of knife was it?'

'It was a Swiss Army knife. He always carried it.'

'Not such an easy thing to kill someone with,' said Edward, thinking aloud. 'How long before the killing had he missed the knife?'

'He can't remember. Look, Edward, you've just got to take it from me: he didn't kill Tilney or anyone else. You've got to come over and find out who did do it.'

Edward heard the desperation in her voice. 'But how much time do we have, Verity?' he said, feeling panic rising inside him. 'I thought you said he was being executed next week.'

'That's right, but I thought if you could get hold of Tilney's parents and ask them to plead for a stay of execution . . .'

Edward's eyes goggled. 'You what?'

'Well, you do know his parents, don't you?'

'I met them,' he admitted, 'but that was a long time ago. But look here, even if I did get to see them and, even more unlikely,

22

if they were persuaded to plead for a stay of execution, I can't imagine for one moment the authorities would take any notice . . .'

'Oh really,' said Verity in exasperation, 'I don't understand you, Edward. Last year you were a different man. Your will seems to have been sapped by good living or something. Didn't your nanny ever tell you there's no such word as "can't"? I haven't got time to argue with you; David needs me. Are you coming with me or not?'

There was such pain behind her appeal, there was no way in which he could refuse. 'Of course I'll come but I can't work miracles. Don't think I can.'

Verity's face lit up. 'There, I knew you had it in you. Weaver has put an aeroplane at our disposal,' she added importantly. 'I must say, Joe has come up absolute trumps over this. Although he has no sympathy with the Party, he has campaigned for David from the moment he was accused. He's been a real duck, but . . .' she added meditatively, 'I'm not sure David likes it.'

'Being beholden to the capitalist press?'

'Yes, still, it can't be helped. I will use anything or anyone to save him.' She spoke with all the grim determination which had made him admire her the year before.

'Even me?' he said nastily.

She grinned. 'Even you.'

'What are you going to do now?' said Edward feebly.

'I'm going in to the *New Gazette*. As I say, Joe – Lord Weaver – is running a campaign in the paper – Free Griffiths-Jones – that sort of thing, but I have to say, it hasn't worked yet.'

Edward paused. If Verity really had persuaded Weaver – who was not a communist and was opposed to everything David Griffiths-Jones represented – to campaign for his release, either there must be something she was not telling him or Weaver had some ulterior motive of which she was unaware. What that could be he had no idea but it crossed his mind that the press lord was a notorious womaniser.

'I have seen some of your reports from Spain – jolly good. I mean, very powerful . . .'

'Oh, shut up, Edward. You don't know what you are talking about. There seems to be no one in this bloody country who knows or cares what is happening in Spain. They don't seem to understand that it's not just domestic politics – it's the beginning of a war. Oh God, why do I bother . . .'

Edward was hurt. Verity seemed to have come to him with the idea he might help her and was now going away in the belief that he was a spineless fish. Also, he did not approve of her language. He was about to say something to the effect that there was really nothing he could do to help her or Griffiths-Jones, and if a Spanish court had found him guilty of murder, then he probably was, when he saw that tears were streaming down her face. He rescued the coffee cup which she was holding so limply the black liquid was running on to the carpet and then went down on his knees and put his arms around her.

'I'm sorry, Verity. I'm not being much help, am I? Look, I'll get going straight away. Do you know where the Tilneys live?'

'Yes, the *New Gazette* interviewed them. They live in Bedford Square. I've got the address and telephone number here.' She thrust a scrap of paper at him.

'Excellent!' he said, taking it. 'When I've spoken to them I'll talk to a few people I know at the Foreign Office and see if there is anything to be done from that angle. As it happens, I am having lunch with a man who might be able to do something.'

Verity looked at him, her strained white face thin enough to make her eyes, filled with tears, seem unnaturally large and luminous. 'Oh, will you, Edward? I know I'm being a . . .' She choked back a sob. 'You see, I'm so tired and I don't think I can manage any more on my own.' She smiled blearily. 'And don't you ever dare quote that back at me!'

A few minutes later, calmer and much more the old Verity, she got ready to leave. She reappeared from a visit to the bathroom, her face washed and a touch of rouge on her cheeks. 'You do yourself well,' she said.

'Oh, you mean the bath? Yes, it's where I go when I need to think.'

'Hmff,' was all she could find to say to that. She was staying with a girlfriend in Holland Park and it was agreed that she would ring him about six to find out what he had achieved, if anything. 'We have to be at Croydon more or less at dawn tomorrow,' she warned him. 'It's a long flight and, if we don't want to be benighted somewhere in France, we have to start at first light.'

24

'I still can't understand,' said Edward, 'how they could convict David of murdering Tilney solely because *his* knife was used to kill him.'

'Oh, didn't I say,' said Verity blithely, going out of the door, 'they also found a jersey covered in blood in David's room. They sort of proved it was Tilney's blood but I expect it was planted on David. That seems to be the most likely thing, don't you agree?' And before Edward had got his breath, she had kissed him lightly on the lips and disappeared down the hallway.

2

At Brooks's, Eric, the porter, seemed pleased to see him and, as he took his coat and hat, inquired after the health of his brother. It always irritated Edward that Eric invariably asked after the Duke despite his not having visited the club for the last five years to his certain knowledge.

'As well as can be expected,' Edward responded airily, hoping to suggest to Eric that the Duke had barely survived a life-threatening illness. The porter would be mortified to feel that he had missed some vital gossip concerning one of the club's most distinguished members. 'Is Mr Thoroughgood in the club yet, Eric? I'm supposed to be lunching with him.'

'Yes, my lord. He is in the morning-room.'

Edward glanced at the teleprinter chattering away in the corner but there was no news from Spain: the country was, as might be expected, absorbed by accounts of the King's funeral. The only foreign news was of Italian 'victories' in Abyssinia. To Edward, Mussolini's efforts to join the imperialists and have his own colonies seemed to be further evidence – if further evidence was needed – of how the world his eldest brother had, in 1914, died to preserve was being torn apart without, it seemed, anyone much caring. He was more than ever convinced that he ought to be doing something to help those who were trying to resist Fascism but what had he to offer? He was still young, rich, healthy and not a complete ass, but would Thoroughgood consider him to be employable? He glanced at the noticeboard. Among the pieces of paper pinned to it, charting the progress of the club backgammon tournament and recommending members purchase cases of the club's own champagne, were cards 'noting with regret' the recent decease of members. Godfrey Tilney's death seemed not yet to have come to the Secretary's attention but one card caught his eye: another near contemporary of his at Eton, Makepeace Hoden, had given up the ghost. Damn it, he thought to himself, was the life expectancy of his generation going to be as short as that of the last? Hoden could not have been more than thirty-seven, surely.

'I see Mr Hoden has died,' he said to Eric. 'Do you know how that happened?'

'Yes, my lord. It was very sad. I understand the poor young gentleman was eaten by a lion.'

'Good heavens, Eric!' said Edward impressed. 'I thought that only happened in music-hall songs.'

'No, my lord!' Eric said, suggesting some disapproval of Edward's levity. 'Mr Hoden was hunting big game in Africa, my lord, and . . .'

'I see,' said Edward hurriedly. He felt it was not quite the thing to gossip with the porter in the hall of the club about a member's demise even though he had not liked Hoden and had seen little of him since he had left Eton, under some sort of a cloud he seemed to recall.

He pushed open the door of the morning-room and surveyed the dozen or so members asleep or reading newspapers in green leather chairs. A coal fire burnt in the hearth and he went over to it and warmed his hands. It had turned very cold and he rather hoped Spain – if he did actually decide to go – would be considerably warmer. Several members nodded to him. The Earl of Carlisle, who all but lived in the club, said, 'Ah, Corinth – not seen much of you lately – been away?' and a very ancient member called Truefitt opened one eye and said, 'Rough weather, eh, Cornford?' Truefitt had an encyclopedic memory for first-class cricket scores but seldom remembered accurately the names of his club acquaintances. It amounted to a rapturous welcome and Edward compared it favourably with the democratic informality of his American friends which had rather shocked him at first. Even a casual acquaintance in New York would think nothing of addressing him by his first name before any formal introduction had taken place. Edward would have been outraged if anyone had called him a snob but he liked the reserve with which the English gentleman protected his privacy.

His closest friends would call him 'Corinth' and only a few intimates would address him as Edward. His brother and sister-in-law called him 'Ned' but the rituals of family life among the English aristocracy were worth a book in themselves.

A face, up to now hidden behind the *Sporting Times*, revealed itself. 'Ah, there you are, my boy.'

'Oh, Thoroughgood,' said Edward without enthusiasm. He remembered now that he did not like the man and certainly objected to being 'my-boy-ed' by a fellow who had been his contemporary at school. Thoroughgood uncurled himself from his armchair. He was tall, skeletally thin with a beaky nose, receding hair and a dusting of dandruff over his shoulders. He wore a perfectly pressed dark blue pinstripe suit, an Old Etonian tie and – this Edward found unexpected – a rather showy gold tie-pin.

It was not done to talk too long or too loudly in the morning-room so they walked through to the bar. 'Gin-and-it?' Thoroughgood inquired.

'Champagne, please,' said Edward, glancing round to see who else was lunching in the club. Two or three acquaintances waved at him and one of these was on the point of coming over when Thoroughgood came back from the bar with the drinks. He was obviously not popular because the acquaintance made a face at Edward indicating that he would wait and talk to him later.

'I see Hoden's dead,' Edward said, sipping his champagne.

'Yes, bad business that. You know how he loved hunting big game. He'd been all over the world: Tanganyika, Kenya, India, the Malay States. You name it, he'd been there.'

'So what happened? Eric said he had been eaten by a lion.'

Thoroughgood snuffled. 'Oh really, did he say that? I'm afraid it was altogether more prosaic. He shot himself.'

'Suicide?'

'Who knows? Probably just an accident but Eric is right in one way: the body was so badly mauled by the time the bearers or whatnot got to him, he was pretty well unrecognisable.'

'But it's rather odd for an experienced hunter, like Hoden, to allow himself to be separated from the others? Maybe he did want to shoot himself but didn't want to sully the family name by being called a suicide?'

'Maybe,' said Thoroughgood, already bored with the subject. 'We'll never know. I don't like huntin' of any sort – not animals anyway.' He gave his snuffling laugh which Edward found rather disgusting. 'I mean, these big game hunters, they like to pretend how brave they are but, as I understand it, they are never put in any danger. Some poor native fella is sent to chase some lion or whatnot into the great white hunter's field of fire and, if he misses, there is a professional there to finish it off.'

'But not in Hoden's case.'

'No, but he was an arrogant ... Oh well, *de mortuis nihil loquitur nisi bonum* and all that. I remember that he was an awful bully at school, though. Perhaps that was where he learnt the fun of chasing animals.' He snuffled again and Edward wondered, if Thoroughgood did offer him a job, whether he could bear to be associated with him.

Over lunch – 'the potted shrimps and then the kidneys, please, George. Same for you, old boy?' – they talked generalities: Abyssinia, the old King's funeral, the new King's raffish companions – 'all cocks and cocktails' as Thoroughgood put it vulgarly – and the inferiority of the club claret of which, nevertheless, Thoroughgood managed to dispose of two bottles. He seemed interested in what Edward had to say about New York's smart set. 'They are anglophile on the whole, are they? Or is it just that they "love a lord" like everyone else?'

Edward was rather put out. It was as if Thoroughgood enjoyed taunting him and he was half-tempted to get up there and then and leave him to it, but something stopped him. Thoroughgood, whatever else he was, was no fool and it occurred to him that he might be being tested in some way. He held his peace and explained that, though the English certainly had some snob-appeal in New York, the Americans he had met could not be considered Anglophile if that meant sharing the British view of world affairs.

Thoroughgood was on to this like a hawk on a rabbit. 'You mean they envy us our empire?'

'I don't know about that,' Edward said. 'I never discussed it with them, but if you mean would they fight alongside us if, God forbid, it ever came to war with Germany, I would say they wouldn't.' Thoroughgood seemed to be considering this because he said nothing but heaped Stilton on to a Bath Oliver biscuit.

29

'Mind you,' Edward went on, 'I was only in New York and its environs, and even there I was meeting a highly unrepresentative slice of the population. I have no idea what they think about England in Washington, or anywhere else. I don't suppose they consider us much at all. I was struck by how little news of Europe there was in the newspapers over there.'

'Shall we have coffee in the library?' said Thoroughgood. 'We can be quiet there and there are one or two things I want to talk to you about in private.'

So I was right! Edward said to himself and he was curious to hear what his host thought wise to keep from long ears.

Thoroughgood seated himself by the fire in one of the huge, dilapidated brown armchairs and rang the bell. He ordered port for himself. Edward declined, wanting to keep a reasonably clear head. As it was, the hot room was making him sleepy.

'You were in the States for six months and never went out of New York?' said Thoroughgood, looking past Edward at the leather-bound volumes on the shelf behind him. 'I thought you were a bit of a traveller. But then I forgot; you had your hands full, didn't you? What's the gel's name? They say she's Weaver's illegitimate daughter, don't they?'

Edward was taken aback by this sudden stab of malice even though he knew it was Thoroughgood's way of trying to put him off balance.

'You mean Miss Pageant?' he inquired mildly. 'She is a friend of mine, yes. Why do you ask?'

'Oh, we thought it was more than that,' said Thoroughgood nastily.

'Who is the "we" you talk about, who have been kind enough to interest themselves in my affairs?' Edward was trying hard to keep his temper.

'Oh, did I say "we"?' said Thoroughgood vaguely. 'It was just an expression.'

'Look, Thoroughgood, if you've got something to say to me for God's sake say it. I don't think the women in my life have anything to do with you.'

'But that's just where you're wrong, dear boy!' said Thoroughgood delightedly. 'Still it's not Miss Pageant who interests us – delightful though she is. It's your little commie friend; D.F. Browne's daughter – Verity, isn't that her name? I believe you met her last year when you were looking into that business of poor General Craig's death. She visited you this morning . . . rather early?'

Edward coloured. 'My God, Thoroughgood, don't tell me I am being watched. Surely England is not yet a police state?'

'No, Corinth, no suspicion is attached to you, I assure you.' He avoided admitting or denying that he and Verity were being watched, Edward noticed.

'Meaning that suspicion is attached to Miss Browne. Is that it?' said Edward acidly.

'Well, of course. We like to keep an eye on political extremists of whatever persuasion and your friend Miss Browne *is* a member of the Communist Party.'

'"We"? You keep mentioning "we",' Edward said coldly, wondering why he did not simply get up and leave.

'Did I say "we" again? I am so sorry. I meant the FO, you understand,' knowing Edward would take it to be the lie that it was. 'The FO is interested in the activities of your friend Miss Browne and that chap of hers – most unpleasant fella – what's his name? They are living in Madrid, are they not?'

'I imagine you know perfectly well that that is where Verity – Miss Browne – is. There is no secret about it; she is a foreign correspondent for the *New Gazette*.'

'Ah yes, back to Lord Weaver, eh Corinth? He has a finger in so many pies.'

'And you doubtless also know,' Edward went on, 'that Mr Griffiths-Jones is in prison accused of the murder of a colleague. As it happens, we both knew him: Godfrey Tilney.'

'Yes, as you say, I did know. Tilney! What an odd lot there were at Eton with us, don't you think? And that was why Miss Browne visited you this morning? She was soliciting your help in staying Griffiths-Jones' execution? I hope you told her there was nothing you could do – because of course there *is* nothing you or anyone else can do. David Griffiths-Jones,' he repeated the name as though he were holding it up for inspection. 'Oh yes, we know a good deal about that young man. He's a bad hat, take my word for it.'

'As a matter of fact, Thoroughgood, that is more or less what I did tell her – that I couldn't do anything, I mean. However, I did say I would try and get in touch with Tilney's parents and see if they might appeal for clemency. Miss Browne is convinced of Griffiths-Jones' innocence.'

'Well, yes, of course she would be.' There was a sneer in Thoroughgood's tone of voice which finally achieved what he had presumably been aiming at for the past hour: Edward lost his temper.

'By God, Thoroughgood,' he said rising. 'I thought you were a nasty piece of work when we were at school but now I see you have become a complete cad. If you think insulting Miss Browne is a way of persuading me to do something for you . . .'

'Sit down, Corinth,' said Thoroughgood, not moving from his chair, 'and don't be a fool. You're drawing attention to yourself. I'm not insulting anyone. In fact, it is just possible we might be able to help her . . . her friend.'

Edward sat down slowly. 'How and why?' he said shortly.

'Two good questions, dear boy.' Thoroughgood, who was only Edward's senior by two or three years, seemed to enjoy patronising him. 'The fact is, we need someone inside the British Communist Party to be our eyes and ears.'

'Let me be clear,' said Edward after taking a deep breath, 'you want me, as your representative, to save Griffiths-Jones' life in return for him working for you – spying in other words – betraying everything he believes in?'

'Oh, come on, Corinth. Don't be so naive. Your schoolboy honour is not appropriate in the dirty, dishonest world we all inhabit nowadays.'

'I have no illusions, I assure you, about the ruthlessness of extremists on whatever side of the political spectrum but I have to say I had hoped . . .'

'What a pompous fellow you are, Corinth. Look . . .' Thoroughgood leant forward so close to Edward's face that he could smell the wine on his breath. 'You don't seem to understand. This isn't cricket. This is not gentlemen against gentlemen, nor even gentlemen against players – this is a fight to the death. Griffiths-Jones and his friends will do everything they can to drag this country into a war. The political situation in Spain is so unstable. The elections, which as far as we can tell were reasonably fair, have brought this hotch-potch of trades unions and left-wing political groupings to power – the so-called Popular Front – but the odds are the army won't stand for it.'

'The new government isn't communist.'

'No and that's the devil of it.'

'Why? Surely we don't want to see a communist government?'

'Listen, the name "Popular Front" was coined in Moscow at the 7th World Congress of the Third International, or Comintern, last year. Stalin was getting panicky about the rise of Nazi Germany – wanted to get on better terms with the democracies – so he decreed that in elections communists should support any party or group of parties however "bourgeois" who are against Fascism.

'The Communist Party comprises the smallest group in the alliance but the Party will do what it always does: destabilise the main parties – which in all conscience are weak enough as it is – and foment civil war. You see, Corinth, the communists are frightened of the ballot box. They know they can never win that way. They want revolution, on the back of which they can seize power. Even more dangerous for us is their intention to lure us into a general European war. They hope a civil war in Spain will be the hook with which they will tow us into the mire. But, by God, some of us will do everything we can to prevent such a catastrophe. The British government will never allow itself to be drawn into a conflict which would destroy us and our empire.'

Edward was silent. Then he said, 'But even if I agreed to help you, can you guarantee to save Griffiths-Jones? I thought you said nothing could help him now.'

'I did. No, we cannot guarantee anything but it's his only chance. We can pull some strings if it's in our interests but you would have to make him understand what is expected of him.'

'And why do you think I might succeed?'

'We can't be sure,' Thoroughgood admitted, 'but you're a persuasive fellow and – shall I be frank?'

'By all means.'

'You are just the chivalrous idiot who feels you owe it to the girl you love to rescue her lover. Griffiths-Jones thinks he knows all about you, so in a sort of way he trusts you. I mean, he probably hates your guts, but he doesn't rate you as an enemy.' Thoroughgood smiled sweetly.

'You're not very complimentary.'

'I don't mean to be. If you are going to do anything in Spain,

33

you must face facts.' He changed the subject. 'I understand Weaver has arranged a plane tomorrow morning at Croydon?'

'Yes, so Miss Browne says.'

'Good! Thank heavens for the very rich. I expect Harry Bragg will be the pilot.'

'The air ace?'

'Oh yes, but he's a modest man so don't call him that to his face.'

'That's all right, I know him a little. In fact, he more or less taught me to fly a year or two back when I was in Kenya. But won't I be rather noticeable when I turn up in Madrid in an aeroplane hired by a newspaper magnate and piloted by Harry Bragg?'

'Certainly! But that's what you've got to do – make a fuss. You're a rich young English milord – a knight on a charger come to rescue . . . well, you know the rest.'

'I seem to recall that lopped heads often end up on chargers,' said Edward wryly.

'Different sort of charger, dear boy. In any case, your head is much too high profile to end up on a plate decorated with limp lettuce. Well, you'd better go now.'

'How do I get in touch with you?'

'In Madrid, through the embassy. Not the ambassador – he's a bit of an ass. In fact, we have brought him back to London for the moment . . . "consultations", you know the sort of thing. You'll liaise with Tom Sutton. He's head of what we call the "political section" at the embassy. Do you know him?'

'No.'

'Well, never mind, you'll like him. Not quite out of the top drawer but very clever.'

'The Tilneys? It's worth my going to see them if there's time?'

'Definitely. It's what you would do in any case if you were thrashing around looking for ways of helping Griffiths-Jones. It's a pity *he* doesn't have any parents alive.'

Godfrey Tilney's parents – once they understood who he was – were pathetically pleased to see Edward. Clearly, the only thing they lived for was perpetuating the memory of their son and here was an old school friend ready, even eager, to talk about him.

The maid had ushered Edward into a drawing-room which he imagined had remained largely unaltered since the reign of Queen Victoria. The room was dominated by a 'baby grand' piano covered by some sort of lace-edged tablecloth which, in turn, was covered with photographs in silver frames and knick-knacks. It looked as though it had never been played. Antimacassars lay primly – like lace bonnets – on stuffed armchairs and a peculiarly offensive silver stag sat on the mantelpiece eternally fending off two hunting dogs.

Before Edward had time to examine the photographs on the piano, the door opened and he saw a large, unhealthy-looking woman with a pale face and eyes reddened from lack of sleep or excessive weeping.

'Lord Edward Corinth?' she said nervously, holding his card in vague puzzlement.

'Yes, Mrs Tilney. I do apologise for calling unexpectedly but I am only in London for a day and I wanted to express my sympathies for your dreadful loss.'

'I remember now. You were a friend of Godfrey's,' she said, brightening.

'Yes, a school friend. I had not seen him for years, don't y'know, but it was a terrible shock . . .'

Edward had thought it might be better to play the amiable ass which, as Verity would say, did not require much acting ability.

'How very good of you to call. Please do sit down, Lord Edward. I . . . we miss him . . .'

'Yes, of course you must,' said Edward gently, seeing that tears had filled the woman's eyes and raw emotion was preventing her from speaking. To give her time to recover he stuttered, 'I've been in America so I missed . . . I've only just heard. Frightful business. How did it . . .? Or am I . . . do you not want to talk about it?' He wanted desperately to comfort the distraught woman but, even more, he needed to know if she had any information which might help him understand what had happened to her son in the hills outside Madrid.

'No! To be frank with you, Lord Edward, it's still all we can think of. Until this man is executed . . .'

'But why did it happen? Who would want to . . . to hurt Godfrey?'

'Well, that's exactly what we can't understand. We – my husband and I – attended the trial in Madrid. A horrible place,' she added, actually shuddering. 'We don't speak Spanish of course and the interpreter's English was not very good so I dare say we missed much of what was said. The evidence seemed quite clear, you know: a knife which belonged to this man – ' she could not bear to say Griffiths-Jones' name – 'and some bloodstained clothes were discovered in his rooms but I never did understand why he had done such a dreadful thing . . . to my poor innocent boy. They were supposed to be friends.' To Edward's discomfort tears poured down her cheeks – tears of which she seemed quite unaware, perhaps because they were as natural to her now as smiling had been before her son's death.

Edward persevered: 'The bloodstained clothes – were they Godfrey's?'

'No, they belonged . . . to that man, but they thought the blood was his. He must have . . . got it on himself when he . . . when he stabbed . . . Oh! How can people be so wicked, Lord Edward?'

'Were the embassy people helpful?'

'Oh yes, the ambassador was very sympathetic and he gave us a nice young man to look after us while we were in Madrid.'

'Would that have been Tom Sutton by any chance?'

'Why yes! Do you know him?'

At that moment the door of the drawing-room opened and an elderly, straight-backed man with a military moustache entered the room. He put out his hand to the grieving mother and looked at Edward reproachfully.

'What is it, Rosemary, my dear?'

'Oh, Henry, this is an old school friend of Godfrey's, Lord Edward Corinth. He has been abroad – in America, did you say, Lord Edward? – and has only just heard.'

'Lord Edward,' said Henry Tilney, 'it is very kind of you to call but you can see we are not in the way of being . . . sociable. You were a friend of my son at Eton?'

'He was a little older than me – two or three years and of course that sort of age difference means quite a lot to schoolboys, but I think I can say we were friends. We weren't in the same house but we played squash together – that sort of thing. I was very surprised and saddened to hear about your loss.'

'Yes,' said the man miserably. 'He was our only son and we had such high hopes ... but there we are. We should not build ...' His words tailed off as if the effort of speaking was too great.

'If I remember, Mr Tilney, you were a Member of Parliament – a Conservative – but Godfrey ... from what I understand he was ... he was on the left?'

'Yes,' said Tilney, smiling wanly. 'I was MP for Marylebone – retired at the last election, but yes, I'm afraid we did not see eye to eye politically. Godfrey was a lawyer, you know. He was very concerned with issues of social justice. Got mixed up with that chap D.F. Browne, do you know who I mean? Can't stand the fellow myself. Anyway, he – Godfrey – suddenly got the idea that he was needed to help ... what do they call it now – you know the alliance of left-wing parties ...?'

'The Popular Front.'

'Yes, that's right. Though why he wanted to go to Spain when there was more than enough for him to do here, or so I should suppose, I don't know.'

'Might I ask, sir, was Godfrey a member of the Communist Party?'

'Of course not!' broke in Rosemary Tilney angrily as though Edward was accusing her son of being a criminal. 'He was just devoted to ... he wanted justice ... and this was his reward. Is that justice, Lord Edward? Is it justice that he was murdered for no reason at all?'

As Edward left the gloomy house permeated by grief, he could not but feel that their mourning was tinged with guilt. Perhaps all parents feel guilt if their child dies before they do; it is against the law of nature. Or was it that they were blaming themselves for not having understood what their only son was trying to do with his life? The father must have thought his son had spat in his face by rejecting his own political values so comprehensively and it was no good trying to tell him that most children rebelled against their fathers.

The anguish of loss: Edward knew something of the pain felt by parents when their children predeceased them. His eldest brother, Franklyn, had died in the first week of the war and his father had never come to terms with the tragedy. He had been in a very real sense a prisoner of war. Gerald, Edward's other brother, who had succeeded as Duke of Mersham, had never been forgiven by his father for surviving while the favourite son had not. It had caused a fracturing of relationships in the family from which everyone had suffered. Edward, very much the youngest of the three brothers, had, in effect, grown up fatherless because the old Duke had gone into a depression from which nothing could stir him except death itself.

One thing was certain: it would have been worse than useless to ask the Tilneys to plead for Griffiths-Jones' life. If he had suggested it, he would have been thrown out of the house. It was better to keep their goodwill so he could go back to them at some future time if he needed their help. Mr Tilney had obviously been puzzled at the absence of any apparent motive for his son's murder and it puzzled Edward too. What reason had Griffiths-Jones, or anyone else for that matter, to murder Godfrey Tilney? Griffiths-Jones was one of the most determined and committed political animals he had ever met and to be behind bars now, just when the new government was taking control of the country, must be, to put it mildly, frustrating. He suspected Griffiths-Jones of being utterly ruthless in pursuit of his ambitions and he was quite ready to believe that he would kill without remorse if he needed to, but to muck up a murder so as to end up in front of a firing squad seemed out of character. He was too efficient to leave evidence all over the place, as he was alleged to have done. No, no, no! Edward was quite ready to believe David Griffiths-Jones capable of murder – capable of murdering *him* even – but not of making a hash of it.

It was an odd way of proving someone innocent but the more Edward considered the matter, the more he felt Verity was right, if for all the wrong reasons. For Verity, her lover was a saint – if the Communist Party had saints – battling tyranny and incapable of anything shoddy or underhand. Edward believed he knew that was nonsense. He had just a few days to try and prove to an indifferent world that the man condemned to death for murdering Godfrey Tilney was guilty of much but not this. He doubted he could do it but, for Verity's sake, he was determined to try. As for blackmailing Griffiths-Jones into becoming a police spy for Basil Thoroughgood, it was just as likely he could turn water into wine but he had to pretend it was a possibility if he was to have Foreign Office help in getting a stay of execution. There would be no point in finding out who really had killed Godfrey Tilney if Griffiths-Jones had already been tied to a stake, blindfolded and shot.

3

Bragg was a piratical figure with only one eye, the other being covered by a black patch. He also boasted a wooden foot. It was a miracle he could fly at all. In the last days of the war he had almost been killed in a dog fight over the outskirts of Albert. A splinter of wood had entered his eye blinding him immediately and causing him almost unbearable pain. Somehow, with extraordinary fortitude, he had managed to land the aircraft before losing consciousness, but his foot had been trapped in the fuselage and had had to be amputated. He ought to have died of blood poisoning or the sheer pain of his wounds but he survived and even learnt to fly again, though, as Edward knew, it could be a frightening experience for his passengers.

Edward had picked up Verity from Holland Park shortly after five o'clock. By the time they got to Croydon – the Lagonda had made good time on the empty roads – it was getting light. It was perishing cold and Verity looked very small buried under a tartan rug and a huge ulster Edward had brought for her. She wore a black beret, a long woollen scarf round her neck and heavy leather gauntlets. Edward was aware they had a lot to talk about. There was so little he knew about the circumstances of her life in Spain. How well did she know Tilney? What was his relationship with Griffiths-Jones? Was one of them senior to the other in the Party? Because, whatever his parents believed, Verity confirmed that he was an active communist. Who else might have wanted Tilney dead? Lots of questions, but somehow he knew that, today at least, he would never ask them. Not having seen Verity for six months made him shy or even guilty – guilty that he had not missed her more. It was ridiculous, he knew, but he felt he had been idling his life away in an unreal world of luxury and artifice while she had been roughing it in the real world, making a name for herself as a journalist to whom people listened. Perhaps it wasn't guilt he felt but envy.

In any case, it was too early and much too cold to ask and answer questions. It was enough to ride in silence through the Surrrey countryside with this feisty, gallant girl beside him, for once silent, vulnerable and trusting. She was so different from the girls he had met as a young man in the drawing-rooms of Mayfair and Eaton Square, waiting complacently or apathetically to be selected for breeding by one of the arrogant males before whom they paraded. Even then the 'deb's delights', as the men were called, had referred to 'the season' as a cattle market and had made jokes about the mothers who chaperoned their girls with such terrible determination.

They had the hood up over the tonneau and Verity snuggled up to him and fell fast asleep, making it difficult for Edward to change gear without waking her. In her sleep she occasionally shivered, whether from the cold or because of her dreams, he could not say. He felt unutterably happy.

Croydon aerodrome was not much more than a cluster of hangars around a tarmacked runway. The one building of character was the control tower and there they found Harry Bragg already prepared for take-off. He fed them hot black coffee and bacon sandwiches to keep out the cold. 'Good to see you, Corinth. Last time must have been two years ago in Mombasa, eh?' The two men shook hands, more or less ignoring Verity, in Bragg's case out of shyness. Since his disfigurement, he felt he was repulsive to look at. Verity, still in something of a trance, did not seem to notice him at all. 'The weather looks set fair,' Bragg said. His voice was a little slurred, not because of drink, though he and Edward both had flasks of brandy with them, but because of his war injury. 'It's going to be cold, old lad – and noisy. This old bus is a goer – no question of that – one of the fastest in the sky but she's noisy and she leaks. Know what I mean?' He grinned. Edward knew what he meant – it was going to be very cold.

Bragg was curious about why his old friend was being whisked off to Madrid in an aeroplane instead of the usual train journey across France but he knew better than to ask. Lord

Weaver had given him his instructions in person but had told him nothing except that he was to deliver Verity, the *New Gazette*'s Spanish correspondent, and Lord Edward Corinth to Madrid with all possible despatch and then return to London to await further orders. Now all he said was, 'We won't be able to talk much on the flight but I will indicate like this if there is anything I think you ought to see.' He waved his gauntlet-covered hands first in one direction and then in the other.

They took off into a gun-metal sky. Verity was awake now but, as Bragg had warned them, the de Havilland Dragon Rapide was too noisy to make conversation possible. At first they flew low over green fields and Edward could see farm workers stare up at them in surprise. Aeroplanes were still objects of wonder when most people never travelled faster than a horse could gallop or went further than their local market town in a lifetime. They gained height over the grey, cold Channel and once again Verity seemed to sleep but Edward was now wide-awake, his brain racing with questions only time could answer. Always, he was aware of the irony: Verity was depending on him to save her lover from a death he probably richly deserved and whose presence in her life he deplored.

They refuelled in Bordeaux and again, just before they crossed the border, at Saint Jean de Luz. The moment they flew into Spain the weather worsened. As they crept over the harsh terrain – almost a desert – Verity began to feel excited and rather scared and wondered what she would do if she *had* to pee. Unlike Edward, she had not flown in an aeroplane before and it satisfied her yearning for urgent action even if in the long run it was fruitless. It was bringing her back quickly to where she wanted most in the world to be but, though she would never admit it to Edward or anyone else, she felt that flying was an unnatural way to travel. Perhaps if she learned to fly herself, she thought, she would feel differently.

Soon they were over the Sierra de la Demanda and the little aeroplane seemed to chug and shuffle over the snow-peaked mountain tops as if some immense magnet was drawing them earthward, to be spiked like an unwanted document on one of the razor-sharp pinnacles of rock. At Burgos, they landed again and refuelled the 'old gel', as Bragg called his steed, for the last time. As Edward and Verity stuffed themselves with sugary buns washed down by scalding black coffee, they exchanged small talk, somehow not wanting to consider the real business of their flight across Europe. The final hop to Madrid's splendid new Barajas airport was made in bright sunlight but to Edward's disappointment it was still very cold. He had been longing to bask in Spanish warmth but apparently Madrid in February could be as cold as England. As they circled the two steel-and-glass control buildings, Verity gripped Edward's hand. Her courage had all but left her during the long, exhausting flight. They were here at last but what could they hope to achieve? David was doomed and Edward had as much as told her so. But oddly enough, as Verity's spirits had sunk, Edward's had risen. As they landed, they could see beyond a huge hangar the solitary figure of a tall woman, standing immobile beside a motor car. Only the long silk scarf round her neck fluttering behind her in the wind gave any life to the picture.

'Who's that?' he shouted to Verity over the roar of the engines.

'That's Hester, Hester Lengstrum. We share an apartment. She's a Swedish baroness.'

This was the first Edward had heard of Hester Lengstrum but there was no time to ask further questions. They landed with a bump, rolling across the grass right up to the stationary automobile. Harry helped them down. It was good to feel solid earth beneath their feet but they were both very stiff and Verity stumbled. She felt light-headed from spinning through the ether but she got out her 'thank you' to Harry Bragg before turning to greet her friend.

As Edward said goodbye to Harry, he watched Verity's friend out of the corner of his eye. She was a striking girl, about twenty-five he guessed, with long black hair flowing down her back which she shrugged now and again almost as if she wanted to be sure it was still there. She was tall, tall as himself, and he was six foot. Verity had to stand on tiptoe to kiss her. It had often amused him how much Verity hated being small; to her annoyance, she was just five foot three or, as he said, five-four when angry. Edward liked the way Hester held herself: straight as a guardsman, as if she scorned trying to disguise her height by leaning forward, as he had seen many tall people do. She was cool responding to Verity's puppy-ish embraces, a calm smile and a toss of her hair saying as much as she wanted about her pleasure in having her back. He guessed she was naturally economical with her smiles and grinned inwardly. She might add interest to his investigations, he thought.

'I'll wait to hear from you,' said Harry, smeared with oil and grease. He had taken off his goggles which had left him with owlish white rings round his eyes. 'I have to go back to London as you know but I can be here or wherever else you command in twenty-four hours. The boss said you only had to telegraph him and he would rub his Aladdin's lamp and, hey presto, I would appear to do your bidding.'

It cheered Edward to know that the aviator would be able to pluck them out of danger if it became necessary. He was not in his element here. His Spanish was rudimentary, though he could speak French fluently so supposed he ought, fairly quickly, to be able to learn enough Spanish to get by. He knew no one in Madrid and did not know how the authorities would react to a foreigner without any official status trying to interfere with the course of justice – or rather he could guess: they would either ignore him, which was the most likely, or push him out of the country if he was too annoying. And then there was the politics: he knew himself to be as innocent as a babe as far as Spanish politics were concerned and, if Tilney's proved to be a political murder, as he suspected it was, he might very well put Verity and himself in danger by some ignorant remark or false assumption.

Carrying their bags, Edward walked over to Hester Lengstrum who held out her hand to him. 'So, I guess you must be Captain Marvel,' she said out of the corner of her mouth. Verity, Edward saw, was blushing prettily.

'Don't take any notice of Hester, Edward, she likes to shock. She wants to see if you mind.'

'No offence, honey, but you have gone on so about *Lord* Edward,' she emphasised the 'Lord' ironically, 'it's quite a relief to see he's a human being after all.'

'And you're American,' said Edward, deliberately sounding disappointed. He dropped his bag and took Hester's hand. 'You were supposed to be a Swedish baroness. I'd rather hoped for a Viking.'

'Oh, I'm afraid I'm no Garbo. I was married to a Swedish baron, I guess I still am, and it's certainly useful to be a baroness in Spain – even Republican Spain. But I'm as American as stars and bars, Lord Edward, as I guess you can hear – from Denver, Colorado.'

'How is he?' Verity asked, impatient of badinage.

'David? He's OK, I guess, that is, considering his situation.'

'Did he have any message for me?'

'No. He seemed to think you were wasting your time though – bringing over Captain Marvel. I don't know what you did to him,' she said turning to Edward, 'but he doesn't seem to rate you highly. I've gotten the impression he thinks you've got the hots for his girl.'

Verity blushed. 'Oh, that's nonsense, Hester. I can't think what gave you that idea.'

'OK, hon. But it's not my idea, it's David's. Maybe it's just he's given up hope, but when I said you were bringing your friend to see him tomorrow morning, he didn't seem to be particularly interested.'

Verity looked vexed and Edward bit his lip. He doubted very much if there was anything he could do for David Griffiths-Jones in his terrible predicament and he feared it might look as though he had come to Madrid to gloat. Whatever Verity might choose to believe, Edward had no illusions: he and David were oil and water. They had disliked each other at Cambridge and, when Verity had brought them together last year, their mutual antipathy had hardened into settled enmity. David saw him, he knew, as a playboy, a drone, a member of a caste he was dedicated to destroying. Edward saw him as the worst kind of bigot, and Verity complicated the whole thing.

Verity's feelings for both men were confused, inchoate. Her instinctive affection for Edward and respect for what she recognised to be his innate decency went against all her political beliefs. She had committed herself to communism as the only political creed a self-respecting libertarian could subscribe to and the only effective opposition to Fascism. David was, in her eyes, the living example of this – Mr Valiant for Truth – though he

45

sometimes frightened her with his seeming indifference to petty human emotions such as – well, such as love between a man and a woman. She told herself this was only to be expected of a knight in pursuit of his holy grail and, in principle, she approved of not letting trivial emotions get in the way of the important work they had to do, but in practice she knew herself to be someone who craved affection of which she had been starved as a child. Had she been silly in persuading Edward to come to Spain? He had been so reluctant; perhaps rightly. He had told her plainly he wasn't going to be able to help and she was beginning to think he was right. But then, she had only turned to him as a last resort, when all other hopes had been dashed. Strangely enough it had been David himself who had suggested it.

'You know, V,' he had said, 'the only man who could do me any good is your pet lord.'

"Edward, you mean?' she said in surprise.

He held up his hands in surrender: 'I was joking,' he had said, but the idea lodged in her mind. She did not quite understand it herself but, despite Edward's deplorable flippancy, she believed there was a vein of seriousness beneath it all which was worthy of respect – a firmness of purpose, to put it at its lowest, which she could recognise in herself. And he was intelligent: everyone admitted that and she had herself had evidence of it six months earlier when he had nosed out the truth behind General Craig's murder. She just wished he wouldn't make those soupy eyes at her.

They strolled towards the white Hispano-Suiza standing haughtily at the edge of the airfield.

'Don't we have to show our passports to anyone?' said Edward, bewildered by the ease with which they were entering a foreign country.

'Sure, Ferdinando will take care of everything. That's him over there.' Hester pointed to a uniformed official who had appeared from behind a hangar and was bustling towards them. 'Ferdy's a pal of mine.'

With much saluting on Ferdinando's part, the formalities were quickly despatched and Hester threw herself into the driving seat of the Hispano-Suiza. 'Get in, both of you. It's a bit of a

46

squeeze but I don't suppose you mind and anyway there's nothing to be done about it.'

Edward, who had a passion for fast cars, stroked the green-painted bonnet lovingly.

'Mmm, how on earth did you get hold of this? It's an Alfonso, isn't it? A bit of an antique but a real beauty.'

'Yeah,' said Hester in her heavy drawl, 'I guess it is something special. The man who sold it me said, when the King abdicated, he left behind thirty Hispanos and this was one of them.'

'Is that why it's called an Alfonso?' asked Verity.

'Yes, after the King,' Edward said. 'It was really the first sports car you could drive on the road.'

'Well, for Christ's sake, stop salivating and get in,' Hester commanded them. 'It's after six and it will take us the best part of an hour to reach the city even with me at the wheel.'

Edward's assumption that Madrid would be warmer than London was naive. He had overlooked the fact that the city was two thousand feet above sea level on a vast, windswept plain. It was a bitterly cold evening to be speeding across the campagna in an open car and Verity was glad she was so tightly squeezed between Edward and Hester. It might be a grand car in its parentage but it was not designed for three and was such a tight fit Verity had almost to sit on Edward's lap, but neither seemed to mind this much.

They started with a violent jerk and Hester swore. 'Fucking clutch.' It was the first time Edward had heard a woman use a sexual swear word and he was shocked but rather excited. After all, he reminded himself, she was American. He had instinctively grabbed hold of Verity to stop her being thrown through the windscreen and now, instead of releasing her, he held her so tightly she complained.

'Edward, I can't breathe!' she laughed, and clung on to him as they bumped over some grass towards the airport gates. Clearly, the Alfonso's suspension was not what it had once been. In a few moments they were bouncing merrily across bare, rust-brown earth. The *mesa* or plain across which they journeyed was something of a dream landscape, red rough scrub for the most part, and Edward thought fancifully that it was as if he had landed on Mars. The roar of the engine and the whistle of the wind, which seemed to sing through every crack and crevice of the car, made conversation difficult. Verity, who had a cat's ability to doze whenever she had an opportunity, fell into a half-sleep, comforted by Edward's arm around her. He hoped the drive would be a long one. He watched the landscape gradually change from barren countryside enlivened by clumps of straggly umbrella pines encircling little country houses to a richer, more fertile country. Hester asked for a cigarette and with difficulty he managed to extract one without waking Verity.

'Be a honey and light it for me, would you,' Hester said and it was true the road was rough enough and the car's steering awkward enough to make it desirable she keep both hands on the wheel. With difficulty he dug out his lighter and then faced having to light the cigarette. In the end he had to put it in his own mouth before he could flick his lighter. When it was glowing he stretched across the sleeping girl and put it between Hester's lips. Nothing was said but an erotic charge – like an electric current – passed between them and he immediately felt guilty of some small betrayal.

At last, they found themselves driving past substantial estates – red-tiled houses set in large uncultivated gardens which in turn gave way, on the outskirts of the city, to groups of houses and then streets.

'We're on the Gran Vía and over there is the Plaza Mayor,' said Hester, gesturing to the left. It was dark now and the car's great gas headlamps probed the city, illuminating the occasional tram. There were very few automobiles, whether because of the hour or because they were rich men's toys Edward did not know. Verity and Hester shared an apartment near the university and, instead of booking Edward into one of the smart hotels on the Gran Vía, they had found him a room in a small hotel, confusingly called The Palace, just around the corner from them.

'Hester thought you would want to hole up somewhere swanky but I said that, though you were often insufferable, you didn't like showing off in that particular way. Was I right?'

'In every degree,' said Edward, pleased that Verity had regained some of the combativeness which had made life so interesting a few months back but which seemed to have been lost in her gnawing fear that her lover would end up in front of a firing squad. In the foyer of the little hotel Edward was consigned into the care of the manager, a Napoleonic figure: rotund, black-garbed, with magnificent moustaches, he seemed to be rather in awe of Hester and half in love with Verity. 'Felipe,' said Verity, 'look after our friend. He is a genuine English milord and don't pretend you've met one before. But he's quite decent, really.'

'*Si, señorita*, welcome to my hotel, milor,' the manager said, proudly displaying his grasp of English. 'Thees is a very good place and I look after you well.'

'Thank you,' Edward said, nodding his head in response to Felipe's bowing and scraping, 'I'm sure I will be very happy here.'

Hester looked unconvinced but managed a wintry smile. 'We'll come and collect you in an hour, if that's all right. We're going to meet some people at Chicote's on the Gran Vía.'

'Chicote's?' queried Edward, who did not feel in the least like going out. 'I thought of going straight to bed.'

'Oh pooh!' said Verity. 'Just because you had to get up a bit earlier than usual you can't not go out on your first night in Spain. Anyway, I'm starving.'

Verity always had had a healthy appetite, Edward remembered, and he was glad to find that she had not lost it in her present anxieties. He hesitated but did not wish to look unenterprising to the two women who were staring at him, Verity accusingly, and Hester mockingly, a little smile playing about her lips.

'You're right. Of course, I would love to,' he said.

'That's good,' said Verity, sounding relieved that this English milord for whose presence she was responsible had not let her down. 'It's the best bar in Madrid. Everyone who's anyone goes there.'

It was half-past nine when Verity and Hester came to collect him. Edward was feeling better. The bath at the end of the passage, which he shared with the other guests on his floor, was inadequate and the water tepid but still he had been able to shave and wash himself. He thought longingly of his clawed monster in his rooms in Albany. He had been uncertain what to wear for the evening's entertainment but the small bag Fenton had packed for him did not allow much choice. In the end, in his clean white shirt, Cherrypickers' tie and tweed jacket, he looked what he was: English to the core.

Hester was looking statuesque in the sort of overcoat he imagined Napoleon might have worn in his Russian campaign but of course she was twice as tall as the Emperor and wide in the shoulders. Her hair had been tidied beneath a wide-brimmed black hat which emphasised what he could see of her face – her black eyes, Roman nose and firm chin. He thought she looked magnificent. Verity, on the other hand, looked almost Spanish, except for the fox jacket which Edward remembered her wearing back in London. She looked a charming, innocent but determined child. Her Mediterranean colouring helped but it was, Edward thought, the black bandanna she wore over the top of her head which made her look 'foreign'.

'It's to keep my ears warm,' she said, seeing Edward eyeing her.

'Very attractive,' replied Edward vaguely. He knew if he said anything more effusive she would think he was patronising her. It came to him that he always thought twice before paying Verity a compliment. He was a little frightened of her finding him a conventional English male and he had had occasion in the past to smart from her biting retort to inanities other girls would have professed to find delightful.

'Well,' said Hester, perhaps a little irritated that Edward seemed to have no eyes for her, 'we'd better get moving. They eat late here but I'm hungry as a stallion.' She marched them through the swing doors into the street. There were some street lights under which their breaths smoked in the cold but for the most part they walked in pools of darkness.

'Hungry as a horse,' Verity corrected. 'Hester has some problem remembering clichés,' she said apologetically to Edward, taking hold of his arm.

Edward thought Dr Freud might have something to say about her seeing herself as a stallion but was wise enough to keep his mouth shut. He looked at Verity intently. Whether it was tiredness or anxiety, she was exhibiting a desperate gaiety which he knew was near to tears. 'You're sure you don't want to go to bed? You have had an exhausting day,' he said to her in an undertone.

'Oh, what can you mean?' said Verity archly, gripping his

arm more tightly, and again, Edward thought she wasn't behaving normally. She obviously regretted what she had just said because she corrected herself fiercely. 'I couldn't sleep. I'm too wound up. Anyway, I want you to meet our friends. They *are* our friends, aren't they, Hester?'

'They have to pass for friends. Beggars can't be rich men.'

'She means,' said Verity fondly, 'that we foreigners have to stick together.'

'You don't mix with the Spanish, then?' said Edward ironically.

'As much as we can but it's difficult. There's a saying, foreigners in Spain should give the men tobacco and leave the women alone, but seriously, the Spanish are so taken up with their own affairs they don't have much time for outsiders. They want us to know what is happening – they want the outside world to help but they are not very good at getting us the information we need. You've no idea how complicated Spanish politics is. Take the new Popular Front government. It's made up of five main groupings each with its own idea of how to govern this ungovernable country. I mean, can you imagine the communists and the socialists agreeing on anything for long and as for the Catalan Separatists . . . I ask you!'

'It's a ragbag of everything from anarchists to communists and they all hate each other,' Hester agreed.

'If there are communists in the pudding, my guess is they will rise to the top,' said Edward mischievously.

Verity looked at him reproachfully. 'We are good organisers and we know what we want. Is that bad?'

Edward was spared from having to answer. 'Yup, they sure do need help,' Hester said thoughtfully.

'Help? Who?' Edward asked. It was bitterly cold and he pulled his coat more closely around him as he walked.

'Economically. The Republic is flat broke,' Hester explained. 'The ordinary worker here in Madrid – the janitor in our apartment building, say – earns less than a dollar a week.'

'Not when you take into account the riches Hester pours over his head,' Verity said. 'She's always giving the family clothes and food.'

'Oh, not really, but when little Francisco looks at me with those liquid brown eyes . . .'

'He's the child,' Verity explained.

'He's so cute. It almost makes me want to have one of my own.'

'Really!' said Verity. 'After all you said against marriage and men.'

'I know, but we can't be consistent – not all the time,' Hester said, confused by Verity's vehemence.

'But, I say, I still don't understand. How can Spain be broke? Look at all this.' They were walking down the Gran Vía and the buildings on either side were larger and smarter than in London's Park Lane. 'This is all so modern and ... and fashionable ...'

'Yes, of course,' Verity said squeezing his arm. 'You wait till you see the shops in the Carrera de San Jerónimo. There are rich people here, very rich – the ex-King's cronies for example – but you have to go away from Madrid, into the countryside, to see the meaning of poverty. The hovels in which the peasants live are ... well, they just don't bear looking at. And that's the trouble; the dukes and marquises maybe own a castle, a palace, a house here in Madrid and another in Monte Carlo, two aeroplanes and six Rolls-Royces. While they may have an income of 25,000 pesetas *a day* all the year round, the *braceros* – that's the landless peasants – if they're lucky earn two pesetas a day for about five months of the year and nothing for the rest.'

This was the old Verity, Edward was happy to see, indignant at social injustice and angry at the indifference most well-fed men, like him, exhibited.

'What has the Republic done then to improve things?' he inquired.

'They are trying to modernise. They are trying to introduce real democracy and they have renounced war ... but they can't do much while the army and the Church oppose them.'

'Yes, but what are they doing about filling the stomachs of the starving?' said Edward drily.

'I think this new government will do something,' said Hester. 'They are pledged to redistribute wealth but of course it's not going to be easy. They want to cut the size of the army and they are taking over education from the Church and making it open to all, paid for by the state.'

'I can see that being unpopular in some quarters,' Edward said.

52

'Yes,' Verity agreed, 'and David says there are no arms, nothing to stop a military coup. In fact, that was what he was doing before he was arrested.'

'What?'

'Buying arms – but that's a secret,' she added hurriedly. 'I don't think David would want me to have told you.'

'I can't help if I don't know the facts,' Edward said sententiously.

'Yes, but you have to make David tell you what he and Tilney were doing in the mountains.'

'It's a mighty queer place to buy arms, out in the country,' Hester said. 'That usually happens in offices or hotel rooms – at least, I guess so; that's what I've always imagined.'

Edward was silent; so this was what Griffiths-Jones was up to: buying arms for a bankrupt government which had renounced war. There might be a few people keen to interfere with *that*, he thought. He shivered. 'Damn it, I thought Madrid – Spain anyway – was supposed to be hot,' he said. 'When do we get to this place?'

'We're here,' said Verity, pushing through big wooden doors.

4

Chicote's was an oasis of warmth and light in Madrid's freezing cold night. There was no hint here of poverty, political unrest or anything disagreeable. At a piano in the corner by a large pot of evergreens, an effete young man in white tie and tails was employed reducing Irving Berlin's 'Cheek To Cheek' to pap. Every table seemed to be occupied. Waiters dodged between them quieting imperious commands with '*Si señor, momento señor,*' which seemed to be the night-time version of '*mañana, mañana*'.

'Over here, over here!'

Edward turned in response to the clear, almost actorish tones of the English in foreign parts.

'Maurice!' Verity responded. 'It's Maurice Tate,' she murmured to Edward. She switched on a smile and weaved her way between the tables towards the man who had called to her, Hester and Edward following more slowly. 'Hello, Maurice,' she said, when they had gained their objective. 'This is Edward Corinth who I've told you about. Edward, Maurice runs the British Council here. If you aren't careful, he'll make you give a lecture.'

'Sit down, you two! Lord Edward – how good to meet you at last. Verity's been singing your praises.' Edward shot a glance at Verity who refused to catch his eye. 'Do you know about the British Council? It was founded a couple of years back to promote the English language and English culture throughout the world. Would you really be prepared to give a lecture? It can be difficult finding interesting lecturers. What would you speak about?'

'I'm afraid I don't know anything about anything,' said Edward, shaking Maurice's warm, damp hand and trying to smile.

'That doesn't matter, does it, Maurice? I don't suppose half the people you get on to the platform actually know what they're talking about. Who was that man we had to listen to the other day? Ugh!'

'Lord Benyon is a famous economist. You mustn't be wicked, Verity. You've heard of Benyon, haven't you, Lord Edward?'

'I'm afraid not, but then, as I say, I don't know anything.'

Maurice Tate looked the typical English intellectual: from the *New Statesman* on the table in front of him down to his grey-flannel trousers, tweed jacket patched with leather at the elbow, and scuffed suede shoes. His hair was thin and brushed over the top of his head in a vain attempt to disguise his bald patch. He was smoking Gitanes through a long, chewed cigarette holder and his white hands, like the flippers of some light-starved fish, flapped foolishly as he talked. Edward imagined he must model himself on Noël Coward – he affected what he obviously believed to be Coward's thin, clipped way of speaking – but he more closely resembled a preparatory schoolmaster.

Edward had occasion to congratulate himself on his perspicacity when Verity added, 'Maurice is directing *Love's Labour's Lost* at the Institute. He wants Hester to play the Princess of France. I think she would be marvellous, don't you?'

'And you, Lord Edward, you would be perfect for Berowne.'

'I fear I won't be here long enough, Mr Tate.'

'Ah no, of course, "lawful espials",' he said in a stage whisper.

'Lawful what, Maurice?' said Hester.

'*Hamlet*,' Edward said. 'But I assure you, I've not come to spy on anyone – just to try and get David out of gaol.'

Edward turned to speak to Hester but she had her back to him, talking to a very good-looking young man who was smoking, drinking and giving tongue all at the same time. Verity, catching his glance, said, 'Let me introduce you to the others. Tom, stop talking for a moment and say hello to Edward – Lord Edward Corinth, Tom Sutton and . . . you know, vice versa.'

The young man rose gracefully and took Edward's hand. 'Hello,' he said. 'Basil Thoroughgood told me to look out for you. I'm at the embassy. Terrible business about David. Anything you want, you only have to ask.'

Tom Sutton was giving every sign of being as ineffectual as Maurice Tate but Edward, looking into his shrewd grey eyes, recognised that he was not to be underestimated. 'Very glad to meet you,' Edward said. 'Perhaps you might allow me to come to your office tomorrow for a chat?'

'Of course,' Sutton responded. 'Eleven o'clock – would that suit you?'

Verity broke in, 'And this is the star of our little party. Edward, you haven't met Ben Belasco before, have you?'

'No,' said Edward putting out his hand, 'but I know and admire your work.'

'Very kind,' Belasco said, not attempting to rise but transferring his cigar to an ashtray in order to put his ham of a hand in Edward's. His voice was a deep growl and it crossed Edward's mind that it might have been practised. The accent was American Midwest.

Belasco would have stood out in any crowd, partly because of his size. He was a head taller than Edward – maybe six-three – barrel-chested and running to fat but, even slumped on the leather banquette, he exuded a charm which almost visibly dimmed the appeal of any other man in his vicinity. His eyes were small, black and very bright; his fleshy mouth was crowned with a silky black moustache which, as he spoke, took on a life all of its own. There was something both ludicrous and impressive about Ben Belasco. 'Half-charlatan, half-genius,' Tom Sutton said to Edward when they were discussing the famous writer the following day. 'I find myself imagining him to be a skin changer. You know what I mean? At night, he shambles across the deserted city in the guise of a brown bear looking for . . . I don't quite know what his natural prey might be, except that he would have prey. Forgive me for being whimsical but he really is a hunter.'

'Yes, I read his book – what was what it called? – *Hunter's Moon*, set in Tanganyika, as far as I remember.'

'It was. A first book and a brilliant debut,' Sutton said. 'And what's more, it was based on his own adventures. They say he's a crack shot.'

'I read his second one too – *Bloodstone* – about his experiences in France during the war,' Edward said. 'I have to admit, I expected it to be bogus but I ended up admiring it.'

'I agree. There *is* something bogus about the man – for example he will let you think he was a front-line soldier in the war but actually he was a medical orderly. Nothing wrong with that but he's a bit of a . . . well, the phrase I've heard Hester use is "bullshitter" – not for repetition but accurate just the same. But if Belasco is bogus, his books aren't. It's odd that, isn't it? A writer may be a fraud in his own life but when he puts pen to paper he can be "the billy", as the Scots say.'

Rather to his surprise, Edward saw Belasco slide along the banquette and signal Verity to sit beside him, which she did after a moment's hesitation, shooting Edward a look as if requiring his permission. Belasco began, absent-mindedly, stroking the back of her neck as though she were a kitten. Edward was not one to gush but he found himself telling Belasco how much his work meant to him and the big American accepted his praise with evident pleasure, notwithstanding the mocking twinkle in his eye. He said little but occasionally nodded his head as if in agreement and sucked on his cigar till the ash glowed. Verity was watching them both with amazement. 'I don't know what's come over you, Edward,' she said at last, after they had ordered more wine. 'I have never heard you so enthusiastic before. In fact, I said to Ben I was sure you two wouldn't get on.'

'Maybe we won't, V,' Belasco said, 'but I would be what Hetty calls a "schlepper" not to enjoy Lord Edward praising my writing. It's the one thing a writer needs: praise and plenty of it and when it comes from an English lord – and not a monocled fool at that – well, I guess we had to "get on" as you put it – but it won't last. When people get to know me they usually find me unbearable.'

'Oh, that's nonsense, Ben,' Tate said. 'Ben always draws a crowd when I can prevail on him to read or lecture.'

'Pshaw!' said Belasco. 'You make me puke, Maurice. You and your British Council! A few old ladies who still think Britain has an empire. You know I hate the whole thing with you Brits. So morally superior! Can't you hear what the world's saying? Brits go home, your time is up.'

'What's "shepper"?' asked a pallid girl with an English accent to whom Edward had not been introduced; indeed he had hardly registered her until this moment. She had a thin, high voice and her whole appearance was tubercular – pallid, almost shiny skin, long limp hair, like Alice in Wonderland, and a peevish mouth.

'"Shepper"?' said Belasco, puzzled, the question having been directed at him. 'Oh, "schlepper". Hetty will have to tell you. It's one of her words.'

Hester said, 'Oh, you know, Maggie; it means "idiot". It's a Yiddish word, I guess.'

Edward thought it would be polite if he introduced himself to the girl Hester had called Maggie. 'Hello,' he said, fatuously, 'I'm Edward Corinth.'

'I know,' was all she said in return, so Edward gave up.

'Who's the girl?' he whispered to Maurice.

'She's my daughter,' Tate said surprisingly.

Edward started to apologise.

'Please!' Tate said, lifting a hand to stop him. 'She lives with her aunt in London – her mother died when she was a baby – but she's here on a short holiday,' he explained in a low voice.

Edward turned once more to Maggie. 'Have you a part in *Love's Labour's Lost*, Miss Tate?'

'No, Dad says I can't miss any more school.'

'Sweetie-pie, it costs me the earth having you boarding at St George's. I might as well get my money's worth.'

Maggie went into a sulk. A thoroughly spoiled child was Edward's judgement.

The waiter was hovering, so they ordered. Edward was feeling very tired but also very hungry. It was ten o'clock and he and Verity had travelled a long way but he thought he would sleep better with something hot inside him. He ordered the *cocido madrileño* which Hester told him was a beef stew. Belasco said it was more likely to be goat. Verity ordered *cabrito al ajillo*. He had no idea what that might be but didn't like to reveal his ignorance by asking.

'You've come to see the prisoner in the tower?' said Belasco when the waiter had departed. Verity looked suddenly stricken and Edward inwardly cursed him.

'Well, he's an old friend . . .' Edward began haltingly.

'V here seems to think she's gotten a miracle man in you. "Open sesame", that sort of thing.'

'I wish I were,' he said, trying to hide his embarrassment by drinking deeply of the strong, garnet-coloured Rioja he had been given. The wine coursed through him making him feel less cold but even more sleepy. 'I have said I can't see what I can do but . . .' The waiter returned with commendable expedition and placed in front of him a plate of steaming meat and cabbage. As he picked up his fork, revived by the wine and the heady aroma of Spanish herbs and root vegetables, he said, 'I must say I feel guilty eating like this when I think of David in his cell . . .'

'Not to worry on that score,' said Belasco. 'Capitán José Ramón is looking after him.'

'He's the prison governor and a friend of ours,' Hester explained. 'You see, David's quite a celebrity here. I mean, he was well known for his political activities before . . . before all this. You were in America and I guess it wasn't reported there.'

'There's never anything about Europe in the New York newspapers as you know.'

'I'm surprised Verity didn't write you about it.'

'Yes, well . . .' said Edward, 'I don't suppose she had time . . . Griffiths-Jones and I were at Cambridge together but we weren't close friends. In fact, it was Verity who reintroduced us.'

Verity buried her face in her wine glass and made no comment.

'Well anyway, you're here now. You're going to visit him tomorrow?'

'Yes, at nine o'clock. I also want to talk to the investigating officer, if that's possible.'

Belasco said, 'Sure. Just ask Ramón to arrange it. The police have a lot to worry about with the new government and the likelihood of political demonstrations of one kind or another but they are surprisingly effective and honest. At least, Capitán Gonzales is.'

'He was the chap who brought the case against David?'

'Yeah, that was "the chap",' Belasco agreed.

Sutton said, 'The last thing the new government wants to do is alienate Britain by executing one of its nationals, but what can they do? The evidence was overwhelming and the verdict was given after a fair trial. There's another problem for the police: David is well in with several senior members of the new government. There was talk of his being the government's unofficial channel of communication with the Soviet Union. I don't know if there's any truth in it and there's no point asking at their embassy because they won't tell you anything. If you could find some way of exonerating David, you would gain the gratitude, not only of the man himself, but the Spanish government as well. It's all an embarrassment to them.'

Edward had the feeling Sutton did not much care for David Griffiths-Jones despite his talk of 'gratitude'. 'You say the evidence against him is overwhelming,' he said, 'but from what Verity has told me it's all circumstantial.'

Verity had managed to keep quiet until now but could not resist saying, as though she needed to convince herself as much as Edward, 'He was framed. I know he was but I can't understand who had anything to gain by it.'

Edward ignored her and said to the table at large, 'By the way, I really would be grateful if you could go over exactly what happened. Verity has only given me the bare facts . . .'

Hester said, 'You don't know? We've heard it all so often it's hard to believe there's someone who doesn't know. Let me see . . .' She began to count on her fingers: 'There was the knife, the bloodstained clothes and the ring.'

'The ring?'

'Yep, didn't she tell you? Hey, you've got to be straight with your man, honey,' she reproved Verity.

Verity scowled, not liking the 'your man' tag. 'No, I forgot,' she said shortly.

'It was the ring clinched it,' Hester went on. 'David left his ring by the body.'

Edward grimaced. 'You would have to be very stupid or very careless to do that and David is neither.'

'They said it must have come off in the struggle,' Hester went on remorselessly. Edward was getting the feeling Hester didn't much like David either. He began to be quite sorry for the man and this cheered him up.

'What kind was it?'

'The ring?' Verity said. 'It was a simple gold one with his initials engraved on it.'

'David's not married.'

'No, silly,' Verity said crossly, 'it wasn't a wedding ring – or rather it was – it was his father's. They shared the same initials: D G-J.'

'I see,' Edward said. 'And we don't know why the two of them went up to the mountains? They were friends – so was it just a companionable trek?'

'David says it was just a trek – you know, hiking . . . for the exercise, but we're all sure it was something to do with politics . . .' Hester responded.

'That's nonsense,' said Verity sharply. 'What could politics have to do with a walk in the mountains?' She had some idea that, whatever she had said to Edward in private, she ought to be discreet about David's political activities in public.

'Well, I guess you should know, darling,' said Hester. Edward wondered if she meant because Verity was David's lover or because they were both Communist Party activists . . . or both.

'In any case,' said Belasco, 'David got back here . . .'

'You mean, Madrid?' said Edward.

'No, I mean here . . . to Chicote's. We almost always meet here about eight for a drink.'

'In your case, several,' said Hester. 'Carlo, behind the bar, he keeps a bottle of bourbon specially for Ben.'

'Good writers are drinking writers, drinking writers are good writers,' Belasco intoned.

'Sure,' Hester continued. 'So he gets back here about eight and is surprised none of us have seen Godfrey. David explains he had gone off on his own to meet some mysterious stranger, but that he should have got back by now . . .'

'Sorry, you mean Tilney was meeting someone in the mountains?' Edward asked.

'Yeah, according to David; it sounds odd but Godfrey was always doing odd things.'

'He was definitely one of your lot?' Edward said to Verity. 'A Communist Party member?'

'Oh sure.' It was Hester who answered for Verity, in her long drawl. 'He was definitely "one of *them*" but he wasn't exactly one of us.'

'How do you mean?'

'Oh, I guess he thought we were all wastrels, capitalists rotten at the core, not worth wasting time on.'

61

Verity said, 'Hester thinks those of us in the Party are ... what is it, Hetty? – "deluded and depraved".'

'Not depraved, darling, but certainly deluded.'

'That was why he was always "doing odd things"?' Edward said.

'Yes,' said Hester. 'He was always going off on mysterious journeys sometimes for weeks on end, so we weren't too surprised that he had gone off on his own instead of coming back with David.'

'But then,' said Tate, 'David seemed to get anxious and we began to wonder if he had got lost or something and whether we should send out a search party.'

'And did you?'

'Yes. Well, there was nothing we could do in the dark, but in the morning David and Ben set out to look for him.'

'Where did you find him?' Edward said as no one seemed to want to carry on.

'We didn't find him,' Belasco said, 'the police found him or rather a shepherd did, at daybreak when he had gone out to see to his goats. We were just about to set off when we had a message from the police chief here: Gonzales.'

'So then what happened?'

'David and I went out to San Martino to identify the body.'

'San Martino?'

'It's a little town in the hills in the Sierra Norte.'

'That's to the north of Madrid?'

'Yes,' said Verity, 'it's directly north on the road to Burgos. I suppose it's part of the Sierra de Guadarrama. It's a very beautiful area; some of it's quite wooded.'

'And that's where the body was discovered?'

'Near there, outside a small village called San Pedro,' Hester said. 'No telephones of course. The goatherd, seeing it was an *extranjero* – a foreigner – rushed to the priest who got on his *burro* and trotted off to town.'

'The goatherd – he knew it was a foreigner?'

'Well, I suppose he would have reported any dead body but he wouldn't have had any difficulty identifying Tilney's body as that of a foreigner unless ... unless it had been very badly knocked about,' Hester concluded.

Edward saw Verity looking very pale so he did not pursue

the matter but clearly the body hadn't been on the mountainside long enough to have decomposed or been eaten by animals.

'San Pedro is a beauty spot. Foreigners do occasionally go walking around there when they want to get out of the city. Of course, Madrid people would never dream of going walking for fun,' Verity said. 'They do enough walking and, in any case, they'd say walking in the hills is something peasants do.'

'So David left Tilney at San Pedro and presumably Tilney did not have far to go to meet his friend.'

'Unless he was murdered on his way somewhere,' Verity said.

'No one in the village saw them?'

'No one admitted to it,' Verity said. Her colour was better now. By putting the whole thing on a 'professional' level – as if they were investigating a stranger's murder – Edward had made her use her brain instead of her heart. 'Probably someone did see David or Godfrey or both but they don't like getting involved with the police. It's quite understandable.'

'And it was definitely Tilney?' Edward had turned to Belasco.

'What do you mean?'

'You identified the body?'

'Yes, well, David did. He was his friend. I looked over his shoulder when Gonzales took the sheet off the body but it was only for a second. Of course it was Tilney. David said it was. Who else could it have been?'

Edward got the feeling that the 'tough guy', Ben Belasco, might have closed his eyes at a crucial moment but, on the other hand, he was a novelist. Wouldn't he have wanted to absorb every little detail of the scene for future use?

'And the knife?' he asked Belasco.

'What about it? Gonzales showed it to us and that was when David recognised it as his own.'

'The ring too?'

'Yep.'

'What did the police do?'

'Nothing then. They said David and I would have to be questioned again in Madrid.'

'I'm surprised they didn't detain him on the spot.'

'Don't forget, David's known as someone with political influence here in Madrid and Captain Gonzales would not have risked detaining him without first discussing it with his superiors.'

'But the evidence was so damning, they had no alternative but to arrest him,' he said brutally.

'I suppose so,' Verity admitted grudgingly. 'The next day – that was the 10th – they searched his flat and found the blood-stained clothing and then they arrested him.'

'Well,' Edward said after a moment, 'I agree with you, David would never have left such an obvious trail if he really had killed Tilney. It looks to me as if someone wanted him out of the way – and Godfrey Tilney too – and this was a way of killing two birds with one stone. Elaborate but effective,' Edward mused. 'First thing tomorrow we go and see David. You've arranged that, Verity?'

'Yes, and then, if you want to, we can go and see Captain Gonzales.'

'Although I doubt whether he will be able to tell me anything useful. I would guess he has done what he considers a pro-fessional job, got his conviction, and won't welcome someone like me trying to reopen the investigation.'

'The crazy thing was,' Hester said, 'when it came to the trial, David would not defend himself. He seemed to have no interest in the proceedings. He wouldn't say what they were doing in the mountains – except that they were out for a walk, which no one believed. He wasn't interested in how his knife was used to kill Tilney and refused to speculate on whom Tilney was going to see. After all, if David didn't kill him – and of course we believe he didn't,' she said hastily, seeing Verity scowl, 'then the most likely suspect was this mysterious "friend".'

'I'll want to go out to San Pedro,' Edward said. 'Is that difficult?'

'You can get a little train part of the way to Montejo de la Sierra, then a bus the few miles to San Martino,' Belasco said, 'then you walk.'

'David's innocent,' Verity burst out. 'Someone's framed him. I don't know why but that's what happened.'

Edward looked at her with affection. He wondered if she would be as vehement on his behalf if he was in trouble and thought she would. 'Apart from David and Ben, did any of you see the body?'

'No,' said Hester, 'but then why should we?'

'I thought they had the custom of showing the body in an open coffin before the funeral?'

'Yes, but Tilney was a foreigner and not a Catholic. His parents came over – poor things – and he was buried in the English cemetery.'

'I see,' said Edward, spooning up the last of his *olla* which was deliciously flavoured with herbs he could only guess at. 'Did any of the high-ups here go to the funeral?'

'The ambassador was in London – still is – but Tom represented the embassy. That was all,' Tate said. 'Of course, I was there on behalf of the British community. And Ben was there . . . he's a high-up in his way.'

'I went just from curiosity, I'm afraid. I didn't much care about Tilney – not a character I warmed to. He didn't drink for one thing. But all writers worth their salt write about death. What else is there worth writing about?'

'No one from the government?'

'No, why should they send anyone? Anyway, there wasn't a government. The elections were on, remember, and the Spanish had other things to think about,' said Hester.

'But if he worked for them . . .?'

'No one says that – not in public,' said Verity. 'Tilney was very secretive. He was officially a journalist but I don't know if he ever filed any stories. He certainly wasn't attached to any particular paper.'

'What was Tilney like? You said you didn't like him, Belasco.'

There was a long silence, then Tate said, 'He wasn't much liked by any of us, I'm afraid.'

'Why?'

'He kept to himself. Didn't mix much with us – seldom came here, for instance. In fact, David was the only one of us who knew him well. That's why . . .'

'. . . why you thought he must work for the Party?' said Edward. 'Surely you would know, Verity?'

'He was a Party member – that's all I know. If you want to know what he did you'll have to ask David,' she said shortly.

* * *

It was after midnight before Edward got back to his hotel. He was very weary and aware that he had a long day ahead of him. As he flopped into bed and tried to get comfortable on the hard little mattress, his mind chewed uselessly on what he had learnt that night. One thing was clear: no one, with the exception of his parents, mourned Godfrey Tilney. Could that mean there might be other people – people he knew nothing about – who had a reason to kill him? The police, busy keeping order in the volatile political situation, might have hesitated to arrest David but, when the case against him was served up to them on a plate, they must have breathed a sigh of relief. They were spared lengthy investigations for which they probably did not have the resources. Their duty was simply to present the case against him in the court. Even Verity did not seem to think the police had conspired against David.

Everyone seemed to feel that David's trial had been fair, except for the odd fact that David had not made much effort to defend himself. Perhaps if the election had not been on, one of his powerful friends might have pulled strings and got him out of gaol but from what he had been told the whole thing had happened too quickly for anyone to have intervened. The evidence had been gathered and the case heard all within three weeks. In England, it took months before a man accused of murder came to trial, but not here in Spain. Edward wondered why there had been no significant protests from the British government. He supposed they had no reason to love David Griffiths-Jones and no obvious justification for interfering in a murder trial carried out with transparent fairness.

The *New Gazette* had fulminated against the iniquities of 'Johnnie Foreigner' but, from what he had seen of Lord Weaver's campaign to have David freed, it was based solely on the principle that an Englishman – however distasteful his political views – could never be guilty of any crime, or, if guilty, should not be susceptible to the authority of a foreign judiciary. It would be interesting to see if David had been surprised by the speed and ease with which he had been condemned to death. On second thoughts, perhaps that might not be a tactful question to put to a man in the condemned cell.

Edward had little doubt that something strange was going on. The evidence against David was absurdly neat and tidy but he seemed to be conniving in his own destruction. Edward had less than a week to find out what was behind it all. If only Thoroughgood could get him two or three weeks more. Might David have something to tell him that he had not even told Verity? As he turned in his bed for the hundredth time trying to get comfortable, he fell asleep.

5

The prison was on the outskirts of the city on the Calle de la Princesa next door to the lunatic asylum. Edward's stomach was churning with apprehension as Hester drove him and Verity past the grim-looking barracks, the army's headquarters in Madrid, to the fortress-like building in which David Griffiths-Jones was incarcerated. Verity tugged at a huge bell-pull outside the prison gates and, as they waited for it to cease jangling, Edward was reminded irresistibly of a production of *Fidelio* he had seen at the Met while he had been in New York .

'Should you go in first, Verity, and make sure David is prepared to see me?'

Verity ignored him and, after a wait of four or five minutes in the cold morning air, Edward was quite glad to be ushered into the great courtyard in which the prisoners exercised. They were then conducted up a stone staircase to the governor's office. Verity and Hester had been there often before, of course, and greeted Capitán José Ramón as an old friend.

'*Hola! José, conoce usted a* Lord Edward Corinth?'

'*Encantado,*' said the governor, coming out from behind his desk to kiss the ladies' hands and shake Edward's.

'*Perdone, no hablo español,*' Edward faltered. He felt a bit of a fraud because he had picked up a little Spanish when he had been in South America but he was shy about using it.

'*No importa,*' said the governor genially. 'It does not matter. It is good I can practise my English. You are the friend of Señor Griffiths-Jones? That is such a hard name for me to say,' he smiled.

'Yes,' said Edward. 'Is he well?'

68

The governor shrugged: 'As well as can be expected.'

Edward cursed himself for having asked a foolish question.

'I'll stay here,' Hester said, 'if the Capitán permits. I think it's better that we do not crowd the poor man. It is important you two go and talk to him. I can't contribute much.'

Verity demurred but Hester was adamant. Just before they were escorted off to see the prisoner, the governor said, 'You must know the day of the execution has been delayed *dos semanas.*'

Verity was delighted: 'But that's wonderful. It gives us the time we need, doesn't it, Edward?'

Edward thought her faith in him was touching. 'Why is that?' he asked the governor.

'I do not know,' said Ramón. 'Orders from above.' He shrugged his shoulders.

'Does Mr Griffiths-Jones know?' Edward asked.

'Yes, I told him this morning, as soon as I received the order.'

Edward wondered if this was Basil Thoroughgood 'pulling strings' or just a coincidence.

David Griffiths-Jones' cell was by no means luxurious but Edward guessed it was considerably more commodious than that in which an ordinary prisoner would find himself. It had a metal bed, a washbasin beside it, a simple wooden armchair with a lamp behind it and a threadbare carpet. On a little wooden shelf half a dozen books were stacked. Griffiths-Jones was reading when they entered and Edward saw that he now wore glasses. As he rose to greet them, he took them off and laid them on the washstand with the book – which Edward saw was *Das Kapital.* Griffiths-Jones was the only communist he had ever heard of who had actually read it. Despite having to wear glasses, David was still a young man and very good-looking. He was tall, blond, though Edward convinced himself, rather spitefully, that his hair was thinning. His eyes were striking – blue and piercing. He was a little thinner than when Edward had last seen him six months before and, unsurprisingly, he looked strained and tired.

Verity kissed him on the cheek and for a moment he held her in an embrace which showed real affection. Then he turned to Edward.

'I'm afraid, Corinth, Verity has wasted your time. I tried to dissuade her from . . . from getting you here but you know how obstinate she is.'

'But he's already achieved something,' Verity blurted out. 'He saw a Foreign Office man in London and now we have got more time to get you out of here.'

Edward broke in hurriedly: 'Verity, you're jumping the gun . . .' Realising how unfortunate this sounded, he pressed on: 'I mean, I have no idea if there's any connection. Basil Thorough-good – he's an FO acquaintance of mine in London, David, – promised to do what he could but who knows what that means in practice.'

Griffiths-Jones was silent for a moment and then said, 'Look, Verity, since you have brought Corinth to see me – and no doubt bullied him just like you bullied me – ' he smiled to take the sting out of his words, 'I think you had better leave us alone to talk. Why don't you go back to José's office.'

'Can I come and see you before we leave?' she inquired meekly.

'Of course.' He signalled to the guard who was standing outside the cell to escort Verity back to the governor's office and, when she had gone, motioned Edward to sit in the chair.

'I'll sit on the bed. No, really,' he said, seeing Edward about to refuse. 'I'm quite comfortable on the bed. In any case, if you don't mind, I might pace around a bit. I have exercise periods but it's never enough. In fact it's what I miss most about this place. But, of course, it won't be for long.'

Edward thought it wisest not to offer conventional prot-estations. 'Look, David – I hope I may call you David?'

'Be my guest,' the other said ironically. 'There is an intimacy engendered in meeting in a condemned cell which it would be idiotic to deny.'

'First of all, I apologise for coming here. I knew you would not want to see me and I told Verity so but, as you said, she won't take no for an answer. She knows we don't get on, for obvious reasons, and I told her you might think I had come to . . .'

'To gloat? No, oddly enough, I didn't think you would come for that reason but I'm almost certain there is nothing you can do . . . in the time available.'

'You think there *is* something I could do.'

70

'There might be,' Griffiths-Jones said grudgingly.

'Well, tell me, for God's sake!'

'You see, Corinth, the thing is, I didn't kill Tilney.'

'I didn't think you . . .'

'No, hold on a moment. I'm sure you do think I did it and maybe I could have. I certainly feel like doing it now!' He hit his fist against the wall. 'I didn't kill Tilney because no one did.'

'No one did? His death was an accident?' Edward said, already disbelieving what he was being told.

'Oh, no. What I mean is when I left him he was very much alive.'

'But you identified the body . . .'

'Yes, well, that was what we agreed.'

'I'm sorry, David, but I'm not following this at all. Can you start from the beginning?'

Griffiths-Jones hesitated for a moment and then said, 'To make you understand, I've got to explain a little about the political situation here. It's anything but cut and dried. Anything might happen. We expect opposition from the army to what we are trying to do. The new government has sent away to the provinces – North Africa mostly – some of the generals they most distrust, like Mola and Francisco Franco, but that may not be far enough. Added to which the Popular Front is by no means united. We have to deal with weak-as-water socialists, Trotsky-ists, anarchists and Catalonian separatists so getting anything done is a battle.'

'You talk about "we" all the time like my friend Basil Thor-oughgood. He means the Foreign Office but I suspect your "we" is the Communist Party as directed by Moscow. Is that right?'

'Look, Corinth, you know I have no time for your sort of "English gentleman" politics. The fight against Fascism is too serious to be left to people like you and in any case – you mentioned Basil Thoroughgood – I happen to know he is a Fascist sympathiser and there are many more like him at the heart of government. Britain is riddled with snobbery, corrup-tion and anti-Semitism. You can't fight evil – by which I mean Fascism – with a broken sword.'

'But you're not Spanish. Is this really your fight? Aren't you interfering in someone else's quarrel and making it worse?'

'For Christ's sake, Corinth, this isn't a Spanish quarrel – or not *just* a Spanish quarrel. It's a fight against the evil of Fascism. This is the first battle in a long and bloody war. Each time we don't stand up to it, it grows like some monster which feeds on blood and treachery. I don't suppose you've ever read Lenin's *What is to be Done?*'

'No, I'm afraid not.'

'Well, you should. It might appeal to you. I read it first at Cambridge, at the Gramophone Society.'

'The what?'

David smiled. 'It's what we called our communist gatherings. We caught "conspiracy" like we caught chickenpox when we were children.'

'I didn't know that.'

'Why should you? Communism could have no appeal for you.' There was a sneer in his voice. 'But you ought to understand what is going to be the fate of you and your class.' He waved a hand at the copy of *Das Kapital*. 'As long ago as 1844 – almost a century ago – Karl Marx described communism as "the riddle of history solved, and knowing itself to be the solution". And to get back to Lenin – ' David was pacing up and down the cell in his eagerness to preach the word – 'he wrote *What is to be Done?* a full fifteen years before the revolution but it is so far-sighted, so brilliantly focused. He stresses the absolute necessity of discipline and he talks about the need for terror – "truly terrifying terror", he says, "is magnificent."'

'Like Robespierre.'

'Yes, like Robespierre, Lenin sees the value of what he calls "*mass* terror" and he emphasises the need for *konspirativnost* – underground political activity. That's what particularly appealed to us in the Gramophone Society. I have said this to Verity but I don't think she understands what I mean – perhaps no woman can: Lenin says there can be "no freedom of criticism" in the Party and those who are unwilling to operate actively under the direction of one of its officials should have membership denied them. Lenin called for miracles, for dreams, but to make them come true one must first have discipline.'

Edward was fascinated by the passion with which Griffiths-Jones spoke. It was almost as though he had forgotten to whom he was talking and was rehearsing in his own mind the faith that sustained him. Certainly, no one listening to him could doubt his sincerity, and the idea that he might accept help from Basil Thoroughgood, in exchange for betrayal of his principles, was frankly ludicrous. Edward was glad that he had not even touched on the subject. Griffiths-Jones might not like him – he certainly saw him as a class enemy – but at least, he fancied, thought him honest.

'And was that why Tilney had to die? Was he undisciplined?'

David ceased pacing and looked at Edward in surprise, as if a child had said something unexpectedly precocious.

'I didn't say that. I told you, I didn't kill him.'

'No, but you said you could have.'

'I was joking.'

'Are you able to tell me what you were doing with Godfrey Tilney on the day he was, or perhaps was not, killed? You said nothing at your trial, I understand.'

'No, I had my reasons for that.' He thought for a few moments, pacing about his cell like an animal in a zoo. Edward waited, curious to see if the man would confide in him. At last Griffiths-Jones sat on his bed and put his head in his hands. 'Can I trust you, Corinth?' he said simply.

'Anything you tell me in confidence now, I will keep absolutely secret unless I think it might damage British interests and then I would tell you what I proposed to do before doing it.'

'Fair enough,' Griffiths-Jones replied. 'I don't believe even you will consider anything Tilney and I were doing to be treasonous.' He smiled thinly. 'Anyway, it looks as though I am going to die unless I get help from someone. I don't want to die now because there is so much to do. Believe me, I have no fear of dying but it has to be at the right time. I'm too useful to the cause to be wasted.'

Edward was filled with revulsion. This man had horribly inflated ideas about himself and his importance. But, like all fanatics, he was in some sinister way impressive.

'Couldn't you have trusted Verity?' Edward said.

'I could but I was afraid she might get hurt. She's a good girl but I don't think she could have coped with . . . with what I was involved in.'

Verity would have been furious – or at least Edward knew she would have been furious with *him* if he had patronised her

73

in this way – but maybe, he reflected, she wouldn't have minded Griffiths-Jones saying she could not cope. She seemed to lose all her critical faculties as far as he was concerned. However, it was something that David did care about her. He was such a cold fish, he could use anyone if he felt it to be in his interests.

'You don't want her hurt because you love her?' Edward blurted out. He didn't know why he said it – why he *had* to say it.

Griffiths-Jones looked at him curiously, his troubles momentarily forgotten. 'I do love her, yes, but I told her, when I brought her out to Spain, that there was no room for personal feelings and that we had a job to do which was too important to be put in jeopardy by bourgeois emotions like love.'

'How did she take it?'

'I don't know. That was not important. She may have been . . . upset.' He meditated for a minute. 'Still, I wish she hadn't fallen into the clutches of that man.'

'Which man?'

'Belasco, the novelist. I can't bear him and when I see him putting his paws on her . . .'

Edward was dumbfounded. 'You mean Verity's . . . Belasco's lover?'

'Yes, didn't she tell you? Naughty girl.' He laughed grimly. 'I suppose she didn't dare. She wanted you to "save" me because that's the sort of bloody fool you are – to save the lover of the girl you're in love with. Lancelot – or was he the one who slept with his master's wife?'

Edward wanted desperately to hit him but knew he couldn't. 'No, I didn't know,' he said, making a great effort to sound calm. 'It wouldn't have made any difference anyhow. I said I thought you would not want me anywhere near you but that, if I could help and you were prepared to trust me, then I would. There was nothing said about my feeling for her or for you.'

'Nothing *said*!' Griffiths-Jones repeated bitterly. 'Spare us the good manners!'

'So are you going to tell me what happened to Tilney?' Edward said, ignoring the jibe.

'I suppose I might as well, but remember, what I have to say to you is in complete confidence.'

Edward thought this rather rich coming from someone whose

whole life was predicated on the premise that the ends justified the means. If Griffiths-Jones were told something in confidence, he would keep that confidence as long as it suited him and not a second longer. Yet here he was appealing to Edward's sense of honour – precisely what he had been sneering at a minute before.

'You must know, Corinth, that the Republic is desperately short of arms and if, as seems likely, it has to face down the army it will have to do it with bare fists and pitchforks.'

'But I thought you said General Franco and – what's his name? – Mola have been exiled to the provinces.'

'Yes, but that was not wise. They ought to have been shot. If you remember your medieval history, the French and English kings liked to keep their "over-mighty subjects" at court where they could keep an eye on them. Back on their own estates, they could more easily plot rebellion and rally their retainers to their flag.'

'You mean you think Franco and his friends are gathering support from the regiments they command in North Africa?'

'Of course! A child can see it, but our good people just want them out of sight so they can be out of mind.'

'How does this relate to what you were doing with Tilney?'

'I'm just coming to that. There are in fact people high up in government who do see the danger and they instructed us – Tilney and me – to buy arms – particularly aeroplanes – from whoever will sell them to us.'

'Why use you – foreigners?'

'Just because we are foreigners, of course. If things went wrong, the Republic could repudiate us. Also,' he added with evident satisfaction, 'as members of the Communist Party we are above suspicion. Spain is riddled with corruption but, if there is honesty to be found, it is from comrades in the Party.'

'I see,' said Edward. 'You were authorised to buy arms using gold . . .'

'. . . from the Bank of Spain. I promise you, Corinth, if any of this leaks out neither your life nor mine will be worth a peseta – another reason I have not involved Verity.'

'But surely,' said Edward, remembering what Hester had said, 'these sort of deals are made in offices and hotel rooms – not on the side of mountains.'

75

'True enough but delivery ... that has to be done with the utmost secrecy as close to us here as possible.'

'But how were these arms delivered? Not by train or motor vehicle – there are hardly any roads up in the mountains, are there?'

'No, that's why it was so safe. The arms came by air along with the aeroplanes. We have no aeroplanes, at least not until recently.'

'The stuff comes by air?'

'Yes, since I'm telling you all this I will have to trust you completely,' he said with obvious reluctance. 'My life may hang on you not revealing what I'm going to tell you – not to anyone.'

'I promise to be discreet. Didn't Lenin have a phrase he used when someone asked how he knew something: "A swallow brought it to me on its tail"?'

'Yes! Wherever did you read that? But I mean it: I must have your word as . . .'

'As a gentleman?' said Edward ironically. 'Look, David, I will keep as silent as the grave.'

'Silent as the grave?' he mused. 'Graves can shout loud enough sometimes. However, I must trust you.' He took a deep breath. 'There's an airfield right up in the mountains in a sort of basin – perhaps it was a volcano once. Anyway, an aeroplane looks as though it's flying over and behind the hills when actually it drops down on to this landing field. The crates are unloaded and taken to a warehouse near Barajas – the airport – where they can be distributed as the government sees fit. The aeroplanes have their markings changed and are flown on to Barajas separately.'

'And is this a regular thing?'

'This was the third delivery.'

'But something went wrong?' Edward hazarded.

'Yes, one of the team got nervy – didn't like something about the job and refused to go on with it. There was the devil of a row and the man got shot.'

Edward guessed this was a partial version of what actually happened.

'So you dressed him in Tilney's clothes and left him to be found by . . .'

'We tried to bury him but the ground is solid rock there so we tossed him down a cliff.'

'So his body would be difficult to identify?' Edward felt revulsion at the coolness with which Griffiths-Jones recounted what must have been murder.

'Yes, and I had to be sure to be the one to identify the body.'

'But why did you leave your knife there?'

'That was just a bad mistake. It must have fallen out of my pocket when we tossed the body down the cliff and, as luck would have it, was found beside the body.'

'And the bloody jersey?'

'Believe it or not, that was nothing to do with it. I got blood on it when I had a fall in the mountains a few weeks back and never got round to washing it.'

'And the ring?'

'I didn't notice it wasn't on my finger until I was back in Madrid.'

'But why did Tilney need to disappear?'

'Well, someone has to organise delivery of the arms we receive and in any case, he believed his life was in danger in Madrid. He refused to give me the details but he had had death threats, so it seemed a good time for him to vanish.'

'But he did not know you would be suspected of his murder?'

'No, we thought it could be blamed on brigands or whatever but it turned out I was the obvious suspect.' He grinned wryly.

'But why didn't he send word or give any sign to prove you were innocent when you were on trial?'

'That's what I don't know,' said Griffiths-Jones in obvious puzzlement. 'Every day I have expected to be released. After all, Tilney must have heard what happened. Even cut off from newspapers, he would have met someone who would have told him. He had to know what was happening in the world.'

'You hadn't quarrelled? I mean, it occurs to me he might want you dead.'

'No, we were both fighting on the same side. Personal feelings didn't come into it.'

'But you kept quiet about why you were on the mountain?'

'Yes, it was my duty, and,' he added grimly, 'if I had started talking about what we were really doing, I would have been found knifed to death even here in prison.'

'Good Lord!' said Edward. 'You are in a hole.'

'Yes,' Griffiths-Jones agreed, 'a hole four foot wide and six foot long unless . . .'

'Unless . . .?'

'Unless you can find Tilney and get him to come forward or something . . . but it's hopeless. I know that.'

'Yes, I suppose it is,' Edward had to agree. 'Is there anyone who might know where he is?'

'I've thought about that. There's a girl he used to . . . he was close to . . . an actress of sorts . . . called Rosalía Salas. I only met her once. She didn't mix with the foreigners much, though I remember she spoke good English. In fact, Tilney kept her away from everyone. I don't even know where she lives. If you could find her she might know something.'

'You didn't see her at your trial, then?'

'No, never, which I suppose was a bit odd.'

Edward sighed: 'Well, thanks to Basil Thoroughgood we've got a bit more time. By the way, in exchange for the help he is giving, keeping you alive, he wants you to spy on your friends in the Party for him.'

Griffiths-Jones laughed for the first time since Edward had seen him, and at once he looked much younger. 'I suppose you told him I would tell you to go and boil your head or you wouldn't have . . .'

'Yes,' Edward said, smiling too. 'As you pointed out, we don't live by the same rules but I would never accuse you of betraying your principles, much as I detest them.'

Griffiths-Jones laughed again: 'No, you're right there, but I don't want to die for them if I can possibly avoid it.'

'Yes, well, I had better get going,' Edward said, getting up from the chair. 'Oh by the way, can you tell me what sort of arms you were collecting that day?'

'Hand-grenades, rifles – mostly Vetterlis, Arisakas and Lebels – whatever we could lay our hands on – pistols, machine-guns – Maxim MG 08s and Hotchkiss M 09s – cartridges of course . . . That last time we took delivery of a Fokker trimotor and a small Nieuport fighter.'

'Good heavens!' Edward exclaimed.

'But not nearly enough and mostly old stuff. You see, the Americans, the French and our own beloved government have refused to sell arms to Spain. They say they want to stay absolutely neutral but actually they want to see the Popular Front overthrown.'

'So, who do you buy arms from?'

'The Soviet Union of course . . . and . . .'

'And . . .?' Edward prompted.

'Well, you'll think it odd and it was this that the Spaniard who died objected to when he saw the markings on the crates. We also buy from Germany. I know what you are going to say but . . . ends justify means and bullets have no smell. If we have to buy bullets from Fascists in order to kill Fascists – then that's what we have to do.'

6

She wasn't sure how it had happened. She had been lonely, of course, and apprehensive, but still . . . The problem was she had no idea how to be a foreign correspondent. There were no instruction manuals, no university courses, and her Baedeker, purchased hurriedly at the W H Smith bookstall in Victoria Station just before she caught her train, restricted itself to describing buildings of historic interest although, to be fair, the author, Albert F. Calvert, Knight Grand Cross of the Royal Order of Alfonso XII, had included some interesting statistics about the population of Madrid and its geography. It was natural, therefore, that she gratefully received the paternal support offered by Ben Belasco. She called him 'papa' which he seemed to like and, though she knew he had a wife back in America somewhere, she put up little resistance when he suggested they spend the long, Madrid siestas in bed together.

It was partly David's fault, she told herself. It was on his orders – he said it was the Party's but as far as she was concerned it was his orders – that she had come to Spain and then he had more or less abandoned her. He seemed to be so busy with Party matters, which he was unwilling to discuss with her, that he had no time left for her. He told her to learn Spanish and get to know the people and wait. It made her fretful and sapped her self-confidence. It had all been so urgent – the call to leave England for Spain – but, now she was here, there was nothing to do but wait. But wait for what? A change of government? Governments were changing all the time but it seemed not to make any difference. Wait for some conflagration, some civil conflict on which the Party would ride to power? Possibly, but there was no real evidence that this would happen.

In the meantime, she travelled round the country, mostly with Hester driving the Hispano. She learnt Spanish at the British Council – and picked it up quite quickly – but it was another matter getting anyone to talk to her. She had somehow assumed that people would want to use her to put across their views on the current political situation and plans for the future. She had taken it for granted that there would be a Ministry of Information through which she could meet ministers and government officials but there was none. Whether it was because she was a woman or a foreigner or both, no one with any influence would let her interview them. Spanish politics was an all-male affair. Women, with a few notable exceptions such as the communist Dolores Ibarruri, were there to cook for their men and breed, not to interfere in matters of state.

Doggedly she set about analysing Spain's political institutions but it was hideously confusing. Governments might change but the cast of characters remained the same and it was almost impossible for a foreigner to make sense of it all – who was who, who was in power this week, who had made deals with whom. She worked out that there were no fewer than twenty-six parties in the Cortes – Republicans, Radicals, Radical Socialists, moderate Socialists, Social Democrats, left-wing Socialists, Anarcho-Syndicalists and pure Anarchists. Most confusing of all, there were two communist groupings, Stalinist and anti-Stalinist, and they hated each other far worse than any of the right-wing parties.

David, as a prominent Stalinist and a foreigner, was always in danger of a stab in the back and Verity suspected that Marxist-Trotskyists were behind his being framed for the murder of Godfrey Tilney. With David ignoring her, bored and homesick for London, it was inevitable that she would drift into the orbit of the most charismatic male of her acquaintance who spoke her own language. She did not quite see it this way. She considered herself to be firmly independent and, if she embarked on an affair with 'papa', that was because she needed . . . not love exactly. Thinking about love made her think of Edward. She missed him badly. It surprised her how much. Sometimes she thought she loved him but she wasn't ready to be in love. To be in lust, yes, but how could she love? She had a career to make. Her whole concentration was on making a success of her time in Spain as a foreign correspondent. Her feelings for Edward were so . . . so complicated. Days went by when she did not think of him, but never whole weeks. Without meaning to, she silently compared him with the little group of English-speaking foreigners who gathered each night at Chicote's on the Gran Vía and found them lacking. She could hear him, in his clipped upper-class accent, dismiss them all as 'second rate'. Even Belasco – for all his animal magnetism, his experience with women, his glamour and fame – lacked something of Edward's gravitas.

At the beginning, she had admired Belasco and felt safe in his company, delighted that this distinguished writer had chosen her as his muse rather than, say, Hester who, on the face of it, was much more his 'type'. It did not take her long to find out his faults. For instance, when he wanted to be, Belasco was a brilliant raconteur but there came a time when she began to find his story-telling tiresome. It wasn't just that he repeated himself. To put it bluntly, she discovered he was a liar. An American journalist passing through Madrid had told her he had spent less than a month in the front line during the war and had spent most of the year he had lived in France not in the muddy, insalubrious trenches he had described so vividly in his book, but in Paris in the luxury of the Hotel Crillon. She had disbelieved the journalist at first but in the end he had convinced her that it was Belasco who was lying. It was odd really because one of his favourite words of condemnation was 'shonky', Yiddish for phoney.

It was not that he was a coward; far from it. She had seen with her own eyes that he had courage. He had insisted on taking her to a bullfight – he was writing a book on the subject – and for a week before had regaled her with stories of death and glory in the dust and heat of the arena. Hester had said to him – in Verity's presence – that he ought to call his book 'Bullshit', but he didn't seem to mind.

He was mad about the colour and frenzy of the bullring. On the day when they elbowed their way through the crowd into the Plaza de Toros, he had been almost beside himself with excitement. The smell of the people, the animals, the dirt in the arena, intoxicated him. 'It's not a sport, V, because the bull can never win. It's a tragedy, a ritual,' he shouted to her above the roar of the crowd.

She watched him getting ever more feverish as the bullfight progressed, ecstatic with the brutalism of the sight, almost as though he was on drugs. When a particularly ferocious bull had beaten down one of the wooden barricades protecting the onlookers, he alone had not run away but had helped the toreadors and the matadors chase the maddened animal back into the ring. He had returned to Verity, hot, sweaty and triumphant. Verity suppressed the thought that it might have been more chivalrous if he had remained beside her instead of dashing off to chase bulls. The event had been the basis of one of her most successful pieces for the *New Gazette* and Lord Weaver had himself wired her his congratulations. It was a secret that Belasco had helped her write the article and, in doing so, taught her how to select just the right word and 'tweak' the facts, as he put it, to give life and colour to a piece of reportage.

Belasco, she now knew, was a liar, a braggart and a bully but she was fascinated by him despite herself. For one thing he was a famous writer, and for another he was so ugly. Once when she had half-heartedly asked him why he felt he needed to lie about his experiences when he had in truth done so much more than most men, he answered her with unexpected seriousness. 'A man is what he hides. A writer's job is to tell the truth and his standard of fidelity to the truth should be so high that his invention out of his experience should produce a truer account than anything factual can be.' He added after a pause: 'What I invent is truer than what I remember.' And on another occasion, when Maurice Tate asked Belasco why he liked to live the life he did – big-game hunting, getting caught up in wars which were none of his business, drinking too much and getting into fights – he said, 'I want to be remembered not as a man who has fought in wars, not a bar-room fighter, not a shooter, not a drinker but as a writer.' It made sense to Verity that he should see his life as 'copy'.

They did not live together – that would have destroyed her reputation – but she spent most of the time at his rather grand apartment near the Plaza Mayor, writing or making love. He was a good lover, if rather brisk. She sometimes wished the men she took to bed were a little more tender. Neither David nor

Belasco went in for tenderness and Belasco, once he had had his orgasm, could not remain in bed another moment. Verity suspected that Edward might be a more imaginative and considerate lover but she reminded herself that could never be – for so many reasons.

Then when David was arrested and, to her amazement, condemned for a murder she knew he had not committed, she realised that Belasco, Tate, Tom Sutton, even Hester, were useless. Not one of them would lift a finger to stop him being executed. As though waking from a nightmare, she suddenly realised what she must do. She had to get hold of Edward; only he could help. That he might not wish to help was not something she ever let herself consider. She was confident that, if she could only appeal to him face to face, he would. She discovered, after wiring Lord Weaver, that Edward was due back in London within the week and determined she would be knocking at his door at eight the morning after his arrival. And now here he was, tired and out of place among the people she now called her friends, but somehow, for the first time in weeks, she felt able to relax. Lord Edward Corinth, class enemy, ineffectual member of a dying caste, was here in Madrid and she felt safe. How mysterious.

7

Tom Sutton was no fool. He looked at Edward through narrowed eyes and said, 'So he told you what he wouldn't tell anyone else. I wonder why? I thought you were sworn enemies.'

'I wouldn't say that,' said Edward mildly. 'I don't approve of his politics and, as far as he's concerned, I represent everything he hates most about the English class system.'

'And that makes for confidences, eh?' said Sutton drily.

'It's quite simple really. David knows – or thinks he knows – that Godfrey Tilney is not dead. There was some sort of arrangement between them which made it necessary for Tilney to disappear. Either through a series of accidents or as a result of someone's deliberate malice, he found himself accused and then convicted of Tilney's murder, but all along David – who's a pretty cool customer as you know – was expecting Tilney to reappear like a jack-in-the-box and apologise for causing inconvenience. David would then brush the dust off his shirt cuffs and walk out of the gaol a free man.'

'But Tilney has not appeared.'

'Quite and, understandably, David is getting anxious.'

'Who was he, by the way – the man buried in Tilney's place?'

'A disgruntled Spanish Republican who did not like the way David and Godfrey Tilney were going about buying arms for the government.'

'I thought that must be it,' Sutton said. 'David Griffiths-Jones is a ruthless man and if he decides something has to happen – then that's the way it does happen. Who murdered this unfortunate Spaniard, then?'

'Oh, from what David says, it doesn't sound like murder –

more like a knife fight which went wrong – and, if we are to believe David, it was actually Tilney who killed the man.'

'But it was David's knife which was found by the body.'

'Yes, he says it either fell out of his pocket when he and Tilney tipped the body over the cliff, or someone added it to the body later.'

'I see,' said Sutton meditatively. 'And you believe him?'

'I do,' Edward said, almost in surprise. 'At least, I think I do.'

'And how does he account for his ring being found on the corpse? It fell off his finger, I suppose.'

'He can't explain it.'

'That almost convinces me he's innocent. Bluff, double-bluff ... I don't understand what he's playing at. So, what are you going to do, exhume the body? I rather doubt the powers-that-be will permit it without some hard evidence. They'll just dismiss his story as a desperate man's attempt to stave off execution. After all, it's rather late in the day for David to say the man he identified as Tilney wasn't him.'

'Quite and, as I understand it from David, after being tipped over a cliff the body was beyond easy identification.'

'So?'

'So, I have to find Tilney.'

'I still think Tilney's dead.'

'There was no point in David telling me this tale if it isn't true. I've got to assume that. I must find Tilney and bring him back to Madrid.'

Sutton was silent. Edward had the feeling he would not be an easy man to know. Superficially, he was a perfect specimen of the imperial Englishman. He ought to be ruling some outpost of the empire in Africa or Asia. His short-cut hair, healthy complexion, firm chin and bright hazel eyes made him appear younger than perhaps he was. Edward guessed he was about his own age – thirty-five or six. But was the real Tom Sutton as frank and straightforward as he seemed to want people to believe? When Edward had arrived for his appointment, after visiting Griffiths-Jones, he had immediately been ushered up to the second floor by a uniformed porter whose considerable physique and muscular forearms suggested he also doubled as 'security'. He had knocked on a door with a label identifying the occupant as 'cultural attaché'. Sutton had peered out cautiously and then –

having established who his visitor was – had dismissed the porter with a nod. It was not a large office and it was sparsely furnished – a simple desk, battered wooden armchair behind it and two uncomfortable visitors' chairs, as though Sutton did not wish to encourage visitors to stay longer than was strictly necessary. There was only one window and that was wide open. The room was very cold. Unless he had been trying to disguise the smell of an illicit cigarette, the man was a fresh air fiend.

'Well, I'm glad you told me all this,' he said at last.

'David did tell me not to,' Edward said a trifle defensively, 'but I assume you will keep it confidential.'

'Oh, yes . . . yes,' Sutton said distractedly, standing up and looking out of the window down on to Calle Fernando el Santo, the busy street in which the embassy was situated. 'I knew most of it anyway.'

'As cultural attaché, you mean?' asked Edward innocently.

Sutton had the grace to smile a little sheepishly.

'As you have been so open with me, Corinth, I won't disguise from you that I do have – as do all of us in the embassy – a responsibility to keep my eyes and ears open. You've only been here a few hours but I expect you realise how complicated and how fluid the political situation is in Spain. We do our best but I doubt if even the President of the Republic has a clear picture of the situation. But, between ourselves, it is the communists who we have to watch closest. Civil war might just suit their book and, if they possibly can, they'll drag us in to support them.'

'Why would it suit their book to have civil war?'

'Oh, because if the Popular Front – the legitimate, democratically elected government – wins, you can bet your bottom dollar the Communist Party – that is the Stalinists – will end up in control of the government. They're the only ones with the single-mindedness, the iron determination, to lead the ragbag of left-wing parties to victory.'

'And if they lose?'

'If they lose, they will have lit the fuse which will ignite a European war.' Sutton looked very grave. 'Find Tilney and for God's sake find out what's going on, Corinth.'

As Sutton was showing Edward out of the building, he said, 'Basil told me you were a friend of poor Makepeace Hoden's.'

'Not a friend. We were at school together but he was older than me and in a different house.'

'But you knew him?'

'By sight, and he was a member of my club.'

'Brooks's?'

'Yes, you seem to have done your homework. Thoroughgood said you had been in Nairobi at the time Hoden was killed. It was a shooting accident, wasn't it? On safari.'

'So I believe. Well, here we are. Good luck, Corinth.' Tom Sutton had the firm handshake of a man you could trust so it was odd that Edward didn't trust him . . . not for a minute. 'Let me know if there's anything I can do and I rely on you to keep me informed of anything you uncover. Are you going to see the police – Capitán Gonzales?'

'I was hoping to,' Edward replied, 'but, when I telephoned, I was told he is not in the city at the moment so it will have to wait. To be honest with you, I'm rather relieved. I fancy he might not relish someone like me asking awkward questions.'

'Hmm, perhaps so, but he's a good chap. I think he will listen to what you have to say patiently enough.'

'There's something I don't understand,' said Verity. Edward was seated in Hester's and Verity's comfortable apartment discussing the situation. 'I didn't know Godfrey Tilney well – hardly knew him at all in fact – but can he really be so . . . so wicked as to let his parents think he is dead, let them "bury" him – knowing what it must do to them – and let a friend or at least a compatriot be executed for his murder?'

'Perhaps he is being held prisoner,' Hester said.

'By the Fascists, you mean?'

'By whoever. Tilney and David had – have – many political enemies,' Hester pointed out.

'Or perhaps he *had* to disappear and the funeral announcing his death to the world was just what he wanted,' Edward suggested. 'I don't think speculation is going to help us understand what happened. Our only hope is to find Tilney's girlfriend. David said her name was . . .' He looked at a piece of paper on which he had made notes. 'Yes, here it is: Señorita Rosalía Salas. David did not have an address for her – apparently, he did not let her mix with "foreigners". I get the impression Tilney was one of those people who kept his acquaintances in different boxes quite separate from each other.'

'So, how do we find her?' Verity said.

'No problem! I got Tom Sutton to look up her address. It didn't seem to be difficult. She lives at . . .' he squinted at the paper again, '16 Calle San Fernando. Do you know where that is?'

'Yes, it's up by the Plaza de Toros – the bullring – on the east of the city. Did I tell you Ben took me to a bullfight?'

'Did he perform himself?' Edward asked a little spitefully.

'He did as a matter of fact,' she said with a laugh.

'Well,' he said, feigning indifference, 'what shall we do? Shall we go there now? I suppose we can't telephone or anything.'

Verity laughed again. 'You're damn right we can't. The one thing I have learnt about this place is the telephone system hardly exists. If you want to, you can always find a boy on the street to take a message but I think it's best just to go. I mean, she has kept very quiet. I don't know what she looks like even, and I never heard she went to the trial.'

'Did she go to Tilney's "funeral"?'

'She may have done but I don't think so. I certainly don't remember any weeping girl and I'm sure someone would have pointed her out to me if she had been there.'

'Perhaps she wasn't there because she knew it was all a show and he was still alive and walking,' suggested Hester.

' "Kicking",' Verity automatically corrected her.

'But if she were in on the deception, wouldn't Tilney have wanted her to go to bolster the whole image – you know, grieving widow, that sort of thing?' Edward said.

'Maybe she was plain scared. I mean, I can't see any sane Spaniard wanting to get involved in the tangled world of Republican politics, especially if she believed her lover was murdered in some political in-fighting.' Hester drew on a cigarette and offered one to Edward.

'I think I had better go alone,' Edward said thoughtfully, lighting his cigarette. 'She might be frightened by a crowd.'

'Crowd?' repeated Verity indignantly. 'If you think you are going without me, forget it.' She crossed her arms in front of her like an angry child and Edward could not help smiling.

'And stop smirking, ratbag,' she said, smiling herself.

'Ratbag?' Edward inquired. 'That sounds like one of Belasco's. Am I right?'

Verity blushed, and Hester said hurriedly, 'And I'm going to be your chauffeur. So let's get cookin'.'

Calle San Fernando proved to be a narrow street close, as Verity had said, to the bullring. It was quiet enough on a weekday morning but Edward guessed it could get lively, not to say crowded, when there was a bullfight. Hester brought the Hispano to a stop in front of a substantial building which must once have been a family house but was now divided into apartments. Immediately the car came to a halt, a crowd of small boys surrounded it, expressing awe and derision in equal measure. Edward chose the fiercest-looking of the little urchins and gave him a handful of small change. 'Verity, tell this child if the car is in one piece when we come back, he gets the same again and a ride across town.'

When Verity had conveyed this in her still less than fluent Spanish, there was much nodding and serious looks among the children punctuated by '*Sí señor, señora*' and '*No se preocupe*' from a child who looked like a pirate.

They were in luck. They walked up a flight of stone stairs to find, stamped on a stout oak door, the name 'Salas' unadorned by any initials or first name. Edward knocked and, after a few seconds, the door was opened a few inches and a voice deep enough to be a man's but, for all that, very much a woman's, demanded, in Spanish, to know who was there.

Edward said in English, 'I'm a friend of Godfrey Tilney, Señorita Salas. I would very much like to have a word with you about his death, if that were possible. I apologise for coming unannounced but Mr Griffiths-Jones said he thought you would be prepared to talk to me and my friends Miss Browne and Baroness Lengstrum.'

He thought he must put all his cards on the table from the very beginning. There was no point in pretending they were here for any other reason than to help David Griffiths-Jones. That, surely, would reassure Rosalía Salas that they were not political enemies.

'*Fuera!* I cannot tell you anything,' the woman said eventually, in heavily accented English. She did not open the door, which was obviously on a chain.

90

'Please, Miss Salas,' Edward pleaded. 'We must talk to you. You see, we don't believe Godfrey Tilney is dead and he may be in great danger. You would not want Mr Griffiths-Jones to die for a murder he has not committed, would you?'

There was a long silence and Edward was just about to turn away in despair when he heard the chain being taken off and the door opened.

'You had better come in,' said Rosalía Salas resignedly.

The woman who faced them was very striking. She was not tall, about five foot six, Edward guessed, sturdily built with broad shoulders and a strong-boned face. Large black eyes under bushy black eyebrows stared at him with undisguised curiosity. Her long, slightly hooked nose and square jaw suggested a woman of considerable character; a magnificent head of hair – black and shiny – completed the picture. This was a woman who once seen could never be forgotten. She led them through into a large drawing-room hung with old portraits of aristocratic-looking men and women. A massive sofa, at least a hundred years old, dominated the room. Around the walls, glass-fronted cabinets held china ornaments.

Seeing Edward's surprise at the solemn splendour of the room, she said grudgingly, 'This was the house of my grand-parents but now I have only this floor, you understand?' Her English was good but she seemed shy about using it.

Edward nodded gravely. 'I am so sorry to bother you, Seño-rita Salas. I am Lord Edward Corinth and these are my friends, Miss Verity Browne and Baroness Lengstrum. We are all friends of David Griffiths-Jones and Mr Tilney and it is of the utmost importance that we find Mr Tilney in the next week. If we do not, David will die.' He spoke formally, repeating their names to give her time to assess them and see that they were respectable and unfrightening because Rosalía Salas was certainly frightened.

'*Su amigo!* You think so? Who told you they were friends?'

'David Griffiths-Jones,' said Edward, puzzled.

'That man,' she said scornfully. 'I think he was Godfrey's greatest enemy.'

'Why do you say that?' Verity broke in. 'Please, tell us: is Godfrey still alive?'

Rosalía looked at the two women and seemed to approve of what she saw. 'Sit down, please,' she said pointing to the sofa.

'Are we right?' Verity repeated. 'Is Godfrey still alive?'

'Yes,' said Rosalía simply.

'But why has he hidden himself and not come forward? Doesn't he know David may be . . . may be executed for . . .'

Verity could not continue and Rosalía, seeing her distress, wrung her hands in almost equal dismay. '*Entiendo*, I understand but what can I do? I can only go to him when I get the signal. I have been waiting for many days but it has not come.'

'Do you think he doesn't know David's predicament?' Edward asked.

'*Qué . . .?*'

'*Su . . . apuro. . . .*' Verity translated.

'*Sí*, when I last saw him . . .'

'When was that?' Verity broke in.

'Ten days ago.'

'But . . .'

'Hold on, Verity, let Rosalía tell us what she knows.'

'I took him up food – he likes English *mermelada* and meat . . . I take him meat.'

'What else do you take him?' asked Edward gently.

'I take him *los periódicos ingleses* . . . the newspapers, and anything else he tells me.'

'But you've had no message to go to him for ten days?'

'He always send to me on the Saturday to go on the Sunday, but this time I had no message so I did not know what to do.'

'You did not go and see if he was all right?'

'No, I . . . I was going to go but . . . but I got . . . scared.'

'You do not look as if you would be easily scared, Rosalía.'

'The men he works for . . . the *comunistas* . . .' she hissed, 'they are not good men.'

'How do the messages come? Who delivers them?'

'Boys, or the messages are put under my door.'

'Have you got one I could look at?' Edward said.

'No, I have orders to destroy them when I have read them.'

'But David . . . he is Godfrey's friend. How could he leave him in such danger?' Verity said, biting her lip to hold back her emotions.

'*Amigos*? Oh no, I tell you, they were not friends. Godfrey . . . he hated your David. They were great enemies.'

'I don't understand. They were working for the same cause.'

'No, *señorita*, they hated each other. *Política.*' She raised her hands up in an expressive gesture of disgust.

There was a silence while Verity and Edward considered this, then Edward continued: 'But did Godfrey say that he was not going to tell anyone he was alive even if . . .?'

'I do not know . . . I think so . . . but I do not know. He said there was one who knew him . . . who he did not want to see.'

Edward was puzzled. 'Not David?'

'No, one other . . . I think from . . . how do you say? . . . from the past, you understand?'

Edward thought about this and looked at Verity. Then, turning to Rosalía, he said, 'Please, can you take us to him? Where is he? Up in the mountains?'

'I do not know. He would not like it. It is a great secret where he is.'

'Well, if you tell us how to find him, we can go without you,' said Verity.

'Yes, we will never say you told us.'

'You would never find him,' she said simply.

In the silence which followed, Edward went over in his mind all the arguments he might use to persuade her to help them find Tilney. He might threaten to tell the police that she had been withholding information; but then she would become their enemy and, if she denied that she had ever said Tilney was alive, the police would just think it was one last despairing fantasy of Verity's. When Edward glanced up from his boots, which he had been studying hard in search of inspiration, he saw Rosalía was looking at Verity and his gaze followed hers. Great tears, of which he was certain she was unaware, were running down her cheeks and dropping on to her lap. These tears were more eloquent than any words.

'Please,' Rosalía said gently, 'do not weep. You are too beautiful to weep. It is I who must weep. All the women of Spain should weep . . . I will take you to see him.'

Verity got up from the sofa and went over to Rosalía to embrace her. For a moment, the two women clung to each other. Edward, embarrassed by this un-English display of emotion, averted his eyes. Was this a new Verity who felt so much and showed so much? If Hester was right, David wasn't even her lover. She had never been one for tears and he had supposed, now she was a journalist, she was even less likely to ... to get emotional. He shook his head. He really did not understand women, but he did know that he ached to hold her in his arms. She was only a few feet away. Why could he not go over to her? He moved slightly but it was already too late. Verity was her old self once more. Smiling with relief and excitement, she was planning with Rosalía where to meet the following morning – it was too late to venture into the hills that afternoon. They agreed to meet at first light at the station and take the little train that ran up towards San Pedro. The women kissed each other and Edward, feeling a fool, thrust out his hand to Rosalía. Before he knew it, she had gathered him into his arms and kissed him on both cheeks. Her hair brushed his lips and he smelt garlic, sweat and other scents he could not identify. He smiled, blushed and went out of the apartment feeling that he had made an ass of himself but that, in doing so, had tasted for the first time the real Spain.

8

They had left the path and were scrambling up the rocky bed of a stream. On either side, stunted pines and scrub scratched at the rock for anchorage. Edward had climbed some awkward mountains in his time – from the red kopjes of Damaraland to the Chamonix *aiguilles* – but never in such unsuitable clothes. Fenton, when he had packed his bag in London, had not envisaged his master scrambling up these cold, cruel slopes, the razor-sharp stones cutting his thin shoes to shreds, allowing the stream to reduce his toes to so many icicles. Verity was better equipped but even she was cursing in a most unladylike way. Hester, to her annoyance, had been left in Madrid. Edward looked at his wristwatch. It was ten twenty. They had been climbing for almost three hours. He was just about to suggest to Rosalía that there was little point in suffering frostbite for the sake of secrecy and perhaps they should find a recognisable road or track, when she left the stream and cut across the face of the rock.

Verity and Edward stumbled after her until they came to the edge of a precipice where she urged them with a wave of her hand to halt. They obeyed with relief, dropping the packs they carried on the ground beside them. Edward peered over Rosalía's shoulder and sank back in some alarm. Surely they must have lost their way. They were right on the edge of the mountain. To go up, they would first have to go back the way they had come. Below, there was a sheer drop of at least a thousand feet. Edward saw at a glance that without proper equipment – ropes, boots and crampons – there was no way in which they could continue their ascent.

He tapped Rosalía on the back but she lifted her hand in an imperious gesture of denial. She lay face down on the rock seeming to be listening intently. She had transformed herself for the expedition into a peasant woman. Her glorious black hair was twisted into a bun and covered with a black bandanna. She wore rough trousers and a coarse sailcloth shirt over which she had slipped a smock. On her feet were strong, rope-soled sandals. She looked a typical, shapeless peasant of indeterminate age and sex.

At the station, in the darkness before dawn, Edward had not at first recognised her and she had had to speak to him before he realised who she was. She whispered to them that she would travel on her own in a different carriage. To be seen with foreigners – and Verity and Edward were very obviously that – was not so unusual; there were many Spanish guides prepared to take foreigners out to see the monasteries and fortresses that ringed Madrid. However, it was early in the year for tourists and Rosalía did not want to draw attention to herself in case Godfrey's political enemies were keeping watch on her hoping she would lead them to his hideout. As far as Edward could see, they attracted no particular attention and he chatted to Verity about Madrid in English as if they were innocent tourists embarking on an outing in the hills to empty their lungs of city air.

They had been glad to say goodbye to the bus which had rattled and shaken them up the unmetalled road to San Martino. The bus, Rosalía had told them, was the pride of the locality and was now three years old but to Edward it already seemed at least as old as himself. From San Martino they had walked. As they drew close to San Pedro, dawn began to break over the hills and the view of the little village, dominated by its church spire, recalled to Edward the spiritually uplifting, crudely coloured pictures in his Sunday School book, over which he had dozed as a child. To heighten his feeling of peace, the bell for mass echoed across the silent landscape as it must have done for centuries.

Rosalía skirted the village along the route he supposed Tilney and Griffiths-Jones had taken on that fateful day six weeks before. They met nobody except a peasant on his donkey who ignored their greeting. Twenty minutes after putting San Pedro behind them the full glory of the rising sun broke over the hilltops, bathing the walkers in light and heat.

'"Full many a glorious morning have I seen flatter the mountain tops with sovereign eye",' Edward quoted, pausing to wipe the sweat from his forehead.

'Stop enjoying yourself,' Verity reproved him. 'We're not on holiday.'

'Oh, don't be so severe, dearest,' he said lightly, his spirits failing to be subdued. '"To one who has been long in city pent, 'tis very sweet to look into the fair and open face of heaven."'

'And don't quote Shakespeare at me. You know it makes me feel inferior.'

'Keats, child,' Edward said, provocatively.

'I said don't patronise me.'

'Verity, forgive me, but this is the first morning for months I have really felt alive. I've been stuck in cities – New York, London, Madrid – when I should have been out walking and breathing in this glorious country.'

'Oh, do shut up, idiot. Looking at the state of your shoes, I imagine you will soon be singing another song.'

Rosalía had confidently taken them off the main track on to a little path, clearly not much used, and soon they were scrambling over rocks and small boulders until even that faint footway had become invisible. Apart from knowing they were going up, Edward was completely lost. He reckoned on having a good sense of direction but, if Rosalía vanished, he knew he would have no idea how to get back to civilisation. It crossed his mind that she might have taken them into the wilderness to kill them but he dismissed the thought immediately. Still, it was comforting to feel that, if anything did happen to them, Hester would know where to begin looking.

They sat for some minutes on the edge of the precipice in complete silence. They were out of the heat of the sun and their sweat began to dry. Verity, despite wearing a thick jumper, shivered. Edward's feet grew numb and he crawled over beside Rosalía and muttered that, if they did not move on, they would get chilled.

'No entiendo, there is always someone on guard here but not today. I fear there is something wrong.'

'Well, let's go and have a look,' said Edward, 'except I can't see where we are going.'

'Look over there,' she said in a low voice.

Edward stared in the direction she was pointing. 'I can't see anything.'

'Do you see that – how do you say? – that thorn bush?'

A little further up the slope, a belt of bramble and brush barred the way. 'I see it,' he said.

'There is a cave hidden behind.'

No one could have guessed it and Edward suppressed a cry of astonishment. 'And that's where Tilney has his headquarters?'

'*Sí, pero no es* . . . it is so . . . *muy tranquilo*. I make a mistake . . . I come without the signal.'

'Well,' said Verity who had joined them, 'we're here now so we had better go and see.'

'You stay there,' said Edward firmly. 'I'll creep round the side and see if I can spot anything.'

'Not likely,' Verity said indignantly. 'You go, I go.'

In the end, they all three moved towards the cave together as though they were engaged in a sinister game of Grandmother's Footsteps. Edward thought what a wonderful fortress Tilney had found for himself. The rocky track which, as they had so uncomfortably discovered, doubled as a stream, ended a hundred and fifty yards from the cave entrance. There was little or no cover between and a man with a firearm could defend the cave from all comers for as long as his food, water and ammunition held out. They had come by the only path, which was invisible except to someone who already knew where he was going. Behind the cave there was thick undergrowth and anyone approaching that way would make enough noise to wake the heaviest sleeper.

Abandoning caution at the cave entrance, Edward called Tilney's name. There was no answer. Gingerly, he lifted part of the bramble and called again. Rosalía was now standing stock still, her hands against her cheeks, seemingly unable to move. If there was anyone in the cave, they would have been aware by now that they had visitors so Edward, his heart beating fiercely, dragged away the brambles which parted quite easily, like a curtain. Crouching, he stared into a narrow aperture hardly wide enough to enter except on all fours. There was the cave but it was too dark to see anything. Verity had a torch in her pack and went back to find it. As Edward's eyes became accustomed to the dark, he thought he could see something pale but the cave was obviously much deeper than he had imagined. He crawled inside. Immediately beyond the entrance, the cave widened and the roof rose to six feet so that he was able to stand. It was at least ten degrees colder here than outside and he shivered. He hesitated and sniffed. There was a noxious smell in the air which made his gorge rise. And then he became aware of an angry buzzing noise.

Verity returned with the torch and, not waiting for Edward, thrust past him further into the cave. Her scream brought Edward to her side. In the feeble orange light of the torch, which seemed unwilling to penetrate the gloom, they saw the figure of Godfrey Tilney. He was seated on a canvas chair, the sort one finds in front of bandstands. Death had clearly taken him unawares. He looked, at least at first glance, almost normal, as though at any moment he might rise from his chair to greet them, but there was a bullet hole in his forehead the size of a florin. The buzzing Edward had heard was made by the flies which swarmed in a black cloud above the dead man's head like some devilish halo. Pulling himself together with an effort, Edward pressed the back of his hand against Tilney's cheek. The flesh, even in that icebox of a cave, was still faintly warm. As Edward helped Verity out of the cave, he found he was very angry. Godfrey Tilney was dead because of his indiscretion. Without a doubt, it was he who had brought Tilney's murderer to him. He must have been killed perhaps only an hour before. Verity, her hand to her mouth, had burst out of the evil-smelling cave and was clasping the Spanish girl to her bosom. A harsh keening wail filled the air. Rosalía was mourning her lover.

Edward was unable to dissuade her from entering the cave to see for herself that her Englishman was really dead. As Edward took her back outside into the clean mountain air, he could not doubt that one person at least had really loved Godfrey Tilney. Edward was anxious to leave the place as soon as possible. It now seemed to exude evil and he was very much aware that Tilney's killer might be tempted to take a pot shot at them if they dallied. He said nothing of this to the two women, unwilling to alarm them further. At first, Rosalía could not be persuaded to leave the mouth of the cave unguarded and Verity announced that she considered it her duty to stay with her. Patiently, Edward pointed out that, if he went off without them, they would be in for a long vigil. It would take him at least two hours to get back to San Pedro and at least another two hours to get the police organised. It might be six or seven hours and almost nightfall before he returned. The police would almost certainly refuse to set out up the mountain until early the next day. The idea of spending a night by the cave made Verity shiver. They had brought some food – bread, salami, chocolate and biscuits – but no warm clothes, let alone camping equipment. There was nothing for it but for them all to return to San Pedro.

It took a further half-hour to persuade Rosalía that she had to leave the body of her lover where it was and go for help. Whatever she might be hiding – and Edward was too cynical to believe she was quite the innocent she pretended – there was no doubt her grief was genuine. They found a large rock, almost circular, which they would be able to roll in front of the entrance to the cave but, before they did so, Edward braced himself to make one final examination of the corpse.

With Verity's torch he crawled inside, attempting not to disturb anything more than necessary. He stared at the corpse using the torch to study it section by section. Then, trying to control his urge to retch, he examined the body to see if there was any other wound invisible to the naked eye, but there was only the bullet hole in the forehead. He felt in Tilney's pockets and, as carefully as he could, removed a wallet from the jacket the dead man was wearing and stuffed it in his own pocket to be investigated later. However, he noted there was a lot of money in it – about two hundred pounds in pesetas, he guessed – so obviously theft could be ruled out as a motive for Tilney's murder. He was touched and surprised to see that the wallet also contained a photograph not of Rosalía but of his mother. Perhaps after all, Tilney was capable of love.

In a corner of the cave, there was a little food wrapped in a cloth – sausage and lentils. For water, Tilney presumably used the stream. There was a simple army sleeping bag in one corner but nothing inside it – no papers or books even. There was no sign of any kitbag; had the murderer removed that? But in that case why not the wallet? Rather surprisingly, Tilney was wearing an expensive Swiss watch, but no other jewellery and, apart from an empty pipe – a Peterson 33 no less – with a pouch of tobacco, there was nothing personal. It dawned on Edward that Tilney was hardly here at all except in the form of an increasingly repellent heap of flesh. He had either had no personality or was a true ascetic indifferent to personal comfort, Edward decided. Maybe it was just that he had known his life was in danger and had deliberately kept his belongings to the minimum so he could speedily disappear into the mountains if need be.

When he had stumbled out of the cave and vomited noisily into a bush, he and the two women rolled the stone in front of the entrance. It moved so easily, it had clearly been used to block the opening before. He felt for a moment that he was taking part in some Biblical drama but, in this case, he trusted the body in the tomb would remain undisturbed for at least twenty-four hours. He was well aware there were foxes and wild dogs in the mountains, and there was always the possibility that the killer might return to destroy the evidence but he considered it unlikely. To remove the body and toss it over the precipice might be possible but what would that achieve? They had seen what they had seen and their story would be supported by scientific evidence, he supposed.

As they scrambled back down the rocky slope, hardly noticing the thorns scratching their flesh, the heat on their backs and the cold water around their feet, Edward was puzzling over the meaning of the riddle. Tilney, who had arranged his own death and burial for safety's sake, had risen from the dead only to be killed again. Either he had been so surprised to see his murderer that he had not even had time to get up from his chair, or he had known his killer and had felt no alarm in his presence. He glanced at Verity. He wondered if she had seen the silver lining from her point of view. Whoever had killed Godfrey Tilney, it could not have been David Griffiths-Jones, ensconced in his prison cell.

In San Pedro, the priest had been praying alone in his little church when they burst in upon him. Edward stood in silence as Rosalía and Verity bombarded the old man with news of violent death. At last, he raised his hands in the air as if to arrest the women in their flow. He summoned them with dignified authority – Rosalía the grieving lover, Verity the principled communist, and Edward the English milord – to kneel and pray for the soul departed. As he knelt beside Verity in the little white church, the walls bare of any ornament except a badly damaged Pietà, Edward was overwhelmed with a sense of the futility of his life. What had he achieved? What good had he done since leaving school and university, and not just any school but Eton, and not any university but Cambridge? A privileged education, the gift of a far from negligible intellect, enough money to do . . . something; since then restless, pointless travel. What did it all amount to? As a New York friend had put it so succinctly: a big zero. He managed a wry smile beneath the hands he held to his face. His self-disgust, which had been growing on him ever since he had embarked on the *Normandie* in New York, washed over him. In this simple church he felt the sharp pain of absence: the absence of any religion which might make sense of his life, the absence of meaning and purpose, and – if he were to wallow in self-pity – might he not add the absence of love. He knelt a few feet from the only woman he thought he could love, in the knowledge that they might as well be thousands of miles apart for all the good it did him.

As the priest rose from his knees, Edward made a great effort to throw off his depression. There was one thing he must do in justice to a man he had not liked but whose claim on him was that of youthful comradeship: he could find out who had ended Godfrey Tilney's life with cool deliberation on the side of a bare mountain and left him a feast for flies. Edward had thought it might take a couple of hours to summon police to the scene of the crime but it was soon borne in on him that this was an absurd underestimate. There was no telephone in the village for one thing. A small boy – there was at least a limitless supply of small boys – was bribed with promises of wealth beyond his wildest dreams to search out the local policeman who, in theory, might be anywhere within a twenty-mile radius. The boy, as it happened, knew exactly where to begin his quest. It was the policeman's custom to spend his siesta in a little drinking shop, hardly more than a hut, in a neighbouring village.

He duly arrived, sweating and exhausted from his uphill bicycle ride, three hours after they had brought the news to the village priest. Unfortunately, the policeman seemed to Edward to double as the village idiot and, when the whole story had been told him, did nothing but shrug his shoulders and sit down in the shade with a bottle of beer. It was by now four in the afternoon, too late to go up the mountain even if the policeman had been in a fit state to do so and, in any case, Rosalía was too distressed to guide anyone anywhere.

Edward then did what he knew he should have done hours before and announced that he and Verity would walk back to San Martino and hope to catch the bus to Montejo de la Sierra where they could get the train back to the city. They were both weary but it was unthinkable to vegetate in San Pedro for twenty-four hours. At San Martino, they could report what they had discovered to the local police and telephone Hester in Madrid so that she could alert Capitán Gonzales. Rosalía would not come with them. She wanted to stay as near her dead lover as possible and be there to accompany the police to the cave the next day.

The priest had a guest room of which he was very proud but his housekeeper – she might very well, Edward thought, be rather more than that – made it plain she was reluctant to have a strange woman in the house, particularly one as beautiful as Rosalía. She looked even gloomier when the priest offered the three strangers food. In the end, the priest had to command her to show what Spanish hospitality meant. A meal of ham, coarse bread and a kind of stew, the contents of which, Edward decided, should not be investigated too closely, made them all feel better. Even the priest's housekeeper cheered up when Edward slipped her enough pesetas to cover her expenses several times over.

Back at the hotel that evening, weary, scratched and bruised with his clothes in rags, Edward was greeted by Felipe, the manager, bobbing and bowing at the front desk, waving a sheet of yellow paper.

'Señor, Milor Coreeth, I have a telegram for you, from London,' he said with awful solemnity, his moustaches quivering with excitement.

Edward grabbed the paper from the little man's hand and

began to read. It was from his sister-in-law, Constance, and it was dated February 22nd and addressed from Mersham Castle. 'GERALD FELL WHILE HUNTING AND BANGED HEAD STOP DOCTOR SAYS YOU SHOULD BE HERE STOP COME IF YOU CAN STOP LOVE CONNIE'

Part Two

9

Edward took a step back and almost tripped over the hotel manager. He knew Connie was the last one to panic so Gerald must really be in danger. He read the message again and then made a decision.

'Felipe, I need to send a wire. My brother is very ill and I must return to England immediately.'

'In the morning, *señor*, in the morning,' he said shrugging his shoulders. 'It is too late tonight.'

Edward repressed a desire to hit this innocent bearer of bad news and with an effort said, civilly enough, 'In that case get me Miss Browne on the telephone, please.'

It was Hester who answered the telephone, her cool American drawl calming him. 'Oh Hester, is that you? Is Verity there?'

Verity had gone out. Apparently, Hester informed him, she always wired her stories through to the *New Gazette* at about this time and, despite her exhaustion, had insisted on tapping away on Hester's ancient Remington as soon as she got into the apartment.

'I told her she was being dumb and needed to shower and rest but I guess you know how much attention she pays when she's set on doing something.'

Of course, Edward thought bitterly, the discovery of Tilney's corpse was just a story to her, to be relished by a million Englishmen as they decapitated their boiled eggs before setting off to work. He knew he was being unfair. Verity had a job to do and could not afford to have another newspaper report a murder she had discovered. It suddenly occurred to him that two of those *New Gazette* readers might be Tilney's father and mother. It struck him as horrible that they should hear of their son's 'second death' in this way and he would not be able to rest until he knew that someone at the embassy, Tom Sutton most likely, had forewarned them.

'Are you still there, Edward?'

'Oh, yes, sorry, Hester. I was just thinking about Tilney's parents – what a shock it's going to be for them.'

'Yeah, you're right there. Is that what you wanted to tell V?'

'No, not really. I wanted to break it to her that I have to go back to England.'

'You mean because David is now out of danger? I guess he can't be tried for killing the guy a second time – while he was in a Spanish prison. It seems crazy . . . V said he had only been dead an hour or two.'

'The body was still warm,' Edward said simply and he shivered remembering the horror of of the scene. 'But that's not why I'm going. My brother has had a fall from his horse and . . . and my sister-in-law thinks I ought to be there.'

'I see. I am so sorry. Is there anything I can do?'

'Well yes. Lord Weaver said Harry Bragg – our pilot – would collect me whenever I wanted but I'm not sure how to get in touch with him. I suppose you couldn't ask Verity to go back to the post office and wire Lord Weaver again and see if he could send an aeroplane for me tomorrow? The train would take two days, perhaps three and . . .'

'Yes, of course. I'll tell her as soon as she gets in.'

'Thank you, Hester, I'll . . . I'll talk to you later.'

He telephoned the embassy but, as he had expected, everyone had gone home except for a sleepy-sounding clerk who refused to give Edward Tom Sutton's home number. Verity must have it or, if not, presumably he would be at Chicote's again tonight. He wondered why he felt so worried – almost guilty – about the Tilneys hearing the news from a newspaper. He could try telephoning them himself but he knew that, even if he could get through, the line was likely to be bad and it would be very difficult to make himself understood. They probably wouldn't even remember who he was. He wondered if he was making excuses but decided he was just being practical.

He went up to his room, took off his jacket and shoes, lay on his bed and settled down to some serious worrying. What if

Gerald were to die? He suddenly realised how much he loved his brother. Gerald had been fortunate in one respect. He had found in Connie one of the few women with the sense to recognise that beneath all his pomposity there lay a genuinely good man. She was the anchor who had given Gerald the strength to lead a useful and fulfilling life. He had not wished to become Duke of Mersham but, as the position had been forced on him, was determined to use whatever influence it gave him to stop England being dragged into another European war.

Edward had no desire to succeed his elder brother. It was a great weight off his mind that Connie and Gerald had had a son, their only child, who had been named Franklyn – or Frank to his family and friends – as were all immediate heirs to the dukedom of Mersham. Frank, now aged sixteen, was at Eton. Uncle and nephew got on well, liking and respecting each other. Edward was young enough – 'unfossilised' as the boy put it – to play the part of the older brother Frank had never had. He pitied his nephew and feared for him. It might seem magnificent to be heir to a dukedom but the silver spoon was poisoned. In the modern world being a duke, Edward considered, was rather ridiculous. It was bad enough to be a duke's younger son with pots of money and no chance of being taken seriously. His birth – his position in society – aroused expectations in some people, suspicion in most, and envy in a few. As far as women were concerned, he knew the girl he wanted was put off by his being a lord while the girls who threw themselves at him were precisely the kind he despised. Would it be worse for Frank?

It made him itch with frustration that he could not at once rush to his brother's side and he knew he would not be able to sleep. It seemed to put everything else into perspective. What did it matter if David Griffiths-Jones rotted in a Spanish gaol or if Godfrey Tilney, whom he remembered as a bully and a liar, had been murdered by one of his enemies? In the mood he was in, he was prepared to believe that anything bad which happened to these political troublemakers was no more than they deserved.

At last, unable to lie still any longer, despite aching limbs and a headache which made him giddy and sick, he got up, grabbed his coat and walked hurriedly towards Chicote's. It was almost eleven o'clock but it was just possible Tom Sutton would be there and could be persuaded to telephone London for him. Chicote's was much less busy than it would have been earlier in the evening. The bar was only half full and the waiters chatted behind the long wooden counter, surreptitiously dragging on cigarettes. There was no one at the table which seemed to be reserved for Ben Belasco and Hester but he spotted Maurice Tate talking to Carlos, the barman. Tate had his back to him. He had his arm around the shoulders of a slim young man in a dinner jacket whom Edward identified as the pianist. He went up to Tate and tapped him on the shoulder. Tate turned round, his face a picture of irritation, but his annoyance quickly turned to something like alarm. 'Ah, Lord Edward, it's you. Um, this is my friend Agustín.'

Agustín looked about twenty-four or five. He had long eyelashes, a swarthy skin and almost shoulder-length hair which fell lank on his none too white collar. He smiled into Edward's face and then looked down at his feet. In that moment, Edward knew that this half-starved-looking Spanish boy was Tate's lover and the knowledge disgusted him.

Tate saw the expression which passed over Edward's face and knew at once that he had been judged and found wanting. Homosexuality was not a crime in Spain as it was in England but not because Spanish society was more tolerant. In Spanish culture there was nothing finer than the comradeship which came naturally between men – it was of a higher order than the love between a man and a woman – and sexual feelings dishonoured it.

'I was looking for Tom Sutton. I suppose he's not here yet,' Edward said a little too quickly, ignoring Agustín.

'No,' said Tate, 'he should be here. He usually comes about now.' It seemed to be an effort for him to speak.

'I'll wait then,' Edward said shortly. Then, his natural good manners insisting he ought not to sound superior or worse still, contemptuous, he added, 'I need to get Sutton to telephone London for me. I have had some bad news which makes it necessary for me to get home as soon as possible.' He cursed himself for coming out with all this but he was embarrassed and that made him voluble.

'I'm sorry,' said Tate. 'Have a drink while you're waiting. Carlos . . . what will you have? Sherry? Cognac?'

'Just a beer, please.'

'*Una caña, por favor, Carlos*. An illness in the family?' he said, turning back to Edward.

'Yes,' said Edward shortly, not wanting to say more to this man for whom he had an instinctive dislike. Then, realising he was being rude, he added, 'My elder brother has had a riding accident.'

'The Duke?' said Tate and Edward again felt the disgust well up inside him. What was he doing talking to this odious man? He hated to think of Verity having friends like Maurice Tate, Belasco and even Hester Lengstrum who seemed to think marriage was a convenience to be shrugged off when it had served a purpose – in her case making her a baroness.

'Look,' said Tate, 'we could try telephoning from here. This is about the best time for getting through – after the end of the business day.'

'Oh, I don't know . . .' Edward began but Tate had said something to Carlos who brought out from behind the bar an ancient-looking instrument which did not hold up much hope of communicating with the next room, let alone England.

Tate spoke into the telephone for some time and then said, 'There's about an hour's wait. Give me the telephone number in England and the operator will call us back when he gets through.'

'That's very kind of you,' Edward said. He suddenly remembered that he did not have the number of the *New Gazette* and that, even if he did get through, Lord Weaver would not still be in the office. He hesitated and then gave the Mersham Castle number. He supposed he ought also to ring the Tilneys but, to his relief, he realised he could not as he did not have their number on him.

Agustín had slipped away during this and was strumming at the piano. 'Who do I pay?' Edward said.

'Don't worry. We'll settle up later. Let's go to our table. Carlos will call us if the operator gets through.'

'Did you say you were putting on a performance of *Love's Labour's Lost*?' Edward said to make conversation when they were seated.

'Yes, the English theatre is quite popular here. In fact everything English here has a certain snob appeal.'

111

'Aren't they all too busy with their politics to go to Shake-speare?' Edward said. There was a touch of scorn in his voice of which he was unaware – scorn for Tate and for the Spanish. Tate looked at him curiously. He was disappointed. This English lord with a ridiculous name was not stupid and yet he seemed to share all the prejudices of his class and nationality. How often had he heard the English insult foreigners – it had made him quite embarrassed on occasion – and how few of them bothered to learn the language. If only the English could hear themselves! Ignorance and superiority; it was an unpleasant combination.

'Funnily enough,' he said, 'despite the difficult political situation, all kinds of Spanish, who would never normally be seen in the same room together, come to watch our plays. I sometimes think we supply a vital channel of communication between the different "faiths" as one might call them. Somehow, in Spain, it all comes down in the end to religion – or lack of it. The odd thing is, the atheists are more fanatical than the Catholics.'

Edward relaxed a little. He was beginning to feel that this man was not quite as odious as he had first thought. *'Love's Labour's Lost* . . . it's one of the plays I know least well. Remind me what the plot is?'

'There's not much plot and what there is is rather absurd, though I believe Shakespeare based the play on real events. It's sort of love's revenge. Four young men – the King of Navarre and his friends – take a vow to forswear love for three years. Then along comes the Princess of France with some ladies but they are not allowed into the palace because of the King's vow. They are naturally insulted at being made to camp outside so they decide to seduce the men from their vows.'

'Yes, I remember now,' Edward said. 'Doesn't it end rather oddly?'

'Yes, just as all the women are paired off with the men and they are celebrating there comes news of the King of France's death.'

'Death triumphs over love?'

'That may be the moral,' Tate agreed.

'And the jokes are dire, aren't they?' Edward said.

'They *are* very literary and *were* very topical so some don't make much sense now but oddly enough the wit is very Spanish. There's even a word for it: *"gracia"* – repartee, as in fencing.

112

Actually, it's not quite as esoteric as you might think and it does have some very good lines. For example, Rosaline tells Berowne that he must earn her love by working in a hospital among "the speechless sick", and he sneers at her: what is the point of struggling against pain and decay – "To move wild laughter in the throat of death"? Perhaps it isn't a sneer but one of Shakespeare's profound poetic truths. I don't know but it's a line which always gives me pause. You must also remember that Shakespeare was writing more of a masque than a play. We have to add the music.'

'Hmm!' Edward said. 'Interesting – I must reread the play. Sounds as if you've given yourself quite a challenge. When's the first performance?'

'Not till the beginning of July. We would like to do it outside so we'll wait till the weather warms up! Perhaps we can entice you back to Madrid then.'

Edward was excused having to answer by the arrival of Hester, Ben Belasco and Verity. As Edward and Tate rose to greet them, Hester said, 'Ah, there you are. We've been looking all over for you. We went to your hotel but they said you had gone out.'

'Yes, I'm sorry, Hester, I was looking for Tom Sutton. I wanted to telephone home and it seems I can't do it from the hotel, so I thought I would try the embassy.'

'Did you find Tom?' Belasco said, seating himself.

'Not yet but Tate – Maurice – has very kindly booked a call for me from the telephone at the bar.'

'Terrible business,' Belasco grunted.

'Yes, horses . . . they're so dangerous,' Tate said.

'I don't mean that,' said Belasco scornfully, 'I mean Tilney.'

Tate looked bemused. Hester said, 'For God's sake! Don't say he hasn't told you. They found Godfrey Tilney half-way up a mountain – murdered.'

'Murdered!' said Tate. 'But . . . but we knew that.'

Verity then had to tell him what she and Edward had discovered. Tate seemed stunned by the news. It was interesting, Verity decided, how differently everyone took the news of Tilney's 'second' death. Hester had been upset but more intrigued than anything else. Belasco had frankly enjoyed it. He had hardly known the dead Englishman and had certainly not

113

liked him. Verity thought she could see him storing away all the details for use in some future book. He made her tell him about the exact circumstances of the discovery – how Rosalía had behaved and what the priest had said – everything. Tate seemed to be taking it most to heart, although she couldn't think why. Of course it was horrifying, but Tate's reaction seemed extreme. It was common knowledge the two men hadn't liked one another.

'So what were you talking about all this time?' Verity demanded of Edward.

'*Love's Labour's Lost*,' he told her.

Verity said nothing but looked at him with disbelief. Then, collecting herself, she said, 'I'm so sorry to hear about your brother's accident.'

'Yes,' said Edward distractedly. His headache, which had abated somewhat, was now worse than ever.

'I have reported everything to the police,' she told him eagerly. 'We are all going up to San Martino at first light.'

Edward, who could hardly concentrate, said, 'Not me. I've got to go back to England.'

'But you can't,' Verity burst out.

'I can,' Edward said brutally. 'What more is there for me to do here?'

'You've got to find out who killed Tilney.'

'No I haven't. I came here to get your David out of gaol and I have.'

'*My* David,' said Verity angrily. 'He's your friend.'

'No he's not. He's your lover, or was. He's no friend of mine.'

Verity blushed and everyone looked embarrassed, particularly Belasco.

'I'm sorry,' said Edward. 'Please forgive me. I ... I don't know. But you see, I must get back.'

'You're a stuck-up, selfish bastard,' Verity said, rising white-lipped from the table. 'What have you done when it comes down to it? You go and see David who tells you how to find Tilney and, when you get there, you find he has been killed, probably because someone heard you gassing about where you were going. And ...' She held up her hand to stop Edward interrupting her. '... and I don't know what makes you think they're going to let David out of gaol. They can probably be persuaded

114

he didn't kill Tilney because, as you so rightly pointed out,' she said sarcastically, 'he was in the clink, in a dungeon, at the time but they will still want to know who killed the man they buried, and they will want to know why David did not tell them Tilney was alive and save them the trouble of trying him for murder. I suppose you didn't think of that.'

Once again, Edward tried to break into this stream of accusations: 'But my dear child . . .'

Edward could not have chosen words more likely to enrage Verity. The tears, which she had been struggling to control, now rolled down her cheeks but she did not notice them. 'How dare you "dear child" me, you . . . you effete relic of decayed capitalism. And what makes you think the Spanish police will let you out of the country? You haven't even met Captain Gonzales yet and I don't for one minute think he will like you when you do. Think about it. A foreigner, after only a day in this country, finds the body of a man allegedly murdered weeks ago. Highly suspicious, I'd say. Do you think they will like being made to look like fools? No, of course not! They will, quite rightly, assume you had information you ought to have passed on to them and they'll think you didn't because you wanted to get to him first and kill him . . .'

'But that's absurd, I . . .'

'Perdone, señor, su llamada telefónica . . .'

'What? Oh, yes, thank you.' Edward followed the waiter to the bar where Carlos proudly passed him the telephone. 'Very good, very queek, eh?'

Still bewildered by Verity's outburst, he nodded uncomprehendingly at the barman and picked up the receiver. 'Hello, hello? Who is there? Connie, is that you? Look, I am speaking to you from a bar and it's very noisy . . . sorry, I can hardly hear you. Listen to me. I am coming back straight away . . . as soon as I can. The quickest will be by aeroplane. Telephone Joe Weaver and ask him to send Harry Bragg to pick me up tomorrow if possible . . . Wire me through the embassy – a man called Tom Sutton . . . yes, that's right, Sutton . . . S-U-double T . . . How is . . . Oh Connie, I am so sorry. I'll be back as soon . . . oh damn it, it's gone dead.'

When Edward got back to the table, there was no sign of Verity but he pretended not to notice. Belasco said, 'I hope . . . I mean, I didn't know you had a thing going with Verity, Lord Edward. If I . . .'

'We had nothing "going" as you put it,' Edward said coldly. 'I suppose she's just upset about David, but really you know, there's nothing else I can do.'

His appeal for sympathy fell flat. Hester said, 'We understand. That's really bad news about your brother. When are you leaving for England?'

'Tomorrow I hope. If not, then the next day.'

'Well, let me know and I'll run you to the airport.'

'Thanks, I'm . . .'

Tate broke in: 'Here's Tom. You had better tell him everything. He's always good in a crisis. Mind you, I suppose that's his job.'

10

'Connie, I'm so, so sorry. How is he?'

'Still unconscious. I spend most days at the hospital but . . .'

'What do the doctors say? Do they think he'll . . . he'll pull through?'

'They don't know, Ned.' Connie, holding Edward's hands in hers, looked him full in the face. 'As far as they can see, he hasn't had a haemorrhage. They just think he has bruised his brain and only time will tell how . . . how badly. It's funny, I suppose I always knew I loved the old boy even when he was at his most annoying but . . . I . . . never knew how much, until now when I may lose him. Oh God, Edward, it's so good to see you. Everyone's been frightfully kind but it's only family who matter at a time like this. Do you mind if we walk round the garden before going in – that is, if you're not too tired?'

'I'd like some air,' Edward said, taking her arm. Words didn't seem adequate somehow.

It was almost dusk and he was mortally tired and very depressed. Fenton had met him at Croydon and driven him straight to Mersham. In the evening light the castle looked at its most serene but for once Edward had no eyes for it.

'When can I see him?'

'Whenever you want. Not today, you're tired after the journey and anyway it's late. Go tomorrow morning.'

'How's Frank?' Edward was prompted to ask.

'He's been wonderful . . . such a help, but I wouldn't let him stay more than a couple of days. He's working for exams, you know and . . . and there's nothing he could do.'

'He's a good boy. How old is he now? Fifteen?'

117

'Sixteen. Oh Edward, he's so grown-up in some ways and in others such a child! He said . . . he said to me so solemnly, "Is father going to be all right? I do so hope so. I love him so much." And then he said, "I don't ever want to be a duke."'

Edward smiled. 'I thought I might go and see him at the weekend.'

'Oh yes, do. He loves and admires you so much, and you can speak to him man to man.'

'Admires me!' Edward exclaimed. 'There's nothing much to admire. All I seem to be able to do is let people down.'

Connie looked at him shrewdly. 'You mean in Spain? You didn't have time to finish what you were doing out there . . . with Verity?'

The Duchess had met Verity the year before when she had come to the castle posing as a respectable journalist preparing an article on Mersham for *Country Life*. It transpired she actually wrote for the official organ of the Communist Party, the *Daily Worker*, and proceeded to anger the Duke by describing the death by poison of one of his dinner-party guests, General Sir Alistair Craig. The Duke had found it difficult to forgive her and the Duchess, though she admired the girl and thought her energetic, determined and basically honest, had been concerned she might hurt her brother-in-law who, she saw, was smitten by her. Verity's priorities, the Duchess thought, were always going to be her career as a journalist and her politics. Love would come a poor third.

'How is Verity?' she asked timidly.

'She's rather upset because her friend – do you remember me telling you about him? An odious man by the name of Griffiths-Jones.'

'Yes, I remember. You knew him at Cambridge, didn't you? Another communist, isn't he?'

'Yes, of the most doctrinaire kind. I can't abide him. Anyway, the Spanish police put him in jug and were going to execute him for murdering another communist, a man called Godfrey Tilney, who as a matter of fact was at school with me.'

'What strange friends you had, Ned. Did your father send you to the right school? I trust Frank isn't getting into bad company.'

Edward was glad to see Connie was capable of making a joke and he smiled too. 'There's nothing wrong with the school, at least *I* think so. Verity wouldn't agree.'

'That's one of the reasons you like Verity.'

'Because she doesn't think the way I do? She doesn't hold conventional views on anything? Yes, you're right. The thing is, Connie, the women I met at dances and tennis parties and so on, when I was a young man, were so boring. They'd been conditioned to please men. They thought if they were assertive – if they had minds of their own – men would find them tiresome or ridiculous and then – horror of horrors – they wouldn't get anyone to marry them. It was bad for us men too. We became bullying, smug and insensitive. You could humiliate a girl and she would think it was her fault. Verity was never a debutante, thank God, and would tick off the Prince of Wales – I mean the King – if she thought he was talking nonsense.'

Connie was fascinated. She had never before heard her brother-in-law talk candidly about why he was so attracted to Verity Browne. It seemed in the end to come down to boredom; these other girls bored him – Verity was unpredictable and exciting. Connie could understand but still wondered if she could ever make him happy.

'You know, Connie dearest, I've been reflecting on what it takes to make someone – I mean someone of our kind – become a communist. Most people are quite happy not to think of politics at all – any regime is acceptable if it provides us with our basic needs. So long as we can feed our families and have a few bob over to go to the pub for a pint or two we won't care about social injustice provided we don't have our noses rubbed in it. I mean, if we're told the Nazis have camps in which they beat up Jews or communists or any other group, we probably say it's none of our business and likely as not they deserve it anyway. All most people want is to be left alone in peace and quiet to get on with their lives. But there will always be a minority, however small, who will care. They will want to change their society for the better and interfere in others where they see what they consider to be injustices. But who are these people – this minority who are so much more politically aware than the majority . . . the people who want to put the world to

119

rights? In many ways they are better than us – altruistic with a noisy conscience. They'll be educated, with enough free time to devote to "the cause" . . .'

'Like Verity you mean?'

'Yes. Most Communist Party members are not starving peasants. They are, as I say, educated, middle-class and comparatively well-off. I respect their commitment; after all, they could be spending their spare time at the dogs or at deb dances, but they are mistaken if they think they can take ordinary people with them. And this is the danger: as they find that working people don't flock to join their banner they get frustrated and angry. They know they're right and that ordinary people are lazy and stupid and, like Lenin, they will have to resort to terror . . . to violence. They may do so with regret. They may say it's only a temporary terror. They may call it by politer names but it will be tyranny. Stalin talks about "the dictatorship of the proletariat". It is a recognition that only force, or discipline as he calls it, can make ordinary people loyal Communist Party members . . .'

Connie was unable to stifle a yawn.

'Oh, I'm sorry,' he said huffily. 'End of lecture.'

'No, honestly, Ned – I'm interested. I'm sorry I yawned. I'm sure what you say is true. It's like you say, we common folk find political theory boring. I know we shouldn't, but forgive me if we go back to Verity. She came running to you to prove her friend wasn't a murderer after all?'

'That's about the size of it, Connie.'

'And did you?'

'Sort of. I was able to find Tilney – but not alive. He had been murdered but not when the police thought he had. When we found him, he had only been dead an hour or so.'

'So the man who was buried as Tilney wasn't him after all? How very complicated! Verity must have been pleased because that presumably let Mr Griffiths-Jones off the hook. Sorry, I didn't mean to put it that way, but he couldn't have done it because he was in prison. Do you know who did?'

'No. I didn't think that was my problem. Verity had wanted me to find a way of getting David out of gaol and, more by luck than anything else, I did. Then I got your wire and I wanted to be back here.'

'Did Verity understand?'

'No. We had a bit of a row about it. There was a lot of tidying up to do which I had to leave to her, and she thought . . . anyway, it doesn't matter. The main thing was, I had to get back here as fast as I could. I have my priorities too, and you and Gerald, and Frank of course, are top of the list.'

Connie pressed his hand warmly. Under the great copper beech that trailed its branches in the slow-running river, they talked of other things – of old memories, of the castle they both loved so much and of their hopes for the future.

'I do so fear – I haven't said this to anyone else, not even to Gerald – specially not to Gerald – I do fear there will be another war and Frank will have to go and fight and . . . die like the Uncle Franklyn he never knew.'

'Oh, I don't know,' said Edward, who was haunted by precisely the same fear but had no wish to admit it to his sister-in-law. 'The next war, if it does come, and pray God it doesn't, will be as dangerous for those who stay at home as those in the front line. Did you hear the Prime Minister say how "the bomber will always get through"? I have a terrible feeling he may be right.'

Connie shivered. 'I'm cold, let's go in, Ned.' She folded her arms, defensively, across her chest. 'Oh, why can't we all be left in peace to live our own lives without interfering with anyone else's! Oh dear! There I go again. That's exactly what I'm not supposed to say, isn't it?'

'Why indeed,' he sighed.

As they strolled back together across the lawn, green and soft as the baize on a billiard table, to the fairy-tale castle innocent of any military attributes, Spain seemed far away to Edward but the cloud of depression which Verity's attack on him and the news of his brother's accident had precipitated, deepened and darkened.

The next day, standing at his brother's bedside in the hospital, he looked gloomily at the pale, lined face of the man who had been more of a father to him than a brother. Was this the state between living and dying, between sleeping and waking, he wondered, which Catholics called purgatory? He thought of the little Norman church in Mersham in which generations of their family had worshipped, married, and been buried. The marble effigies of Sir Marmeduke Corinth and his lady lay on a dais near the altar in cold splendour, Sir Marmeduke's legs crossed to remind strangers that he had been a crusader. How often had he as a boy knelt in the family pew and glimpsed through his fingers the feet of the ancient warrior warmed by lifelike effigies of his favourite hunting dogs. He had, during dull sermons, fantasised about what exploits would bring him the honour and glory which had brought Sir Marmeduke eternal fame.

In 1921, a war memorial had been unveiled in the church. Thereafter, when his attention wandered during the service, his eye would stray to the plaque on the whitewashed wall. Beneath a few words from Laurence Binyon's 'Poem for the Fallen' were inscribed the names of those from Mersham who had given their lives so that he and his generation could live in peace. It was a burden which weighed heavily on both Franklyn's surviving brothers. In 1914, from a population of four hundred and seventy-five, twenty-nine able-bodied young men from the village had marched to war, leaving only old men and women to till the fields. Only seven had returned to their families in 1918 and, of these, four had been wounded. Franklyn had died first – as perhaps old Sir Marmeduke might have expected of him. These were the empty places to fill and Gerald, for one, had tortured himself with the fear that he was not worthy to do so. He had devoted himself to preventing a second, even more savage war which would destroy a new generation, and he had failed.

On an impulse, and after checking that there was no one in the corridor who might come in upon him without warning, Edward knelt beside the hospital bed, as simple as any soldier's cot, and prayed. After a minute, he rose from his knees, self-consciously wiping the dust from his immaculately pressed trousers. Finding to his relief that he was unobserved, he took the flower out of his buttonhole – it was a daffodil head he had picked just outside the front gate as he left for the hospital – raised it to his nose and inhaled the scent of spring. Then he placed it on the pillow beside the head of the unconscious man.

A nurse came in, saw the flower and smiled at him, and Edward returned her smile. Neither spoke a word but something passed between them. In the Lagonda going home, Edward felt strangely refreshed as though he had done his duty or, more than that, had expressed, however inadequately, the love he felt for his brother. In ordinary life, Englishmen, and brothers in particular, seldom touched each other beyond the occasional firm handshake. The nearness of death, the final farewell, after which there could be no embraces, only regrets, made it absurd not to show his feelings. However, like Prince Hal at his father's deathbed, if Gerald did wake up, Edward knew they would revert to their usual outward show of mutual indifference. As he drove through the castle gates, the phrase from *Love's Labour's Lost*, which Maurice Tate had quoted, came back to him: 'To move wild laughter in the throat of death.' He thought he almost understood what Berowne had meant.

11

The following Saturday, he drove down to Eton in the Lagonda
to see Franklyn.

'I say, Uncle Ned, she's a stunner. May I drive her?'

'No, dash it, your mother would kill me,' then seeing the
boy's face fall: 'At Mersham you can have a turn at the wheel,
on the drive mind you, not on the road. But, you're right, Frank,
ain't she a beautiful thing.' The two stood in companionable
silence admiring the car before the boy said, 'What's the news of
Pa?'

'The same, I'm afraid. All we can do is hope and pray.'

'Mother's being most awfully brave.'

'Yes, she's been amazing. And she worries about you.'

'About me?' said Franklyn in surprise. 'Why me?'

'Well, why do you think, you young idiot? She doesn't want
this to spoil things for you here or prevent you doing as well as
you might have done in your Trials.'

'Oh, I say, Uncle, tell her not to worry. I just feel the only way
I can help Pa is by doing the very best I can in exams so, when
he wakes up, he will be proud of me.'

Edward ruffled his nephew's hair but was temporarily unable
to speak.

He was not a particularly good 'old boy'. He had enjoyed
Eton but it was at Cambridge that he had really blossomed. He
had not been back to the school for several years and it was an
odd feeling walking past his house – Mantons – in Common
Lane. His housemaster, a man called Hobbs whom Edward had
not liked, was now dead. The boys streaming in and out – the
little ones in their 'bum-freezers', the bigger ones with coat tails

flying – brought vividly back to him the schoolboy past he thought he had forgotten. He was particularly struck by one boy, about Frank's age he guessed, his top hat perched precariously on the back of his head, almost hidden behind a pile of books in a strap, crossing the road in front of them. He could not see his face at first but, when the boy looked his way, he experienced a shock of recognition.

'Frank, see that boy over there – do you know who he is?'

'Yes,' his nephew said without hesitation, 'his name's Thayer, Charles Thayer. Why, do you know him?'

'I knew his father,' Edward said. 'We were in the same house, this one, in fact,' he said, indicating Mantons. 'I was his fag.'

'Good Lord, Uncle Ned, what a lark. Charles is one of my best friends. Wait there, I'll just go and get him. I'm sure he would like to meet you.'

Edward put out a hand to stop him but it was too late. Frank had hared off down the street and was now talking animatedly to his friend and gesturing towards Edward. Edward smiled weakly. He hoped, at least, that Thayer's father was not in the offing. That didn't seem likely as he was clearly going off to some lesson or lecture.

Two minutes later, Edward was shaking the warm, wet hand of his friend's son. 'I say, sir,' said the boy eagerly, rescuing his top hat which had fallen into the gutter, 'how absolutely ripping to meet you. My father was only talking about you the other day ... when I mentioned Frank here,' he punched his companion affectionately with his free hand, 'was my greatest friend.'

'Ah well, please give him my regards.'

'But, sir, you can do that yourself, if you have the time. He's having lunch with the Head Man and the Provost – you know, he's a fellow and all that rot – but then he's going to have tea in my room. Do say you will come, with Frank of course.'

'Oh well, I don't . . .'

'Oh please, Uncle Ned.'

'Yes, of course,' Edward said, not wishing to be rude to his nephew's friend. He was curiously hesitant about renewing his acquaintance with Thayer whom he had not seen in over a decade.

'Oh good, that's splendid, sir. Now I will be off. I've got to see m'tutor – Mr Blanchard. Of course you won't know him, sir. He's quite a young man.'

Edward admired the boy's effort of imagination to see that it might be tactless to designate Mr Blanchard, who was probably Edward's age, as one of the ancient.

'He's your classical tutor?' Edward said.

'That's right, sir. M'tutor is Mr Caine.'

'An ominous name,' Edward joked.

'What? Oh yes, I see what you mean. His nickname's 'Whacko' Caine but actually he doesn't like beating boys. He's very popular.'

When they had said their goodbyes, Edward watched in amusement as the boy loped off down the street, employing that peculiar, careless, almost simian gait known as the Eton slouch.

'I haven't seen your friend's father for some years and I had no idea he was a fellow and all that.'

'Yes, he's quite a swell, but he has no side. I like him.'

With that compliment, all the more effective for being unconsidered, they strolled back to Frank's house, which was in the High Street, so that he could change for a house match.

The Field Game, a combination of rugger and association football, was never a favourite sport of Edward's when he had been at school. He had played it with some success because he was a natural athlete but his enthusiasm had been then, and still was, cricket. He had been captain of the eleven, no less, in his final year – and he had rowed a bit too – but now, muffled against an unseasonably cold wind, he cheered on his nephew with as much enthusiasm as he could muster. Inevitably, his mind went back to his schooldays. Stephen Thayer was three years his senior, which meant a lot at school. Edward had been his fag. He had brought him tea in bed in the morning, blacked his boots, toasted cheese sandwiches at tea time and run errands for him.

Thayer had been a glamorous figure: he was in the sixth form and a member of Pop. But, more importantly, he displayed elegant unconcern for the honours which accrued to him. Nothing was more attractive to Etonians than achieving triumphs – sporting, social or academic – without seeming to strive for them. If he was arrogant, he hid it behind a mask of courtesy;

if he was selfish, it was disguised as sophistication. At home in the holidays, he mixed with famous actors and actresses, politicians and 'society people' whose faces regularly appeared in the illustrated papers, and this gave him a superficial maturity, a world-weary tolerance of school regulations which even his masters – the beaks – found winning.

And yet, Edward had a feeling that Thayer had left under something of a cloud. He couldn't quite remember exactly what sort of cloud. He had, nevertheless, gone up to Oxford but remained there for just a year, whether at his own desire or the university's Edward did not know. He had gone into the City and was now, he had heard, a successful merchant banker. Edward had always been mildly surprised that his old schoolfellow had not made more of a splash: become Prime Minister, climbed Mount Everest or even become a newspaper tycoon like Lord Weaver. He had charm, he was not afraid of hard work when this was absolutely necessary, but perhaps there was some fault-line in his character which prevented him achieving everything his friends had hoped and expected of him. Could the same be said of himself? Edward thought wryly.

It was hard to explain why he had lost touch with Thayer. There was the age difference, of course, but that became less significant as time passed. They had gone to different universities and made different friends. For a year or two after that, Edward had seen his friend at London parties and he seemed just the same: charming, interested in what Edward had to tell him of his travels but reluctant to talk about his own affairs. They had made those very English assignations to meet, so vague as to be meaningless. When Edward was in Africa, he had heard from a friend that Thayer had married and that his wife had died in childbirth. He had been saddened by the news and meant to write to him but had put it off from month to month until it became too late to write at all. And now they were to meet again through the happy coincidence of his nephew being Charles Thayer's best friend. Fate had a way of bringing everything full circle.

As they strolled back to the house after the match, Edward felt an immense affection for Frank – perhaps because he was seeing his own youth in the boy beside him. He found himself wishing Verity could meet him. He thought they would like

127

each other. Also, he wanted her common sense, her contempt for privilege and tradition, to cauterise the sweetness of nostalgia which threatened to overwhelm him. He wished he had not parted with her so abruptly and on bad terms. He decided he would make a few telephone calls when he got back to Mersham and find out what was happening in Madrid.

With Frank showered and pink with good health and excitement, they walked the few hundred yards to Thayer's house. Close friendships between boys in different houses were rare unless they were related in some way and Edward asked his nephew how he had become such good friends with Thayer.

'I suppose we got to know each other because we both play the clarinet – very badly in my case – and in the summer half we both play cricket. But it's not that. It's just that we both . . . we both liked each other as soon as we met.'

Edward wondered if there was a schoolboy crush involved but would not have dreamed of even suggesting such a thing.

'Edward! How very good to see you again. It's been much too long. Why is it one never sees the people one really *wants* to? It is so good that my Charles and your nephew should be such friends.'

'Yes indeed, Stephen,' Edward said, shaking the hand of his old school friend. They scrutinised one another as men always do when they haven't met for some time, looking for signs of their own mortality. Both looked young for their age: Edward still had the figure of an active man and Thayer was tall and willowy. There was perhaps a puffiness round his eyes which betrayed late nights and too little fresh air, but Edward could still recognise in the middle-aged man the schoolboy he had once been.

'I'm so sorry to hear about your brother. I do hope he will recover quickly,' Thayer said, still grasping Edward's hand.

The words were commonplace enough but the look in his eye, the expression of concern, was altogether captivating. Although Edward knew he was being, in some sense, manipulated, he could not help but feel a surge of warmth towards the man. Thayer was displaying the ability most public figures have for making anyone they speak to feel that, at least for those few seconds, they are the most important person in the world. Edward wondered again why he had chosen not to go into politics.

The boys were gathered round the little grate attempting to set fire to stapled brown-paper strips called Burn-A-Witch. When the coals were hot enough, toasting forks would be got out and crumpets attached to their prongs. There was a whole ritual to tea-making which every small boy – every fag – had to learn if he hoped to escape chastisement. Toast had to be laid against the teapot and not flat on a plate where it would become soggy. The teapot had to be warmed before tea was spooned into it and the boiling water – it had to be bubbling not just hot – poured over it. The pot then had to rest for two and a half minutes. Although each boy, even the most junior, had his own room, two or three would choose to eat together in what was called, in naval style, a 'mess'. Edward, conscious of schoolboy etiquette, asked if they were inconveniencing Charles's messing partners.

'Oh no, sir, thank you, sir,' said the boy politely. 'When we have parents, it is quite all right for us to eat in our own rooms, not with our friends.'

'But please don't smoke, Uncle,' said Frank firmly, seeing Edward take out his cigarette case.

'Oh no, of course, I forgot for a moment. I don't want to get you into trouble.'

After ten minutes discussing the boys, Thayer took Edward to one side and said, 'It's so good to meet you like this, Edward. As it happens, there is something about which I want to consult you. I imagine you know that Makepeace Hoden's dead?'

'Yes, I gather he was killed on safari. It was a shock.'

'It was, and I gather you have just got back from Madrid investigating the death of another of our old friends, Godfrey Tilney.'

'Good Lord! Where did you hear that?'

'Thoroughgood mentioned it to me.'

'Of course! You know Basil Thoroughgood.'

'Do you think the two deaths are connected?'

'Hoden's and Tilney's? Heavens no! Why? Do you?'

'It's just possible. I wondered if I might have had a word with you about it, in London.'

129

'Of course, but ... I was hardly "investigating" Tilney's death. In fact, it's still a bit of a mystery. I would guess he was killed by one of his political opponents. Spain is a chaos of competing factions, as I'm sure you know.'

'But you did discover Tilney wasn't killed when everyone thought?'

Edward's brow darkened. 'I did, but what use was that? I fear it is possible my own clumsiness might have led his murderer to him.'

They glanced up to see the boys looking at them curiously so they quickly changed the subject to one of universal interest: the food. However, when they were parting, Stephen Thayer repeated what he had said about having things to discuss with him. 'I'll phone when I can see what's in my diary. Brooks's perhaps? Better than the office, I think.'

Edward was greeted back at Mersham by a jubilant Connie: 'Ned, he's regained consciousness!'

Edward threw his arms round his sister-in-law in an unaccustomed display of affection and kissed her heartily on both cheeks. 'That's such wonderful news, Connie. Can I go in and see him tomorrow?'

'Yes, of course, but you can't be with him more than a few minutes. He tires quickly. The doctors warned me, we're not out of the woods yet. He's still not able to speak and we don't know if he's ... if he's lost his memory or ... or anything.'

'No,' said Edward, still with his arms around her, 'but it's a start. Now he can begin to live again. I'm so pleased, Connie. It's what we've been praying for.'

He felt, rather than saw, his sister-in-law break into deep, panting sobs. She had kept herself determinedly cheerful and optimistic but, now there was something to give her hope that Gerald might regain his health, she broke down. Edward said nothing but held her to him, gently stroking her head. When he felt her begin to calm down, he said, 'First thing tomorrow we'll telephone Frank's housemaster and ask him to pass on the good news.'

'Oh yes, I was so excited that I forgot to ask how you got on at Eton.'

'Everything was well with Frank. He's so proud of you and says he's determined to show it by doing well in Trials.'

'The darling boy. It's he who has been brave. Did you meet anyone you knew?'

'As a matter of fact I did – Stephen Thayer, he was in my house. It turns out his son is Frank's greatest friend. Small world, eh?'

They had dinner together, not 'dressing' as the Duke always insisted even when there were no guests. Like naughty children, they sat cosily in front of the library fire and Edward, who had always had a soft spot for his sister-in-law, felt how pleasant it might be to sit as a married couple and chew over the day's events. He thought he might be getting weary of being single. As if reading his mind, Connie, daring on the intimacy engendered by their situation and relaxed by the good news and the wine with which they had celebrated it, said, 'What about you, Ned? You look as if you need a bit of affection. Am I allowed to ask if there's anyone . . .?'

'No, Amy Pageant turned out not to be . . . I mean we're still great chums and all that but . . .'

'Verity?'

Edward looked into the flames. 'I just don't know, Connie dearest. As I said, we rowed . . . about my leaving, but what else could I do?' His brow darkened and then cleared. 'You're the only person I could possibly talk to about it and . . . and there's nothing to tell.'

'Have you spoken to her?'

'About my feelings for her? No.'

'Why not? If you don't ask her, how is she to know what you feel about her?'

'The trouble is, Connie, I don't know what I do feel about her. Sometimes, I think I love her to bits and then she reduces me to gibbering rage. I don't want to sound a prig but there's so much about her I disapprove of.'

'Her politics?'

'Yes, but I don't mind about them really. She's a thoroughly good-hearted girl – just naive – and she's under the influence of that man David Griffiths-Jones.'

'Still?'

'Well,' he said reluctantly, 'since you're being my father confessor, I had better tell you everything.'

Connie felt slightly guilty, knowing just how much Verity would hate being discussed in this way, but felt her first loyalty was to her brother-in-law . . . and she couldn't help unless she knew what the situation was between them. 'Can I ask . . .' she said nervously, 'is she in love with this man Griffiths-Jones?'

'I don't know. I don't think so. He doesn't think so. He actually told me she was "having a fling" – to use his words – with this American writer, Belasco, who's there in Madrid.'

'Belasco! Gosh, I 've heard of him. I read one of his – it was a "Book of the Month" choice. I can't remember what it was called. It was very well written but I didn't like it.'

Edward laughed. 'Oh Connie, you're so loyal.'

'No,' she said blushing, 'I really didn't like it. I got the impression from the writing that he was . . . I don't know . . . fantasising about being such a "tough cookie" – isn't that what the Americans say? – but really he was just self-obsessed.'

'No, no,' said Edward, struggling to be fair, 'he is a good writer – maybe even a great one. Anyway, the point is that he seems to have dazzled Verity.'

'You really must tell her what you feel?'

'I will but . . . she isn't in the mood for love-making. She's trying to make her name in a tough job where women are usually conspicuous by their absence. It takes up all her energies.'

Connie leant forward and put her hand on Edward's. 'I'm so sorry, Ned. One is rarely forgiven for being generous, but maybe . . . maybe fate is trying to tell you she isn't . . .'

'Gosh, this is jolly,' Edward said, gently removing his hand from under hers, thereby signalling that he didn't want to talk about his love life – or lack of it – any more.

Later, when they were going to bed, Connie said, 'I think it's partly due to that nurse, that Gerald's getting better.'

'Which one is that?' Edward asked casually.

'Elizabeth Bury – she's the pretty red-haired one. Wasn't she there when you went to sit with him?'

'Yes, I think I know the one you mean,' he said lightly. 'Well, tomorrow, if she's on duty, I'll make a point of thanking her.'

Before he went to sleep, Edward wrote a long letter to Verity apologising for leaving her in the lurch and asking for news of David. He ended: Thank God, Gerald has regained consciousness – I'm going to see him tomorrow. In a week or two, I will probably feel comfortable about leaving Mersham and, if by any chance I can help, I will be delighted to come out to Spain again. If, as I hope, everything is all tidied up, then of course you won't want me. You probably don't want me anyway . . .'

He sucked the end of his fountain pen: . . . but I want you, he longed to add but did not dare. This was the first letter he had ever written her and she had never had occasion to write to him. He wondered if she would even read it. She might not even be in Madrid but chasing some 'story' the other side of the country. There hadn't been much about Spain in the papers recently; they had been filled with gossip about the new King, as though England was grateful for having some pleasant domestic news in which to bury its collective head.

In the end he just wrote: 'I do hope you are not still angry with me, your friend from the politically unacceptable class, Edward.'

He read the letter through once quickly, grimaced, and sealed it. Then he rang for John, the footman, and asked him to make sure it caught the first post.

'Very good, my lord,' said the footman. 'May I say, my lord, how happy we are in the servants' hall to hear of his Grace's recovery.'

'Thank you, John. Yes, it is very good news, isn't it, but it's early days. We must keep our fingers crossed that he continues to improve. These head injuries . . . well, they are so unpredictable.'

'Yes, my lord.' Then, presuming on his status as a servant who had known Edward since he was a schoolboy, he said, 'Might I ask, my lord, if the Duke will be coming home? It is the opinion of the servants' hall, my lord, that we could look after him better here than any hospital.'

Edward was touched. 'I'm inclined to agree with you, John, but of course, it's up to the doctors. But if the Duke can be brought back here and properly nursed, I do think he might get better more quickly. As you know, he's always hated sleeping even a single night under a strange roof. I will be seeing him tomorrow morning and I promise to keep you all informed.'

'Thank you, my lord. That would be appreciated.'

When the footman had gone, Edward, still seated at his desk, smiled to himself. How Verity would spit if she had been privy to his conversation with John. She would have seen it as grovelling subservience by a representative of the oppressed working class to a representative of the decayed aristocracy. 'She would probably have strung us both up from the same lamp-post,' he muttered to himself. He was astute enough to recognise that the fact that he could imagine how Verity might see the situation meant that she had influenced him. A year ago, it would never have occurred to him to question his own behaviour. It was not that for one moment he saw his and his family's relationship with the servants as being anything other than natural, hallowed by tradition and based on mutual respect. They were all – Duke and scullery maid – in some profound sense servants of the castle but with different duties. But Edward could see that, before this horrible, shoddy decade was over, there would be seismic social changes and, he was honest enough to recognise, not all for the worse.

The next day, to his great happiness, he discovered that Gerald was definitely on the mend. Edward was able to say a few words to his brother who recalled that he had been in Spain, which was evidence his memory was unimpaired. The matron would not permit him to stay for more than fifteen minutes and Edward saw that, even after so short a time, his brother was slurring his words and showing every sign of extreme fatigue.

He raised with the doctors the idea of Gerald being nursed at home and, to his surprise, they were not opposed to the plan. 'If he progresses as fast as he has in the last forty-eight hours, in ten days or so I see no objection to his being nursed at Mersham Castle,' Dr Wild opined. 'I have had considerable experience of patients with head injuries, as you know, and I have often observed that they benefit from being in familiar surroundings. I must tell you, Lord Edward, that the next ten days are critical. The great danger is that there is a blood clot or some other obstruction to the flow of blood to the patient's brain which might suddenly bring on irreversible brain damage. It is far too early to say that the Duke is going to achieve a full recovery. I tell you this because it is my principle to tell relatives the truth. In the end, it is more merciful than buoying them up with false hope. Now, it is up to you whether or not you pass this on to the Duchess but, as I say, I thought it was my duty to warn you this could be a false dawn.'

'Yes, thank you, doctor. It was quite right of you to warn me. May I ask when, or perhaps I ought to say if, you judge the Duke to be well enough to return to Mersham, what special nursing requirements would be needed?'

'Nothing more than rest. I would recommend you spoke to Nurse Bury. I have noticed the Duke seems to have taken a fancy to her. He appears to find her presence soothing. I am sure I speak for Matron,' he said, turning to the large, starched-looking woman beside him, 'when I say we could spare Miss Bury for, say, a month to look after the Duke. Of course, you would have to talk to Miss Bury yourself and see if she was agreeable.'

Matron looked less than overjoyed at the prospect of losing one of her nurses for a month but could only nod her agreement.

'Is Miss Bury here now?'

'She comes on duty at five. If you would like to return then, Lord Edward,' Matron said firmly, 'I would allow you a brief conversation with her. However, we are very busy at the moment, as I am sure you can see, so I would ask you not to take up too much of her time.'

Thus rebuked for a sin he had not yet committed, Edward went back to the castle in good spirits. He found he was looking forward to having Nurse Bury there – that is if she could be persuaded to come. He had not even spoken to her yet but his one glimpse of her had convinced him he would like to know her better. He could hardly admit it to himself but, now that the immediate crisis was over, he was in danger of being bored. He loved the castle better than anywhere else in the world but it was very empty without the Duke and, of course, it was not the time to have guests.

It was not until the middle of March, a full fifteen days after the Duke had regained consciousness, that he was brought home to Mersham. He looked desperately pale to Edward and, when he helped Elizabeth Bury put him to bed, he was shocked at how little flesh he had on him. His legs and arms were as thin as sticks, and his paunch, of which he had been embarrassed, had degenerated to flaps of unsightly skin.

The days went by more quickly now and Edward began to be much taken by the red-headed young woman nursing his brother so devotedly. There was still a cold wind blowing but there were hints that summer might not be far away. Connie used to chase Elizabeth out of the sick room to walk along the river, while she stood guard over the patient. Sometimes Edward accompanied her. His efforts to make his meetings with Elizabeth seem accidental amused his sister-in-law. She liked to watch the two of them from the bedroom window – Edward, tall and supple, striding beside the girl, her hair escaping like flames from a silk scarf. Edward suddenly seemed to have found his tongue and she longed to hear what he was telling her. She watched her turn her head towards him now and again, hardly saying anything in response to his flow of words. Over the little wooden bridge they would go and Connie would see them disappear among the trees with something like envy. Her days of romantic walks by the river were, she fancied, over for good. She could not help but hope that, in Elizabeth, Edward might at last have found a woman he could be happy with. She knew she was being absurdly premature, like an old mother hen, she chided herself but . . . he had written to Verity – John had been indiscreet under her close questioning – and had had nothing from her in response. She had heard him trying to telephone Madrid on more than one occasion but it seemed almost impossible to get through, as if Spain had decided to cut itself off from the rest of the world while it sorted out its future.

Finally, in desperation, at the end of March, Edward decided to ring Basil Thoroughgood at the Foreign Office but was told by an unhelpful assistant that he was on leave. Defeated in his attempts to keep in touch with the outside world, he relaxed into a dream world circumscribed by the dry-stone walls around the estate. He drove up to London once but found the noise and the dirt gave him a headache and, after a sleepless night, returned gratefully to a bucolic existence. He thought Fenton was rather worried by his retreat into unsociability. Certainly, Connie was getting a little perturbed and occasionally invited over neighbours, including on one occasion the Chief Constable, Colonel Philips, in an effort to take Edward out of himself.

Colonel Philips had one item of news: Inspector Pride, who had investigated the death of General Craig at Mersham the year before, had been promoted to Chief Inspector and was now highly thought of by Scotland Yard. There had existed a mutual antipathy between Edward and the Inspector, the latter considering him a tiresome meddler in affairs which did not concern him, while Edward only just refrained from asking the Chief Constable if he thought Pride's promotion was in recognition of his ability to hide embarrassing truths under the carpet. He was too polite to say any such thing but was amused when the Colonel offered him what might have been an apology for the way Pride had treated him the year before.

'Dashed good fellow, don't y'know. Amazingly thorough but don't quite know how we work in the back of beyond, what? He cleared up a nasty blackmail case a few years ago and, since then, I've always had the utmost admiration for the man. A bit blunt, I grant you, but I like him,' he ended defiantly.

Otherwise, Edward gave offence to the dull daughters of the local gentry and their even duller mothers when he proved unable to disguise his yawns. Connie got so exasperated that she actually suggested he go away. 'I mean, I'm terribly grateful to you, Ned, for flying to my rescue but, thanks to Elizabeth, Gerald is so much better.'

'Thanks to Elizabeth,' repeated Edward dreamily, and Connie looked at him closely.

As far as she had been able to discover, Elizabeth was entirely respectable. She was a clergyman's daughter but both her parents were dead. She had been in Africa – Kenya – but not nursing. She was older than Verity, about Edward's own age. Connie had the feeling she had a little money of her own. She was always nicely dressed and she wore clothes she could not have afforded on what she was paid at the hospital. She was not exactly secretive but Connie, who was usually so good at extracting information from people, could get little else from her.

As the days passed, Edward and Elizabeth, as the only two young people in the castle, found they spent more and more time together. Elizabeth was interested in Edward's views on world affairs and on the situation in Spain in particular. She claimed to be in complete ignorance of the political turmoil in that unhappy country which, to judge from *The Times*, seemed to be getting ever more unstable. He, of course, considered himself an expert on all things Spanish having spent less than a week in Madrid and delighted in instructing this attractive young woman who – so unlike someone he could mention – gave every evidence of enjoying being lectured by him. Elizabeth said little or nothing about her own political opinions. As far as he could gather she was an admirer of the Labour leader and former Prime Minister, Ramsay MacDonald, and hated what was happening in Germany.

He scanned the *New Gazette* for articles by Verity but, whether because there was nothing sensational enough to interest *New Gazette* readers or the news from Spain was judged by the editor to be too depressing, there were only two reports carrying Verity's by-line in the whole time he was at Mersham. Neither, if Edward was honest with himself, made riveting reading and he hoped Lord Weaver, the proprietor and Verity's sponsor, would not tire of her. He knew she would not last long without his support; the editor certainly did not care for her.

Then came a telephone call from Basil Thoroughgood which galvanised him. He was sitting at the breakfast table consuming, without much appetite, kippers and scrambled egg when Bates, the butler, came into the room.

'Excuse me, my lord. There is a trunk call for you – a Mr Thoroughgood. I informed him you were at breakfast but he insisted it was urgent that he speak with you.'

'Thank you Bates. That's quite all right. I'll take it in the hall.'

The instrument in the hall was one of only two telephones in the whole castle – the other being in the Duke's study. If any of the servants wished to use the telephone, they had either to ask permission from the Duchess, which she almost always granted, or walk to the village. The Duke was inclined to think that telephones were a necessary evil and the source of bad news. Edward had to admit that, at least in this instance, he was right.

'Thoroughgood, that you?' he shouted down the mouthpiece in his clipped, high-pitched, rather nasal drawl which Verity, in one of her moments of irritation with him, had described as 'equine'.

'Corinth? Yes, it's me, Thoroughgood. I wondered if you had heard the news?'

138

'What news? Has something happened to Ver...? What news?'

'It's Thayer ... he's been murdered.'

'Stephen, murdered? I can't believe it. Surely not! Murdered? There was nothing in the papers.'

'Well, there wouldn't have been. His body was only discovered this morning when the maid went into the study. He had been bashed on the head.'

'How do you know all this?'

'The Commissioner's a friend of mine and he knew I was a close friend.'

'I didn't know that.'

'Sorry, what did you say? This is a bad line.'

'I said ... oh, never mind. Look, Thoroughgood, can I come and see you? There are things we need to discuss.'

'Of course, that was why I was ringing. What time can you be in London?'

'I'll come on the eleven-ten and be with you about one. Oh ... and Thoroughgood, will you talk to the Commissioner again and find out all you can about the circumstances of poor Thayer's death – who was in the house, that sort of thing? Do we know who's going to be in charge of the case?'

'Chief Inspector Pride. I believe he's a good man.'

'Pride?' Edward groaned.

'Of course, I had forgotten you know him. He handled the unfortunate business at Mersham well – kept the whole thing quiet, didn't he?'

'Never mind about that. I'll see you later. Goodbye ... and thank you for ringing.'

Edward found Connie in the breakfast-room looking worried. She had overheard his side of the telephone conversation. 'What is it, Ned? Did I hear you say Stephen Thayer is dead?'

'Yes, murdered ...' He rang the bell for Bates.

'That's terrible and there's that poor boy too, Frank's friend. I must ring the school and see if there's anything I can do. It's too awful. It's the Easter break next week. I wonder if Frank will want to bring Charles here to Mersham?'

'Yes, do that, Connie: speak to Frank. I think this may upset him quite badly. Do you remember I said I had met Stephen for the first time in years when I went to see Frank at Eton? I am kicking myself for not having followed it up. I might have been able to help in some way. Thayer told me he had something he wanted to talk to me about but because of one thing and another – Gerald mostly – it went right out of my head. Now I'm wondering whether if I had talked to him, I might have been able to do something which would have prevented this.'

'Please, Ned, don't start torturing yourself. If Mr Thayer had wanted to see you, there was nothing to stop him telephoning you here.'

'I know but . . . Ah, Bates, have the papers arrived?'

'Yes, my lord. I have them here.'

Edward grabbed *The Times* and Connie took the *New Gazette* but, as Thoroughgood had said, there was nothing about Thayer's death in either.

'Connie, I'm going up to town on the eleven-ten. I feel in my bones there's a connection between Godfrey Tilney's death and Thayer's – something Stephen said when I met him at Eton. And now I think about it, someone else who was at school with the two of us was killed – a chap called Makepeace Hoden. It's all too much of a coincidence.'

'This man Hoden – you mean he may have been murdered?'

'I don't know,' Edward said grimly, 'but I'm beginning to wonder. His death was reported as a shooting accident. He was on safari in Kenya, but now I am beginning to think his death may be part of a pattern. Makepeace Hoden,' he murmured to himself, 'a singularly inappropriate name.'

12

'It's damned odd, Corinth. There's got to be something going on.'

Edward was seated on an upright chair like a naughty school-boy, while Thoroughgood lounged back in his armchair behind a desk empty of anything except a telephone and a blotting pad.

'You've talked to Pride? How did you get him to confide in you?'

'I know the Commissioner. I told him I was a close friend of Thayer's and he instructed Pride to keep me informed of pro-gress. I went to see him at the Yard on my way here. He was quite helpful though he says he doesn't have much to go on.'

'What does he think happened?'

'The murder must have occurred after the servants went to bed – I understand that was about eleven. There's no evidence that anyone broke into the house so whoever killed Thayer must have been let in by him.'

'And you don't turn your back on someone you think may have a reason to kill you.'

'Not unless you are very arrogant.'

'Hang on, though, what about the servants?'

'There are only three who live in, according to Pride, the butler – a man called Barrington – a cook and a parlourmaid. They would appear to be beyond suspicion.'

'What time was the body discovered?'

'Seven this morning, when the maid went in to tidy up.'

'You say he was killed by one of his own ornaments?'

'Yes – or rather not an ornament but a work of art. Thayer had a valuable collection of oriental figurines – jade mostly. The killer brained him with a Buddha – late seventeenth-century Japanese, I believe.'

'Hmm. That suggests the killer acted on impulse.'

'You mean, he used whatever was at hand?'

'He – or she. Could a woman have done it? I'd like to see the figurine.'

'Women don't go bashing people over the head. Anyway, they're not strong enough. Thayer was tall and . . .'

'Maybe – yes, you're probably right,' Edward admitted. 'Did he have any obvious enemies?'

'I don't think so but Pride may turn up some skeletons. You don't found and run a successful merchant bank without breaking a few bones.'

'No, I suppose not.' Edward paused. 'It was successful – the bank?'

'As far as I know.'

'You must forgive me, Thoroughgood, but I don't quite understand why you're so worked up by all this. It's terrible, of course, but, as I remember it, you were never a great friend of Thayer's.'

'No, not at school but afterwards our paths crossed quite a lot, you know,' he said airily. 'I was able to do him a few favours, gave him a tip now and again – early warning of what was happening abroad, that sort of thing . . .'

'And in return he made you money?'

'Yes, he cut me in on a few deals. You know how it is – old school tie . . .'

'So, you've got money in the firm?'

'Between ourselves, Corinth,' said Thoroughgood, leaning forward confidentially, 'I've got a lot at stake if the bank goes down.'

'But why should it go down? You said it was successful.'

'Merchant banks are all a matter of trust, Corinth, you must see that. Thayer *was* the bank. With him dead . . . murdered . . .'

'There must be other partners.'

'Just the one – a chap called Hoffmann.'

'German?'

'Yes, Heinrich Hoffmann. You haven't heard of him?'

'Should I have?'

'I just thought you might. He's based in Frankfurt. Thayer was well in with the Fatherland.'

'Hoffmann's a Nazi?'

'No, he's not actually a Party member, not yet anyway.'

'I see, so you're afraid this business will uncover some deals with the Nazis which you wouldn't want your name connected with?'

'I'm being quite honest with you, Corinth. After all I can trust you; we were at school together.'

'And if we went to war with Germany . . .?'

'God forbid . . .' said Thoroughgood, passing a hand through his thinning hair. 'I'm trying to get my money out of the bank but it's not easy, and now . . .' he shrugged, 'as I say, I've got a lot at stake: money, reputation – everything to lose.'

'How can I help?' Edward said easily, taking some pleasure in seeing the man squirm.

'Well, you know, I can't really be seen to be asking too many questions. I thought, as a friend of the dead man, you could keep an eye on the investigation. Maybe even drop Pride a hint or two. Anyway, keep the whole thing quiet. It's for the good of the country.'

Edward was beginning to feel his stomach churn. 'I thought you were worried you might be next on the list?'

'To be murdered? Well, there's that too. That's why we need to find out who killed Thayer . . .'

'And Tilney and Hoden.'

'You think the deaths are all connected?'

'Don't you?'

'Maybe . . . I have thought so but I have no idea why or how.'

'Thayer hinted to me, the last time I saw him, that something was . . . I don't know . . . worrying him.'

'Blackmail?'

'I'm not sure. He was going to tell me about it but he never did.'

'You've got to find out why Thayer was killed. You can ask people – people at the top – questions the police can't ask or, if they do, they won't get answered. It will be good for you, too.'

'What do you mean: "good" for me?'

'Well, if you do your country a service . . .'

'My country!' Edward exploded.

'The FO, then. If you deserve well of us, we can help you. You want a job, don't you? That's what you've been saying. And then your girlfriend: Verity Browne. She's got some undesirable friends. She may need protecting. Another thing, for all we know this madman may have *you* next on his list, not me.'

No one had ever attempted to bribe him before and it took his breath away. He wanted to stretch across the desk, take the fellow by the throat and throttle him. This man, with a job of trust and responsibility in one of the great departments of state at a critical time in British history, was prepared to lie, bribe and blackmail to preserve his worthless hide. His influence in the Foreign Office would be directed at keeping his financial dealings with a potential enemy secret and safe. Regardless of the national interest, Thoroughgood had only one aim: to keep Britain on good terms with Germany.

Edward got up carefully, holding back the anger which threatened to overwhelm him.

'Let me tell you something, Thoroughgood. I didn't like you at school and I don't like you now. There is nothing you can offer me which I would take with a pair of fire tongs. As it happens, I have my reasons for wanting to get to the bottom of this killing, otherwise I would tell you to go to hell.'

'Steady on, old chap. Don't take that tone with me. I've done nothing wrong. I'm not a rich man, you understand, and this was a way of putting aside something for my retirement. I've done nothing illegal.'

'Listen carefully, Basil my boy,' Edward said with studied contempt. 'You will send me, to Albany, a letter of introduction to Mr Heinrich Hoffmann requesting him to answer any question I might put to him. As soon as I have left this office, you will telephone Chief Inspector Pride and ask him to give me any information I may require and, if he makes a fuss, get on to your pal, the Commissioner. Savvy?'

'Yes, of course, Corinth, just as you say.'

'But I warn you that if, in the course of my investigations, I uncover any dealings between the bank and your Nazi friends which affect the case, I will not hesitate to inform the police. I shall try and forget what you have said to me today but, if at any time I have reason to believe that you are annoying any of my friends or putting obstacles in my way, I will not hesitate to speak to Sir Robert about you. Vansittart ought to know the value of the advice given him by his officials.'

'But, Corinth, we were at school together,' bleated Thoroughgood.

'And I am ashamed of it,' said Edward rising.

Without another word, he left, closing the door behind him as quietly as if he were leaving a sick room. As he passed Thoroughgood's secretary, she looked up with a startled smile which faded as she saw his face. When he reached the street, he gulped down mouthfuls of the smog which had settled on London like a dirty blanket, despite a persistent drizzling rain. At that moment, after what he had had to listen to inside, it tasted sweeter than the air on his beloved hills above Mersham.

Edward found Pride at the Yard but, as he had feared, the Chief Inspector was not willing to co-operate. His mention of Thoroughgood's name merely made the policeman curl his lip and raise an eyebrow, and he saw he had made a tactical error. Pride made it quite clear – with icy politeness – that the last thing he needed on the investigation was some meddling aristocrat asking questions of him or his officers.

'I was a friend of the dead man, Chief Inspector. We were at school together and his son is a close friend of my nephew's. I'm naturally keen to do anything I can to help you find his killer.'

'Very good of you to have come forward,' said Pride, with a smile of wolfish insincerity, 'but it's best to leave these things to the experts, no offence mind. If we need to ask you any questions you can be certain we will be in touch with you . . . my lord.' He added 'my lord' with studied irony.

Edward knew it was hopeless but he tried one more time. 'I am aware that you don't like me, Chief Inspector, but I hope you won't let that prejudice you. There may be something . . . some enemy in his past . . .'

'I don't know where you got the impression I don't like you,' said the policeman, grinning, 'but I assure you that is not the case. However, I am confident we shall quickly find Mr Thayer's murderer. He had enemies in the world of banking but I don't think you are able to help us with that side of things.'

'No, but . . .'

'Please, Lord Edward, as you can appreciate I am very busy

right now. Don't hesitate to ring my sergeant if there is any information you wish to pass on.' A thickset, amiable-looking man, with a face badly scarred by acne, came into the room. 'Sergeant Willis, this is Lord Edward Corinth ... a friend of the late Mr Thayer's. I have asked him to tell you if he picks up any interesting titbits. Perhaps you would be kind enough to see Lord Edward out. Goodbye, sir. I am sorry we seem always to meet in circumstances like these.'

As Sergeant Willis led Edward through to his office, which adjoined Pride's, he said, 'I was explaining to the Chief Inspector that the murdered man was a friend of mine – an old school friend, in fact. If there's anything you need to know about his background, please feel free to ask me. Here's my card.'

'Very good, my lord,' said the sergeant. 'I'm sure we're very grateful.'

'Oh, by the way,' Edward said casually, 'might I see the Buddha – the murder weapon?'

'I'm afraid not, my lord. It's still in the lab. They're running all sorts of clever scientific tests,' he added patronisingly.

'Of course. Have you a photograph?' The sergeant hesitated and glanced towards Pride's office. 'Please, Sergeant. I can't see what objection there could be to me looking at a few photographs.'

The sergeant glanced once more at the door behind which his superior laboured and then took a decision. 'These only arrived an hour ago.' He passed Edward a brown file tied up with ribbon. Edward fumbled with the tie, almost tipping the sheaf of glossy photographs on to the floor. When he had them in his hand, the first image was so horrific he had to check the exclamation that came to his lips. Even in a black-and-white photograph, the brutality of the scene shocked him. His friend was lying on his face, his head a pulp of blood and brain. The frenzy of the attack was unmistakable. This was not a cold, planned killing but someone giving way to ungovernable rage.

'Not a pretty sight,' the sergeant said.

'No indeed, Sergeant. This was a savage attack.' He put the photograph on the bottom of the pile and looked at the second. This showed the Buddha clearly. It had rolled a few feet from the body and lay against the fireguard. He judged it must be about eight or nine inches high and five wide – it would easily have fitted in the murderer's hand and the heavy jade had smashed Thayer's skull as if it were eggshell.

'It must have been a man,' he said, thinking aloud.

'Or a strong, tall woman. If you get a good swing with a heavy object, it will act like a hammer head. The force of the blow is concentrated. It looks as if the killer hit much harder than he – or she – needed to.'

'Yes, it was rage all right.'

'There's one odd thing, my lord. Do you see here?' The sergeant stabbed a chubby finger at the photograph.

'What is it? It looks like a fountain pen.'

'That's just what it is. See, this next photograph – it's a close-up.'

Edward studied it carefully. 'It's one of those fountain pens clerks use, isn't it?'

'Yes, it's a Waterman. You can get them at any stationer.'

'There's no cap on it.'

'No, we haven't found that yet. It seems as though either the murderer or Mr Thayer was going to write something and it got knocked on to the floor.'

'It doesn't – it didn't belong to Mr Thayer?'

'No, the servants are adamant that it was not his. In any case, his Parker was still in his jacket pocket. We've looked at cheques and letters Mr Thayer wrote recently and they were all written with his Parker.'

'So this is an important clue?'

The sergeant sighed. 'Yes, but there are thousands of people with pens like this.'

'No fingerprints, I suppose?'

'None we have been able to make out.'

Edward continued leafing through the photographs. 'The time of death?'

'Well, as you can see, Mr Thayer was in his dinner jacket – the servants said he dined alone and then dismissed them before going into his study. That was about eleven or eleven fifteen. Apparently, he often worked in his study after dinner. There's a half-smoked cigar in the ashtray on his desk – one of the Monte Cristos from the box you can see in that photograph. He normally went to bed about one in the morning so it looks like he was killed between, say, eleven thirty and maybe one or thereabouts. The medical evidence supports that.'

'No glasses? I mean – he didn't take a glass of brandy in with him?'

'There was brandy in the study with one glass on the tray, but he hadn't touched it so, if he expected a visitor, he made no obvious preparations we can see.'

'Was he working on anything special when he was killed?'

'No. It looks as if he had been sitting in his chair smoking his cigar and thinking.'

'Or waiting.'

'Or waiting, yes, my lord.'

'Thank you, Sergeant. You have been most kind to satisfy my curiosity.'

'No bother, my lord.'

'I suppose I can't keep this photograph . . .'

'Oh no, sir, that would be more than my life's worth.'

Before Edward could say anything more, the communicating door opened and Pride appeared. 'Ah, Lord Edward, not gone yet? Willis, will you come in here.'

With an apologetic smile, Sergeant Willis left him alone. On an impulse, Edward took the photograph he had been examining, slid it into an empty envelope from a pile on the sergeant's desk and left hurriedly. Damn it, he thought, I'm reduced to thieving now. What would Verity say!

As it happened, he had an opportunity of asking her because, on returning to his rooms in Albany, Fenton informed him that she had visited while he had been out.

'Good Lord, Fenton, I didn't even know she was in England.'

'No, sir. The young lady asked me to convey to you her disappointment at having missed you and inquired whether you might be free to take her for dinner this evening.'

Edward had no difficulty in interpreting this as: 'I'm hopping mad not to find you in and I demand you meet me tonight.'

'Very good, Fenton. Did she leave a telephone number?'

'Yes, my lord. She said to tell you she is at the *New Gazette*.'

Edward looked at his hunter. It was two o'clock. 'Get her on the blower for me, please, Fenton.'

Edward was both pleased and alarmed to hear that Verity

was in town and wanted to see him. Was the little termagant going to tear him limb from limb for having abandoned her in Madrid or was she going to forgive and forget? Hardly the latter, he decided.

'My lord . . .' Fenton passed the telephone receiver over to him.

'Verity, is that you?'

'Of course it's me! You've just rung me, haven't you!'

'I mean, it's very good to hear your voice again.'

'Hmf,' she said. 'I don't know whether you will say that after dinner tonight. I assume that's why you're ringing – to invite me to dinner.' She went on without letting him get a word in: 'I suppose I must accept, even though my father doesn't approve of you . . .'

'Your father?' said Edward puzzled.

'Yes, he's been in Madrid helping get David off the hook. He thinks you abandoned me without just cause . . .'

'I thought you never listened to your father . . .'

'Don't be smart with me. Your wicket is a sticky one and don't you forget it.'

Verity's father was a distinguished left-wing lawyer called Donald Browne. As D. F. Browne, he was known on committees up and down the country as the respectable face of the Communist Party. He had defended in the courts many well-known figures on the left of the political spectrum: union leaders, Party members and, notoriously, an MP accused of passing state secrets to a foreign power. He was respected and execrated in equal measure.

'Sorry! As it happens, I have got things to discuss with you . . .'

'About Tilney?'

'Sort of, but I'll tell you tonight. Where do you want to go – the Ritz?'

'No, idiot, why not Gennaro's – for old times' sake.'

'Gennaro's at eight then.'

Gennaro's was the Soho restaurant where Edward had first taken Verity when they had decided to join forces to discover who had murdered General Craig. He thought he knew Verity quite well

149

by now but he was never sure how she would react to anything. She had no respect for him as a male, as the brother of a duke or even for being rich – and he wouldn't have had it any other way. If Verity stopped treating him like a precocious but rather irritating child of seven, he would know their relationship – and he could never be sure they even *had* a relationship – was dead.

As Edward rose from his seat to kiss Verity on the cheek, almost knocking over his champagne glass as he did so, he thought she looked even thinner and paler than when he had last seen her. However, he knew better than to comment on her appearance.

'Verity, how good to see you. Damn difficult to get under the brim of that hat though. When did you get into London? Have you forgiven me for deserting you?'

'Oh gosh, yes. I didn't really need you after all,' she said, smiling at the head waiter who was pouring her champagne. 'Thanks, Freddy. How are you?'

'Most well, thank you, Signora Browne, an' you are well I 'ope?'

Freddy was as English as bully beef but liked to pretend he was Italian. Once they had ordered and Freddy had made himself scarce, Verity said breezily, 'Yes, your absence was not remarked upon. I'm afraid I was a bit unreasonable when you jumped ship without warning.'

Edward was nettled. 'The Spanish police – they didn't make a fuss?'

'No, not with me. Why should they?'

'Rosalía?'

'She did say she always thought you might prove unreliable, but we didn't discuss you. Oh, by the way, how is your brother? I wasn't very sympathetic when you told me about his accident.'

Verity had reason to be wary of the Duke. He distrusted all journalists and her behaviour, when she had been at Mersham the year before, had confirmed his prejudices.

'He's regained consciousness but he's still very weak.'

'He's at Mersham?'

'Yes, fortunately there's a marvellous nurse who looked after him in hospital and she agreed to come back and nurse him at home.'

'Huh!' said Verity, reddening. 'I might have known it! Can

you imagine some poor injured miner being able to hire his hospital nurse to come and look after him – that is if he even got to hospital. I'm surprised your brother didn't hire the whole place.'

Edward might once have risen to the challenge but now he just grinned at her and dug into his huge plate of *ravioli al sugo*. 'The old Verity!' he said sententiously.

'Less of the old, if you don't mind, Comrade Corinth. I think I will have to start calling you Comrade, just to annoy you.' She smiled and touched his hand as it lay on the tablecloth.

In her cashmere twin-set, fur tippet and string of pearls, she looked like any ordinary upper-class girl with nothing more pressing on her mind than her rather absurd hat – she had always liked hats. And yet Edward knew it was just a disguise – or rather not a disguise, because there was a part of her which longed to be conventional, but the *active* part of her hated the whole charade. He guessed it was quite hard for her always to be swimming against the current. It was what had puzzled the Duke: she was, as he put it, 'one of us' and yet the whole purpose of her life was to war against her own class. She wanted to redistribute wealth from rich to poor and to take away economic power from the small group of men who had run the country and the empire for generations – men like Edward Corinth.

Edward sympathised with her dream of a fairer, less class-ridden society in which there was no yawning gulf between the very poor, living – and often starving – in slums unfit for animals, and the very rich like himself. What he could not share, as he had told Connie, was her preferred method of achieving her objective. He believed in gradual change brought about through the ballot box. Verity scorned this as unrealistic: 'Whoever's voted themselves out of power?' she would inquire, with some justice, though ignoring the fact that she certainly would. She subscribed to the view that revolution was the only way of achieving a just society.

Edward was too much of a cynic to believe that change would necessarily be for the better. If one economically dominant class were destroyed – and he was quite prepared to accept that it might be, even that it might *deserve* to be – he believed another as bad or even worse would emerge to take its place. In his mind, the slogans and catch phrases of the left – 'class struggle', 'the dictatorship of the proletariat', 'monopoly capitalism', 'exploitation of the workers', 'nationalisation of the means of production' – were nothing to do with democracy. After the revolution it would be people like David Griffiths-Jones – ruthless ideologues – who would decide what the workers wanted and the result would be an even more pernicious system of government. However, Edward did not despair: the working-class people he came across – and they were surprisingly numerous and varied – were too bloody-minded, individualistic – too conservative with a small 'c' – to be taken in by Griffiths-Jones and his ilk.

'How's world revolution?'

'Don't joke, Edward,' she said, removing her hand. 'Sneer all you want, but history's on our side. Whatever you say, it is a class struggle. Until you understand that – until you change your life and come over to the progressive side of the conflict, the side of the workers – your life will be unreal, a fantasy. You and your class can't cope with reality so you play the ostrich. If you're not an activist you're nothing.'

For a second, Edward was tempted to brush aside her words, ascribing them to some lecture of David's. What could she know about his life – about life, period, as they said in New York. Then, looking into her eyes, earnest and intense, it was borne in on him that there was something in what she said. His life *was* purposeless – it was a fantasy. He would always hate Griffiths-Jones' communism – brutal and self-serving – but he was prepared to admit his life was . . . not what he wished it to be. He did need to change it if he was to achieve . . . if not happiness, at least contentment. But how . . .?

'Is the struggle over in Spain?' Edward inquired.

'No. David thinks it hasn't even begun. The Republic is thriving – chaotic but thriving – but the Church and the army are dragging us down. There may be blood spilt before the new Republic is safe,' she added darkly. 'But let's get off politics. Tell me what you meant when you said you had learnt something which might bear on Tilney's death.'

'Dragging "us" down? Come on, V, it's not your fight.'

'Of course it's my fight,' she flared up, 'and yours, too, if you would only recognise it.'

Edward thought it was time to change the subject. 'I've just come from Scotland Yard.'

'Stephen Thayer? He was a friend of yours, wasn't he? We've just been discussing him at the paper. In fact, to be honest, that's why I wanted to talk to you. I thought you might give me an insider's view. I rather need a scoop. Absolutely nothing seems to happen in Spain – at least nothing people over here care about.'

'No, Verity. I absolutely forbid you to write about Stephen's murder.'

'But I only want to . . .'

'No, and no. I mean it, Verity. If you want me to tell you . . . things, you've got to promise me on whatever you hold most sacred that you won't write about it in any Fleet Street rag – and that includes the *Daily Worker* – unless I give you my express permission. Understood, Comrade?'

'Oh, I suppose so,' she said scowling, 'but . . .'

'No buts. I can just see the headline in the *DW*: "Old Etonians murdered by class enemy". Just finish your *foie gras*.'

Verity saw he was serious and was rather impressed. Maybe he had some spirit in him after all.

She put down her fork. 'I can't eat any more.'

'Well, pass it over. At one and nine, I'm not letting it go to waste.'

'Old Etonians?' she said meditatively. 'So you think Tilney's death may be linked with Stephen Thayer's?'

'Yes, and perhaps Makepeace Hoden's too. I told you about him, didn't I?'

'Yes, he was eaten by a lion.'

'More or less. Actually, that's high on my list of things to do – find out exactly how he did die. It may have been an accident, but it's a bit of a coincidence that three of my school friends – exact contemporaries, all of whom knew each other well – should die within the space of a few months.'

'Hmf. A coincidence but why do you think it's anything more? I mean the *New Gazette* report says Thayer was hit on the head by a rock or something in a – what was it? – "a frenzied attack".'

'Look at this,' he said, taking out the photograph he had stolen from Sergeant Willis.

'It's a pen.'

'Yes, a cheap fountain pen belonging not to poor Thayer, so almost certainly to his killer. But that's not all. Do you see that white thing a few inches from the pen?'

'Ye . . . s, but I can't make out what it is.'

'The police missed it too,' Edward said smugly. 'I stole this photograph from under Chief Inspector Pride's nose.'

'Cripes! Did you really? I didn't think you had it in you. Is Pride a Chief Inspector now?'

'Yes, but that doesn't matter. Look at this, girl!' Verity considered protesting at being called 'girl' but was too intrigued to bother. Edward took a magnifying glass out of his pocket and gave it to her.

'Sherlock,' she said predictably. She glued her eye to the glass. 'Good heavens, it's . . .'

'Yes, it's one of those little matchboxes they have on the tables at Chicote's. Do you see?'

'Golly, yes, you're right. You must be right. So . . .?'

'So,' said Edward sombrely, 'Stephen Thayer's last visitor and probable killer has to be . . . is likely to be . . . someone we know.'

'Mmm. Yes, but I suppose the matchbox might have been on the floor for some time.'

'With servants in the house? I doubt it. Anyway, I was going to try and inveigle myself in to talk to them. If you want to come with me . . .'

'Pride still hates your guts?'

'Yes. It's a bit of a nuisance but it does mean I feel no compunction about not sharing my thoughts with him. I offered and he turned me down like a bedspread.'

'Mmm, I can see why you are worried: you expect to be the next corpse.'

'Verity!'

'Oh, sorry. Can't you take a joke? It's interesting, though. I mean, the chances of anyone making that connection between Tilney, Hoden and Stephen Thayer are remote, though you might be jumping to conclusions. There's certainly nothing to link Hoden's death with the other two. There must be Old Etonians being murdered all over the world most of the time.'

'Verity!'

'You know what I mean!'

'Yes, I wonder how I can find out more about how Hoden died. I don't have time to go to Kenya at the moment and, even if I did ... Wait a moment, though, I wonder if the Colonial Office might have reports of the inquest or anything. There must have been an inquest. I'll ask Thoroughgood to see what he can get me.'

'The *New Gazette* has people who report from Africa. I'll find out if there's anyone in Nairobi who could do some snooping on our behalf.'

'Good idea.'

Verity tried not to look pleased. 'What else can I do?'

'You can find out if anyone we know who frequents Chicote's happened to be in England when Stephen was murdered. How long before you have to go back to Spain?'

'Soon, but I can stay a few days if there's a good enough reason.'

'Well, it might be better for you to go back sooner rather than later. You might be able to make some discreet investigations in Madrid. If you're establishing who was where when, you can also get a list together of who was in Kenya when Hoden died. Didn't Ben Belasco say he had been in Africa before going to Spain?'

As soon as he said it, he remembered that, according to David, Verity was having an affair with Belasco. Seeing her in London like this had, for a blessed moment, put it out of his mind.

Verity blushed a little but Edward pretended not to notice. She had no idea that David had told him about Belasco, so had no reason to object to his remark. He hurried on: 'In the meantime, I've got two visits to make. You can come with me on one if you like. It might be educational in every way. The other would be too dangerous for you.'

'Tell me all, oh great one,' Verity ordered, bowing her head and putting out both her hands in supplication.

Edward ignored her play-acting. 'I want to go to Eton to see if I can dig up any evidence of a connection between the three dead men – beyond the obvious one. If you came with me, you could research a horrible article about the place for the *Daily Worker*. You can explain how it perpetuates class divisions.'

'Well, it does,' Verity said stoutly. 'Look at the number of

Etonians there are in positions of power in the government, the Foreign Office, the Civil Service. I expect even the Archbishop of Canterbury went to the "old school" – not all appointments are made on merit, I fancy. Anyway, look at the fees: what are they – two hundred pounds a year?'

'Eton's the best, I grant you, but it's not exclusive. When I was there, we had boys from . . .'

'Of course Eton's exclusive. If it didn't exclude, it would lose half its appeal.'

'Oh, stow it, Verity. You don't have to preach to me.' He added shyly, 'I'd also like you to meet Franklyn, my nephew, don't y'know. I have a sort of feeling you might get on. I may be wrong. He'll be back for the Easter holidays next week but I don't want to wait till then to talk to him. As I say, I want to chat to a few people there who might remember why Stephen left under a cloud. Then there's Charles Thayer. I want to talk to Frank and to his housemaster about him as soon as I can. I want to do something for him if I'm allowed. I don't think he has many living relatives.'

'Is Thayer's son called Charles?'

'Yes, why?'

'Oh, I don't know: he just would be, that's all.'

'What on earth do you mean?'

'Oh, I don't know – Charles – it's so snobby.'

'There's nothing particularly snobby about Charles,' Edward said irritably. 'What about Chaplin?'

'That's Charlie, idiot. Charlie's a good name, but Charles . . . I ask you. You either have to be a duke or a hairdresser.'

'Well,' said Edward, shortly, 'Charles Thayer is neither; he's just a boy who has no mother and has just lost his father in the most awful way imaginable.'

'Oh gosh. Sorry. I didn't mean to sound like a hard-faced bitch . . .'

Edward tried not to look shocked at Verity's language. 'I know, but wait until you meet him. You'll like him.'

'And what's the other visit you think is too dangerous for me?'

'I've got to go to Frankfurt to meet this man Heinrich Hoffmann, Thayer's banking partner. He may have something to tell us, but with your politics it would be madness for you to go.'

'I could go in disguise.'

'What about your passport?'

'I could get it changed. Joe will help.'

Joe, Lord Weaver, the proprietor of the *New Gazette*, was a friend of both of them, but Edward didn't trust him as far as women were concerned. He'd never dare suggest to Verity that Weaver's motives for employing her as a foreign correspondent were not solely on her merits as a reporter, but she did seem to be very intimate with the man. Of course, he was old enough to be her father. After all, he actually was the father of the girl Edward had thought himself to be in love with in New York, but still . . .

'No, I don't want you,' he said roughly. 'I've got to prise information out of a Nazi banker. It won't be easy but your presence would make it impossible. You're more use in Madrid.'

'Oh stuff; bankers go for . . . well, you know . . . girls like me.'

'Well, you're not going. What you can do is go through the files at the *New Gazette* and find out if there's anything interesting on Hoden or Tilney or, for that matter, Stephen Thayer. Oh, and find out which reporter the *New Gazette* puts on the case. You never know, a good chap might find out something useful.'

'OK,' said Verity. 'When do we go to the "old school"?'

Edward was encouraged by how meekly Verity had taken his refusal to let her go with him to Germany. Perhaps she was at last beginning to see him as the dominant male and treat him as such. Unwisely, he felt confident enough to rebuke her for her use of slang.

'I wish you wouldn't say "OK". It's so sloppy.'

Verity turned on him a look which the Spanish call the *mirada fuerte*, a gaze fierce enough to cool porridge.

'Don't you dare criticise me. I'll say exactly what I want to say, when I want, in the way I want. I made a resolution not to tell you what I thought of you leaving me to sort out Tilney's murder but blast you . . . You never once telephoned to find out . . .'

'I tried but I couldn't get through . . .'

'Pathetic. You just hadn't got the guts. I saw the way you got the wind up when it came to dealing with the Spanish police. And who do you think had to telephone Tilney's parents and tell them their son had been murdered *again*?'

'Oh God, I'm sorry, Verity. I know I left you in the soup but there was no alternative. I did at least get your David out of gaol.'

'Rubbish! The police absolutely refused to let him go.'

'But they couldn't have thought he had killed Tilney. He was in gaol.'

'I don't know what they thought or rather they just thought there was something very fishy going on . . . which, of course, there was. They said if he hadn't killed Tilney . . . and they weren't convinced he hadn't magicked himself out of gaol to do it . . . he had probably murdered the man they had buried. At best, David had perverted the course of justice by mis-identifying the first corpse as Tilney's. It was a nightmare. I had to get my father to come out from England, which he was very reluctant to do, to sort it out. I made Tom Sutton ring everyone in the Spanish government with any influence . . .'

'I'm sorry, Verity. I'm really sorry. What more can I say?'

'You can keep bloody quiet, that's what you can do . . . Comrade.'

In a typically British way, people at neighbouring tables were pretending they could not hear the argument between the pretty girl in the big hat and the impeccably suited young man, while breaking off their own conversations to listen intently.

'I'm sorry,' Edward repeated in a low voice. 'Please, Verity, keep your voice down. Everyone can hear us.'

'I don't care . . .'

'I know, but we don't want the whole world to know what we're planning.'

Edward had skilfully implied they were still a team with a plan to pursue and Verity was partly mollified. It was probably no bad thing that she had broken her resolution and aired her resentment rather than let it fester. She felt better now and was tempted to apologise for her outburst but decided it might weaken her position if she did. So instead she said, 'When do we go?'

'To Eton?'

'Yes.'

'Tomorrow? I could pick you up at ten and we could motor down. I could see if we can take Frank out to lunch. It's a Thursday, isn't it?'

'Yes, why?'

'As far as I remember, it's a half-holiday – no work in the afternoon – just games.'

Edward had telephoned Connie who had reported that she had spoken to Frank who was understandably upset and worried about his friend. He was anxious to talk over the murder with his uncle: he said he had something to show him – he wouldn't say what. Charles was staying with an aunt in London at least until after the funeral, which was to be the following Saturday, as soon as the police released the body. It was to be private, for family only, but Charles had particularly asked that Edward and Connie should be there. There would be a memorial service at some later date.

'I wonder why he wants us there,' Edward said to Connie.

'I don't know, but he wants you to bring Frank if the house-master will give his permission.'

'Frank! That will be an ordeal for the boy.'

'Yes, but I've discussed it with him and he wants to go. He knows his friend needs all the support he can get from the people who love him.'

13

The next day proved sunny and warm for early April. He picked up Verity about midday from the flat where she was staying in Bayswater. It was oddly pleasurable, Edward discovered, to be spinning down the Great West Road in the Lagonda to visit his old school with Verity at his side. Fenton had packed a lunch basket for them and, since it turned out they could not see Frank until half-past two, they found a place by the river, spread a rug on the grass, which was only slightly damp, and tucked into smoked salmon, cold chicken, and early strawberries which Connie had sent from the Mersham greenhouses. They washed it all down with champagne and discussed David Griffiths-Jones, the situation in Spain and Verity's plans for the future.

'It's terrible, really, but I just can't wait till war breaks out. Promise you won't ever tell anyone I said so, but you can see what I mean. I know it's wrong to put my career above the happiness of hundreds and thousands of ordinary Spaniards, but I do.'

Edward was always amazed by Verity's honesty. She was able to look at herself quite dispassionately, examine her motives and judge herself against her principles in a way he could never do. It occurred to him that, if he ever asked her if she could love him, she would give him a totally honest answer and that terrified him. Better perhaps not to know than to be certain of rejection.

'But you have already made a reputation for yourself,' he said. 'Anyway, if war broke out, you couldn't report it. Only men can be war correspondents.'

Verity, lying on her back, her head on a cushion from the car,

160

raised herself slightly to see if he was joking. He did not appear to be. She almost loved him for being so predictably male in his expectations of what was and was not possible for a woman.

'Of course I can be a war correspondent,' she said levelly. 'Don't you see, this war would be my great chance. There are not so many of us in Spain. Most newspapers think Spain is boring and they concentrate on what's happening in Italy and Germany. I've done my homework. I know how Spanish politics work. I know which of the dozens of political groups are important. I know most of their leaders and they're beginning to know me.'

'On the left.'

'Oh yes, on the left. I'm a communist so I could never pretend to be neutral in that way. I could never get close to General Franco, say, nor would I want to.'

'But how can you keep your reports fair if you are only hearing one side of the argument?'

'Because I have my intelligence. I can tell when I'm being lied to and I only report what I know to be true. Or if I report what I'm told, I give my source and put a value on it for veracity so my readers can judge for themselves. In any case, I make it absolutely clear what I believe in: the legitimate government of Spain, the Republic, religious tolerance and so on. I can't pretend every side in the Spanish political world is as good as any other. I have to make judgements otherwise what I say would be literally valueless.'

Edward pursed his lips. 'It sounds a thin line between news and propaganda.'

'I would never report anything unless I believed it to be true,' repeated Verity stubbornly.

'Yes, but would you ignore something unpleasant – like corruption – if, by reporting it, you would damage the Republic?'

'Damn you,' said Verity smiling. 'I suppose the answer is "I don't know."'

'I was thinking,' he said, bravely, 'of David buying arms and equipment from the Nazis.' He had not meant to break his promise to David not to tell anyone what he had been up to but Verity had questioned him so relentlessly when they had got back from the prison that in the end he had told her everything,

161

swearing her to the secrecy which he had been unable to command. He supposed he had half-hoped Verity would see her lover for the unscrupulous manipulator he was but in that he had been disappointed. She had made no comment then or afterwards on the morality of David's activities. 'It's a great story – a scoop – but you also know the enemies of the Republic would make hay with it. The *Express*, the *Telegraph* . . . they'd make a few headlines with the story.'

'Oh God, Edward. You've got me there. I have thought about it a lot but in the end I did decide to keep silent. I told myself it's because I couldn't prove anything but, of course, that's not the reason. It would be just too damaging to our cause. I know David feels the ends justify the means but, I admit, it seems wrong to me, as it would to a lot of other people . . . I have to keep silent.' She sat up and looked at him like a serious child. 'Does that make me a liar and a cheat?'

'I can't answer that,' he said gently. 'For what it's worth, I think I would do what you have done – keep quiet about it – but I don't have much faith in politicians of whatever persuasion. I believe, on balance, the Popular Front is the best government for Spain and we should support anybody who fights Fascism but I think all these "isms" are poison . . . I'm sorry, but I do.'

Edward felt a heel for having made her acknowledge her hypocrisy, if that was what it was. He had had some vague idea that sitting beside the Thames drinking champagne, he might have the opportunity to take Verity in his arms and . . . but the conversation had gone another way and the sun now went behind a cloud in recognition of a lost opportunity.

Verity shivered and looked at her watch. 'Let's get on, shall we. Look, I'm doing what you think I should be doing: entering the enemy's camp with an open mind.'

'Eton? It's a camp you belong to by birth and education,' he said sententiously, 'but still – let's go on. I have this feeling that it's there we may find out who murdered Stephen Thayer.'

As Verity folded up the blankets and put the dirty plates and glasses back in the basket, she risked saying – getting her own back for some of the things Edward had said to her – 'Does it really matter so much if three Old Etonians bite the dust when there are hundreds of deaths in German concentration camps every day?'

'You don't know that. It may be just Communist Party propaganda. I don't doubt there is brutality in the German prison
camps because these are brutal times and the Nazis are brutal
people but they are like us, from the same civilisation – the
civilisation that gave us Goethe, Mozart and Beethoven. They're
not mass murderers.'

Verity looked at him oddly. 'You really believe that?'

'I do,' Edward replied defensively.

'Then you are more naive than I believed,' she said, snapping
shut the wicker picnic basket. 'I thought you understood what
we are up against but you don't. You're cynical about politicians
but these people, the Nazis, are not politicians. They're thugs
and until people like you understand it . . . we'll . . . we'll slide
further and further and faster and faster into hell.'

Edward could see she was deadly serious but he thought she
was exaggerating because of her political loyalties and told
himself, smugly, that he was better placed to judge the truth of
the matter than she.

As the Lagonda came to a halt outside Frank's house, Edward
took a deep breath. Eton was looking ancient and tranquil. He
was pleased to have the opportunity of showing Verity his old
school but apprehensive that she would say something deroga-
tory in a loud voice in Frank's hearing. When a man shows a
girl over his old school, he is inviting her to investigate his
childhood. Consciously or not, he is laying bare a cherished part
of himself and only invites such intimacy when he anticipates
being offered something even more intimate in return.

Fortunately, he was sensible enough to say nothing to Verity
about not criticising Eton in front of his nephew and, as it turned
out, he had no need to worry. She charmed Franklyn, she
charmed his housemaster, and she charmed Edward most of all.
They agreed to defer all discussion of Charles until later in the
day. It was first of all necessary to show Verity Eton's glories.
Sightseeing can be a wearisome business and certainly tolerable
only in small doses but, to his surprise, Edward found himself
enjoying strolling around in the sunshine. As they walked into
School Yard, Verity slipped on the cobbles and would have
fallen if Frank had not grasped her arm. Edward noted with

amusement that his nephew was still holding on to her as they climbed the steep stone steps into College Chapel. Inside, he had to relinquish her arm to indicate where he normally sat. Unlike most churches half the congregation faced the other half rather than all facing the altar. 'It's because what we have here is only the choir. The nave was to have stretched right down Keate's Lane,' Frank explained.

He showed her the fifteenth-century wall paintings which had been almost obliterated in the previous century, only to be rescued by Provost James fifteen years ago. He talked about the organ – he was passionately musical – and introduced them to the Precentor who was teaching him how to play it. They examined the Founder's statue in the ante-chapel and sat in silence not exactly praying but drinking in the peace of the place.

Verity was unusually silent and Edward wondered if she was impressed by the beauty of the building or waiting for an appropriate moment to voice her disapproval.

'How often do you use the chapel?' she inquired.

'Once a day and twice on Sundays,' he replied, 'except, of course, the little boys who go to Lower Chapel down Keate's Lane, and the Jews and Catholics.'

'Where do they go?'

'I've no idea,' said Frank. 'I'm afraid I'm not religious. I mean, I believe in goodness, courage, truth, honesty – the Christian virtues – but I can't see how there could be a god. If there is, he must be blind or vicious, otherwise he wouldn't have let the world get into the state it's in.'

Verity nodded and Edward guessed the boy had expressed her own views on the subject. It was touching to hear Frank express his beliefs so unaffectedly. Had Edward said something similar, he knew he would have sounded priggish or hypocritical but the boy's innocent statement of what he considered incontrovertible made him rather ashamed of the cynicism, the compromises and the half-truths which had infected his own faith. At thirty-five, he felt his own youth to be brown at the edges, sere as a leaf in winter.

They walked out into the sun, Verity's high heels clicking and clacking on the uneven stone. College, the ancient crenellated building in which the black-gowned scholarship boys known as 'tugs' lived, glowed bronze. They strolled round the mildew-green statue of King Henry VI, the school's founder, into the cool and pleasant cloisters where they read the names of those Old Etonians who had fallen during the war. Solemnly, Frank pointed out his uncle's name which was, of course, also his own. Edward shivered, assailed by memories and forebodings.

'I wish I had known him,' he said wistfully. 'They don't make heroes nowadays. I can't wait till I'm old enough to go out to Spain and fight for the Republic. It's the only government in the world doing something to stop the Fascists. I just don't understand why our people are being so stand-offish.'

'There's no one to fight yet . . .' Verity said.

'Not with guns,' said Frank, looking at her earnestly, 'but we must fight the Fascists now, before it's too late. Don't you agree? I know you do because I've read your reports in the *New Gazette*.'

Verity blushed with pleasure but said quickly, 'Please don't think I take any satisfaction in the idea of war and young men killing and being killed like last time . . .'

'But we have to fight for what we believe in,' the boy said, gripping her arm again. 'You believe that, don't you?'

'Yes,' said Verity soberly, 'I do.'

Edward was pleased with his nephew. He might have known that he would side instinctively with the underdog and the liberal-minded but even he was a little startled by the boy's ready espousal of communism. Verity was gracious and a little impressed: it was, after all, flattering to have a good-looking young Etonian, a duke in the making, look at you with admiration, ready to accept without protest even your most outrageous statements.

'I agree,' Frank said earnestly to Verity at one point, 'the aristocracy is finished. I have terrific arguments with my Pa about it. He calls me a "pinko", but I'm right, aren't I? Dukes and earls and so on – it's all bosh, isn't it?'

With some amusement, Edward saw Verity actually being driven to defend the Duke of Mersham.

'Your father's a good man, Frank. He has a great sense of responsibility and he means well. My only quarrel with him is that he has not been elected. He's probably a better man than many MPs but . . .'

'That's what I mean,' the boy said fervently. 'He oughtn't to be put in that position. I know it's a burden to him. Why should

Pa have a castle and lots of servants and all that "my lording"? I'm going to give it all up.'

Edward and Verity looked equally shocked.

'No . . .' Verity began.

'No . . .' Edward said at the same time. 'You have responsibilities, Frank, whether you like them or not. Surely it's better to work within the system in order to change it rather than run away?'

Frank looked at his uncle critically. 'It's easy for you to talk, Uncle Ned. You have all the fun of being a rich aristocrat without any of its burdens.'

'*Touché*,' Edward said, and Verity smirked.

They went back to Frank's house and were introduced to Mr Chandler, his housemaster. He was about Edward's age, good-looking with a rather shaggy beard but a sensible, humorous man whom Edward liked immediately. He seemed much taken with Verity and went so far as to suggest that she might like to come and give a talk to the sixth form about the situation in Spain.

'I thought public school housemasters wanted nothing to do with women,' Verity said in surprise.

'Oh, we try to change with the times,' Chandler said mildly.

'It was different in my day,' Edward remarked. 'I remember my mother saying my housemaster, Henry Hobbs, never addressed a word to her in all the years I was in his house.' He turned to Chandler: 'I suppose he must be dead now?'

'Yes, I believe so but, if your Dame was Miss Harvey, she's still very much alive and lives in the town.'

'Goodness me,' Edward exclaimed. 'Old Miss Harvey still alive! She seemed ancient to me twenty years ago!'

'Why don't you call in and see her if you have time? She loves it when old boys drop in. Her memory is excellent, better than mine, and I'm sure she will remember you.'

'Perhaps I will,' said Edward thoughtfully.

'Miss Browne,' said Chandler, turning to Verity, 'I wouldn't be surprised if Lord Edward hadn't told you about his sporting triumphs here at Eton?'

Verity gave a little moue. 'He played cricket, didn't he? Isn't the phrase "a useful bat"?'

'Oh come now,' said Chandler laughing. 'Frank, you know what your uncle did here?'

'Of course!' the boy said proudly. 'He was captain of the eleven and scored a century at Lords against Harrow.'

'He did indeed, but did he tell you about his success at rackets?'

'Oh please, Chandler,' Edward begged, 'spare my blushes. I had a good eye, nothing more.'

'What's "rackets"?' said Verity belligerently. She was getting a bit fed up of all this praise of Edward. Wasn't it enough to be rich and a lord and not altogether an ass? Was she now to be told he was a sporting hero?

'Rackets, Miss Browne,' said Chandler solemnly, 'is generally considered to be the fastest game in the world. It's played with a small hard ball in something like a big squash court. It's been estimated that the ball travels at over a hundred miles an hour.'

'And you were good, Uncle?' said Frank appraisingly.

'Oh I . . .' Edward began in some confusion.

'You didn't know then?' Chandler broke in. 'Just as I supposed. Your uncle, Frank, played doubles with Stephen Thayer and they were almost unbeatable. They won the Public Schools championship and the Noel Bruce Cup – that's right, isn't it, Lord Edward?'

'Yes,' Edward mumbled, 'but the Noel Bruce Cup – that was with someone else. I had rather lost touch with Stephen by then. Anyway, what does it all matter?' he said testily. 'I'm sure the last thing Verity or any of you wants to hear is tales of my schooldays.'

'On the contrary, Mr Chandler,' Verity said coolly, 'I'm very interested in what Lord Edward got up to at school, before he went off to rule the empire. From what you tell me, I'm surprised he's not in our Olympic team.'

'I don't think rackets is an Olympic sport, is it?' said Chandler, taking her seriously, which irritated her. 'Do you still play, Lord Edward?'

'Oh, occasionally, at Queen's Club, don't y'know.' He was distinctly uneasy now, seeing the expression on Verity's face. 'Chandler, might I just have a word with you about Charles Thayer?'

The two men went into a huddle in the corner. Verity and Frank amused themselves talking politics. Verity discovered that, if anything, Frank's views were more extreme than hers but, when she tried to temper his enthusiasm with a bowdlerised account of the left's factional fighting in Spain and the Party's problems in England, he did not want to hear. 'Don't try and put me off, Verity. By the way, you don't think it cheek me calling you Verity but I seem to know you so well . . .'

'No, of course not,' Verity said faintly.

'I know you want to put me off – all my family try it. They say – Pa specially – that I'm just a child and know nothing. Well, I agree. I know I've no experience but even a child can tell right from wrong. As soon as I'm twenty-one – earlier I hope – I'm going to fight for . . . Oh, you've finished, Uncle,' he said looking up, annoyed at being interrupted.

'Yes, I've fixed up things with Chandler. He's going to speak to Caine, Charles's tutor, and keep me in touch with . . .'

'Fixed things up!' Frank exploded. 'You see what I mean, Verity? Grown-ups are always "fixing things up".'

'Hey, steady on, old lad. I'm just trying to help your friend.'

'I know you are, Uncle Ned, but I wish you wouldn't . . . oh, I don't know.'

Edward was a little hurt. He had thought Frank would be pleased he was taking an interest in his friend's future but somehow he had managed to say or do something wrong; he didn't know what. He looked at Verity for help, but she was looking interestedly at her feet. He said more coldly than he had intended, 'I'm going to take up Chandler's suggestion of visiting my old Dame. Will you two be all right if I leave you together?'

'I think so, don't you, Verity?' Frank said with exaggerated consideration.

'I think we'll muddle on along somehow,' Verity agreed. 'Dames? They sound like they belong in a pantomime.'

'Very funny; matrons are called "Dames" at Eton,' Edward said.

'Uncle Ned . . .'

Edward put a hand on Frank's shoulder. 'I know you want to talk about this dreadful thing which happened to Mr Thayer, and I do too, but I want to do this first – talk to old Miss Harvey. It's not just nostalgia. I think she may be able to explain one or two things which are puzzling me about ... about what happened when Stephen and I were at school. What I suggest is that you do a bit more sightseeing and meet me at the Cockpit – that's the teashop in the High Street, Verity – at four thirty. I've booked a table and then we can all three go over what we know about this murder. I promise you, Frank, I intend getting to the bottom of it, for both our sakes.'

'And for Charles's,' Frank added.

'For his sake too,' Edward agreed.

It was with mixed feelings that he knocked on the door of the little house in the High Street where Miss Harvey now lived in retirement. It took the old lady some time to answer but she recognised him immediately and with evident pleasure. She had put on a lot of weight since he had been a boy at Eton but in every other respect seemed to Edward much as she had always been: sharp-eyed and benevolent. She had had an ability to spot immediately when a boy was feigning illness to get out of an exam or a cross-country run and the shrewdness to know when one of her charges was genuinely ill or unhappy. She had no favourites and she was not 'soft'. She did not attempt to be a surrogate mother but was conscientious in returning the boys to their homes at the end of each half, sound in mind and body. Her responsibility was all the more onerous when she knew the housemaster, Henry Hobbs, was shirking his.

Edward had been impressed with Chandler and compared him favourably with the man who had been his housemaster. Hobbs had been a strict disciplinarian, when he remembered, but most of the time had ignored the boys in his care and left the house to run itself. In retrospect, Edward considered him to have been guilty of gross dereliction of duty, whatever his personal problems, and, inevitably, Miss Harvey had had to bear more than her share of the burden in the running of the house. It was all right for Edward, who was a high-spirited, confident boy, but there were others who suffered from not having anyone to monitor their development, encourage and direct them. By modern standards, conditions in the house were primitive. The food was plentiful but virtually vitamin-free, and beating and bullying, which a good housemaster would have repressed, were rife. The lavatories were outside and in winter froze. Indeed, one of the early morning duties of a fag was to sit on a scuffed and none-too-clean wooden seat and warm it for his master.

Edward wondered if it was possible to feel nostalgia for a period one had not particularly enjoyed. On the whole, he thought it was. As a child, every setback and every triumph is branded on the memory – the caning he received for three 'rips' in a week, for example. It was a solemn moment when the form master ripped the top of a bad piece of work and told the erring boy to present it to his tutor, and Hobbs had been brutal with him. But these moments were, at least in his case, outweighed by moments of joy more intense than any he had experienced as an adult: the memory of getting his house cap for cricket, and that glorious day in his last summer when he had carried his bat against Harrow at Lords. Had he ever been happier? He realised now that he had been protected by Stephen. First as his fag and then as his friend – though always his dependent because of the three-year age difference between them. He had basked in the reflected glory of being Thayer's 'boy'. There had been nothing overtly sexual in their relationship – Edward was totally innocent of any such emotion – but, looking back, it had all been a little unhealthy. A good housemaster might have nipped the friendship in the bud.

Thayer had been a glamorous figure, tall, good-looking, good at sport and no fool academically. He had been elected to Pop much earlier than usual. In fact, most boys never were elected. He had collected a host of sporting honours, coloured caps and scarves, and had been much liked by the beaks who relied heavily on boys of his stature to run the school. During the war, Eton had been short-staffed and beaks past their retiring age had been kept on. In their dotage, they sometimes found discipline a problem. And yet, in the end, it had all gone wrong. When, in 1917, Thayer had left a few weeks before the end of the summer half, Edward had been surprised but, as boys do, had taken it in his stride. He had asked a few questions but had allowed himself to be fobbed off with bland remarks about his friend having been ill. Life was too full to allow him much time to dwell on such little mysteries, but now he blamed himself for not having made more effort to discover what had really happened. Children then were used to grown-ups having secrets and when, a few months later, rumours reached him of some unpleasantness, he had resolutely shut his ears to them. It was part of schoolboy honour that one did not listen to stories of friends' misfortunes.

It seemed odd to him now but, even when he met Thayer at parties after he himself had left Eton, he had not asked him whether there was any substance in the rumours. Verity would think it absurd but he had, quite simply, been too embarrassed. In just a few months one of the most important friendships of his life had atrophied. Thayer had said no goodbyes, left no messages, written no letters – at least none to Edward. Now he was dead, he thought it was time to find out what he ought to have discovered all those years before. He had a hunch it might shed some light on why his friend had not enjoyed as an adult the success he had achieved as a schoolboy and, perhaps, even why he had been beaten to death in his own home.

Miss Harvey welcomed Edward literally with open arms. 'Of course I remember you, Lord Edward,' she said when she had released him from her embrace. 'I remember all my boys and twenty years doesn't seem so long a time. It's yesterday and tomorrow I have problems with.'

She put the kettle on a gas ring and then sank back into a large armchair which still managed to seem too small for her bulk. Around her on the mantelpiece, on little tables perilously placed to impede her movement, Edward saw dozens of photographs, some in frames, others propped up behind ornaments – all of boys or young men. It was a custom at Eton that when a boy left, he presented his friends, his tutors and his Dame with a likeness. In the eighteenth century, it might have been a portrait but, even before the war, it had degenerated into photographs pasted on to stiff board. Miss Harvey saw Edward looking curiously at one he recognised.

'That's Stephen Thayer. You remember him. He was a little older than you but . . .'

'Yes, Miss Harvey, I remember him very well and it is partly about him that I came to see you. I hope you don't mind.'

'Tut, tut! I had a feeling you had some reason to be visiting me.'

'Oh, please don't think I didn't want to see *you*. My nephew, Franklyn is in Mr Chandler's house and he suggested I might like to have a chat.'

171

'Mr Chandler,' the old woman said vaguely. 'I have met him, I'm sure, but you see I don't get about much . . . You have a nephew here? Well I never. But, may I ask, have you got sons?'

'Not yet, Miss Harvey. I have to find a wife first.'

'Oh, fiddlesticks,' said the old lady sounding annoyed. 'You must be being picky, as we used to say. Everyone loves a lord . . . but I'm sorry. Forgive me for treating you like a small boy, Lord Edward. It's a natural fault for us old folk to get time muddled.'

'You're not so old . . .'

'Eighty-four!' she said triumphantly.

Edward thought he would try to steer her back to the subject which had brought him. 'But you have an excellent memory for the old days and I wanted to ask you a few questions about Stephen Thayer.'

Miss Harvey looked at him shrewdly. 'I read in the *News Chronicle* that he had been murdered.'

'Yes, that was so shocking. I had not seen much of him since I left Eton but I considered him a friend and his son is a great friend of my nephew.'

'I didn't know.'

'Do you remember him?' Edward persisted.

'I remember him.' There was something steely in her voice and Edward had the impression she had not liked him. 'I . . . I don't want to talk about him if you don't mind.' She took the photograph off the table and put it in a drawer.

'But please, Miss Harvey, just a couple of questions. I think it might be important.'

'He was a bad boy. They were all bad boys. They all had to go,' she said, twisting her hands in her lap. 'Oh, the tea!' she added brightly.

As she struggled to her feet to fill the teapot, Edward tried again. 'I was three years younger than Stephen so no one ever told me why he left Eton early. There was some sort of a scandal, wasn't there?'

'I don't remember,' the old lady said shortly. 'Sugar?'

'No . . . no thank you. Please, Miss Harvey, I'm not just scandal-mongering. I want to find out who killed Stephen and I think it might be something to do with . . . with what happened here.'

'Scandal-mongering! I should think not! The newspapers, I'd never have believed it. The things they got up to . . . reporters, they call 'em, climbing trees to look in windows, questioning the "boys' maids" . . . disgusting!'

The newspapers! It was that bad a scandal. He must get Verity to look in the files.

'I never heard . . .'

'They said if Mr Hobbs had been looking after his house properly it would never have happened. It nearly killed him.'

'What might never have happened?' Edward said in frustration.

'Godfrey Tilney, he was a bad boy too, but at least he wasn't in our house,' she continued, as if he had not spoken. 'It was a bad time but the next year . . . we had some good boys. You . . . we always liked you. So well-mannered, always so courteous. I remember once I tripped and fell down the stairs and you . . . you tried to catch me . . . and I rolled on top of you. I might have hurt myself . . . but you caught me . . .' She mopped her eyes: '. . . a good boy.'

Godfrey Tilney! There was a connection after all. Miss Harvey was not going to tell him what she knew about Stephen Thayer's 'scandal' but she had told him more than she had meant. It was bad news, shameful news, and she did not want to be reminded of it. He thought the best thing was to leave it for the moment. He would find out what the papers reported at the time and then, if necessary, come back with some specific questions.

He finished his tea and got up to go. 'It has been so nice talking to you about old times, Miss Harvey. I hope I haven't upset you with my questions but it is important. I must go now as I have to meet my nephew. I am sure I'll be back soon and, if I may, I will visit you again. Here is my card. If you remember anything about Stephen Thayer which you think might help me discover who did this dreadful thing, I would be so grateful if you could telephone or write to me.'

'Oh, are you going, Lord Edward?' said the old woman and, for a moment, he thought she might bribe him to stay with a little information but the moment passed.

'Yes but, as I say, I'll be back. Now I've found you, Miss Harvey, I'm not going to lose sight of you again.' She looked slightly worried by this remark but said nothing. 'Perhaps I can bring my nephew to meet you next time,' Edward said. 'It would be good for him to hear what the school was like before he was born. Really, a historian ought to interview you for your memories.'

Edward left the little house and walked down to the Cockpit wondering if he had stumbled on something interesting or whether he was following a false trail. He would ask Thoroughgood if he remembered anything of the scandal and he must find out what Chief Inspector Pride had discovered. Maybe the murder had already been solved and no one had bothered to tell him.

It amused Edward, when he pushed open the glass door of the tea room, to see Verity and Frank deep in conversation at a little table in a corner. His first thought was that they looked like lovers and he had to check a surge of ridiculous jealousy. They were both leaning forward so that their heads almost touched and were ignoring the scones covered in clotted cream and strawberry jam on the plate in front of them. As he walked towards them, he saw that Verity had a smear of cream at the corner of her mouth and, for a moment, he wanted more than anything else in the world to bend over and kiss it off her. He was actually standing beside the table before they noticed him and jumped apart almost guiltily. He imagined that this might be how the dead felt, aimlessly hanging about in the corners of the lives of loved ones left behind on earth – invisible, frustrated, inconsolable. He pushed away such morbid imaginings and said, meaninglessly, 'Well, here we are then.'

'We were talking about Spain,' said Frank brightly. 'It sounds most awfully interesting. Verity says in the holidays I can come and see for myself what's happening. She says I ought to join the YCL.'

'The what?'

'The Young Communist League. What do you think?'

Edward frowned and Verity giggled nervously. 'Only if your parents agree,' she said, as though she had just remembered that Frank was only a boy. She made haste to change the subject. 'Did you get anything useful out of your Dame?'

'Yes, I did, at least I think I did. Apparently there was a terrific scandal which actually got into the papers and resulted in several boys being sacked, including Stephen Thayer.'

174

'What about Tilney and Hoden?' Verity said.

'She mentioned Tilney was another "bad boy" but said nothing about Hoden and I didn't press her. She really didn't want to talk about it.'

'So what was the scandal?' Frank inquired.

'I don't know. She clammed up. I think she was ashamed of it.'

'Why? It was nothing to do with her, was it?'

'No, I don't expect it was but Thayer was in her house, in her charge. She knew Hobbs, our housemaster, was worse than useless so she must have felt doubly responsible for the boys in her care.'

'So what happens now?' Verity said impatiently. 'I must go back to Madrid on Monday.'

'Well, today's only Thursday. If you could spend tomorrow seeing what the *New Gazette* has in its files, it could be just the lead we are looking for. Oh, and we need to go and talk to Barrington, the butler, tomorrow. You are coming with me? Then, we all go to the funeral on Saturday. You're sure you feel you want to, Frank?'

'Yes, I do. Charles needs me. Look, I've had a letter from him. It's what I wanted to talk to you about. He left it for me when his aunt came to take him home. I had only had a few words with him when we heard the news and there was so much we didn't have time to say to each other.'

Frank dragged out of his trousers' pocket a crumpled sheet of lined paper covered in a childish scrawl. Edward began to read and, seeing that Verity had sat back in her chair obviously not wanting to look as though she was prying, he asked, 'May I read this aloud?'

'Yes, of course. I want Verity to know everything.' Frank leaned forward over the table again. Spontaneously, he put out his hand to the girl who, at that moment, seemed only a little less of a child than he. She smiled at him and took his hand in hers, but said nothing.

Edward took a sip of the tea which had been put in front of him by the white-smocked waitress and began to read. ' "Dear Frog . . ." '

'He calls me Frog because he says that's what I look like,' said Frank.

'And what do you call him?' Edward inquired.

'Charles. I call him Charles,' Frank said in surprise.

Edward began again: '"Dear Frog. Thank you for being so sweet to me when I had the news about my father. He was murdered you know. Isn't that awful? I mean, he was the gentlest, most wonderful father I could ever have had. I can't believe anyone wanting to kill him. Perhaps it was all a dreadful mistake. Chief Inspector Pride doesn't think so though. He says they will catch whoever did it. He thinks it might be one of the people he did business with. He says he has 'got some names', whatever that means. I do hope you can come to the funeral and bring that nice uncle of yours. I don't know why but I think I trust him. I do miss you, Frog. Love, Charles."'

'I don't think I ought to go with you to the funeral,' said Verity after they had sat in silence for a moment. 'It's a private affair and I don't even know Charles.'

'No, please,' said Frank. 'I would like it so much if you came. I want to introduce you to him.'

'Yes,' said Edward, 'we'll all go, Connie, me, you and Verity. I'm sure Charles won't mind.'

When the time came for them to say goodbye, Frank took his uncle aside for a moment, with a polite apology to Verity. 'Uncle Ned . . .'

'Yes, Frank?'

'You will find out who killed Charles's father, won't you?'

'The police . . .'

'No, I don't think the police . . . they don't have the same *reason* to find out as we do.'

'I'll do my utmost,' Edward said, holding out his hand.

'I do so like Verity,' Frank said confidentially. 'Is she your girlfriend?'

In his bright, candid eyes, Edward saw neither prurience nor vulgar curiosity but the benevolent interest of a child wanting those he loved to be happy.

'Not exactly,' was all he could manage. Frank raised his top hat. It was not quite their style to kiss, or even hug, but uncle and nephew shook hands gravely. Edward felt another surge of jealousy as he watched Verity kiss Frank on both cheeks, holding her hat by the brim so it did not fall off.

Part Three

14

'I've found it!' Verity's excited voice squeaked down the telephone line. 'Edward, are you there? I've found it!'

'What have you found?' he said, taking the cigarette holder
out of his mouth.

'There's quite a fat file of reports and it's really hot stuff. I'll
come round later, shall I, and you can give me a bite of lunch?
I'm absolutely famished. I've been working here since eight and
I didn't have time for breakfast.'

'What's the date?'

'April 8th 1936 – why do you want to know?'

'No, idiot. What's the date on the newspaper reports?'

'Oh, yes, I see what you mean – July 12th 1917. It's
sensational . . .'

'Good girl! Don't try and tell me any more over the phone. I
was thinking of going round to Stephen's house to see if I can
talk to the butler, Barrington. I gather he's still there.'

'Oh, I'm afraid I can't come with you. I've got a meeting with
Weaver in half an hour and I daren't miss that. In any case, I'm
not very good with menservants. I seem to remember I rather
messed things up last year when we interviewed General Craig's
valet.'

'No, you didn't, but if you trust me to go it alone . . . Anyway,
I rather doubt he will have anything useful to report.'

'That's OK by me. I'll come round about one. Bye.'

'Verity, I've told you before about "OK" . . .' He stopped and
shook the receiver but it was dead. Verity was not in the mood
for a lecture on the English language from anyone, especially
him.

Edward pulled on the gold chain around his waistcoat and looked at his hunter; it was almost ten thirty. 'I say, Fenton, Miss Browne's coming to lunch. Can you find another chop?'

'Without difficulty, my lord.'

'Oh, and make sure there's champagne on ice. I think we may need to do some celebrating.'

'Indeed, my lord. Might I inquire if congratulations are in order?'

'What? Ah, no ... don't be an ass, Fenton. I simply mean we're making some headway in our investigation. I'm going round to Belgrave Square to talk to Mr Thayer's butler, Barrington. He may slam the door in my face, of course.'

'Hmm.' Fenton coughed.

'Got a cough?'

'No, my lord. I was about to say that I might be of some assistance. Mr Barrington is an old friend of mine.'

'Good heavens! I never knew that.'

'We both belong to the ... to the Pipe and Port.'

'The Pipe and Port? What's that when it's at home?'

'Well, my lord, that's precisely the point. It's a club for gentlemen's personal gentlemen, butlers and other senior staff of gentlemen's establishments.'

'You amaze me. Do you mean to tell me you go out to this club on your days off?'

'Yes indeed, my lord. When I am at leisure ... I trust you have no objection?'

'None in the world. It just strikes me how unobservant I am. All these years you have been in my employ and I never knew ...'

'There is no reason, my lord, why it should have come to your attention. I mentioned it merely because, as I say, Mr Barrington is also a member.'

'What a coincidence!'

'Not really, my lord. A gentleman of Mr Thayer's eminence in the world of banking would be very likely to have a butler of sufficient seniority to be eligible for the club.'

'I see,' said Edward, feeling that in some undefined way he had been put in his place. 'And Mr Barrington ... is a good egg?'

'He is highly respectable and respected, my lord.' Fenton drew himself up another couple of inches.

'I mean, he's not likely to have bashed his master over the head with a jade Buddha?'

'Certainly not, my lord. If I were to telephone Mr Barrington, he might be more ... approachable than if you went to the house unannounced.'

'A good idea, Fenton. This is going to be a spiffing day, I can tell. We'll probably have the whole thing cleared up before tonight.'

'That is very much to be desired, my lord.'

'Nothing special I should know about Mr Barrington? Is he married? Does he drink?'

'My lord!'

'I'm sorry, Fenton. I seem to be in good spirits today. You haven't talked to him yourself about poor Mr Thayer's death?'

'No, my lord. I was going to ask you whether I could be of any assistance in this respect but you forestalled me. I believe that Mr Barrington has been – or I should say was – employed by Mr Thayer for the past four years. His character is of the highest and I can asseverate that he would not be party to any action which might be in any way suspect. And no, my lord, Mr Barrington is unmarried.'

'Excellent, Fenton. Yes, please do see if he would be willing to talk to me this morning. I would be much obliged.'

'Mr Charles is with his aunt in Fulham, my lord.' Barrington was a large, grave-faced man of indeterminate age who spoke of Fulham as though it was beyond the bounds of civilised society. 'I understand Mrs Cooper ...'

'That's the aunt?'

'Yes, my lord ... I understand the lady has not yet decided whether to move into this house or remain in Fulham.'

'And you would stay here if that were to happen ... if she and her nephew were to make this their home?' He saw Barrington frown and he wondered if he had gone too far. 'I'm sorry, I am prying into something which is by no stretch of the imagination my business.'

'No, my lord. To be truthful, I have not yet made up my mind.' The butler's mask of imperturbability slipped. 'A gentleman's establishment is what I am used to but on the other hand . . . if it is not presumptuous of me to say so, I am very fond of Mr Charles.'

'I quite understand, Barrington. I am sure you would be very much missed if you do decide to leave.'

The butler bowed his head in acknowledgement of the compliment. Edward made a mental note to reward Fenton when he returned home. It was clear that he must have spoken well of his master if Barrington was prepared to confide in him to this extent. He was very grateful that Verity had decided not to accompany him. He had no difficulty imagining the impression she would have made on this solid, rather forbidding figure. She would hardly have been able to resist the opportunity of telling the butler to throw off his shackles and join the revolution, and Barrington would not have been amused. Edward had the impression he had not been amused since the death of Queen Victoria.

'To get back to the reason I am taking up your time, Barrington. As an old friend of Mr Thayer, I am naturally anxious to discover who did . . . who killed him. You must have been appalled to discover the body of your master in the way you did.'

'Indeed, my lord, it was a very great shock. It was not of course I who found the body but the house parlourmaid, Betty. She came into the room – this room – and did not immediately see the master. It was only when she opened a curtain and the light fell on the fireplace that she saw his body.'

'What did she do?'

'She screamed, my lord. I came to see what the noise was and there was my poor master.'

'Is Betty still here?'

'No, my lord. With Chief Inspector Pride's permission, I sent the girl back to her mother in Tooting. She is highly strung and finding Mr Thayer dead affected her spirits.'

'Of course, it must have done. What other staff are there, Barrington?'

'Apart from myself and Betty only the cook, Mrs Harris. She

has gone to stay with her sister until it is decided what is to happen here.'

'Did Mr Thayer have a chauffeur?'

'He used to, my lord, but at the end of last year he dispensed with his services. He explained to me that he was feeling ... "hipped" was the word he used, and had decided to take more exercise.'

'But he couldn't walk all the way to the City?'

'He walked some of the way, I believe, and then either took an omnibus or a taxi. If I may say so, my lord, he had very simple tastes. He disliked show.'

'That's interesting, Barrington. As I remember him at school, he was a colourful figure, a bit of a dandy. But perhaps that was just how he seemed to us younger boys. It sounds as if he was getting a little eccentric.'

'Particular in his habits is how I would put it, my lord.'

'Now, let me see: only you, Betty and Mrs Harris live in? It seems a small staff for a house of this size?'

'Yes, my lord, but we had no difficulty bringing in outside help when Mr Thayer entertained.'

'Was that often?'

'No, my lord. The master seldom entertained at home. I think he used his club a good deal.'

'He was a member of White's, wasn't he?'

'Yes, my lord, and he was often away ... abroad. I think he kept this house largely so that Mr Charles should have a home to go to in the holidays.'

'There was no female to ... to look after Charles in the holidays?'

'No, my lord. Mr Charles's nurse, of whom he was very fond, died this time a year ago. Mrs Cooper was good enough to come last holidays to help sort out his clothes and that sort of thing but, if I may say so in confidence, my lord, I do not think Mr Charles ... liked the lady.'

Edward was suddenly struck by the loneliness of the child. His father was dead and his new guardian was a middle-aged lady who probably had no wish to take on the burden of looking after a boy at her time of life and, from what the butler said, he had no particular affection for her. It made him quite determined to take his nephew's friend under his wing. He knew Connie, when she heard what the position was, would also be concerned.

There was also the question of money. If Thayer's financial affairs were in a mess, as he was beginning to suspect . . . well, he had spoken on the telephone to Caine, the boy's housemaster, and made it clear that if there were any problems on the fees he would make up any shortfall. He must talk to this Cooper woman as soon as possible and try and put things on a formal footing. He wondered who Thayer's solicitor was. He ought to talk to him too.

'The evening he died . . . I understand Mr Thayer had dinner in the dining-room and then went into his study – into this room – to work, saying he would not need you again that night. Did you go straight to bed?'

'Yes, my lord. It took Mrs Harris and me about twenty minutes to clear up Mr Thayer's dinner. He had eaten very lightly and, of course, we had eaten earlier. We then went up to our rooms.'

'And you heard nothing? You did not hear a knock at the door, or voices?'

Barrington hesitated. 'The servants' quarters are at the back of the house, on the top floor, but I thought I did hear something.'

'What was that?'

'Well, it must have been just before I fell asleep . . . about one or half-past. I did not think to turn on my bedside light and look at my alarm clock. I thought I heard the front door slam.'

Barrington was beginning to sound defensive and Edward was quick to reassure him. 'Of course not. I expect Mr Thayer did occasionally have late night callers, or perhaps he went out for a final walk before turning in?'

'Maybe, my lord, but I can't say I ever knew the master to have visitors so late before and I am not aware he was given to late night perambulations.'

'I see. You can say nothing else about the visitor, if indeed there was one.'

'No, my lord.'

'Did you tell Chief Inspector Pride about this?'

'No, my lord. I suppose I should do so. I only remembered

the noise some time after I had been interviewed by the Chief Inspector. It went out of my head with all the ... with all the distress of finding the master's body ...'

'I quite understand and I'm sure the Inspector will too, but I think you ought to inform him. It helps establish the time of Mr Thayer's death, you understand.'

'Yes, my lord.'

'And is there anything else? Did anything strike you about the body ... I mean apart from the horrible savagery of the killing? Or this room ... was anything moved, apart from the Buddha, or taken?'

'No, my lord, nothing was stolen. The police checked with me very carefully about that. All the jade was there. There was the fountain pen, but I expect you know about it. I told the Chief Inspector that it didn't belong to Mr Thayer.'

'I wanted to ask you about that.'

'About the pen, my lord?'

'I noticed in one of the police photographs that there was a box of matches from a Spanish restaurant lying beside the pen. Do you know anything about that?'

'No, my lord. I never noticed it and the police never brought it to my attention.'

'Could it have been there on the floor a day or two before the murder?'

'I would very much doubt it, my lord. Betty is a most conscientious girl and she cleaned the master's study every day ... but, of course, you can ask her.'

'No, I am sure you are right about Betty. Did Mr Thayer have any visitors in the few days before he was killed?'

'No, my lord. He was a solitary man, if I may say so.'

'He had no ... no lady friends?'

'Not that I am aware of, my lord.'

'It seems strange that an attractive, rich, comparatively young widower had no ... no personal friends.'

'No doubt he had friends, my lord,' Barrington said a little stiffly, 'but he did not bring them home.'

'He must have gone out in the evenings. Did he ever go to night-clubs ... anything of that sort?'

'Not to my knowledge, my lord. I don't think he was the kind of gentleman to go to night-clubs. He did go out to dinner-parties on occasion but, as I say, he was a solitary man. He liked to keep his own company.'

'Yes, of course, and I suppose he would have seen his . . . his business visitors at his office in the City.'

'I imagine so, my lord.'

'Well, you have been most helpful, Barrington, and I am grateful to you for talking to me so frankly. Here is my card. If anything else does occur to you or, indeed, if I can be of any help in the . . . domestic arrangements, please do let me know.'

'There is just one other thing, my lord. I don't expect it is at all important but . . .'

'Well, spit it out, man,' Edward said a trifle impatiently.

'You were asking about lady friends. I do remember about a couple of months ago – at the end of January – when he came in. I opened the door and saw that he had just got out of a taxi. He had turned to say goodbye to a red-haired lady who I presume was being taken on to another destination. That was the only occasion I saw Mr Thayer with a lady in the past six months, my lord.'

15

'Oh God,' said Verity wiping her lips. 'Eton, falling for a handsome young dukeling and now champagne. I just hope the comrades don't find out. They'll never believe it's all in aid of the class struggle.'

Edward grinned and leant over the table to wipe away a few errant drops of the forbidden drink from the crease at the corner of her mouth. For some reason, when he had reported to her on his interview with Barrington, he had failed to mention the 'red-haired lady'. That was something he wanted to brood about.

'You're not trying to get me drunk, are you? I've read about what evil aristocrats do to innocent young girls: they lure them into their apartments and ply them with drink and then ... and then ...'

He wondered, without meaning to, what it would be like to kiss the laughter lines around her mouth which signalled her inability to be totally serious, even about Marxist-Leninism. 'I shouldn't worry,' he said. 'I would wager Comrade Stalin is enjoying a glass of champagne with his caviar at this very moment.'

'Don't tease, Edward,' she said, making faint efforts to prevent him refilling her glass. 'I suppose a girl can be forgiven for straying off the narrow path of rightchess ... righteousness – oh cripes, I can't even say the word – I must be squiffy ... once in a while. No! ... no more bubbly. You represent everything David dislikes about British society and it's just annoying that I happen to like you. It muddles me, or the champagne does.'

'Gosh! I would hate to confuse you,' Edward said. 'I mean, I know how difficult it is – or ought to be – for intelligent people to believe in generalisations. The moment one gets anywhere near the individual, one's favourite generalisation starts to look as full of holes as a string vest.'

'You're not going to lecture me again, are you? I don't want to be lectured.'

'I remember Gerald saying,' he went on regardless, 'that it was the civilians – particularly the women – who hated the Boche most fiercely in the war. The men in the trenches were too busy surviving to hate the enemy. They tended to feel that Jerry, a few hundred yards away in trenches as insanitary as their own, was very much in the same boat as they were. Of course, all private soldiers hate their officers – or rather not the young captains and majors who were being killed with them but the generals sitting in chateaux far behind the lines. It was probably unfair – old General Craig would have said so – but there it is.'

'Yes,' said Verity earnestly, 'that's the purest example of class war. It's precisely what destroyed the Romanovs, and it accounts for the mutinies in the French army . . .'

'But . . .'

'Don't "but" me, please, Edward. The trouble with you is you're afraid of ideas. You consider yourself a pragmatist but all that means is you can't stand back and see the whole picture. You don't deny the social order is changing . . . perilously slowly in this country, I grant you. Look at women, for instance. Women found freedom to live their own lives and earn their own bread in the munitions factories during the war and they'll never give that up. Mrs Pankhurst, much as I revere her, could never achieve what economics has.'

'Of course! I welcome change . . .'

'You do?'

'Yes, but as I've had occasion to say to you before, what I do not welcome is revolution. Change, at least in Britain, has always been gradual . . .'

'Very comforting . . .' Verity expostulated, the champagne loosening her tongue. 'Generations have to live and die in poverty so your feathers aren't ruffled by something as distasteful as naughty old revolution. I don't think so. You honestly believe it's possible in a world without honour, in a country like ours – morally defeated, ready and even willing to do deals with murderers and worse – to have change without bloodshed? We have had to suffer a world war even to get your "gradual" change. The miners – when they reached the trenches – discovered conditions to be much better than in the mines. The food was better, the chances of being killed were only a little greater . . .'

'Yes, and all those coal owners living the life of luxury in London comfortably unaware of what they were inflicting on the people who made them wealthy . . . I agree . . . I agree: things had to change.'

'Shaw said and I agree,' Verity continued, unstoppable now in her indignation, 'that even good solid folk, the middle class, with their investments in companies owning coal or slum property, are accessories to murder . . .'

'Murder! That's going it a bit, Verity.'

They looked at each other, surprised at the vehemence of their exchange. Verity wondered at how quickly a moment of happiness, in which Edward could wipe away the champagne from her lips without her objecting, had changed to violent argument. Edward sighed. It was the temper of the times; politics were extreme. Verity was right: one had to stand up and be counted. Gentle liberalism was no longer enough.

'Sorry about that,' she said gruffly. 'I told you not to get me drunk. I remember now, I get quarrelsome when drunk. That's before I get maudlin.'

Edward accepted the olive branch gratefully. 'Don't be silly, V, it was my fault. So much of what you say is right. One gets on one's high horse when one is in the wrong. Henceforth, discussion of politics will be banned at table. I don't know how we got on to it, anyway. Let's go back to Thayer's murder.'

Verity grimaced. 'I've seen things in Spain that . . . that frightened me,' she said suddenly, still a little drunk. 'I sometimes think . . . I sometimes think politics are going to tear us all apart.'

They were silent for a few moments and then Edward said, 'Well, show me what you've found.'

'Oh, yes, of course. Here we are.' She pulled a sheaf of press cuttings from a brown envelope and passed them over to him. 'It seems your friend Thayer was a naughty boy at school.' She watched him in silence as he scanned the papers with increasing amazement.

'This is absolutely extraordinary. I just can't understand how I never knew anything about it. Look at this headline: "Actress siren threat to Eton morals".'

'From what I can gather, the powers-that-be quickly stamped on the press. They didn't want this sort of thing being read by the "common people",' she said ironically. 'Actually, I think ordinary people like reading about the aristocracy behaving badly. It confirms their prejudices.'

'Yes, but I saw newspapers even when I was at school.'

'I doubt they would have let you see these. My schools – note my use of the plural – all had one thing in common: they censored the newspapers. I remember seeing one of my headmistresses solemnly cutting out stories she didn't approve of and then handing us something which looked like the paper streamers we hung up at Christmas. And I don't suppose your father would have . . .'

'No, you're right,' Edward said, continuing to read, 'he wouldn't. I say, none of the papers mention Stephen by name.'

'Yes, but I happen to know it was him. Look at this one from the *New Gazette*. It's one of the most detailed. It's dated July 15th 1917.'

Edward read the article aloud with furrowed brow. '". . . Inspector George Yarrow told our reporter that, in the course of two Sundays' observation, he noted well over a hundred expensive motor cars bringing weekend revellers to dance to bands from fashionable London night-spots such as the Kit-Cat club. He says that among these were the actress Miss Dora Pale with theatrical friends and three or four young men whom he was able to identify later as boys at nearby Eton College. The Hotel de Paris in Bray is a favourite meeting place for the 'fast set'. The hotel lets suites for three guineas a night and Miss Pale is thought to have been 'a habitual visitor'."'

'Look, here's an article in the *News Chronicle* a few days later: "Eton boys ordered to leave – punished for an unauthorised night out – three ringleaders . . . indecent and unnatural acts at a riverside hotel." Pretty strong stuff.'

'But we can't be absolutely sure this was about Stephen,' Edward said, reluctant to believe what he was reading.

'Yes we can. I tried to find out if the policeman . . . what was he called?'

'Yarrow.'

'Yes, I tried to discover if Yarrow was still alive but unfortunately he died last year. However, I found out that the *New Gazette* reporter, retired of course – a man called Mike Nadall – *is* alive. I got a telephone number from the file and bingo – there I was!'

'Gosh, that's brilliant!'

'Yes, it is rather,' said Verity modestly. 'But that's not all. Nadall was quite happy to talk about the scandal. He said that when he read Thayer had been murdered, he got out his notes to refresh his memory. He was quite definite; it was Thayer who was sacked from Eton on account of the brouhaha. But what is more . . .' Verity looked at Edward with undisguised triumph, 'he gave me the names of the two other boys expelled with him . . .'

'Makepeace Hoden and Godfrey Tilney?'

'You got it, pal. Oh yes, and I also talked to Peter Weiss who is covering the story for the paper. He says Pride is certain Thayer was murdered by someone he crossed while doing business. The bank was teetering on the brink, apparently, and Thayer needed to pull off one of three or four deals he was doing if it was to survive.'

'Well,' said Edward at last, 'we may be barking up quite the wrong tree. Pride's no fool. We had better go and see this Mike Nadall and find out if he knows anything which might help us. Where does he live?'

'Seventeen Riverside Drive, Putney, and he's expecting us for tea.'

Edward looked at Verity with frank admiration. 'Sherlock Holmes, you're a genius.'

'Elementary, elementary, my dear class enemy. Now, let's finish the champagne. I want to be in the right mood to discuss high jinks among the upper classes.'

191

16

'I'm beginning to think Pride may be right,' Edward said as he negotiated Hyde Park Corner. 'I really don't see how schoolboy escapades could possibly end in murder years later. I probably ought to be in Germany talking to Thayer's business partner – what's his name? – Heinrich Hoffmann.' He swung the Lagonda in front of a tram, to the driver's fury.

'But the fact that the three boys who were expelled . . .'

'We say "sacked",' Edward interjected.

'Sacked then, as if I care about your jargon. It's just another way in which you can make yourself special and feel superior to us lesser mortals.'

'What is?'

'A secret language. Instead of tuck you say "sock", and your "halves" instead of terms, and "dames" and "beaks". Please don't try and make me feel small.'

'But you are small,' said Edward unwisely. Verity punched him so hard he almost drove the car into a roundsman's cart and was sworn at once again.

'Joke, Verity, just a joke.'

'Yes, well, remember Napoleon was small.'

'I know, that's so interesting. Dr Freud says . . .'

'I don't care what Dr Freud says. The point is the three boys sacked from Eton nineteen years ago have all died within a few months of each other. When was it Hoden died?'

'At the beginning of January. I have to find out much more about that. But I agree, all our instincts say there is a connection and maybe Mr Nadall can spell it out for us.'

Edward eventually pulled up the Lagonda in front of a black

Ford Prefect which, if it belonged to Mr Nadall, suggested that he was not without means. It was parked directly in front of number 17, a small house separated from its neighbours by shrubberies and from the road by a privet hedge. This was what estate agents described as a cottage or – Edward had seen the phrase somewhere – a bijou residence. A wicket gate opened on to a gravel path which led up to a front door painted green and boasting a brass knocker. Before he could raise it, the door swung open and a cheerful, red-faced man in his late sixties or early seventies appeared before them.

'Lord Edward? Come in, come in. This is a great honour. And Miss Browne – I have read your articles on Spain in the *New Gazette* – most absorbing.'

There was still a hint of cockney but, over the years as a reporter, Nadall had taken on that neutral 'London' accent designed to put duchesses and serving girls equally at their ease.

'Now what may I offer you?' he said, rubbing his hands. 'I have some very acceptable elderberry wine, or bottled beer.'

'Oh, no thank you. A cup of tea – if that's possible . . .?'

'Of course, of course. And you, dear lady?'

'Tea please, Mr Nadall. Driving in an open car dries out the vocal cords.'

Verity wasn't quite sure why she had said this except that there was something so arch about his way of speaking that it invited imitation.

'What a beautiful motor car, Lord Edward . . .' Nadall began, and Verity blushed as she saw that she might legitimately be accused of having drawn attention to the Lagonda in order to 'show off'.

'It is splendid, isn't it, Mr Nadall,' Edward said.

'Mike, please; everyone calls me Mike.'

'Mike, then, but your Ford – it is yours?'

'Oh yes. I wouldn't be without it for the world. The wife and I take a spin in it most Sundays – she has a sister in Clapham – or else we go out to Hampton Court . . .'

Edward called the meeting to order. They were standing in the tiny front room, as clean as if it had never been used, which he thought was probably the case. 'It is so kind of you to be so helpful about Mr Thayer. May we ask you a few questions about that business at Eton?'

'Oh, but I'm delighted to help, my lord. The fact of the matter is that now I'm retired I get a little bored and I welcome the chance of reliving old days. I've kept all my notebooks, you know.'

'Very wise. May we sit down?'

'Of course! I don't know what I'm thinking of. Make yourself comfortable. Ethel,' he shouted, 'tea for our guests.'

A large woman, as red in the face as her husband, put her head round the door. 'The wife,' Nadall said apologetically.

Edward rose politely but Ethel was too shy to acknowledge his presence and Nadall seemed unwilling to introduce her into the conversation. 'It's the maid's afternoon off,' he said as he packed her off to the kitchen to make the tea.

Edward rather doubted that there ever was a maid.

'You see, the thing is, Mr Nadall – Mike – we have a hunch there might be a connection between Mr Thayer's murder and that affair at Eton. I know it must seem unlikely but . . .'

'Not at all. It crossed my mind it might have something to do with the boy.'

'You mean Stephen Thayer?'

'No, the boy who was killed.'

'The boy who was killed? I'm sorry, Mike, but I have no idea what you are talking about.'

'Well, fancy that,' Nadall said, and a sly look came into his eyes. 'May I ask, my lord, why you want to know about all this? The police . . .'

'Yes, it must seem a bit odd,' Verity said. 'The fact is, we don't think the police quite know where to look and so we thought we'd give them a bit of help,' she ended lamely.

Edward decided he had better tell the truth. 'Stephen Thayer was a friend of mine at Eton; older than me by about three years so I was never told the reasons behind his being expelled.'

'Sacked,' Nadall corrected him officiously. 'That's what they call it there, but then you would know that, my lord.'

'Yes, sacked. You're quite right, Mike.' Nadall looked pleased. 'And we discovered – Miss Browne and myself – that the two other boys sacked at the same time as Thayer – Makepeace Hoden and Godfrey Tilney – were also killed recently in suspicious circumstances.'

Nadall whistled. 'Fancy that. That is a rummy thing, eh, my lord? Three murders!'

'We're not sure Mr Hoden *was* murdered,' Edward explained. 'I don't want to leap to conclusions. He died on safari in Kenya. Mr Tilney was killed in Spain. Perhaps there's no connection, but that's why I am so interested in what you can tell us about this other boy.'

At that moment, Ethel came in with a fine porcelain teapot on a tin tray emblazoned with a picture of Hampton Court. They were clearly being honoured with the best tea set. She began to pour the tea, managing to slop a little on to the tray. 'I'll do it, woman,' Nadall said brusquely, and for a moment his geniality was replaced by something close to anger. Edward wondered just what Mrs Nadall had to put up with.

When she had left the room, Nadall silently poured very black tea into three small cups, passed one to Edward and a second to Verity, and sat back sipping at his own, looking shrewdly at his guests. It occurred to Edward that the man was computing the value of the information he had to give but, in the end, he said, 'Maybe the best thing is if I tell you the whole story as I learnt it.'

'That would be best probably,' Edward said encouragingly.

'Well, see, it was like this. We got a tip-off that Dora Pale, the film actress . . . you remember her, my lord?'

'Yes of course, though I don't believe I have ever seen any of her films.'

'Ah, there you've missed something, if I may say so, my lord. Silent films, of course, but what a looker she was. Sultry they called her and that about sums it up. When I was starting out in Fleet Street, she was the cat's whiskers. Whenever there was nothing much doing, the editor would say, "What's Dora Pale up to?" and we would scuttle off to find out. It became quite a joke in the newsroom. We would always refer to a quiet day as a Pale day. Ha! But her films! *Faithless*, that was one of hers, *Tarnished Woman*, and *The Sin*. For my money, she was better than Tallulah Bankhead or even Jean Harlow. She was a stunner but that wasn't the half of it. She smouldered. She had a drugged look and that was no coincidence. She was a dope fiend – no doubt about it. She never tried to hide it and, for the most part, the authorities turned a blind eye.'

'She was American?'

'No, my lord. She lived mostly in America, naturally, but

195

I do believe she was born in Tunbridge Wells – the daughter of a Colonel of the Guards, I heard tell. Tunbridge Wells, I ask you!'

'Was she married?'

'You've put your finger on it there, my lord,' Nadall said admiringly. 'She was married to a rich Jew. His name was Federstein – Max Federstein. Ever heard of him?'

Edward shook his head.

'He owned one of the big department stores in Oxford Street, but I believe his millions – he was a millionaire and needed to be, mind you, married to Dora Pale – came from oil. Persia – that was where he lived most of the time.'

'And while he was away . . .?' chipped in Verity.

'Exactly, miss, the mouse played – and played hard.'

'But why was she at Eton so often? In one of the cuttings it said she was "a habitual visitor" at the hotel in Bray.'

'That was because she had her boy at the school.'

'Ah ha!' Edward exclaimed. 'She had a son, did she? Would that be the boy who was killed?'

'Yes, my lord. It was her little lad who died.'

'How did he die?'

'It wasn't exactly her fault, my lord.'

'She was a good mother?' Verity inquired.

'Maybe, maybe not. The thing was – and you must excuse me being coarse, miss – she had a thing for boys. A penchant for young flesh. That was why she liked visiting the school. I don't know that she was much interested in her son, but that's just a guess.'

Nadall rolled the words about in his mouth like a fine wine. Edward was revolted but dared not show it.

'Drugs, sex. . . It was frustrating. The *New Gazette* couldn't report the smallest part of it. In fact the Old Etonian brotherhood, if you will allow me to so describe it, my lord, came down on us like a ton of bricks. Lawyers, politicians . . . after that first couple of days we had to put a sock in it; the editor's orders. They didn't care what we said about Dora Pale but there must be no scandal touching boys at the college. They talk about the Freemasons but Old Etonians are much worse when they want to hush something up – begging your pardon, my lord.'

'But the three boys were sacked,' Edward said.

'The boys' parents took them out of the school – which is different, I understand.'

'But you say Dora Pale's son was killed. How did that happen and when?'

'I'm not sure,' said Nadall reluctantly. 'I was off the story by then but I heard he had committed suicide or maybe was even murdered . . . It must have been soon after the events we were talking about.'

'But if it had been either murder or suicide, surely it would have been reported?'

'Yes, miss, but I don't think there was ever such a verdict in any coroner's court. As I say, it was all kept very quiet. It was never reported that Dora Pale even *had* a son, let alone that he was at Eton. You see, his name wasn't Pale. There was a biography of her a year or two ago and I got it out of the library. There was nothing in it about her family – just the very briefest mention of her being married to Federstein.'

'So the boy's name was Federstein?' Edward persisted.

'Yes, Oliver Federstein.'

'Dora Pale's dead, isn't she?'

'Yes, my lord. She died shortly after her son, I believe.'

'In 1918?'

'Yes, in the flu epidemic, according to the book about her, but I expect it was more likely to have been the booze and dope.'

Edward rubbed his forehead. 'I must say I can't believe I never heard anything about this.'

'Don't blame yourself,' said Nadall comfortably. 'There's nothing like the upper classes for keeping a secret and suppressing information when it's in their interests.'

Edward was beginning to get annoyed at being patronised by this unpleasant fellow. 'Well, Mike,' he managed, 'that was most interesting. We're most grateful to you. There may be a connection between this boy's death and Stephen Thayer's murder but I can't quite put my finger on it yet.'

'Will you tell the police what I have told you, my lord?'

'Yes, we must. You don't mind?'

'No, why should I?' said Nadall, as though he had been accused of something.

'Thank you again, Mike,' said Edward, rising with relief from the sofa which had been specially designed, he thought, to torture anyone foolish enough to sit on it. 'We'll let you know what happens and, please, get in touch with me if you think of anything else which might be of interest. Here's my card.'

'Yes, my lord.'

'And you will keep all this confidential?' Verity added, rising with difficulty from her uncomfortable armchair.

'You're afraid I might "scoop" you, miss?' Nadall said mischievously.

Verity gave him one of her sweetest smiles. 'Oh no, Mike, that hadn't occurred to me. I merely thought if Stephen Thayer's murderer knew you had information which might lead to his being found out, well . . . you might be in danger.'

The smile left Nadall's lips to be replaced by naked fear. 'You don't really think, do you, my lord, that I might be in danger?'

'Probably not,' said Edward, 'but Miss Browne is right. Best keep mum, don't y'know.' He put on one of his silly-ass expressions but, when they were safely in the Lagonda speeding away from the prim little house behind whose net curtains so many secrets were hidden, Verity said, 'Cripes! Didn't he remind you of . . . of one of those little men who murder their wives in the bath or something?' She shuddered. 'My flesh is still creeping. Perhaps he's our murderer?'

'I don't think so, much as I would like it to be him. It sounds far-fetched but . . .'

'. . . someone was taking revenge for the boy's death?'

'It has to be that!' Edward hit the steering wheel, sounding the horn and scaring a bicyclist.

'But who . . . who? Dora Pale is dead. Her husband is either dead or very old.'

'Yes, we must see if Federstein senior is still alive and find out whether Dora Pale had any other children or close relatives.'

'I'll get down to that in the archives.'

'Yes, and talk to Lord Weaver. He may well have come across Federstein if he was a millionaire businessman. It's a small club, that one.'

'And what will you do?'

'I'm going to talk to Thoroughgood – see if he can add anything. After all, he was at Eton when it all happened. And I must tell Chief Inspector Pride what we have discovered.'

'You have to?'

'It's our public duty,' said Edward pompously. 'But never mind, Verity, he'll take absolutely no notice! After the funeral, I'm going to Frankfurt. I must talk to Hoffmann even if he's got nothing to tell us. I wonder if Pride has been over to Germany? I somehow doubt Scotland Yard finances run to foreign travel.'

'And I have to get back to Madrid. Hester wired me. Things are hotting up. I don't want to miss an important story when I've done all the work.'

'My little bloodhound,' said Edward, risking a tease.

Verity ignored the remark. 'Apart from the politics, I want to find out if any of our friends in Madrid are suspects. Don't forget we may have a motive but we also need an opportunity. Someone has to have been present at all three deaths. It might be someone we don't know – a complete stranger – but it might be . . .'

'. . . someone we do know,' said Edward grimly.

17

Chief Inspector Pride stared at him and Edward stared back. Across Sergeant Willis's pockmarked face passed the ghost of a smile.

'Now, let me get this straight,' said the Chief Inspector at last. 'You have taken it upon yourself, for reasons I have yet to fathom, to interview a number of people who knew Stephen Thayer when he was a schoolboy.'

'Well, it's natural that I should want to know who killed my friend.'

'And you have come up with some story . . .' Pride persevered, as if Edward had not spoken, 'some theory that he was killed in revenge for the death of a film star's son.'

'Come on, Chief Inspector, be fair. I have given you good reasons why there may well be a connection.'

'Good reasons? I'm sorry, Lord Edward, but I must reiterate what I said earlier. It can only confuse things if you and your girlfriend . . .'

'She's not my girlfriend.'

'If you and Miss Browne go around asking people questions, causing alarm and upsetting old ladies. Leave it to us. We have a number of leads and we expect to make an arrest before very long. I will go as far as to tell you this, Lord Edward. Your friend Stephen Thayer had enemies about whom you know nothing and whose motives for wanting him dead are much stronger and more recent than some schoolboy enemy. You think you are investigating this murder but really you're just dabbling in things you don't understand. At best, you may muddy the pond and, at worst, you may cause us to miss vital evidence. As for your plan to go over to Frankfurt to see this Mr Hoffmann, I absolutely forbid it. Our friends in the police over there are investigating on our behalf and I believe them to be most efficient.'

There was something about Lord Edward Corinth which made him sick with anger. How dare this rich, idle aristocrat interfere with his investigation? How dare this supercilious nincompoop imply that he – Chief Inspector Pride, with more than a decade of experience investigating crime – might not be up to catching this murderer? All this stuff about Eton – it made him want to spew.

Edward sighed: 'You know best, Chief Inspector. I merely thought it my duty to tell you what I had discovered but, as you say, it may well be irrelevant if you are just about to arrest the murderer. I'm afraid, though, I cannot promise not to travel to Frankfurt. There is no law – at least not yet – against taking a train across Europe, is there?'

'I must warn you for the last time that if you are detained in Germany for making ... a nuisance of yourself, there will be nothing we can do about it.'

'Very good, Chief Inspector. I quite understand. Thank you for giving me so much of your time.'

'Not at all, Lord Edward,' said Pride, positively genial in victory. 'Sergeant Willis will show you out.'

As Edward left Pride's office, he caught sight of the policeman's face reflected in the glass door. There was almost elation there and he thought, rather uncomfortably, that along with Verity and his nephew Frank, Chief Inspector Pride saw him as a class enemy – a silly ass with too much time on his hands and too little responsibility. It was hard, he thought, that a man in his position could be so despised for the silver spoon which had been thrust into his mouth at birth, before he was in any position to object.

Sergeant Willis, showing him out of the office, said, a little conspiratorially, 'My lord, don't think we won't take what you say seriously. You will understand, I am sure, that the Chief Inspector is under great pressure. There are several influential figures watching this case closely and ...'

'Thank you, Sergeant,' Edward said with a smile. 'I do understand. Do you think the Federstein connection is just my overexcited imagination?'

'I don't know, my lord. I truly don't know. But we will be talking to this Mike Nadall and I will keep you informed of any developments.'

'I most grateful, Sergeant,' said Edward and he walked out into Whitehall with a lighter step.

Breathlessly, that evening over the telephone, Verity reported on a conversation she had had with Lord Weaver. She considered what he had told her to be highly significant but Edward, though not wishing to be a wet blanket, could not see that it left them very much further forward.

'Joe said he had never met Federstein but that stories about him were legion. By the time he arrived in London towards the end of the war, he was already known as an eccentric but he kept very much to himself. In any case, he spent most of his time in Persia looking after his oil interests.'

'What about Dora Pale?'

'Joe couldn't tell me much. It was said she was the great love of his life but that, after she had borne him a son, they had agreed to live more or less separate lives. Joe doesn't know the reason but her lifestyle was already becoming notorious. She collected around her a group of "theatrical" friends whom she entertained with a succession of parties which the press liked to describe – how accurately one does not know – as orgies.'

'Sex and dope?'

'Supposedly. Then came the tragedy of the boy's death, followed quickly by the mother's and then, a few years later, by Federstein's.'

'Oh, so Federstein is dead?'

'Yes.'

'He was much older than Dora?'

'About twenty years.'

'There were no other children?'

'Not as far as we know.'

'Do we know how Federstein met Dora Pale?'

'Not for certain. Joe thinks Federstein met her in Hollywood when he was in California looking at oil prospects.'

'I see,' Edward mused. 'Lonely old man falls for femme fatale.'

'Something like that,' Verity agreed.

'Is that it?'

'Not quite. I went back to the files and found a cutting from the *News Chronicle* which someone had marked with a red exclamation mark.'

'Yes?'

'It was about the boy's death. It said – wait, I'll read it to you. I copied it out. Ah, here we are; it's dated February 8th 1918. It's only one column but it's on the front page. The headline is: "Eton boy's tragic death."

' "Oliver Federstein, aged fifteen, was found dead at Eton College yesterday. It is believed he drowned while bathing in the river. His father, the millionaire businessman Mr Maxwell Federstein, was not available for comment but the boy's housemaster, Mr Harold Banville, said he was very distressed by the accident. He said Federstein was a popular boy and a member of Upper Sixpenny" – whatever that is,' Verity said, breaking off.

'It's the under sixteen eleven,' Edward said shortly.

'Oh, cricket,' Verity sighed theatrically.

'Is there anything else?'

'Not really. The housemaster is quoted as saying that "swimming in the river was against school rules except in the pool designated for this activity". Reading between the lines, he seems more irritated than upset at Federstein's death, but maybe that's unfair.'

Edward was silent, straining to bring to mind some faint memory which was nagging him.

'Are you still there?'

'Oh yes, sorry, V. I was just trying to recall something. Do you know, as you read me that cutting, I think I do remember hearing that a boy in another house had died in an accident. It's dreadful that I don't remember the details. I certainly can't put a face to Oliver Federstein. I wish I could.'

'From what I hear about the way things were done at Eton, probably the whole thing was hushed up. One of the papers has a photograph of Oliver. Shall I bring it to the funeral?'

'Oh yes, do. What does he look like?'

'Just ordinary – quite cheerful. It's not very clear . . .'

The funeral was over and the congregation had spilled out into Chester Square. Verity had insisted on going on her own as she knew that, if she went with Edward, Frank and Connie, she would be seated in the front pew alongside Charles and his aunt. She dreaded anyone jumping to the conclusion that she had been a girlfriend of Thayer's or, even worse, of Edward's. In any case, as an atheist, she didn't approve of the Christian burial service. It was all the more annoying therefore that, when she slipped into the back of the church, an usher grabbed her by the arm and insisted on escorting her up to sit beside Edward. Worse still, entirely against her will, she spent most of the service in tears. She wept for Charles and for the mother she had never known and for herself but she knew people would think she was crying for Stephen Thayer, a man she had never met and whom she believed she would have disliked. Edward kept glancing at her, passed her his handkerchief which she accepted, and unwisely tried to squeeze her hand which she angrily shook off.

St Michael's was a gloomy church at the best of times but the day was dreary, threatening rain and the lights had had to be turned on in the nave. Only Charles's courage and noble bearing illuminated the occasion and it was a great relief to Verity when at last the coffin had been carried out of the church and normal life could be resumed.

'Here it is,' Verity said, taking an envelope out of her handbag. They were standing on the kerb, Edward in his top hat and tails looking, she had to admit, rather distinguished. He felt curiously reluctant to take it from her. He feared the boy would look at him accusingly like the murdered children parading before Richard III at Bosworth. But it was more upsetting than that. The photograph, grainy and blurred, showed the smiling, open face of an ordinary boy. He was dressed in a jacket and tie and behind him Edward could just make out the front door of a big house. Just ordinary, as Verity had said. That was the real tragedy! A normal child with every right to expect a normal upbringing and a normal life had had it taken away from him.

'Don't look like that,' Verity said, putting her arm in his. 'It's not your fault.'

'I know it isn't, but it makes me feel guilty all the same. Do we know who took this?'

'I'm afraid not.'

Edward stared at the photograph as if he were willing it to speak.

At that moment they were joined by Charles, Connie and Frank. He hurriedly pushed the photograph into his breast pocket. Most of the congregation had dispersed though some still milled about chatting to friends. He noticed Thoroughgood getting into a taxi with Chief Inspector Pride.

Frank said, 'Charles, you haven't properly met Verity Browne.'

'It was so kind of you to come,' the boy said with deliberate courtesy, shaking her by the hand. He looked round. 'I had no idea my father knew so many people. He seemed so solitary but the church was quite full.'

'Yes indeed,' Edward said, 'but you were very brave, Charles, and you read the lesson beautifully.'

'Did I? I am glad. I didn't feel like crying then. I just wanted ... I just wanted to do ... him proud. You see ... I never had time to say I loved him ... to say goodbye.'

Charles, who had shed not a tear during the service, was now unable to restrain his grief and, to Connie's slight embarrassment, wrapped himself around her as if he needed a woman's comfort. After all, Edward thought, he was just a child ... a child like Oliver Federstein.

The undertaker signalled to Edward that they must get into the car which was to take them to Putney for the cremation. Verity said her goodbyes, kissed Charles, which he didn't seem to mind, and jumped into a taxi. The others piled into the limousine. There were six of them: the two boys, Mrs Cooper, Edward and Connie, and Stephen's solicitor and executor – an elderly man called Jameson. The latter was obviously deeply relieved that Edward was taking an interest in Charles and was noisily effusive which made Edward want to kick him.

Charles recovered his self-possession during the journey and talked of his father with respect and affection which made Edward look at his nephew longingly. He hoped he might have someone to say such good things about him when he departed this life but he rather doubted it. It made him even more determined to act as Charles's unofficial guardian, if it were permitted. The boy had no father, no uncles or male cousins to watch over him – just the solicitor, Jameson, of whom Edward expected little.

The cremation took only fifteen minutes and, as they walked out of the so-called chapel which resembled a railway station waiting-room, Jameson asked Edward if he had time to go back with him to his office. Edward explained that he had an engagement that evening and could not.

'Ah well, another time, perhaps,' Jameson said. 'The thing is, I don't know what to do with a letter I found which had slipped down behind a drawer in Stephen's bureau. I suppose I ought to give it to the police but I don't want to stir up any scandal. Poor Thayer should be allowed to rest in peace – and Charles too of course. I mean, he ought not to be worried more than . . .'

'What are you driving at?' Edward inquired irritably. The two men were walking down a narrow gravel path edged with flowers left by mourners at other ceremonies. It had occurred to Edward during the funeral that, what with one thing and another, he had quite forgotten to order a wreath but, as he left the church, Mrs Cooper had surprised him by thanking him for his 'beautiful offering'. It appeared that Fenton had taken it upon himself to send a spray of lilies, for which Edward was grateful although somewhat taken aback by his enterprise.

'What do you mean? Give the police what?' He had a sudden fear that the solicitor had found some evidence of fraud – or worse.

'It's a blackmail note . . . rather vague but threatening, which refers to a woman called Dora Pale. Do you know who she was? My secretary says she was an actress . . . a film actress,' he said with contempt.

'Who was the letter from?' Edward demanded, his heart in his mouth.

'A man called Nadall . . . Mike Nadall. Have you heard of him?'

'Indeed I have, Jameson. A nasty little journalist. Retired now, but I went to see him just a day or two ago. When was the letter dated?'

'December last year.'

'Can you remember what it said?'

'I think it must have been the last of a series – though it was the only one I found. It said: "I am waiting to hear from you. I need the money now or they'll have the whole story of Dora Pale at the paper." I may have got it slightly wrong but that's as near as I can recall.'

'Well, I'm afraid you will have to give it to the police. Chief Inspector Pride might find it useful in his investigations. Stephen was involved as a schoolboy with this woman, Dora Pale. She seduced him – it was a sordid business.' Jameson looked shocked. 'There was a scandal which even got into the newspapers. Nadall was one of the journalists involved. As a result, Stephen had to leave Eton a few weeks early. I doubt, so many years later, Nadall would have got anything out of him by threatening to drag it all up again but I blame myself. When I last saw Stephen at Eton a few weeks ago when I was visiting Frank, he said there was something he wanted to discuss with me and I think it must have been this grubby little attempt at blackmail. Unfortunately, we never got round to talking. I don't expect Pride will do anything with it except give this man Nadall a roasting, which he richly deserves.'

'You don't think this Nadall might have ... might have murdered him?'

'I doubt it, but Pride will follow it up.'

Back in town, Edward parted from Charles and Frank promising to come and see them when he returned from Germany. Connie was taking the boys and Mrs Cooper back to Mersham. Edward, as he kissed his sister-in-law on the cheek, whispered in her ear, 'You're a good woman, Connie, and I would marry you myself if you weren't spoken for.'

She blushed and tapped him on the cheek. 'And you're a naughty boy who ought to find a nice girl and settle down instead of rushing around Europe like a ... like a ... like I don't know what.'

'Like a blue-arsed fly, as Herbert used to say.' Herbert was the gardener's son with whom Edward used to play as a child.

'Edward, behave!'

Charles said, 'Lord Edward ...'

'Give an old man pleasure and call me Edward.'

'Oh, are you sure,' the boy said smiling, 'I don't want to be ...'

'I mean it, old lad,' Edward said. 'I think we're going to be great friends – at least, I hope so.'

'I would like that very much,' the boy answered gravely.

In his rooms in Albany, Edward felt suddenly weary. He had no wish to go out tonight but he had promised Elizabeth Bury and he could not possibly stand her up.

'Bring me a whisky and soda, would you, Fenton, and run me a bath.'

'Yes, my lord. I trust the funeral went off as well as could be expected.'

'Thank you, it did and the flowers I sent were much admired.'

'I am very glad to hear it,' Fenton said imperturbably. 'Miss Browne telephoned twenty minutes ago and asked whether you could ring her on your return, my lord.'

'I'll do that now, but please . . . a whisky before I drop.'

'You're all packed up?' he asked when he had told Verity about Jameson finding Nadall's blackmail letter.

'Yes, I'm going first thing tomorrow.'

'By air?'

'Yes, Harry Bragg's taking me.'

It was quite absurd but, once again, Edward suffered a pang of jealousy though of whom he could hardly say – not Harry Bragg surely. He really had to take a pull on himself.

'I see,' he said cheerfully. 'You've done wonderfully well to turn up all that information.'

'I've asked the librarian at the *Gazette* to look out Dora Pale's obituary and Federstein's. He must have had one – prominent businessman, store owner and so on. And I'm going to do a bit of sleuthing in Madrid – politics permitting.'

'Be very careful, won't you,' Edward said. 'We're floundering around in the dark but, if we panic a murderer, there's no knowing what he might do.'

'Or she. The murderer may be a she. It was last time.' Verity was referring to their investigation into General Craig's death.

'Or she, then. Verity . . .'

'Yes?'

'Oh . . . nothing.'

'You're going to Frankfurt tomorrow?'

'That's right. I will let you know what I find out, if anything.'

'What are you doing tonight?'

'Oh . . . I . . . I am going out.'

'That's a pity. I was going to suggest we . . .'

'I'd have loved to but this is a long-standing . . .'

'Of course, not to worry . . .'

'I don't think I can . . .'

'Bye then,' Verity said breezily.

'Bye. Oh gosh, I'm really sorry about this evening because actually there is something I have been meaning to say . . . Verity, are you there?'

But she had hung up and the line was dead.

'Fenton! Fenton! Damn it, man, where's that whisky?'

'At your elbow, my lord.'

'Oh, I see. My bath . . .'

'I have drawn it, my lord, and I have laid out your evening clothes on the bed.'

18

Even after his whisky and bath, Edward was still in a bad temper.

'This shirt has been starched to blazes, Fenton.'

'My lord? I will speak to the laundry tomorrow.'

'Yes do, and where's my tie . . . oh, there it is. Blast it, why can't . . . Yes, thank you, Fenton. I don't know what the matter is. I'm all fingers and thumbs.'

Fenton dextrously completed tying his master's tie and sighed inwardly. He wanted this evening to be a success. He knew exactly what was biting his employer: it was that girl Verity Browne. What right had she to go and upset his lordship? He had never liked her, or rather he had a grudging respect for her courage and grit, but he thought no well-bred young lady should be rampaging around Europe pretending to be a journalist. In Fenton's view, girls ought to know their place. They ought to be mothers and wives, not whatever it was Verity Browne thought she was. He had been very glad when that charming young lady who had nursed his Grace had seemed to . . . like his lordship. Now *there* was someone who knew how to behave to servants. She was polite, gracious even, but not condescending. One knew where one was with Miss Bury and you never knew where you were with Miss Browne. It was the difference between tranquillity and turbulence. He sighed again – more deeply this time.

Elizabeth had an aunt with a small flat in Pimlico and it was from there that Edward picked her up in a cab. He had booked a table at Claridge's but, when the taxi stopped at the large shabby house now divided into flats, he wondered if he had made a mistake. Perhaps she had not got the clothes for the evening he had planned and would be embarrassed or even humiliated. He guessed she rarely came to London. In fact, he thought he remembered her telling him so when, on an impulse, he had invited her to dine with him and perhaps go on to a night-club.

He rang the bell and, as he waited, nervously reached into his breast pocket for his cigarette case. Before he had time to extract a cigarette, the door opened and he gazed with admiration verging on astonishment at the apparition before him. Elizabeth was dressed in a white silk-organdie sleeveless dress revealing long, graceful milky-white arms, lightly freckled. Over her shoulders she wore a black fur cape and on her head, quite failing to cover her flaming red hair, a pillbox hat covered with tiny black organdie flowers. In her hand she was grasping a little net evening bag.

'Lord Edward,' she said. 'Do I look too awful?'

'Oh, I'm so sorry, was I staring? How incredibly rude of me. I was just thinking how . . . how splendid you looked.'

Elizabeth lifted her head and laughed aloud, showing her white teeth and letting a few auburn strands escape from under her hat. 'I think that must be a compliment.'

'Please,' Edward said, gathering his wits, 'it's cold.' He held open the taxi door and took her arm, quite unnecessarily, as she got in.

Geiger's Hungarian Orchestra was playing in the foyer as they entered the hotel and guests were sipping cocktails before going in to dinner. He saw several women look at Elizabeth speculatively and he was irritated to think that they would be the subject of gossip at luncheon the following day in many fashionable London houses. Edward left his hat and Elizabeth her cape with the cloakroom attendant, a pretty young thing who smiled at Edward. For a second, he thought she might be going to wink. In a bad mood, he took Elizabeth by the arm and guided her towards the restaurant.

'Shall we go straight to our table?' he said, and then feared that this might look as though he did not wish to be seen with her. Before she had time to answer, he said, 'No, come to think of it, I don't know about you but I could do with a cocktail.'

'Whatever you wish, Lord Edward.'

'You're not going to call me "Lord Edward" all evening, are

you?' Edward felt he was being rather boorish and told himself to relax. Here he was with a beautiful woman about to eat in one of the best hotels in the world before going on to dance with that same beautiful girl in a night-club. To be cross about this was frankly ridiculous. They ordered Manhattans and Charles Malandra, the maître d'hôtel, brought them menus.

'Elizabeth, I've ... I've so much looked forward to ... to seeing you. You have been so kind to Gerald.'

'It's only my job, but I have become so fond of him and of ... The Duchess asked me to call her Constance.'

'Connie, yes, she's wonderful. Much too good for Gerald, I sometimes think.'

'Oh no, he's a duck.'

'A duck! I don't think I've ever thought of him as that.'

'You know, when he came out of his coma but still had difficulty speaking, he used to want me to sit beside him and hold his hand.'

'He always did have an eye for a beautiful woman,' said Edward without thinking, and once again felt he had been guilty of boorishness. 'No, but seriously, you have worked miracles.'

'Is that the only reason you asked me out?' she said, gazing at him with wide eyes. 'I mean, it's going to be jolly dull for you if all we can talk about is your brother's health.'

'Dull – it's not going to be dull for me, I promise you, and I won't mention Gerald or Connie or anything else about my family until you tell me it's safe to do so.'

Elizabeth chuckled. 'That's good then. Now tell me, what should I eat? I've only once been to Claridge's before and that turned out to have been a mistake.'

'Whose mistake?'

'Mine, and probably his, but it's much too early to tell you things like that about myself.'

Monsieur Malandra directed them towards caviar. The oysters he did not recommend. He suggested the *Consommé Yvette*, which he said was turtle, and *Filet de sole Cambacérès*, *Becasse au fumet* with *salade Coeurs de Laitues*. 'Ze sole is finished with lobster and mushroom, madame, and the woodcock is done with brandy and served on toast adorned with its own liver.'

'My goodness,' said Elizabeth when the head waiter had gone, 'I think I know how the woodcock must be feeling.'

'Adorned with its own liver? Surely not.'

'No, but I do feel a little like mutton dressed as lamb. I have to confess, when you asked me to go out with you I almost refused, not having anything suitable to wear, but the Duchess . . . Constance . . . persuaded me.'

'But you look beautiful,' Edward said sincerely.

'Well, if I do, it's thanks to her. She took me shopping and she lent me this dress. She said she never went out any more and it was criminal letting her evening clothes go to rack and ruin and so . . . here I am.'

'Well, God bless Connie! But I thought we said we would not mention my family.'

'Yes, that's right, I had forgotten. Tell me about your investigation. You said you were going to see if you could discover anything about why your friend was murdered.'

'Oh, I wouldn't call it an investigation. I thought I had discovered something but Chief Inspector Pride didn't want to know.'

'Tell me,' she ordered.

They were still discussing what he had learnt when they were tucking into the woodcock. 'Verity thinks . . .' Edward was saying

'Verity Browne. Constance has told me about her. She sounds . . . intrepid. I wish I had the guts to go and be a foreign correspondent.'

'Intrepid, yes, that about describes Verity,' and he went on to expatiate at some length on Verity's virtues, ending by saying, 'Actually, I was supposed to be having dinner with her tonight . . .'

'I'm so sorry,' broke in Elizabeth coldly. 'Here am I taking up your time when you wanted to be with Verity Browne. You should have told me.'

'No, no . . . I didn't mean that at all. I . . . wanted to see you, Elizabeth. There's nothing between me and Verity, I promise you. I've told you, she has a . . . a friend in Madrid.'

'The communist or the American novelist?' inquired Elizabeth, unappeased.

'Oh, I don't know,' he said, feeling that he was in some way betraying Verity and insulting Elizabeth at the same time. 'Please, Elizabeth, I must have sounded like the most awful cad

213

but really, I do want to be with you. Nothing to do with Gerald or anything. I thought we seemed to get along so well at Mersham, I wanted to know you better. Please forgive me if I have been saying idiotic things. It's just that it's so easy to talk to you that I didn't think.'

At that moment, a friend of Edward's who was dining with his wife came up to their table. 'Edward, how are you, my dear boy. I haven't . . .'

The introductions were made and it was a full five minutes before they were left alone again. They were silent for a moment or two. Then Edward said, 'Forgiven?' and put out his hand across the table.

'Forgiven,' Elizabeth said, putting her hand in his before quickly withdrawing it. 'Not that there was anything to forgive.'

'Shall we go on somewhere?'

'I 'd like that,' she said, smiling at him.

They ended up at the Four Hundred in Leicester Square. In the dim religious light, the sound deadened by walls and ceiling swathed in red and beige silk, they danced scarcely exchanging a word. She wore a scent Edward did not recognise but, as he held her closer and she inclined her head against his shoulder, he breathed it in and forgot about the murder, about Mersham and about Verity Browne.

It was past three in the morning before they got into a cab and directed the driver to take them to Pimlico. 'Your aunt won't be waiting up for you?' he inquired anxiously.

'No, she gave me a key.'

Edward tried to turn her head towards him so he could kiss her, but she twisted away.

'Edward, that was a wonderful evening but, before we say goodnight, there is something I have to say to you which perhaps I ought to have told you before – in fact, I *know* I ought to have told you before.'

'What is it, Elizabeth?' he said, taking her hand in his. 'You can tell me anything.'

'No, I'm serious. Let go of my hand. I don't think you will want to touch me after I've told you.'

'For goodness' sake, what are you talking about?' Edward said, now irritated and suddenly feeling slightly drunk and very tired. Perhaps he was too old for these late nights. It crossed his mind that he might not sleep well despite being so weary.

'I was married to Makepeace Hoden.'

Edward's fuddled brain took some time to register this. 'But Hoden's dead.'

'I know he's dead but I was married to him . . . and then I . . . I left him.'

'But you're not called Hoden. Your name's Bury – Elizabeth Bury.'

'Bury's my mother's maiden name and, when the marriage failed, I decided to use it. I didn't want anyone to know I had been married.'

'Hoden? But what made you leave him?'

'I didn't actually leave him. I found out something . . . discreditable about him. I can't tell you what. It made it impossible to live with him, that's all.'

'So you were still married to him when he was killed?'

'Yes, technically.'

'But you didn't go out to Africa with him?'

'Yes, I did. I was there when he was killed.'

'Did you kill him?'

'No, but I was thinking about it.'

'Do you know who did?'

'It was probably one of his native bearers,' she said, as if it was a matter of no importance. 'They hated him. Or it might have been Captain Gates. He was the white hunter. It wasn't any of the other people on the safari, I'm almost sure.'

'And . . .?'

'What do you mean . . . "and"?'

'And you knew Stephen Thayer?'

'How did you know that?'

'You admit it, then?'

'Am I in the dock?'

'Elizabeth! It was you who suddenly sprang this on me . . . that you were married to Hoden. I don't want to have this conversation. It's three – no four – in the morning and my head is buzzing like a wasps' nest. Can we talk about this tomorrow?'

'You're going to Frankfurt tomorrow.'

'Yes, of course, so I am. Well then, when I get back.'

215

'Yes, when you get back.'

The taxi drew up in front of the house in Pimlico. Elizabeth opened the door and made to get out, but Edward stopped her.

'Look, I don't understand any of this but then I know I'm stupid. But I want you to know that anything you tell me is in complete confidence and, more important than that, nothing you tell me will change the way I feel about you.'

'How do you feel about me?' The light from a street lamp illuminated her face, which was as pale as the moon.

'I . . . I think I love you,' he blurted out, and then wished he had not said it.

She smiled, leant toward him and kissed him on the lips. He closed his eyes and the scent of her made him dizzy. 'Don't get out,' she told him. 'I don't want to wake the neighbours. I'll see you at Mersham when you get back from Frankfurt. And Edward . . .'

'Yes?'

'I think I love you too, but nothing said after midnight in the back of a taxi means anything, so don't worry about it in the morning.'

'But I mean it,' said Edward, not knowing if he meant it at all.

'And so do I, Edward dear, but there's still a lot you have to learn about me. But thank you for . . . a memorable night out.'

She got out quickly and lightly, closing the door of the taxi behind her. Edward fumbled with the catch but his fingers seemed unwilling to obey him. She had said something to the driver as she got out and, no sooner had she shut the door, than the taxi shot off tossing him on to the floor. With some difficulty, he got himself back on the seat and turned to look out of the small rectangular window at the back. For a moment he could see a pale form standing in a doorway and then the taxi turned the corner.

In the morning, Fenton found a pile of clothes on the bathroom floor and noted, with a smile, lipstick on the collar of the starched shirt and on the white bow-tie. He judged the evening to have been a success but, of course, he was not in full possession of the facts.

19

Verity slipped out of bed and wrapped a towel round her. She took a cigarette out of a packet on the table and then draped herself over the chair, leaving one leg hanging – she hoped provocatively – over the arm. She looked back at the bed where Belasco lay sprawled. It was odd, she thought, that she who cavorted shamelessly naked during their love-making was shy enough, the moment the blood cooled, to have to cover her body. Belasco, on the other hand, gloried in his nakedness despite being in many respects repulsive to look at. As he stretched himself and reached for one of the horrible little cheroots he liked to smoke after sex, she once again wondered at his hairiness. The thick pelt, which covered his chest and ringed his neck like a choker, continued down to his groin. His back, too, was felted and bear-like. In retreat, she noticed, his penis was entirely hidden in a great ball of fur sprouting like coarse brown grass.

Verity had had little experience of men. Her only previous lover had been David Griffiths-Jones, efficient enough but, she now realised, uninventive. Belasco, whom she had at first considered repellent, was by comparison ... extraordinary. She blushed inwardly at what he had taught her to do to his body and the excitement he had generated in hers by his playful nuzzling and ... She stopped herself.

She had never intended to take Belasco as her lover, but he had given her no say in the matter. He had invited her back to his apartment 'to look at some drawings by a guy named Pablo Picasso; ever heard of him, kid?' Verity hadn't – and he had taken her with a suddenness some might have considered perilously close to rape. One moment she had been looking at a charcoal drawing of a bull on its knees before a matador and asking him about the wine stain which disfigured it, the next she had been thrown on the unmade bed and was having her skirt torn off her. She had slapped him hard on the face and he had stopped. With as much dignity as she could manage, she had told him there was no need to tear her clothes. He had climbed off her and watched with an amused smile as she had removed first her shirt and skirt and then her undergarments. 'You're just a kid,' he had said with some surprise, eyeing her small breasts with displeasure. Verity was indignant: 'And you are just a pig – a hairy pig.'

That was when he had laughed at her and she had impulsively laughed back.

After that first coupling, he told her he had been provoked by her prim, virginal Englishness. He said he had wanted to 'kick her neat little butt' – by which she gathered he meant shatter her self-esteem, disturb her equilibrium and liberate her from her class and culture. As an enemy of convention and with an almost obsessive fear of being thought ordinary, she could only approve his aims. He was not, it turned out, normally a violent or even an energetic lover. He was a prankster, teasing her, arousing her and then letting her hang suspended in a state of sublime anticipation, before satisfying her with the passionate casualness of a beast. And all the time – or at least when he was in a position which allowed him to do so – he would watch her with his small, porcine eyes as though he was playing with her, as a lion plays with its food before devouring it. And always there was his fur, which stroked her flesh and set her blood screaming.

It was strange, she thought, how much she could enjoy sex without love. It went straight across everything she had been told, which might be summed up as the only sex worth having was sex within marriage. Verity could not imagine herself loving anyone to whom she was not sexually attracted, so it was peculiar the opposite was not true and she could be exhilarated by sex with someone who ... disgusted her. Perhaps it was because Ben was so strange, so foreign to her. Maybe that was the source of his interest in her. She wondered if she would turn up in one of his novels as a prissy English girl, inhibited about sex and naive about everything else.

She found herself idly imagining what Edward Corinth might be like as a lover. She suspected that beneath his hauteur – the coolness of an English gentleman who had been taught since the nursery that it was not good form to show his feelings – there might lie a passionate nature. Might he not be tender? Her whole body ached for tenderness, to be stroked and ... pampered. Edward Corinth was everything she had been taught to admire in a man – smooth, strong-featured, muscular, athletic, always perfectly dressed even when he considered himself to be in rags, courteous, patronising, intelligent, considerate ... inconsiderate ... Verity's mind wandered. But for the moment what she wanted was the man now noisily peeing in the basin because he was too idle to go down the passage to the lavatory. He frightened her and he thrilled her to the core ... and he knew it.

'What's bugging you, V?' he asked, coming over to her still stark naked, drops of urine dropping from his penis. 'Come back to bed, baby. I'm still hungry.'

'You're always hungry,' she said with nervous petulance. 'I suppose I'm just a snack...'

'Hey, kiddo,' he said, lazily pulling away her towel and drawing her to him. 'What's up? Maybe you'd like it better with that lord of yours,' he added as though he had been reading her mind.

'What can you mean?' she said, trying to pull herself free of him.

'That Lord Corinth or whatever he calls himself. I've seen him looking at you.' He laughed happily. 'When you came to sit by me that time you brought him to Chicote's, the guy almost had apoplexy. That man – if he is a man and not just a stick – wants to get into your drawers, V.'

'Oh really, Ben, you're absurd. Anyway, as you might have noticed, I don't wear drawers.'

'Knickers, then ...'

'And if you don't let me go, I will push this cigarette into you and you'll probably go up in flames.' His flesh smelled of dried sweat, sex and pure maleness ... something she had never smelled before but recognised instinctively.

'Hey! V, don't be so violent. You don't have to stab me with a cigarette to send me up in flames.'

'I expect that's what you say to all your women.'

'Women, what women?' he said, throwing up his arms so she could duck out of his embrace. Naked, she ran back to lie on the bed but, to show how liberated she was, did not cover herself this time. 'I don't have any women . . . besides you.'

'You have a wife, don't you?' she said sharply.

'Oh, sure.' He was quite unmoved. 'But Gloria knows the score. I love her . . . sure I do . . . but she knows I need other women. It gets so lonely in these foreign places.'

'I thought you said you didn't have other women. But it's good to know I can keep you from feeling lonely for an hour or two.'

'What's eating you, V? Haven't we just been having a great time? Why spoil it? You're not really mad at me, are you?'

'No, but . . . you are the limit . . .'

'I'm the limit, am I?' he mimicked her prissily. 'I've heard about you English girls. You don't have sex till you're married and then you have babies and stop. Christ! England must be a dull place.'

'It probably is,' Verity agreed. It was true that after Madrid and the life she had been living – 'rackety' her father had called it – she did not think she could ever go back to running around London making banners and getting indignant about 'the proletariat' and the 'class struggle'.

'Maybe I am English and dull, but isn't that just what you like about me?'

Belasco laughed again, his easy throaty chuckle. 'Gee! I never said you were dull. You ain't dull – no way.' He looked admiringly at her eyes which sparkled with indignation as she momentarily forgot her nakedness. 'You're a firecracker. I guess I've gotten bored of American women. Look at Hetty . . .'

'Was she your lover . . .'

'I tell no stories – ask her yourself,' he said annoyingly.

'When you were in Africa?'

'I guess I rescued her . . . You'd never believe that Swedish Baron . . . what a cocksucker.'

'For goodness' sake, Ben. You know I hate that sort of language.'

'Sorry.' He raised his hand in mock contrition and she once again marvelled that anyone could be so hairy under the arms, on the shoulders . . . everywhere.

'Who was he?'

'The Baron? God knows. I guess his title was real enough. He had a castle to prove it and Hetty ... why she was just an innocent Jewish kid from Denver ... of all places. There aren't many Jews in Denver, I can tell you. She was lonely, came to Europe, met the Baron in Paris, I think ... and they were married a few months later.'

'And then ...?'

'Hetty knew she had made a bad bargain the moment she saw the castle.'

'You mean they hadn't even been back to his home before they got married?'

'I know. Sounds crazy, doesn't it, but she was so desperate to stop being a boring American and lose her virginity, I guess she just sort of went off with the first European who made eyes at her.'

'And what happened when she saw the castle?'

'It was just a ruin and Lengstrum, he just wanted her money to rebuild it. But Hetty had regained her senses by then and she just walked away ... taking the title of Baroness with her.'

'Did he follow her?'

'I guess the poor sap didn't have the money.'

'When did you meet her?'

'I met up with Hetty in the States.'

'And you took her to Africa?'

'Yeah. Can we skip the rest of the interrogation?'

'Were you married by then?' Verity persisted.

'Sure, I was married to Gloria practically in high school. I just adored her and she wouldn't let me sleep with her unless we were married ... so I guess I went through with it.'

'Just like an English girl ... Why don't you divorce? It's easy in the States, isn't it?'

'I don't want a divorce. I don't intend to marry again and I still love Gloria ... and I guess she loves me. Anyway there's Star.'

'What is Star?'

'Star is my daughter and she needs a father.'

Verity was fascinated by all this autobiography. She had never heard him say so much about himself. Before he became maudlin about Star, she wanted to ask him one more question. 'While you were in Africa, did you and Hetty hear about that Englishman, Hoden . . . Makepeace Hoden, who was eaten by a lion?'

'Yeah, we did, I guess. I used it in a story I was writing. Look, honey, let's stop talking and start f . . .' Verity put a hand over his mouth and he removed it, gently but firmly. 'I tell you, kid, I only do three things – fucking, writing and fighting – and I only do one of them well.'

'One last thing, Ben. Was anyone else we know in Kenya when Hoden was killed?'

'Sure, Tom Sutton. He was the British consul there or whatever they call it . . .'

'Was Maurice Tate there?'

'Maurice? No! What makes you think Maurice might have been in Kenya?'

'Oh, nothing. I must have got muddled.'

Verity had more questions she wanted to ask but it was too late, at least this time. She had got much more out of Ben than she had ever expected. It looked as though Edward might be right. It was certainly a coincidence that so many of her friends in Madrid had also been in Nairobi just when Makepeace Hoden was killed.

She felt the now familiar excitement rise in her as Belasco spread her legs with his hands, as though he was opening the doors to her soul. It was strange but, as Belasco buried himself inside her, the last thing which crossed her mind before she became incapable of thinking at all was the image of Edward Corinth at his most disapproving.

20

The boat train, the Gare de Lyon, the border – surly, unshaven French, smartly uniformed, polite Germans – and at last Frankfurt – the Hauptbahnhof. The upright figure of the Englishman, closely shaved, head up, aquiline nose twitching a little as if it were some sensitive radio transmitter – Fenton had good reason to be proud of himself. The bedraggled young man of the night before, befuddled by drink and the scent of a woman, had been transformed into one of the most immediately identifiable figures in Europe: the English milord. The navy-blue, double-breasted suit, trousers creased to a knife edge, discreet silk tie, heavy overcoat and trilby set him apart from his fellow travellers. Edward stood out like a lighthouse: the product of an English public school and a pedigree which never doubted its superiority to all others. Quite unconsciously, his demeanour and deportment proclaimed it was enough to be English, but to be an English aristocrat was – despite world war, democracy and an economic slump – to be only a little lower than the gods. Policemen saluted him and railway officials touched their caps and hastened to ease his passage. Other passengers looked curiously at him, wondering, perhaps, why he travelled without half a dozen trunks and a manservant to organise his food and toilet. Was he a diplomat? Not quite – the hat perhaps a trifle too rakish. A businessman? Certainly not. He was simply an Englishman abroad.

Comically unaware of the impression he was making, and unconcerned that the French thought him arrogant and the Germans, half-resentfully and half-admiringly, strove to impress on him their own commitment to order and degree, Edward stared out of the window watching the steam cloud the land-scape, concealing and revealing features which seemed for a moment significant and then were lost for ever.

It was the same with this investigation. He kept on feeling he was on the point of making a major discovery, of seeing exactly what had been going on, and then something else would come along and confuse his vision. Damn this journey. How he hated feeling dirty and sitting still for so long. It seemed absurd to go so far for one meeting. Chief Inspector Pride would never bother to travel across Europe to question Thayer's business partner. He was content to rely on the local police, even though they were hardly likely to be interested in inconveniencing a rich businessman with close links to their political masters. No, however tiresome it was, it had to be done.

He opened an envelope which had been delivered to him at Albany by hand just as he was leaving for the station. It was from Verity's friend at the *New Gazette* and contained obituaries of Dora Pale and Max Federstein. A paragraph at the end of Federstein's obituary made him sit up. It said that only two years before he died he had married again and was survived by his wife. There cannot have been children from this marriage or they would have been mentioned but the wife might still be alive. It was a lead he must follow up as soon as he got back to London.

In Frankfurt, he directed the taxi driver to take him to an address given him by Basil Thoroughgood. It proved to be a large house in extensive grounds in the city's Westend, near the Eschenheimer Landstrasse. The villas in this exclusive neigh-bourhood, including the one Edward sought, had been built in parkland in the middle of the previous century and, because of their size, elegance and seclusion, were now owned by the richest and most powerful men in the city. As the taxi dropped him off at the elaborately sculpted iron gates, Edward went over in his mind the questions to which he needed answers. A sleek butler opened the door to him and took his card. He was taken to a small drawing-room where, despite the day being warm, a fire burned in the grate. Edward hardly had time to examine a painting of a particularly savage crucifixion, which he was almost certain was an Altdorfer, before the butler reappeared and led him up a flight of stairs, heavily carpeted, to knock on a wooden door more appropriate to a monastery than a suburban villa.

'*Herein!*' a hoarse-sounding voice commanded. The butler opened the door and showed Edward into what was obviously an office but the most luxuriously furnished he had ever seen. Outside it was still daylight but in this room a sepulchral gloom persisted. His eye was immediately drawn to the walls from which hung half a dozen paintings subtly illuminated from hidden lights in the ceiling. He caught his breath as he recognised a Dürer he could have sworn he had last seen in Munich's Alte Pinakothek. There was a painting of the interior of a Dutch house in which a young woman was playing a musical instrument of some kind. If he had not known there survived only fifteen authenticated Vermeers in all Europe, he would have said it was by that great master. He was, however, certain that the landscape behind the great ebony desk was a Jakob Philipp Hackert because there was one similar, which he had always loved, in the library at Mersham.

'I see you like my paintings.' A little man, with a lined face and flowing white hair, speaking perfect English, got up from the huge carved chair – almost a bishop's throne – that stood behind the desk. It was almost ludicrous – this tiny man with his great desk and massive chair – but, as he approached Edward, he appeared anything but laughable. He could have been any age between forty and seventy. He walked lithely, like a young man, but his eyes were very old and the duelling scar down the side of his face must have been cut before the war as such badges of honour were no longer permitted to officers of the new German army.

'I'm so sorry, Herr Hoffmann, but I could not help noticing the Hackert because my brother has one very like it and that must be . . . surely Piero della Francesca?'

'Ah! I see you are an art lover, Lord Edward.'

'But these are all great masters.'

'I have been very fortunate,' said the little man modestly.

Edward wanted to say that it was not luck that had brought these paintings into this room but huge wealth. Instead he said, 'It is very good of you to see me, Herr Hoffmann. I can guess how busy you are so I will take up as little of your time as possible.'

'You were a friend of Stephen Thayer? Such a sad business!'

'Yes, we were at school together.'

'Really? At Eton. Stephen was good enough to take me over "the old place" on your Fourth of June. That is your Founder's Day, is it not?'

Edward suppressed a smile. Hoffmann was evidently vain of his grasp of English idiom, and it diminished him in Edward's eyes. 'The old place' indeed. 'The Fourth is not actually Founder's Day,' he said, 'but it's the school's main "feast day".' He paused and then said: 'His son is a pupil at the school, along with my nephew. We were all very . . . distressed . . .'

'I, too, was very distressed,' said Hoffmann, though he did not sound it. 'He was my partner, as you know, but I also counted him my friend.'

'I apologise if I ask you about things which you have already discussed with the police . . .'

'The police? The English police? No one has been in touch with me from that excellent body of men. In fact, I was surprised that they had not been . . . No, wait, I tell a lie . . .'

And not the first one, Edward thought wryly.

'I had a letter from – let me see – ah yes, here it is, Chief Inspector Pride, but I have not yet had time even to read it. You see, I have only just returned from a business trip.'

'To England?'

'To England, yes, and to Paris, Madrid and Lisbon.'

'I'm so sorry,' said Edward, hearing a note of sarcasm in Hoffmann's voice. 'I did not mean to sound inquisitorial.'

'Inquisitorial! Yes, I like it. Of course you must be inquisitorial. We both want to find out who killed Stephen Thayer, do we not?'

'We do,' Edward agreed. 'When you say Stephen Thayer was your partner, what exactly did that mean? To put it bluntly, I would not have thought my friend was in your league.'

'My league? Ah, I understand. No, Lord Edward, you are right. I had business with him. In London he was useful to me. He provided me with information. He acted on my behalf on occasion. He was not, as you surmise, my partner in any real sense.'

'Basil Thoroughgood said you and he were partners in the bank. That's what confused me.'

226

'I think it is possible Stephen – how do you say it – liked to "show off".'

'You mean you were not partners or there was no bank?'

'Ah, Lord Edward. There was a partnership, there was a bank . . . on paper. But I am the sole owner. A year ago, Stephen was in something "of a hole" . . .' He smiled, clearly pleased with the expression. 'Yes, he was in a hole and I bought his share off him. I was generous,' he said, momentarily defensive.

'So you think Stephen might have lost money somewhere else?'

Hoffmann shrugged, 'Perhaps. How would I know?'

'You did not ask him?'

'No. His financial affairs did not concern me.'

'But they might have if they brought the bank into disrepute.'

'Disrepute? No, how could they? I do not deal with – what do you say? – the general public. My clients know me and trust me.'

'So why did you need Thayer in the first place?'

'It's useful having a representative in a foreign capital – London above all. As you know, London is the world's financial capital.'

Edward had the distinct feeling he was getting nowhere. While being courteous, Hoffmann was obviously going to tell him nothing. He decided to try shock tactics.

'Do you think Thayer was being blackmailed?'

'Blackmailed? Why should he be blackmailed?'

Was there something just a little too vehement in his repudiation of the idea? Or was it just his way with English? Well, he had learnt one thing: Thayer had been short of money. He had always thought of him as rich but perhaps he had not been in the sense that the rich define rich. Or perhaps he was having to find money for some other reason. He would have to find out. There was nothing more to be gained here.

Edward got up from his chair. 'That was very kind of you, Herr Hoffmann. I'm so sorry to have bothered you.'

'Not at all, not at all,' said Hoffmann visibly relaxing. 'And how is my friend Basil?'

He said 'Basil' as though he was holding between two fingers a dirty handkerchief.

'He's well. Worried about his money,' Edward added on an impulse.

'Tell him he has no need. His investments are with very profitable armaments companies.'

'Such as Krupp?'

'Why yes, such as with Herr Krupp,' Hoffmann said smiling.

'But what if there is a war?'

'There will be no war,' Hoffmann said, getting up and coming round from behind his desk.

'Herr Hitler seems set upon war.'

'Oh, but he is of no account. It is we bankers and the great financiers who control Germany. Nothing can happen without our permission.'

'You believe that, do you?' Edward said drily.

'I do,' he replied firmly. 'There will be no war. Maybe a local war – in Spain perhaps. Soldiers need to try out their toys – but no European war.'

'And the war against the Jews in this country?'

'Oh, the Jew has always been hated. But many of our greatest bankers are Jews. That will all pass. In the meantime it gives people someone to blame for our economic failures. My own feeling is that we did wrong in Germany to introduce a sewerage system in our cities.'

'But why?' inquired Edward, puzzled.

'Because, in the last century, regular outbreaks of cholera and other diseases of the poor killed very many people who are now starving – who are now "a drain" on our resources. That is what you call "a pun", is it not?'

Edward found it hard to speak. This was what chilled the blood: a man in a suit, so civilised he decorated his walls with great art, talking about killing the poor like vermin. He shuddered.

'You are not cold, Lord Edward?'

'No, not at all.'

He would dearly have liked a drink – a cup of tea at least – and saw once more that the man he was talking to did not know the meaning of hospitality.

'Did not your namesake, the author of *Struwwelpeter*, live near here?'

'Hoffmann? Yes, in Schubertstrasse, but sadly I am no relation.'

'It is a favourite book in English nurseries.'

'So I understand and here also, naturally.'

Hoffmann sounded bored. No doubt many other people had asked him the same question.

'I have always thought the book a little cruel,' Edward added. 'Struwwelpeter was always being burnt or cut.'

'Only when he misbehaved,' Hoffmann said, smiling. 'You know "Struwwel" means "slovenly". We Germans are not slovenly.'

Out in the street, Edward looked up at the shuttered villa. It sent shivers down his spine. How could somewhere so orderly, so decorous, be so sinister? But, as Hoffmann had said, the Germans – so civilised in so many ways – were capable of extreme cruelty. Was Hoffmann in some way responsible for his friend's death? He did not suppose the man had actually hit him over the head, though Edward had no doubt he would commit murder if he had to. But had he driven Stephen into a position which resulted in his death? It was possible. He had clearly used him and then, when he had finished with him, had spat him out to fend for himself. Hoffmann could have ruined him financially whenever he chose but, even worse, Stephen's reputation would not have survived his friends in the banking world knowing that he was the cat's-paw of a man like Hoffmann.

He spent a sleepless night in a small hotel near the station. The trams appeared to live just beneath his bedroom window and clanged and clattered amongst themselves throughout the night. It was a relief to get back to London the following day. For a week he busied himself to very little effect pursuing possible leads which invariably led nowhere. He spent hours in the archives of the *New Gazette*. He looked up several Eton friends of his and Stephen's and, to Fenton's alarm, passed one whole day supine in an armchair in his chambers looking blankly into the middle distance. He had, he knew, to go and see Elizabeth Bury and conclude the conversation he had begun when he had taken her out to dinner. He put it off day after day but at last, on the seventh day after his return from Frankfurt, he realised he could procrastinate no longer. He decided he would go down to Mersham that afternoon after he had fortified himself with lunch at his club.

However, in the event, he had once again to postpone his interview with Elizabeth. Fenton telephoned him at Brooks's where he was lunching. 'Bad news, I am afraid, my lord. Lord Weaver has just had a cable from Madrid. Apparently there has been an attempt on the young lady's life.'

'Verity? Is she . . . is she . . .?'

'She is not dead, my lord, but she is in hospital with a suspected fractured skull. She was hit over the head by some unknown assailant.'

'Oh my God! I told her to be careful. When did you hear?'

'Lord Weaver telephoned with the news a few minutes ago. He asked me to tell you he was completely at your service.'

'We must bring her back to an English hospital.'

'I understand the doctor says she cannot be moved for the time-being, my lord,' said Fenton.

'I must go to her immediately.'

'I anticipated that that would be your wish, my lord. I have arranged with Lord Weaver for Mr Bragg to fly you to Madrid tomorrow at first light.'

'Fenton, I see now I've been a damn fool. I've been looking in the wrong place for the wrong man. It's time I did something right for once.'

Fenton knew the tone of his master's voice. Lord Edward Corinth was no longer playing games; he was seeking vengeance.

21

Verity was behaving 'like a cat on a hot stove', as Hester had put it. In London, she had been possessed by panic. She had convinced herself she was going to miss some crucial event in Spain's history. She imagined she would for ever more be known as the foreign correspondent who was where the battle was not. When she was back in Madrid, however, nothing had changed and nothing looked like changing. Now she decided she might just as well have stayed in London or, better still, *insisted* on going with Edward to Frankfurt. She craved excitement, even danger – anything to justify calling herself a journalist and prove she was right to be here in Spain rather than Italy or Abyssinia – or Germany. Few people in England were interested in Spain but she was certain . . . except sometimes at three in the morning when she could not sleep and twisted and turned in sweat-damp sheets . . . she was *certain* Spain would be Europe's tinderbox. All her instincts told her the political crisis was coming to a head. There was going to be a smash – a coming together in open war of the forces of reaction – the Church and the army – and the new Republic. So why didn't it happen?

If only she could get information from North Africa, where the generals plotted and planned, but this was impossible and she could find no one in Madrid who knew any more than she did. Or, if they did, they would not confide in her. She blamed herself for not having made closer contacts with the Spanish political leaders but none of them was willing to take a foreigner and a woman into their confidence. She even managed to see Manuel Azaña himself. The new President of the Republic was charming but told her nothing she did not already know, mouthing complacent clichés with which she had to pretend to be satisfied. She was reduced to flirting with him and despised herself, particularly as it achieved nothing. The Republic was 'safe', 'in good shape', 'would face down its enemies', and so on. '*Sol o sombra*,' he intoned, using a metaphor taken from the bullring where seats are so named depending on whether they are in the sun or the shade. 'Spain is a country of contrasts, always in the sun or the shadow.' His great moon face looked at her as if she were a child asking for sugar-plums, which in effect was all he would give her.

She wondered idly if she *could* somehow ingratiate herself with the 'other side', with the army, but she knew it was impossible. For better or worse, she had identified herself, very publicly, with the Republic. She was a known communist. The idea that she might be accepted as a nationalist was ludicrous. So she could only wander about Madrid annoying her friends – all of whom seemed to have better things to do than listen to her complaints about how bored she was. David had vanished. She thought he might be in Barcelona but she wasn't sure. Tom Sutton was working long hours at the embassy and hardly ever went to Chicote's. Even Maurice Tate was busy. He had discovered the Spanish did not trust the news they read in the newspapers and he had set up what he called the British Council News Bureau which issued a newsletter in the form of several sheets of cyclostyled paper distributed free at the Institute and the embassy. It gave world news, in Spanish, as he – with Sutton's assistance and advice – wanted it to be read. 'My dear, I really don't have time,' Maurice said with exasperation when she badgered him to come on an expedition to take another look at the cave where Tilney's body had been found. 'Why don't you help me with the newsletter if you've nothing to do?'

'Oh pooh, Maurice, I'm a journalist not a propagandist.'

'Very well then,' he said huffily, 'don't let me detain you.'

Disconsolate, she withdrew into herself, finding relief only in fierce sex with Belasco, but even he seemed able to resist her when he wanted to write. 'Snap out of it, V. Go get a story some place else. I ain't got time to listen to you bewailing the absence of world war.'

Hester was concerned. 'Look, honey, I never interfere with what my friends do in their spare time. Sleep with *el burro* if you want to – donkeys have big dicks – but just remember, Belasco is another way of spelling bastard. I should know, cherub.'

Verity blushed deeply. She liked to think of herself as modern, hard-boiled, unshockable, but she still found Hester's uninhibited discussion of sex profoundly unsettling.

'Oh, I don't ... I don't think Ben's the love of my life or anything stupid like that. I know he's married,' she ended defiantly.

'Yes, Gloria! Poor bitch! He's married all right, but that's not what I mean. He is just a phallus on legs. He *uses* women, damn it! One day, you'll find a note on your pillow saying, "Bye babe, I'm off to the war" and he'll be out of your life.'

'But he's a great lover,' Verity said, trying to match her friend in frankness.

Hester looked at her with a blend of pity and envy. 'Well, kiddo, never say I didn't warn you.'

A week after she got back to Madrid, a visit from Rosalía Salas depressed her even more, despite the spring weather which had overnight transformed the city. In just a couple of days, the women threw off their heavy coats and thick shawls to dawdle about the town in thin cotton dresses, while the men lingered in groups at street corners viewing the girls critically as they passed, cheering or whistling at the pretty ones and spitting tobacco juice out of the corners of their mouths at those unblessed by a good figure or a quick wit. Verity was depressed because Rosalía had come to remind her of another failure. She had asked her, quite meekly, if she had discovered who had killed her man.

'The *policía* – they have given up looking. They think your friend David Griffiths-Jones is his murderer but they don't know how he did it.'

'Oh no, Rosalía, I am certain he was in no way responsible. In any case, he was in gaol when Godfrey was killed.'

Rosalía sighed. 'I know, Doña Verity, but it is strange is it not?'

'How are you managing?'

'How am I managing? Oh, I manage. I work in a bar near where I live.'

'I thought you were an actress.'

'Unemployed actress. Did you know,' she continued with more animation, 'I have joined the Communist Party? When Godfrey was alive, I loved him but I was not so interested in the work he was doing but now . . . now I get satisfaction from being like him.'

'I've been thinking. Why don't you and I go and have another look at the cave?'

'But why?'

'I don't know, but I feel we may have missed something. We were all so . . . upset when we were there.'

'But the *policía* . . . your friend Lord Coreent . . . they have all looked.'

'I know . . . I know, but . . . at least it's doing something.'

Verity had plenty of time to think about who killed Godfrey Tilney and Stephen Thayer. She was English enough to find it difficult to sleep during the long siesta the Spanish thought essential, even in times of political turmoil. She sometimes went to Ben's apartment, to be made love to, but only when he invited her. He often preferred to write in the middle of the day and he made it quite clear that, while sex was entertainment – *necessary* entertainment but still entertainment – writing was what he lived for.

Her room in the apartment she shared with Hester was pleasant and airy. It was at the back of the building – Hester's was across the passage at the front – and, with the shutters closed, it was cool and quiet. When Rosalía had left, she had taken up Ben's novel based on his experiences in the war but she was unable to concentrate. Her mind was awhirl with thoughts of Edward and of their visit to Eton – she reminded herself she must send Frank a picture postcard as she had promised. She gave up trying to read Ben's book and lay back in the semi-darkness, her hands behind her head, trying to think things through.

She couldn't quite make up her mind if she believed that there really was any connection between the two deaths – Tilney's and Thayer's. As for Makepeace Hoden's 'accidental' death in Africa – she really had no opinion about that. It ought to be possible to say for certain if anyone in Madrid who might possibly have killed Tilney had also had the opportunity of

234

killing either of the other two. For example, she knew Hester and Belasco had both been in Africa before coming to Spain; Maurice Tate, she had discovered, had been in England before coming to Madrid. He'd been a teacher and then a school inspector. Belasco had said Tom Sutton had been in Nairobi before being posted to Madrid and it should be easy to check that.

Then there was Thayer's murder. She ought to ask each of them whether they had been in London at the time he had been killed. She was almost certain Ben and Hester had been in Madrid but she supposed it was possible that one or other of them might have slipped out of town without her being aware of it. Yes, she would ask each of them – her 'friends' – whether they could have killed Thayer. They might not tell her the truth but, if one of them was the murderer, it might – what was the expression? – rattle the bars of his or her cage.

She closed her eyes; she felt a headache coming on. She couldn't seriously believe that any of them could be a killer. She hesitated. Wait, was that really the case? Could she be absolutely certain that Ben wasn't a killer? He was a hunter, after all, but then, what motive could an American novelist have for killing Tilney – an Old Etonian communist activist – or Thayer whom, as far as she was aware, he had never even heard of – let alone met? For that matter, what possible motive could any of them have had for stabbing Tilney? Nobody had liked him, but that was a long way from saying he was *hated*. Only David might have had a motive: some sort of political quarrel, but he at least – thank goodness – was *proved* to be innocent. She shook her head in frustration and then wished she hadn't as her headache worsened.

It was probable that Tilney had been killed by someone quite different, someone she did not know: a Spaniard, a political enemy. It was a comforting thought. There was another thing: Hoden and Tilney had both been shot but Thayer had died from a knock on the head and the weapon had been a Buddha from his collection. She wished she had met him. Edward had described him to her but she found it difficult to get a grip on his personality. In many ways, it seemed, he had been exactly how most people imagine an Etonian: smooth, charming, arrogant – but that was all superficial. In one respect at least he was sincere: he was a devoted father. If anyone had threatened Charles, his father would have acted to protect him. Of that there could be no doubt. But had anyone threatened Charles? There was no evidence of it.

Edward had called him sensitive and even generous but Verity had the feeling he had never really liked Stephen, otherwise surely they wouldn't have lost touch. He had been under his spell at Eton but Edward appeared to feel that his 'dependence' on his friend had been . . . unhealthy. Perhaps dependence always was since, by definition, it was one-sided. She shivered. She had no understanding of homosexuality. She thought of it – when she thought of it at all – as perverse and unnatural. It was a relief to her that she could absolve Edward of any sexual feeling for his friend. If there had been anything of that kind on Stephen's part, Edward had been unaware of it. Anyway, Stephen had proved himself to be a red-blooded heterosexual with Dora Pale. Was he *abnormally* highly sexed? She examined her own sexual adventures and blushed. If anyone had told her two years ago that she would be fornicating with a married American novelist with no thought of love or marriage, she would have been disbelieving . . . horrified. Now, she understood more clearly how powerful sexual feelings were and how they could make someone throw caution, principles and respectability to the winds. Any red-blooded boy would surely welcome the chance of learning about life and sex in the arms of a beautiful, older woman: it was probably most schoolboys' fantasy.

Was it about money then? Thayer was a banker and she had a deep-seated suspicion of all bankers. Edward was investigating his financial affairs and they looked pretty murky. And his politics? Was he a Nazi sympathiser or just an amoral businessman doing deals where he could? In short, was Thayer a victim of his own weaknesses or an out and out villain? From what Edward had told her, she was inclined to give him the benefit of the doubt. One hard fact in all this speculation: Thayer's killing had been different from Tilney's. The latter had been 'executed' by a single bullet at close range. Thayer had been battered to death by someone in the grip of an uncontrollable impulse.

Tussle with it as she might, Verity could get no further forward. David was safe; that was the main thing. She put a hand to her forehead, which felt damp, and could feel a pulse throb in protest. She wished David was with her now. She really didn't like Belasco but at least he was here and the sex ... she could not put into words what she felt about that. She was partly ashamed. She belonged to a tradition of English motherhood which decreed that sex was something the man enjoyed and the woman suffered in order to bring forth children. That was not how it was for Verity, so surely it must be wrong. Without seeing any connection, she wondered what Edward had found out in Frankfurt and wished ... She fell into a deep sleep.

When she awoke, she felt better. Her head had stopped aching and she was calmer. She looked at her watch. It was half-past three and the day was cooling. She didn't dare imagine what Madrid would be like in July and August. She had a feeling that her ancestors must have been Norsemen because she worked and thought much better in the cold. She mentally shook herself. It was so unlike her to sink into lethargy and despondency. There had to be *something* she could do. She considered for a minute; since she had time, the most useful thing was to be methodical. She would compile two lists showing precisely where all her friends were at the time of Hoden and Thayer's deaths and uncover any hint of a motive for murder. She was sure it would be a futile exercise and there would be no connections beyond the ones she knew; that Ben had written a story based on Hoden's death, for instance – she really *must* read that. It ought not to be difficult but, thick-skinned as she was, there was some embarrassment about going round asking friends for alibis. She would have to be tactful and she wasn't sure tact was her strong point.

She would begin with Hester. She put on a dressing-gown and padded out to knock on her friend's door.

'Come in,' Hester called.

'Are you awake?' she said unnecessarily.

'Sure. What can I do for you?'

'Oh, I just wanted to talk. You know, I'm still in a muddle about Godfrey Tilney and all that.'

'Forget it, cherub. Who gives a shit?'

'I know it's silly. Tell me about Ben instead. How did you meet?'

'In the States. I was just drifting around. He said come to Africa, so I did.'

Verity was shocked. 'It can't have been that casual?'

'It was too. I know he's a man and therefore a bastard, but at least he's a different kind of bastard from my husband.'

'What was he like in Africa?'

'Ben? Oh, can't you guess? It was Tarzan stuff. Ben waving his gun in the air and killing anything which came into his sights. It just had to be bigger and stripier and have sharper teeth than anyone else's.'

'But you're a crack shot, Hester. Ben told me. Did you kill a lion?'

'Ben told you that? Bullshit. Bullshit Belasco.'

'He said he knew all about Makepeace Hoden being killed. In fact he said he wrote a story about it.'

'Yeah, he did. One of his best. I think I've got a copy of it. It came out in *Transatlantic Review*. I'll give it you. It's about a man who committed a great sin.'

'A great sin?'

'Yep, but we never get to know what it is. It's an odd thing but, as I've said, Ben's full of shit except when he gets a pen in his hand. It's as if his pen *has* to tell the truth even though his tongue doesn't know the meaning of the word.'

'But you didn't meet Hoden, I mean before he was killed?'

'Not before or after. Why, do you think I killed him?'

'No, of course not,' Verity said hurriedly.

'But you do,' Hester teased. 'I *might* have killed him. He was a bastard too, by all accounts.'

'Did he commit some terrible sin, do you think?'

'Maybe. You'll have to ask Ben next time you're in bed together. I suppose you do have time for conversation?'

Later, for want of something better to do, Verity accompanied her friend to the Institute to watch her rehearsing *Love's Labour's Lost*. At the back of her mind, she wondered if she might get a chance to ask Maurice Tate a few leading questions.

The British Institute was on Calle Alcalá Galiano. It had once been a school and still had a smell of chalk and disinfectant about it. In what had been the gymnasium there was now a theatre – a primitive stage, a few lights and simple oil-cloth curtains. Verity had heard Hester's lines for her until she knew them as well as her friend. As the French Princess, Hester was marvellously haughty with Ferdinand, King of Navarre – one of the lusty young men who had forsworn love for three years. He was played by one of the few Spaniards in the cast. José was one of Maurice's protégés: very good-looking, muscular, prone to taking off his shirt at the slightest excuse, with a six o'clock shadow whatever time of day it was. Verity suspected that Hester and José might be having an affair but, if they were, they were discreet about it and she had never seen the boy in the apartment.

At first, Verity found the play hard to follow and wondered what the Spanish in the audience would make of it. It seemed to abound in word play; Elizabethan puns, inexplicable jokes which must have been highly topical when they were penned, displaying what Maurice called Shakespeare's drunken delight in the sound of words. He explained Shakespeare was exhibiting his skill with 'wit' as a fencer might dazzle onlookers with his foil. But this wit, which had once been the height of fashion, had over time become almost unintelligible. On the other hand, the preening and flirting in which the characters indulged was very Spanish. Verity had watched young men strolling along the Gran Vía flaunting their sexuality in just this way. And the sense of honour, which now seemed antiquated to a young British girl, made perfect sense to the Spanish.

Verity sat at the back of the room and prepared to be bored but, in fact, she was soon engrossed in what was happening on stage. She was impressed by Tate's direction. He had thrown off the feeble air of a provincial aesthete and assumed control of what could easily have been chaos. He not only knew the play through and through but also seemed to know exactly what it was about and how it should be played. He was lucid and patient but quite ruthless in getting what he wanted. It was a new Maurice, as far as Verity was concerned, and she found herself thinking that this was a man who could commit murder if it were essential to his gaining a particular end.

She was much taken with the character of the braggart Armado – the so-called 'fantastical Spaniard' – an absurd, clownish figure made more appealing by Shakespeare softening his absurdity with a vein of melancholy. She could not decide whether the Spanish in the audience would be offended or whether they would see in Armado a prefiguring of Cervantes' Don Quixote. Armado – 'his humour lofty, his discourse peremptory, his tongue filed, his eye ambitious, his gait majestical and his general behaviour vain, ridiculous . . .' – was most amusingly played by, of all people, Maurice's friend Agustín, the pianist at Chicote's. Verity thought he was so good that he should take up acting professionally.

Armado and some of the other clownish characters were performing a play for the 'great ones' who were mocking their efforts unmercifully. Verity was laughing at their antics when suddenly she was arrested by some lines of Armado's in which he upbraided his betters for jeering at his efforts to portray the Greek warrior, Hector. If they mock him, he says, they mock Hector and 'the sweet warman is dead and rotten'.

'*Diga me, Maurizio*,' said Agustín, coming out of character, 'what does it mean when I say, "beat not the bones of the buried. When he breathed he was a man"?'

'It's another way of saying, speak well of the dead and respect the chap because he was once a living, breathing man like you and me,' Maurice explained.

It made Verity think. Three men were dead: Hoden, Tilney and Thayer. They had all in some way offended someone. And there was a dead child: dead and rotten these eighteen years.

'Maurice,' said Verity, during the break for 'tea and recriminations', as Hester termed it, 'you were wonderful. I had no idea you would be such a good director. I'm impressed.'

Maurice blushed with pleasure and immediately reverted to being the effete 'man of letters' which so irritated her.

'I'm glad you like it, my dear. José, now – isn't he gorgeous?'

'He's a very good actor.'

'Yes, he is, isn't he?' Maurice said with feeling.

'And Agustín, he's so good as Armado. Like Don Quixote, I thought.'

'Yes, you're right,' he said, seeming surprised at her perspicacity.

'I was struck by the phrase he asked you about.'

'Which one?'

' "The bones are buried", that bit. I was thinking about Tilney.'

'For goodness' sake why, child? You think he was a "sweet warman"?'

'Not quite but . . .'

'He was a piece of garbage – nothing more,' Maurice said with cold contempt. 'It was the best thing that could have happened – him being shot like a mad dog.'

The vehemence of his words rendered Verity speechless and Maurice, seeing her expression, quickly corrected himself. 'I don't know why I said that, my dear, forgive me. The play . . . I was thinking of the play, but he was a nasty piece of work.'

'Because of his politics?'

'Oh no, what do I care about his politics? He could have believed in . . . in Hector for all I cared. But he was – forgive me, dear, but I must say it – a complete and utter bastard. He tried to blackmail me once.'

'Blackmail?'

'Yes, he said if I didn't do . . . some dirty political thing for him, he would tell everyone I was queer.'

'Queer? Homosexual? But that's ridiculous. You're married . . . with a daughter.'

Maurice looked at her oddly and seemed about to say something, but changed his mind at the last moment.

'So what did you do?' Verity prompted.

'I told him to go to hell, of course. I said the Spanish – in spite of all the Catholic stuff – were a surprisingly broadminded lot and had a different sense of honour to him. In fact, I think I said – I certainly meant to – that he had no idea what the word "honour" meant.'

'Gosh! Was that the end of it?'

'No, the pool of vomit – excuse my French, dear – said he would tell the people back home and ruin my career, blast him.'

'And did he?'

'No, he died. Or, at least, we thought he had died. But of course he wasn't dead – not then anyway.'

'Did you kill him?'

'I would like to have done,' Maurice said with evident sincerity, 'but, as it happened, I didn't – either time.'

'You went back to England a couple of weeks ago, didn't you? Not bad news, I hope?'

'As a matter of fact my mother was ill. They thought she might die.'

'But she was all right?'

'She pulled through – unfortunately.'

'Unfortunately?'

'She's not been in her right mind for years. I hoped she might fade away peacefully.'

'Oh, I'm so sorry.'

'She's a Catholic and she's in a Catholic home. Maggie, my daughter, has to live with her aunt and I'm afraid she doesn't like it. I told you my wife died when Maggie was only a baby. The people who look after my mother are very good but, as Catholics, they are morally bound to keep someone alive – bring them back from the dead – when it might be more merciful . . . She had pneumonia during the winter . . . She should have passed away but . . . I'm . . .'

Verity saw that he was in tears and she upbraided herself for being callous. She put a hand on his arm and squeezed it gently. 'Please forgive me, Maurice. I didn't mean to upset you.'

'Oh, it's not your fault,' he said, pulling out a grubby hand-kerchief and mopping his eyes. 'My mother's the only woman I've ever truly loved and I hate myself for wanting her to die.'

'Of course you don't. You just want her to be at peace.'

Maurice looked at her gratefully and smiled wanly.

When, at half-past seven, they were strolling back to the apartment in the warm, sweet-smelling air of early summer, Verity, emboldened by the semi-darkness and by Hester's unshockability as far as sex was concerned, said, 'You seem to get on very well with José. He's so beautiful I wondered if you were . . . having an affair.'

To Verity's puzzlement, her friend broke into peals of laughter that made others strolling along the Gran Vía look at her and smile in sympathy.

'My dear, sweet, innocent cherub,' she said when she had at last stopped laughing, 'José is Maurice's new boyfriend. Surely you noticed the way the two of them were looking at each other?'

'Boyfriend . . .? Then is he really . . .? Oh God, what a fool I am. But I thought his special friend was Agustín . . .'

'Well, of course! Goodness, you are unobservant. Didn't you

pick up "the atmosphere"? I quite thought Agustín would hit Maurice, or at least walk out, but he so loves being in the play . . .'

Verity felt very foolish. As a journalist, being called unobservant was worse than being biased or corrupt. It meant she was no good at her job and that was the one thing she clung on to – that she was a good journalist. Angry with herself, she became angry at Hester.

'Oh no, that's disgusting! José's a real man. I'm sure you're quite wrong.'

'Wrong, am I?' said Hester indignantly. 'Well, I have seen them in bed together.'

'You haven't!'

'I have. I went to Maurice's apartment because he said he wanted to give me some notes on my part. He had obviously forgotten I was coming because, when he opened the door, he was in nothing but a silk dressing-gown and behind him, through the bedroom door which was open, I could see José, naked as a baby sprawled across the bed.'

In the darkness, Verity coloured. She decided to change the subject: 'Maurice says Tilney was trying to blackmail him. Do you think that's possible?'

'Quite possible,' said Hester firmly. 'That man . . . there was something reptilian about him. I hated him.'

'But Rosalía liked him – loved him – and she's not a fool.'

'Maybe. Maybe he was kind to her but he was a cold fish – a bully and a coward. I don't like saying it, but he deserved to die. I have a feeling Rosalía, bless her, may be a bit of a masochist.'

'But no one likes being hurt.'

'Yes, they do. Some people like to be physically hurt. Haven't you ever heard that some men go to prostitutes to be beaten with birch rods?'

'No!' exclaimed Verity, horrified. 'That's . . . that's horrible.'

'It's so common in your country, the French call it the English disease.'

Verity was, for once, speechless. It seemed she knew nothing about sex after all. She shook her head. She saw herself as broadminded – even immoral. After all, she was the mistress of a married man. It made her feel very cosmopolitan. Edward

243

would probably call her a scarlet woman. She wondered why she should think of Edward at that particular moment. It wasn't as though she cared how he might view her behaviour. He wasn't her conscience.

'Some women like to be tortured mentally, or psychologically,' Hester was saying. 'But perhaps the worm turned.'

'What do you mean?'

'Well, to be truthful, I have always wondered if Rosalía didn't murder Tilney. I wouldn't blame her if she had.'

Verity thought about this. 'No, I don't believe she's capable of murder and I do believe she loved Tilney. I can't forget her wailing when we discovered his body. In fact, tomorrow I'm going up to the cave with Rosalía to hunt for clues.'

'But why? What could be there now after all this time?'

'I don't know. Nothing probably, but I was so shocked when we found the body I didn't have a chance to look around properly.'

'I think you're mad, cherub, but don't let me stop you. But keep a weather ear open. The stab in the back . . .'

'Oh, don't be absurd, Hetty. Anyway, it's weather *eye*.'

'I'm absurd, am I?' Hester said, pretending to take umbrage. 'I guess you know best, but don't blame me if you get pushed off a cliff. I'm going to change and have a wash – then shall we go down to Chicote's?'

They all sat round the table laughing, telling stories, happy. Ben Belasco was drinking hard. When he was working well, he almost never drank but, when he had finished a story or even a piece of journalism, he would celebrate by what he called 'bingeing'. He had finished a story that afternoon while Verity was watching *Love's Labour's Lost* and was in cracking form. He told stories about his childhood in Colorado: how he had been running with a stick in his mouth and had fallen and gouged out his tonsils, how at high school he had taken the part of the playwright Sheridan in a play called *Beau Brummel* and had felt 'damn queer', how he had become a keen boxer and after being knocked out had woken to find a beautiful girl massaging his face with a wet sponge. 'Gee, was I a humdinger in those days,' he remembered fondly. And all the time he told stories, he was stroking Verity – her neck, her leg, her thigh – and she knew there would be energetic love-making later that night. It was as if the adrenalin he needed to finish a story then had to be washed out in sex.

Maurice, too, was in high spirits because rehearsals for the play were going so well and Hester, José and Agustín were infected by his enthusiasm. Even the enigmatic Tom Sutton had deserted his desk for Chicote's and was unwontedly cheerful. He had thrown off the veneer of world-weariness which he usually wore about him like a mantle and was telling stories of his ambassador's *bêtises* with biting sarcasm. The merriment was interrupted by the unexpected appearance of David Griffiths-Jones, grim-faced and exhausted. He smiled thinly at the assembled company, refused Maurice Tate's offer of a beer and summoned Verity – like the Commendatore in *Don Giovanni*, Belasco said later – to follow him to a relatively quiet corner of the restaurant.

'What is it?' Verity asked, when she had disentangled herself from Belasco and joined him on a banquette out of sight of the party. 'Where have you been?'

'Never mind that,' David said coldly. 'I haven't got much time, so listen carefully. Our informants tell us that General Franco and his cronies are planning to mutiny and, unless we can nip it in the bud, God knows where it will end.'

'Mutiny! You mean rebellion? But Franco's still in Morocco, isn't he?'

'Yes, but the tentacles of conspiracy are spread widely. I am off to Casablanca first thing tomorrow to see what I can do to frustrate them. But before I go, I wanted to warn you to be ready.'

'Ready for what?' Verity asked.

'I don't know yet but, when you get a message from me, you must come immediately. I shall want you to begin the war of words. We have to put our side of the story and capture public opinion in England and America. Only then can we put enough pressure on the British and French governments to declare their support for us openly.'

'Won't they do that anyway?'

'Don't be naive, Verity. The British government is virtually Fascist. It will do everything it can to prevent itself getting drawn into a civil war on the side of the left. All it needs to do is nothing and the Republic will fall. Only public opinion can persuade Baldwin to live up to his obligations. But you know all that. That's where your friend Belasco will come in useful. You have to bring him with you wherever I send you and make him report what we want him to report. His name carries great weight in Washington and New York.'

'But I can't make him do anything.'

'Don't be a little fool. This is your job, this is why you're here. That's why I haven't minded you disporting yourself with that creature.'

'Ben?'

'Yes,' David said bitterly. 'You don't think I would have stood for it otherwise?'

'Are you jealous?' Verity asked.

'Not at all. Why should I be? But just remember that you are not in Spain on holiday but to do a job of work.'

'Yes, I'm a foreign correspondent.'

'Stop play-acting, Verity,' he said scathingly. 'You're not a child, even if you behave like one sometimes. Your one reason for being here is to serve the Party. Discipline – I have told you before – discipline. The Party demands it.'

'And by discipline you mean I must do what you say?'

'That is correct, at least for the moment. You take orders from me or some other senior Party member.'

Verity held back tears with difficulty. She was being bullied and she hated it – she hated David, she hated the Party, but wasn't he right? Wasn't that why she was here?

'Look,' David said, making an effort to appear less dictatorial, 'we've obtained a copy of this.' He pushed a paper into her hands. 'How good's your Spanish? Can you read?'

'Yes.' She scanned the paper. 'It's from General Mola.'

'Yes, he's one of the ringleaders.'

' "The situation in Spain is becoming more critical with every day that passes," ' she read. ' "Anarchy reigns in most of her villages and the government presides over . . ." What's this word?'

'Tumults.'

' "Tumults. The Motherland is being torn apart . . . the masses are being hoaxed by Soviet agents who veil the bloody reality of a regime that has already sacrificed twenty-five million lives . . ." What does it mean?'

'It means we are almost at war. We will be in a matter of weeks.'

'So what do you want me to do now?'

'Nothing, just wait. I will give you a signal and tell you what needs to be said.'

Verity wasn't certain that she wanted to be told what to say but she was frightened. She suddenly felt very small, a minnow in an ocean full of sharp-toothed fish who would use her and toss her aside without a moment's consideration when she had served her purpose. She suddenly wished she had Edward Corinth beside her. Thinking of him made her think of the murders he was investigating – that they were investigating together.

'Do you know yet who killed Godfrey Tilney?' she asked suddenly.

'Tilney? For God's sake, what does that matter now? He was a Trotskyist, a traitor. What does it matter who killed him?'

'But was it you?' she persisted.

'I was in prison, remember.' He looked at her with cold eyes. 'Who's put you up to this? Is it that streak of idiocy, Corinth?'

She ignored the question. 'But you could have had him killed.'

For the first time since he had broken in on the party, he looked at her as though she was more than a tool to be used. 'I could have, yes, and I probably would have sooner or later but someone beat me to it. Satisfied?'

'Yes thank you, David.' She hesitated: 'Why not come over and talk to Ben? Get him on your side. Give him some titbits of information to send back to the States. Make him feel "in the know".'

He thought about it for a moment. 'I haven't got the time. I'll just say goodbye. I leave Belasco to you.'

They walked back to the table and David was as charming as he could be but, after five minutes, he excused himself, kissed Verity on the cheek and disappeared into the night.

Belasco shivered. 'I guess he's the future but I don't pretend that young man doesn't send shivers up my spine. When he walks, I get the feeling he walks over graves.'

The following day Verity met Rosalía at the station and they travelled together on the little train to San Martino. It seemed so long since she had made the journey with Edward and found Godfrey Tilney's body. She had an odd feeling that it was more of a pilgrimage than an investigation, or rather a journey of reparation. At that stage, it had not seemed an impossible job to discover the killer but, two months on, they were no nearer finding out who had murdered him and why. The Spanish police were no longer interested, Rosalía confirmed. The last time she had been to the police station to inquire about progress she had been told to go away. They had much more important things to worry about than a man who had twice been killed and twice buried. The police were having to decide whether, in the event of an insurrection, they would side with the elected government or support the army with whom they had close links. It was one of the areas in which David had been most active and he had told Verity that he suspected the Madrid police would stay loyal to the Republic although this might not be the case in other cities.

The two women, on this occasion properly dressed for the climb, struggled up the mountainside to the cave. The sun was hot and Verity mopped her brow, stopping every fifteen minutes to drink from cupped hands the cold, clear water in the stream which ran beside the path and then became the path along which they had to splash. They reached the cave at about eleven and flung themselves down on the little patch of greensward at its mouth to suck the oranges they had brought with them. They felt sleepy in the sunshine and reluctant to enter the cave. It was only with an effort that they roused themselves.

'I don't know why we came,' Verity complained, forgetting that it had been her idea and not Rosalía's.

'We may find something the police overlooked,' the Spanish girl replied.

'They seemed an efficient bunch. In any case, it's two months since we were here. Anybody who wanted to remove anything would have done so already.'

'*No sé. Tiene razón.* You're right. I know there's nothing to be found but still . . . I think we were right to come. I owe it to him to try to revenge his death.' Rosalía spoke wearily, as if she did not have much faith in her words. She would not admit it, but her lover, who had always been so hard to know and who had been absent from her for long periods, was already fading from her memory. She had no photograph of him and found it hard to recall his features.

Gingerly they pulled away the curtain of brush and bramble – the stone had not been rolled back in front of the cave when the police left – but to their relief there was no evidence that Tilney had ever been there, alive or dead. There was no smell of decayed flesh – it had been this which Verity had feared most even though she knew that she was being irrational. After so long what could there be to remind her of the horror upon which she and Edward had stumbled? There was nothing now to suggest that a killing had taken place unless it was that the cave was too clean and tidy. The police had been thorough in their examination.

Disconsolately, the two women began their search, looking in cracks in the walls of the cave and feeling in the sand for hard objects, but there was nothing. 'I don't even know what we're looking for,' Verity said. They were just about to leave when she caught a glint from something in a niche near the opening. It was a gold ring.

'Rosalía, come over here. See what I've found,' she called excitedly.

They stared at the plain yellow band in the palm of Verity's hand. Rosalía took it and turned it over but there was no inscription on it – nothing to indicate if it was a wedding ring or just a keepsake.

'It must have been put there deliberately,' Verity said. 'It would hardly have got into that crack in the wall by accident.'

'It's a woman's ring,' said Rosalía, fitting it on her little finger. 'I have thick fingers *lamentablemente* and see, it only fits my small finger.'

It fitted Verity's middle finger as if it had been made for her. 'It can't have been here when the cave was searched by the police,' she mused. 'They would certainly have found it. It must have been placed there later on.'

'But there are no foot-marks,' Rosalía objected. 'A few animal footprints but no human.'

'Whoever left it must have been careful to cover up their footprints.'

'*No entiendo*. I do not understand. What is the meaning of the ring?' Rosalía sounded put out, insulted, as if someone had laid a claim to her man.

'Well, it's odd, I know, but what if someone had wanted to leave it here for remembrance – like leaving flowers on a grave?'

'Shall we give it to the *policía*?'

'No, what would be the use? I think I will wear it. Maybe someone will ask me where I got it.'

'But that might be dangerous,' said Rosalía, alarmed.

'I don't think so. It's so anonymous. No one need fear being identified through the ring. There must be hundreds, if not thousands, like it.'

'It is strange. No Spanish woman would have a wedding ring with nothing marked on it – no names, no dates.'

'Well, we shall find nothing else here,' Verity said. 'Let's go back. I feel better somehow for having come here and I have a feeling that the ring is an important clue, but what it means I just don't know.'

That evening she had dinner at Chicote's as usual. No one remarked on the ring she was wearing on her right hand – not even Hester or Ben – and Rosalía had persuaded her that it was safer to make no mention of finding it. Verity had invited Rosalía, who was rather shy with foreigners, to eat with them and was glad she had as they were made to describe their pilgrimage in great detail. Maurice Tate was particularly interested and questioned her closely. Tom Sutton, on the other hand, was distracted and Verity wondered if he had heard news of General Franco's putative rebellion. Rosalía's presence made even Ben a little less aggressive than he might otherwise have been; she was in effect 'the widow', the only person who seemed to mourn the dead man.

It was difficult to know why Tilney had been so disliked. Verity concluded that it was probably not so much what he was as what he wasn't. He was solitary, unclubbable, hardly bothering to conceal his indifference bordering on contempt for expatriates like Hester Lengstrum and Maurice Tate. He had apparently disliked Americans on principle as capitalists and exploiters, so he had nothing to say to Belasco. At least Verity was a communist but, in his eyes, of the wrong sort. He tolerated her and David as necessary allies in the fight against Fascism but that was all. His extreme political views, David once said, made him hate Party members whose views he disagreed with even more than his enemies on the political right.

'He hates Stalin,' David had explained to Verity, wonderment in his voice, 'even though Stalin is the true defender of the revolution. He believes Stalin has betrayed Lenin. All nonsense, of course, and dangerous nonsense at that. I've warned him dozens of times he will put his life in danger if doesn't come into line.'

This was a couple of months before Tilney was killed but it accounted for many people's lack of surprise at his death and why the police had immediately suspected David.

Rosalía had loved him, that was certain, but Verity thought she might be getting over her loss. Their visit to the cave where he had died might, she thought, complete her mourning and allow her to get on with her life. Joining the Party had obviously helped her. It had in some way made sense of his death. It was sad, she thought, to leave this world, as Tilney had, mourned only by parents with whom he had nothing in common except blood, and a Spanish girl whom, Verity suspected, he had treated with nothing more than the casual affection he might have offered a stray dog which had attached itself to him. After a moment's thought, however, she decided that Tilney himself would not have cared; he would have thought it bourgeois sentimentality to be mourned. His work for world revolution was the only thing which was important to him and he would have approved of Rosalía's new political life.

By midnight, Verity felt tired and drained of energy so she said her goodnights and walked back to the flat alone. Outside in the soft Spanish night, not yet heavy with the heat of full summer, she felt better. Instead of going straight home, she let her feet take her towards the Puerta del Sol which had once been at the edge of the city but was now its hub and from which most of the main thoroughfares radiated. Restaurants were still open and the occasional tram rattled by but there were not many pedestrians – a few single men looking for female company and two or three pairs of lovers who had found privacy among the trees which lined the square. Deep in thought, Verity was surprised to be addressed. She looked up to see the anxious face of a working man in his fifties. He was speaking to her but so fast that she could not understand him. At first, the man was annoyed but, when Verity was able to pull herself together sufficiently to explain that she was a foreigner, he looked shocked, lifted his hat and passed on hurriedly.

It took Verity a minute or two to realise she had been mistaken for a prostitute. What other single woman would be wandering alone in Madrid at this time of night? She blushed at her own foolishness and turned towards home. She thought she might catch a tram but her apartment wasn't far and she decided it was quicker to walk. She prided herself on how well she knew the city so it was absurd to lose her way, but she did. One moment she was in familiar streets illuminated by the occasional street lamp or bright window and the next she was walking in darkness. After twenty or possibly thirty minutes – she could not tell – she came not to the Gran Vía as she had planned but to the Buen Retiro, two hundred acres of unkempt woodland. She kicked herself for being so stupid and losing her sense of direction. She knew this area could be dangerous at night and a dozen stories of murders and robberies crowded into her mind as she made a great effort not to panic.

She made herself stand still and take stock of exactly where she was. At last, she realised she was quite near the Prado and felt easier in her mind. However, it was still a full hour of fast walking before she found herself at her apartment. She was feeling exhausted and angry with herself but mightily relieved to be safely home. She wondered if Hester was back from Chicote's but, as she could see no light, she had either not returned or had gone straight to bed. She tried to unlock the door quietly and did not turn on the light. She did not feel like explaining to Hester how foolish she had been. She was just about to open her bedroom door when she caught a glimpse of a figure with a raised arm beside her – she could not tell whether it was a man or a woman. She opened her mouth to cry out and lifted her own arm to protect herself but, before she could utter a sound, she felt her arm break as she fended off a heavy blow from a stick or club. Then she did let out a cry of pain but a second blow, this time undeflected, made her feel her skull was exploding as she subsided through red into blackness.

22

'Isn't it all rather primitive?' Edward whispered, as he sat down beside the simple iron bedstead.

'No, they've looked after me so well. Apart from setting my poor broken arm, they just needed to let me rest.'

'You must have a thick skull.'

'Thanks,' Verity said, and tried to smile. She was still feeling weak and woozy.

'No, I mean, I should think it's a great asset for a foreign correspondent. I expect they're always dodging bullets and falling downstairs – that sort of thing, what?'

'Ass,' said Verity, affectionately. 'It was good of you to come. My father says he's coming sometime but he's frightfully busy at the moment.'

'Of course I came,' said Edward, shocked, 'as soon as I got Joe Weaver's message.'

'Have you seen Hester?'

'Yes, she said she found you just a few moments after it happened.'

'I don't remember anything of course ... just the raised arm...' She shuddered. 'Hetty thinks my attacker may even have heard her coming and that was why he didn't finish me off.'

'But he took the ring.'

'Yes, ouch! Sorry, I still get shooting pains in my head but the doctor seems to think they'll go soon.'

'Forgive me. I shouldn't be asking questions. I don't want to tire you.'

'No, it's lovely to see you.' She saw Edward look disbelieving.

'I mean it.' She smiled and slid a hand from under the blanket. He took it and squeezed it. 'You make me feel safe.'

Edward tried to conceal his pleasure. 'You saw absolutely nothing which might identify your . . . your assailant?'

'No, I'm afraid not, except he looked tall, but even that might have been an illusion given that I was cowering below him.'

'Not cowering. I think you were very brave. You realise this alters everything?'

'How do you mean?'

'In the first place, no one can attempt to murder someone I love and get away with it.'

'You dope,' said Verity, feeling tearful and not wanting to admit she had heard the word 'love'. 'And in the second place?'

'It wasn't, obviously, a robbery because your bag wasn't stolen – just the ring.'

'So whoever left the ring in the cave wanted it back?'

'Yes, but why? A simple, plain ring like the one you described could never be traced back to the owner. It couldn't be evidence of anything.'

'But someone recognised it and wanted it back badly enough to . . .'

'Yes, it was probably rather foolish of you to wave it round the table at Chicote's. Did you say where you'd found it?'

'No one asked. No one mentioned it but I had told everyone where I was going.' She closed her eyes. 'You think my attacker was at Chicote's?' Verity shuddered and looked even paler.

'I'm sorry, Verity,' Edward said, squeezing her hand again. 'I know it's horrible to think one of your friends could have done this but I can't see how it could be anyone else.'

'But why should they? As you say, it's not evidence of anything,' she said weakly.

'I've been thinking about that,' Edward said, sitting back on the upright chair, which was uncomfortable enough to discourage long visits. 'I think – and of course it's just a hunch – someone was infuriated to see that ring on your finger. It was a special ring they had left as some sort of offering.'

'Offering?' Verity murmured.

'Yes, as one might leave flowers at a graveside.'

'Oh dear!' Great tears began to roll down her cheeks and Edward was immediately furious with himself. He had upset her when she should be resting peacefully. He looked up and saw a nurse. He tried to find the Spanish for explaining he needed help, but could not. The nurse, a sweet-faced woman in a uniform as clean as any at Guy's or the Middlesex, gently pushed him to one side to stroke Verity's forehead.

'She must rest now,' she said in English. 'Come back tomorrow. She needs to sleep.'

Edward wanted to kiss Verity, felt he couldn't with the nurse present but then did so on the forehead. 'You're the dope,' he whispered. 'I'll come back tomorrow. I've got one or two people to see. I think I'm beginning to get an idea of . . .'

He stopped speaking. Verity had closed her eyes and seemed to be sleeping. It made him angry to see her like this, very angry. His angular face seemed to sharpen – his eyes narrowed and hooded, his lips thinned and his beak of a nose twitched as if it scented blood. His features took on a startling resemblance to the falcon in the Mersham coat of arms.

For fifteen days, Edward took turns with Hester to sit by Verity's bed, often holding her hand. She liked to have her head stroked too. She said it soothed her. Belasco came once while Edward was there; he said hospitals gave him the creeps and it was proof of what he felt for her that he had made himself come at all. Tom Sutton appeared but looked so harassed that Verity found herself comforting him. He had dark circles under his eyes and said the political situation was getting ever more dangerous. The armed forces were reported to be planning violent protests in the streets of Barcelona and Madrid but the government seemed incapable of decisive action.

The hospital did its best to look after the foreign girl: she had a room to herself so she could rest undisturbed by the continual noise of the long tiled wards which echoed with footsteps, talk and cries of pain. The doctor, young and ridiculously over-worked, was brisk but efficient. The nurses were experienced and sympathetic and two of them spoke some English, but there were few medicines – even aspirin was in short supply and the food was uneatable. In any case, Verity insisted that she did not take food away from poor sick people with no friends to minister to them. Whenever a visitor brought her fruit or chocolates, she asked the nurses to distribute them in the wards as soon as they had left. She had very little appetite and both Hester and Edward were worried that she was losing too much weight.

Maurice came once with his two Spanish boys, who now seemed content to share his favours. He brought books but Verity wasn't up to reading. Her eyes were still hurting and she had difficulty focusing. Although the pain in her head was easing, she felt deathly tired. She slept a lot, which the doctor said was the only medicine worth taking, but when she was awake she liked being read to and Hester brought along Ben's story based on Hoden's death in Kenya. Edward was delighted to see that dissecting the story between them seemed to animate her and help slough off her lethargy. Tom Sutton had offered to have her shipped back to London but she would not hear of it.

'And miss all the excitement!' she exclaimed indignantly. 'I'm feeling better every day. The doctor says I can go home the day after tomorrow so long as I promise to stay in bed and rest.'

A pleasant police captain, who spoke very good English, came to talk to her about what she remembered of the attack but she could tell him no more than what she had told Edward: that a tall dark figure had loomed over her just as she was opening her bedroom door.

The policeman confirmed what Edward had already established for himself – that there was no sign of a forced entry to the apartment but that meant little. The simple lock to the front door could have been picked by a child of ten. Hester and Verity had nothing worth stealing except for Hester's camera and a little money, so they had never worried much about security. If you weren't a political activist, Madrid was one of the safest cities in Europe. Rape was almost unheard of and murder was rare and usually the result of a husband finding his wife in bed with a lover. It was clear to Edward that the Spanish police, though curious as to why Verity had been attacked, had no idea how to go about investigating it.

By the middle of May Edward confessed to Verity that he was now reasonably sure who the murderer was. He thought she had been attacked because the murderer was frightened she knew, or almost knew, his or her identity and was enraged to see her wearing the ring which had some special significance.

'The list you drew up – where everyone was at the time of

the three deaths – was useful. I'm not quite sure about motive yet but I am pretty sure the answer lies back in England, at Eton in fact.'

'At Eton?' Verity asked in surprise. 'But . . . but none of our suspects went to Eton.'

'No,' Edward agreed cheerfully, 'but nevertheless that's where all this terrible violence has its source. So you see, V, I need to go back.' He saw her face fall. 'Not for long – probably just a couple of weeks – but I want to get this whole horrible business cleared up.'

'But . . . who do you . . .'

'I'm almost certain you have nothing to fear,' he carried on, disregarding her half-asked question. 'The attack on you has put you out of action, so the murderer won't feel he has anything to fear from you, but you must be very careful. As you know, I've had the locks on your doors changed and strengthened but you must discourage visitors, and what's more, you must pretend to be iller than you really are.'

'That won't be difficult!'

'It would be too suspicious to lock you away in isolation but you need to keep the lowest of low profiles for as long as I'm away. Sorry to be so damn mysterious but . . .'

'But what about you, Edward?' Verity said, grasping his hand. 'Are you safe?'

'I can look after myself,' he said with more confidence than he actually felt. 'You see, I know who to look out for.'

'But you won't tell me?'

'Not for the moment. I think it's safer you don't know. That way, you can't give anything away by look or word which might rouse our man – or woman – to do something silly.'

'You think it could be a woman?'

'I have to ask just a few more questions before I answer that.'

'Such as?'

'I need to ask Hester about being a Jew in Denver for one thing.'

'Hester! But . . .'

'Don't worry, V. You know I wouldn't leave you alone with someone I suspected of being a murderer.'

'No . . . I know Hester would never want to hurt me but, please Edward, hurry back.'

Edward asked his questions of Maurice, Tom Sutton and Hester who told him what he wanted to know with a laugh and a shrug of her shoulders. She drove him to the airport in the morning. Harry Bragg was waiting for him or rather he was munching his way through a substantial cooked breakfast. He had made quite a few friends at the airport owing to the frequency of his visits, most particularly Ferdinando Diego – Hester's friend Ferdy – who was in charge of passport control and customs. It was a powerful position and he owed it to having a cousin in the government. Ferdy ought to have become rich on bribes and no doubt his cousin had counted on it but, in fact, he was too honourable – or, as he said, too lazy, to take advantage of the opportunities he had for 'doing favours'.

Shortly after take-off, Harry started complaining of stomach cramps. 'Sorry, old man,' he shouted over the engine noise. 'Ferdy insisted on my having the mushrooms even though I said they tasted funny. They must have been poisonous or something. I'm a damn fool. I say, I think I'm going to have to find a field to land in.'

Anxiously, Edward stared out of the window, looking for some patch of grass flat enough and long enough for the Rapide to land in safety, but they were passing over a rocky landscape without even a road or track worth the name. The aeroplane began to shake and judder as Harry was convulsed by agonising pains. Edward had never flown a Rapide but it was becoming increasingly obvious that he was going to have to now. With startling speed, Harry's condition worsened until he was groaning pitifully. In a few moments, Edward decided, he would be unconscious. He had no time to consider whether he was competent to fly the machine. It was much more advanced than the 'knitting machines', as Harry had called them, which they had flown in Africa. The Rapide was a modern machine capable of carrying six passengers and flying long distances at speed.

With the utmost difficulty, he climbed over the seats and hauled at the pilot, who was now moaning and semi-conscious. As Edward discovered, unstrapping the body of a man from a cramped seat and tipping him to one side in the confined space of the cockpit while the aeroplane bucked like a bronco, was almost impossible. However, knowing his life depended on it, he drew on reserves of strength he had no idea he possessed and finally, the sweat running off him as if someone had left a tap running, he obtained sufficient leverage to push Harry away from the stick. He made a grab at it, almost turning the machine over on its back. Harry's body was half in and half out of the pilot's seat and, in the end, Edward could do no more than crouch in the lap of the unconscious man. The Rapide was making every effort to spin out of control, diving and swooping across the sky, sometimes so high his ears popped and some-times so low that the taller peaks threatened to end its journey in a fiery ball. For five long minutes, which Edward never forgot, he struggled with the plane as if it were a living thing and, when he finally gained control, he was vomiting, his stomach protest-ing vigorously at being tossed about like a pancake. The sweat salted his eyes so that he could hardly see and he had an ache in his back which he thought must mean he had pulled a disc.

He checked the fuel gauge and heaved a sigh of relief. There was plenty of fuel. He tried to find a map or chart and eventually discovered what he wanted stuck underneath Harry's left foot. With some difficulty, he prised it away. He knew he was only about twenty minutes from Barajas airport but, in the cavorting about the heavens, he had quite lost his sense of direction. He climbed as high as he could but saw nothing – no landmark, no river or recognisable mountain. Finally, he took hold of himself and, using chart and compass, worked out where he must be. With a heartfelt prayer, he turned the Rapide in what he believed to be the direction of the airport. After fifteen minutes of flying, it was with enormous relief that he recognised the outskirts of Madrid and then, shining like a beacon in the sun, the control tower.

When he was over the airport, he flew in front of the tower and waved at the astonished Ferdy, who recognised him in the cockpit. It crossed his mind that either Ferdy had not eaten the mushrooms he had pressed on his guest, or Harry's poisoning was caused by something quite different. He had no way of alerting Ferdy, or anyone else, that he had no idea how to land the Rapide but they seemed to understand his predicament all the same. When he had made another circuit of the airport, he could see several figures running around on the tarmac waving their hands and signalling wildly. Edward grinned. Presumably they knew what they wanted him to do, but he hadn't the foggiest idea. However, the landing strip was clear so, taking a deep breath, he reduced speed and height.

It was a close-run thing. He landed much too fast and hard, careering well beyond the end of the runway and jerking to a halt on the grass a few yards from some bewildered-looking sheep. With his last remaining strength, he pushed open the door and almost fell on to the blessed earth – blessed even though he had chosen to fall on a pile of sheep droppings. He was soon surrounded by a dozen or more men who raised him to his feet and lifted out the unconscious Bragg, exclaiming the whole time in a mixture of English and Spanish.

'Is there a doctor?' he asked, when he could make himself heard. His voice sounded unnaturally hoarse and his throat felt as dry as the landscape he had been flying over. 'He has eaten something . . . poisonous.'

There was no doctor but one of the men in uniform seemed to have some medical training. He tried to make Harry vomit and succeeded in rousing him enough to make him throw up some of his breakfast. Then they carried him to a car and drove off at high speed.

'But you must go back to the city and rest,' Ferdy was saying. Edward lay exhausted in Ferdy's armchair in the control tower, sipping gratefully at black coffee laced with brandy.

'I've got to get to London. I think I've got the hang of the Rapide now,' he said, trying to sound confident.

Ferdy was horrified. 'No, no, meelor, I forbid it. You cannot fly. It is not possible.'

'I don't see why not. There's nothing wrong with the machine as far as I can see. My landing was a bit rough, I admit, but practice makes perfect.'

Edward had considered trying to find out how Harry had been poisoned but really, what was the point? He didn't believe Ferdy was involved. The latter had taken it for granted that the poisoning had been accidental and it would be unforgivably mean-spirited to rub his nose in the reality. Someone in the airport kitchen had been suborned into eliminating Lord Edward Corinth and, if it meant killing someone else as well, it wasn't going to hold him – or her – back. It rather pleased Edward to feel that he was so close to the truth he had got his murderer worried enough to try and bump him off. He never doubted for one moment that the same hand had also been responsible for the attack on Verity and the murder of Godfrey Tilney. And yet, paradoxically, he still believed he would discover what lay behind the murders in England rather than in Spain.

'We shall send to Madrid for another pilot.'

'No, Ferdy, old lad, no time for that. Just do us a favour and top up the tank and I'll be away. I think I've got navigation and landing licked but I don't want to do either in the dark.'

He wanted to be off before his enemy could try anything else to stop him getting to England.

'The English! You are mad,' Ferdy responded, shrugging his shoulders to indicate admiration mixed with exasperation. His surrender was absolute and he went over the charts with Edward, pointing out the difficulties he might face. The Rapide was refuelled and Ferdy watched with apprehension as Edward taxied it across the grass to the beginning of the runway. He had to close his eyes as the aeroplane roared down the tarmac and then sighed with relief as it climbed into the sky and disappeared towards France. He decided to telephone his friend the Baroness. She would want to know what had happened. Edward had absolutely forbidden him to tell Verity how close he had come to ending his life over the ochre plains of Léon but he had said nothing about not communicating with Hester Lengstrum.

23

At Croydon, he was met by Fenton in the Lagonda and was driven not to London but to Mersham Castle.

'A good flight, my lord?' Fenton inquired, as he accelerated through Croydon.

'Not bad, thank you, Fenton. Harry Bragg got taken ill so I flew the bird myself. Easy to master, I'm glad to say. Got lost just the once and almost had to land in the Champs Elysées but saw the Eiffel Tower . . . in time, thank goodness.'

'Indeed, my lord!'

'Just my little joke, Fenton.'

He had, in truth, had some extremely anxious moments over Paris and some minutes later a passing seagull might have heard him abusing the Almighty for the width of the English Channel as he watched his fuel gauge drop perilously close to the red. He considered that, for an idle aristocrat with more money than sense, he seemed to be busier than many of his friends who took the nine-five from Sevenoaks each morning and spent the day behind an office desk.

'Ned, you look tired out. Was the flight exhausting?'

'Not particularly, Connie. Just getting old.'

'How is Verity?'

'On the mend, but it was a near thing. The blow on her head was meant to kill.'

'How dreadful! You must be so worried. I have written to her.'

'Yes, that was good of you, Connie.'

'Come and have tea in the gun room. Gerald is itching to hear what you've been up to.'

'Gerald's up and about then? That's very good news.'

'Yes, he's almost his old self – complaining about the weather, the food, and blaming it all on the government.'

Edward laughed. 'And Elizabeth? She's gone back to the hospital?'

'Well, I don't know that she has. She was supposed to. She's been wanting to leave for some time but we've pressed her to stay on. Finally, at the end of last week, I had to agree that Gerald was well enough to manage without a hospital nurse. The trouble is, of course, she's become essential to him – to us both. She's been a true companion and I really don't know what I'm going to do without her. Gerald is already beginning to play up. That's one reason why I'm so pleased you're here. He is better of course – much better – but he's still not quite right. He gets very tired and he's irritable. He likes to be entertained.'

'Sounds to me like he's got very selfish,' said Edward bluntly.

'Oh well, I'd just say he's got used to being the centre of attention and being waited on hand and foot.'

'Looks to me as if he needs to be shaken up a bit.'

'Part of the problem is that he feels so useless. He reads *The Times* and gets depressed by the news and feels he can't do anything about it. You know how badly it hit him when he had to give up those dinners.'

The year before, the Duke had planned a series of dinners at which influential people from all sides of the political spectrum could meet important Germans informally to exchange views and seek ways of cementing Anglo-German relations. Unfortunately, the poisoning of General Craig at one of these occasions had made it impossible for them to continue, even though the murder was in no way connected with politics.

'You do look tired, Ned. Can't you take a holiday?'

'I can't take a holiday because I'm not one of the world's workers, am I?' he answered cheerfully. 'As Verity's always telling me, I'm a fully paid-up member of the idle rich.'

'But you must rest from all this travelling. What are you doing anyway? I thought David Griffiths-Jones was no longer in prison.'

'No, but I have still to find out who killed Stephen Thayer

and who knocked Verity on the head. The same person perhaps – but then again, perhaps not.'

'But can't you leave that to the police, Ned? You're not ... you're not Sherlock Holmes.'

'Spanish police, bless them, have other things to worry about. As for the egregious Chief Inspector – I have absolutely no faith in him whatsoever. Charles wants to know the truth about his father's murder and I gave him my word that I would find out. It's as simple as that.'

'It doesn't sound simple.'

'But tell me more about Elizabeth. I don't quite understand. Why hasn't she gone back to the hospital now Gerald doesn't need her?'

'I'm not sure she's ever going back. I'm rather worried, actually. I wondered if you could go over and see her and find out what the problem is. I felt she and I could talk about anything but, after you left for Madrid, she ... changed. She couldn't have been sweeter. I don't mean her manner to me changed except that she wouldn't confide in me. Did you upset her in some way before you went? I may be wrong but I think it's to do with you.'

'Me?'

'Did you say something to upset her?'

Connie had had hopes of Elizabeth Bury but something had happened which had made her fight shy of Mersham. She guessed it was to do with her brother-in-law because she had first talked about leaving soon after she had returned from London when she had had dinner with him. It was all most unfortunate: Gerald had behaved like a spoiled child when she insisted on leaving and Connie had had moments when she could cheerfully have strangled them both.

'I thought you might like to invite her to the Fourth of June. Gerald feels he's well enough to go and, to be honest, I think either he or I will burst a blood vessel if he doesn't get out of here soon. Anyway, I know Frank is counting on you being there.'

She wondered if she was being too direct. Would her brother-in-law feel he was being manipulated and shy away from taking up with Elizabeth again? To her relief, Edward said, 'Good idea. She hasn't got a telephone, has she? I'll walk over to Lower

Mersham and surprise her.' Elizabeth had a cottage in the village, which was hardly more than a hamlet, about three miles away. 'Of course, she may not be there.'

'As far as I know, she is. I had a rather cross call from the matron at the hospital almost accusing me of kidnapping her but I explained it was nothing to do with us . . . I am right, aren't I?' she added, looking at her brother-in-law questioningly.

Rosemary Cottage was a tiny house – one up, one down – approached by a wicket gate and a narrow gravel path beside which sweet peas draped themselves over bamboo stakes and hollyhocks stood sentry. On that first day of June, it seemed that English summer had finally decided to appear in all its buxom beauty. The cottage eaves were embraced by wisteria which seemed to break over them like spindrift. Pink and white roses climbed carelessly over the porch, threatening to engulf it, and jasmine and honeysuckle mingled their sweet scents so intoxicatingly that Edward forgot the speech he had rehearsed that morning in the shaving mirror. He had been to the cottage before, of course, but had never gone inside. He had walked Elizabeth over from the castle two or three times in the spring when she had been nursing his brother, but had always left her on the step, raising his hat and saying goodbye as if she were just an acquaintance. Now he knocked on the door with some trepidation. It was hard to believe that in this most English of paradises a snake might lurk. How could evil breathe such air and survive? And yet . . . he had unfinished business with the occupant of the cottage which he very much feared might . . . might not be pleasant to conclude.

He sighed and knocked once more on the door, disturbing a flake of paint. He stood there for a minute hoping that Elizabeth might be away from home. It was not quiet there on the doorstep. The songs of many birds, most of which he could not hope to identify, assailed his ears but he did recognise the 'pink-pink' of the chaffinch and the almost devilish scream of the swift. But louder than birdsong, he heard the beat of his own heart and the sound of his own breath. He could not forget that he had told Elizabeth he loved her and she had answered . . . how? By telling him that she had once been married to Makepeace Hoden. Then, there had been no time for questions to be asked or answered. Now there was time but, on Edward's part, very little inclination.

'I'm so sorry, were you looking for me? Oh Edward, it's you. I heard you were back and I wondered if you would come and see me.'

He started at the sound of the cool, clear voice behind him. She had not been inside the cottage but out walking. While he had been away in Madrid he had almost forgotten why he had thought he was in love with her but now it all came back. She had the serenity of an old-fashioned English rose – a cool, clean beauty which relied on a clear eye, a faultless complexion and a grace of movement which had captivated him before and which did so again now. She was wearing a straw hat with a white rose attached to the brim, a long white dress, flat-heeled 'sensible' shoes and carried a trug on one arm.

'Elizabeth! I didn't think you were in and I was just about to depart in sorrow . . . Here, let me take that from you,' he said, reaching for the trug. 'It looks heavy. You've been stocking up, I see.'

'Yes, I've been over to Mersham.'

'To the castle?'

'No, to the village. I needed a few things from the shop. And you were just passing, I suppose?' she inquired with a smile.

'No,' he admitted. 'I came over to talk if you have the time. We never got round to finishing that conversation we were having about . . . about your husband.'

'About Makepeace?' she said vaguely. 'Oh,' she said, putting a hand on his arm and looking at him earnestly, 'I meant to ask: how is Verity? Is she better? I do hope so. Did you find out who attacked her?'

She seemed disinclined to pursue the subject of her marriage.

'I've got a good idea who it was.'

'The same person who killed Stephen Thayer?'

'Perhaps, but I rather think not. That's why I'm here, to make sure.'

'I don't understand. What can I tell you? I would like to help if I could but I don't see how I can.'

'But I think you can, Elizabeth. You can start by telling me what you meant about Makepeace.'

267

'Yes, of course, but I don't see what it's got to do with . . . but don't let's stand here. Come through to the garden and I'll get you a drink. I'm afraid it has to be either water or lime juice.'

'Lime juice, please.'

Instead of opening the front door Elizabeth led him round the outside of the cottage to a small patch of grass upon which two ancient deck-chairs rested wearily. Gingerly, he sat himself down, half-expecting the canvas to tear under his weight. Elizabeth opened the back door, which was unlocked, and he heard her filling a jug. When she returned and had poured two glasses, she sat down beside him. 'This is such a peaceful place, isn't it?'

'And so beautiful,' he answered her, looking out over the flower beds to the fields and a streak of water in the distance which was the River Mersham. 'You know,' he said seriously, 'whenever I think of England, I think not of London, nor even of Mersham Castle, but of this. I have a favourite walk on the hills behind us and, looking down from there, this is what I see. I believe this is what my elder brother Frank went to fight for in France.' He sipped his juice, which was sour but refreshing.

'And shall we have to fight for it again?' Elizabeth asked gently.

'I pray not but I fear . . . I fear we may have to.'

She looked at him wide-eyed. 'But not yet,' she said falteringly.

'No, not yet. Perhaps never. You mustn't let me frighten you. I suppose I'm just a little depressed.'

'Because of what happened to Verity?'

'Yes, and I feel surrounded by evil somehow. Oh God! There I go again. I'm being absurdly melodramatic.'

'I suppose, as a nurse, I ought to be used to pain and suffering but I'm not.'

'Is that why you haven't gone back to the hospital?'

'I don't know. I ought to have gone back but somehow I didn't think I could face it . . . not just yet.'

'I know so little about you, Elizabeth. Your father was a clergyman?'

'Yes, but he died when I was very young and my mother married again.'

'A wicked stepfather?'

'Oh no! Certainly not. I loved him and he . . . loved me. But he too died.'

'I'm so sorry. You don't seem to have had much luck.'

'I've nothing to complain about. Many people have had much worse a time.'

'You mean because of the war?'

'In the war . . . yes,' she said looking into the distance. Then, visibly taking a grip on herself she added, 'You said you thought . . . I could tell you something which would help you . . . My husband's death – might that be connected with Stephen Thayer's?'

'Yes, it might, and also Godfrey Tilney's in Spain.'

'But how could anyone have possibly been involved in all three deaths?'

'That's what I want you to help me find out. Maybe I'm wrong but I think the deaths are linked.'

He glanced at Elizabeth. She looked 'the picture of innocence', as his nanny used to say. 'You didn't come here by accident, did you Elizabeth?'

'To Mersham?' she prevaricated, but there was a quiver in her voice.

'To Mersham, to look after my brother. You see, I'm not easily convinced by coincidences. When you look at a coincidence carefully, it usually begins to resemble something else.'

She hesitated. 'I knew you would say that, Edward, and I was determined to lie to you but . . . I can't.'

She turned away her head and took a sip of lime juice as if to steady herself.

'I wish you would tell me the truth. So many horrid thoughts cross my mind which I would like to banish.'

'I did come to work here at the hospital on purpose so I might get to meet you, but nursing your brother was . . . accidental.'

'You mean it was a happy coincidence he had his fall?' Edward inquired sarcastically.

'No, of course not. I did everything I could to help him get better. I'm a nurse . . .'

'So why did you want to meet me?'

'It was something my husband told me, the day before he was killed.'

'So you are sure he was killed? It wasn't an accident or . . . suicide.'

'No, I'm sure of it. He had been very nervous for about a week but I hadn't taken much notice of it. He was very secretive. I thought . . .'

'Yes?'

'I thought he might be being blackmailed.'

'Blackmailed! What about?'

'Oh God, do you really want to hear about it? It's . . . it's so awful . . . I can hardly bear to think about it. It was just so . . . such a relief when he . . . when he wasn't there any more. A weight was lifted off me – off my heart. That's a wicked thing to say, I know.'

Edward saw that she was crying. He put down his glass and took her hand. If she were acting, then she was a consummate actress. 'Tell me,' he said firmly.

'It's so horrible,' she repeated in a low voice. 'I believe it was Eton.'

'Eton?'

'Yes, it made him what he was – and his parents, of course. I think they call it a pederast. I looked it up in the dictionary.'

Edward blanched. Whatever he had imagined, he had never thought of this. It was . . . disgusting. 'He liked boys?'

'Yes.' She still had hold of his hand but would not look at him.

'You were married – how long?'

'Long enough . . . two years.'

'And did he . . .? You didn't have any children.'

'That wasn't the reason,' she said breathlessly. 'He made love to me. I thought it was all normal . . . but he was away a lot. Then things happened . . . I found some photographs . . . of some Venetian boys – naked – taken by a German a long time ago, fifty years ago, Makepeace said. He told me they were art, and I tried to believe him.'

'How do you know they were Venetian boys?' asked Edward fatuously.

'They were gondoliers – they were photographed against famous views of Venice,' she answered, without seeming to mind.

'What else?'

270

'Oh, I don't know ... little things. After a bit, it was as if he didn't care.'

'Didn't care?'

'He didn't really mind if I knew. I found ... I found other photographs ... horrible things. Then he started telling me things.'

'Telling you things?'

'About what he did when he was away ... abroad. I told him I didn't want to know ... that he disgusted me. That was when he began to hit me.'

'He hit you? Once?'

'Often ... mainly when he was drunk but, worst of all, when he wasn't. That was when he seemed evil. It was as if he liked making me suffer. He said he should have been like Tolstoy and given me his diaries to read before we got married. I said I didn't know what he meant so he explained. Apparently, Tolstoy had disgusting habits ... about sex, I mean, and he made his fiancée read his diary so she would forgive him and they could begin their married life with a clean slate. But she was disgusted by him ...'

'But you went to Africa with him ... on safari?'

'Yes, it was supposed to be a fresh start. I had threatened to divorce him but he begged me not to. He said he would commit suicide if I did.'

'I don't understand. Do you think he still loved you?'

'In a way I think he did, but it wasn't that. It was his reputation. The scandal ... he couldn't have faced people.'

Edward thought for a moment. That certainly rang true. If what Elizabeth hinted at had become public knowledge, no one respectable would have had anything to do with him. He might even have gone to prison.

'Also, as I told you, I think he was being blackmailed and I was ...'

'Cover?'

'Protection. I think he thought I could protect him.'

'And you think he *was* being blackmailed?'

'Yes. Of course, I didn't have much idea about money but he always seemed to have plenty.'

'Yes, I know.'

'Of course, I'd forgotten for a moment that you were at Eton together . . . His father was a wastrel. He hated his father. He said he beat him and he beat his mother. Do you think violence is hereditary?'

'Perhaps. If as a child you learn that bullying weaker members of the family is "normal", it must affect you. But you were saying – about the money.'

'Oh yes, the money. When we were first married we seemed to be very rich and, after his parents died, he inherited a lot from them. I don't know how much. He would never discuss money with me. He said it wasn't women's business.'

'But later there seemed to be less money?' Edward prompted.

'We always had money. I don't think it was that which worried him. As I say, it was his reputation. He didn't want to be "drummed out of his club".' Elizabeth smiled wryly. 'His behaviour changed. He got nervy and . . . and he took it out on me.'

'I see. But you have no idea who was blackmailing him?'

'No, but the day before he was killed he said if anything happened to him I was to try and find you.'

'Me? Why should he suddenly think of me, I wonder?'

'Makepeace said a friend – he didn't tell me his name – had said you had helped him and had been good at getting to the bottom of . . . of problems – something like that. I can't remember his exact words. Didn't you investigate a murder at the castle last year?'

'Yes . . . I wonder who he meant.'

'He said the friend had killed himself in the end but that you had tried to help him.'

Edward was silent. He knew now who Hoden's friend had been. It was a young Member of Parliament who had been at that fateful dinner at Mersham Castle when old General Craig had been poisoned. He had been destined for a cabinet post but money troubles and women had put paid to it all. He sighed.

'Yes, I do know who he was talking about. So your husband . . . what did he say? Try and remember his words as closely as you can.'

'He said that if anything happened, there was money enough for revenge. He didn't want to "die like a pig" . . .'

'That's what he said?'

272

'Those were his words, yes. He didn't want to die like a pig and if he did he wanted justice . . .'

'Revenge or justice?'

'Revenge, he said revenge. And you might get it for him. It was I who wanted justice,' she added.

'Did he say anything else?'

'Yes. He said you were an Etonian so you would understand. Do you know what he meant?'

'Maybe. Look, will you come with me to Eton for the Fourth of June? Connie's very keen on it.'

'The Fourth of June? The Eton holiday, you mean. I remember Makepeace talking about it but he never went back – at least not with me.'

'Yes. I think it's important.'

'Why?'

'Trust me.'

'Of course I trust you but . . . but won't it be embarrassing? People would wonder why I was there.'

'They would think it was because I invited you; simple as that.'

'Not quite, Edward. You see, don't think I'm being . . . silly, but I get the feeling Connie thinks you and I . . . well, you know. I don't want to give her any false hopes.' She smiled at him.

'Would she be so wrong . . . in her hopes, I mean?'

'Edward, I . . . I think we ought to clear all this up first before we talk about anything else.' She spoke seriously and obviously meant what she said but left her hand in his. 'Anyway, what about Verity?'

'What do you mean: "what about Verity?"' Edward said crossly, removing his hand. 'I wish people didn't jump to conclusions all the time. I like Verity, I respect her but we're not . . . we're not that way. She's in love with an American novelist – a man called Belasco. But then, you know Belasco, don't you? Wasn't he in Kenya when your husband died?'

'I believe he was,' Elizabeth answered vaguely, 'but I never met him.'

'So you'll come?' Edward said brusquely.

'I haven't got anything to wear.'

'Oh bosh. Connie will lend you something.'

She smiled at him. 'You really want me to come?'

'Yes, I do. Otherwise I wouldn't have asked you.'

'Well then, I'll come. What time do we have to be there?'

'About twelve. I'll pick you up from here about ten. We'll wander round with Frank, if he's not playing cricket, look at the school and watch some cricket perhaps. Don't be alarmed, it won't be for long. Then we'll have lunch and after that watch the afternoon parade of boats.'

'What's that?'

'The school eights and a few other odds and sods row up the river in all their finery. But the fun is that they try and stand up holding their oars and, with any luck, at least one of them falls in. Childish, I know, but fun all the same. The whole thing is repeated when it's dark and then there are fireworks. But I want to get there a bit early because I want to talk to my old Dame again. I think she has the secret.'

'What secret?'

'She told me something about why your husband, Godfrey Tilney and Stephen Thayer were thrown out of the school but she wouldn't tell me the whole of it. I think I can persuade her now.'

'And you think all three were murdered because of something that happened when they were schoolboys?'

'I know it sounds preposterous, but yes, I do. You know the expression "revenge is a dish best served cold"?'

'Yes, but that cold? You really think someone would wait – what is it – nearly twenty years before taking revenge for some schoolboy prank?'

'I think this might have been more than a prank. But yes, I do think people can harbour hate in their hearts for years waiting for the moment when they can do something about it.'

Elizabeth shivered. 'I'm not sure. You see, I think I know why my husband was killed.'

'You do?'

'Yes. You know I said we went on this safari as a sort of new beginning – a second honeymoon, Makepeace called it.'

'But the safari didn't really help?'

'Well, he made an effort to be nice to me, and I quite enjoyed myself.'

'Did you shoot game yourself?'

'No. The animals are so beautiful. It was enough just to see them. I hated the idea of killing elephants or lions.'

'But your husband . . .?'

'He'd never done it before but he loved it. He said he would die happy if he could kill a lion first. We had separate tents because I didn't need to wake up at dawn like Makepeace.'

'Yes, you have to be in position before the sun gets up and the heat drives the animals into the long grass to sleep.'

'I'd forgotten, Connie said you had been in Africa.'

'It was the happiest time of my life. One day I want to go back and live there.'

Elizabeth looked at him strangely. 'I hate the place,' she said.

'Of course, you must do,' Edward said in confusion. 'So what happened?'

'Well, as I say, I didn't have to get up so early but I wasn't sleeping very well so I often *did* wake before dawn. We weren't allowed to wander around but I liked to walk to the edge of the camp and watch the dawn. It is the most beautiful sight in the world, don't you think? The mist rolling back to reveal great expanses of grassland and maybe some animal walking across the view as though . . . as though you weren't even there.'

'Yes,' Edward said, remembering the African dawns he had seen.

'Anyway, on the day Makepeace died, I was up before dawn and sat myself in a favourite place to watch the sun rise. And, just as the sun broke through the mist, I saw something out of the corner of my eye. Joe, one of the boys who carried our stuff, was coming out of his tent.'

'Your husband's tent?'

'Yes.'

'Perhaps he had gone to wake him?'

'That wasn't his job.'

'So you think . . .'

'Yes, I do. I was disgusted,' she said vehemently.

'Did anyone else see what you saw?'

'Yes, the head boy, a man we called Barny. I don't know what his real name was. We gave all the boys names we could pronounce.'

'And Barny saw this boy, Joe, come out of the tent? When you say "boy" . . .?'

'Yes, I know, they call all the Africans "boy", but Joe really was one.'

'And you think that Barny . . .?'

'I found out later Barny was Joe's father.'

'I see,' said Edward gravely. 'Tell me, was this a private safari? Were you the only white people there?'

'Yes, except for Captain Gates, the hunter, and his assistant. I can't remember his name, I'm afraid.'

'That was a bit unusual. Normally, there would be several people – white people – on a safari.'

'Yes, but Makepeace was adamant he wanted to be alone.'

'I see,' said Edward again, but he wasn't altogether sure he did. Elizabeth was at great pains to say that her husband had been murdered although, at the time, she had acquiesced when the authorities concluded that he had died in a shooting accident. And she was even telling him who had murdered him. Why? What wasn't she telling him? He had heard of Gates. He was a famous 'white hunter'. It was extremely unlikely that he had been involved in anything shady. But he was rumoured to be something of a ladies' man. Might he have been 'entertaining' Elizabeth . . .? He looked at her sitting beside him. She seemed to be innocence itself – her skin a little browned by the sun, her auburn hair escaping from under her hat so that she unconsciously swept the strands away from her face with the back of her hand. No, damn it, he could not believe she had murdered her husband.

As if she read his thoughts, Elizabeth said, 'I didn't kill him. I won't say I did not want to . . . sometimes, but I didn't kill him.'

'I don't believe you did,' Edward said.

24

'Chief Inspector Pride says they expect to make an arrest in the next day or two.' Basil Thoroughgood looked at Edward musingly. 'I say, you look a bit off-colour, Corinth. Did you have a bad time in Spain? I was sorry to hear about Miss Browne. I gather she's on the mend though. Had the attack on her anything to do with your investigations? By the way, I should say, Pride hates your guts. But then you knew that, didn't you?'

Edward, despite Connie's protests, had taken the early train to London. 'You're not fit to travel, Ned. You must rest,' she had insisted when he had told her what he intended to do. Privately, Edward agreed with her. He had telephoned Lord Weaver and explained briefly that his pilot had been taken ill and he had flown the Rapide to Croydon himself. Weaver had expressed surprise that he knew how to fly the aeroplane and Edward had gone so far as to say it had been a surprise to him too.

He had then called the Foreign Office and Thoroughgood had told him he had the reports from Nairobi on Hoden's death but preferred not to discuss them in detail on the telephone. It was these which Edward was scanning while Thoroughgood talked. 'Hoffmann said you were polite and knew a lot about art,' he continued.

'And you, Basil. I take it from your relaxed tone that you have got your money out of his clutches.'

'I have,' Thoroughgood said smugly. 'Mind you, I think I panicked unnecessarily. I'm seriously thinking of joining one of Herr Hoffmann's schemes. He thinks I might be helpful.'

'Oh really? And what does Vansittart say?'

Thoroughgood had the grace to blush. 'Well, it's only an idea.

277

I probably won't but, you know, I have it on the best authority that the German Chancellor has no idea of engaging in a war with England. He admires the British Empire.'

'That's what your chum Hoffmann says, is it, Basil? If I were you, I'd treat anything he tells you as if it came from the father of lies himself.'

'Miss Browne must be pleased her friend is out of gaol?'

'Yes, and I'm sure David Griffiths-Jones is very grateful for all your help – that is, if you provided any.'

'What do you mean, you ungracious man? Didn't I get you a vital two weeks' grace to find out . . . that Tilney wasn't dead after all? Or rather . . .'

'Yes, well maybe. But these reports . . .' Edward waved the papers in the air. 'Do you see who they're signed by?'

'Of course, Tom Sutton. He was the official who dealt with it. You knew he had been in Nairobi before going to Spain.'

'Yes, but . . .'

'He says it was all an accident . . . and he should know. After all, he was actually there on the safari when Hoden died.'

'What!'

'Yes, didn't he tell you? He knew better than anyone what had really happened . . . the man on the spot, so to speak.'

Edward scratched his head. 'No, he didn't tell me. I thought . . .'

'What did you think?'

'I thought I knew who killed Stephen Thayer but now . . .'

'Damn it, you're not saying you suspected Tom Sutton? He's above suspicion. He's one of ours. Pity about his politics, of course . . .'

'What are his politics? It occurs to me that everyone in Madrid talks politics all the time, but not Tom Sutton. I assumed he had to be neutral because he was working at the British Embassy.'

'He's very discreet but I'm afraid he's on the left, a communist possibly. By the way, how did Griffiths-Jones take it when you asked him to be our eyes and ears in the Party?'

Edward made no reply. He was thinking furiously. At last, he said, 'Was Sutton in London when Thayer was killed?'

'No, he was in the south of Spain, I believe, getting intelligence on Mola's activities. Good man, Sutton. He's here now if you want to see him. He's being debriefed and will be going back to Spain at the end of the week.'

'He's here now, in London? Has he got a flat here or something?'

'Yes, at least I think he stays with friends but I can get his address if you want it but ... are you going down to Eton for the Fourth? I'm taking him down – trying to get him to see it's not quite such a bad place after all. If you're going, I'm sure you'll see him there.'

'That reminds me: do you remember a scandal when we were at Eton?'

'A scandal?'

'A film star "entertained" Eton boys at a hotel near the school. Thayer was one of them. Hoden and Tilney too, I believe. It got into the papers.'

'I do remember something about it. Thayer was sacked, wasn't he?'

'Yes. They all were.'

'So what?'

'The film star – a woman called Dora Pale – had a son at the school. He was younger than Thayer – in my year though I didn't know him. He committed suicide. His father was Max Federstein – the Jewish oil millionaire. Thayer never said anything to you about it?'

'No, never! You think it has some bearing on all of this?'

'Maybe. I'll know for sure soon enough.'

It was almost a tradition that the Duke travel to Eton on the Fourth of June in his Rolls-Royce. The least likely of men to advertise his wealth and position in society, there was something about visiting his son at school which made him throw off all his natural reserve. When Connie had once questioned him about this uncharacteristic desire to display himself like a peacock, he came up with a host of explanations – none of which were altogether convincing. He wanted Frank to 'keep his end up' amongst all those tradesmen's sons; he had no fear of embarrassing anyone because 'they're all a damn sight richer than me, Connie dear'; he loved his Rolls-Royce – a Phantom II he had bought in 1930 and the last car actually designed by Royce before his death in 1933. The Duke had considered Royce to be a friend and, when he died, he had the RR grille badge, which was red, replaced with a black one. It was a magnificent beast and the Duke liked to ride in it, particularly when he was feeling depressed. He sometimes drove it himself with his chauffeur sitting beside him like a stuffed dummy but not, of course, on occasions like the Fourth of June.

As it happened, the Duke's chauffeur was ill so Edward volunteered Fenton's services. 'He's the best driver I know, far better than me,' he said encouragingly.

The Rolls stopped at Elizabeth's cottage to collect her and was at once surrounded by half a dozen admiring village children who received halfpennies from the Duke, who was at his most avuncular. He was in high spirits. He was going to see his son of whom he was inordinately proud. He had Edward beside him with a girl he credited with saving his life and whom he considered the epitome of feminine grace and beauty.

'You know,' he had said to Connie that morning at breakfast, before Edward had surfaced, 'I know I'm an old fuddy-duddy, but I think Elizabeth is just the sort of gel a chap with any sense would be proud to make his wife. She's no fool, she's warm-hearted, pretty as a picture, and gentle. That's what I like about her: she's gentle, not aggressive like . . .'

'For goodness' sake, Gerry,' said his wife in alarm. 'If you even hint at any of this in front of Ned, he'll run a mile. No young man with any spirit wants to marry a chintz sofa.'

'Whatever do you mean, Connie? Who said anything about sofas? I just . . .'

At that moment Edward appeared, bleary-eyed but not so sleepy that he could not pick up the atmosphere. 'Have you two been fighting?' he inquired, waving a finger in the air.

'Don't be ridiculous, Ned,' Connie said.

'I've got it! You've been talking about me. I can sense it,' he said, scooping scrambled egg from a silver chafing dish on the sideboard. He turned round and saw his brother trying – but failing – to look innocent. 'You're trying to marry me off to Elizabeth. That's it, isn't it?'

'Of course not,' Connie interjected just as the Duke said defiantly, 'Well, why not? Dem' fine gel, if you ask me. Absolutely pukka, as our pater used to say, God rest him. He'd expect you to be married by now, Ned. And Connie, it's no use you making faces at me. I will say what I want to say.'

Edward smiled. 'Tut, tut, Gerry. Didn't Connie tell you, it puts people off if their family actually *like* the girl they're thinking of marrying.'

'Poppycock!' exclaimed the Duke. 'Everyone loved Connie, when I introduced her to the family. Even awful old Aunt Matilda said she was a sensible gel and she had never been known to say anything nice about any woman.'

'Oh well,' said Edward comfortably, 'Connie's a remarkable woman and much too good for you, Gerry. The least you can do, since for some extraordinary reason she agreed to marry you, is what she tells you.'

'Cheeky young pup,' began the Duke when perhaps fortunately the butler entered the room.

'Excuse me, your Grace, but cook says will you be requiring the asparagus as well as the gulls' eggs?'

Connie had slipped away to speak to the cook, and the Duke, for once letting discretion overcome his natural urge to lecture his brother, had hidden himself behind *The Times*.

When the cottage door opened and Elizabeth appeared, Edward was quite taken aback. He had thought her lovely when he had seen her in starched white uniform at the hospital and, even more, dressed up in borrowed finery at Claridge's. Then, as she sat in her garden wearing an open-necked summer frock, her face and throat browned by the sun, he had thought her lovely but troubled. Now, chameleon-like, she had turned into an elegant, self-assured, 'Bond Street' lady in a low-waisted yellow silk dress with a flared skirt and padded shoulders. Her shoes were black and she carried lemon-yellow gloves. On her head, she wore a smart beige hat at an angle which suggested both jauntiness and untouchability.

Connie, sitting in the back, smiled at Elizabeth as Edward helped her into the car. 'My dear, you look ravishing. Gerald, doesn't she look lovely?'

'Lovely, but do buck up, Edward, or we'll be late.'

Connie was delighted to see that her husband was almost his old self again.

As Edward settled himself opposite her, Elizabeth said, as

though apologising, 'Oh, please, Connie, don't embarrass me. Connie has been so good to me, Edward. When I explained I hadn't a thing to wear she insisted on taking me in hand.'

'Well,' said Edward gallantly, 'I don't know what "taking in hand" means. Whatever you chose to wear was good enough for me, but now you look good enough to eat. No, not to eat – to dazzle.'

As he spoke, his eyes fell on Elizabeth's left hand in which she held her gloves. Perhaps the word 'dazzle' had made him think of rings. He had never seen her wearing a ring but she was wearing one today: a simple gold band. He suddenly wondered if it could possibly be the same one Verity had found in the cave and which had been taken from her finger when she had been attacked in Madrid. He was just about to dismiss the idea as wildly unlikely when, raising his eyes to her face, he saw that she had coloured. He thought about what she had told him of her marriage to Hoden. Was it possible she was wearing *his* ring? But why should she? She had hated him. Elizabeth must have seen the questions in his eyes. The mute appeal she now made to him for understanding or at least patience until they could speak in private made Edward keep silent.

The Duke had been talking away, oblivious to the involuntary communication that had passed between them but Connie – with her quick understanding and feminine insight – had seen that something had interrupted Edward's frank appreciation of the beautiful woman seated opposite him.

As Fenton drove the Rolls-Royce out of the village, she said hurriedly, 'Do you know, Ned, I think it's frightfully unfair, Frank says he has Early School, just like on any other day.'

'What's Early School?' asked Elizabeth, grateful for the diversion.

'It's the work period before breakfast,' Edward explained.

'Before breakfast?' Elizabeth was shocked. 'How can boys be expected to concentrate before they've been fed?'

'Oh, I do so agree,' Connie chimed in.

'It toughens you up for the real world,' the Duke said.

Edward said: 'This is the only day in the year when the boys can dress up as if they were in Pop – you know, the Eton Society.' Elizabeth still looked blank. 'Pop is the school's self-electing club. Prefects or monitors you would call them.'

'Oh, don't try and understand all the cant,' Connie interjected. 'It's supposed to make us women feel out of it.'

'Yes, but why is the Fourth of June the one day the boys can dress like Pop?'

'Well, members of Pop dress in colourful, flowery waistcoats while everyone else is in black – black top hat, black tails. But on the Fourth, boys can wear grey waistcoats, stick-ups – you know, a stick-up collar – and a button-hole.'

'And they can roll their umbrellas,' the Duke added impressively.

Edward grimaced. 'It's all very childish but, you see, all these little rituals and traditions bind us up, make us feel part of an elite.'

'And that's good?' Connie inquired mildly.

'Well, you sent Frank there, so you must think so,' Edward said a little crossly.

'So tell me what happens today,' Elizabeth asked.

'Oh, it's terribly tiring,' Connie said. 'You walk for miles looking at unimaginably boring cricket matches and art exhibitions. Still, some of the boys are easy on the eye.'

'Connie, I'm shocked,' Edward mocked, 'and you haven't even been at the champagne.'

'Don't be absurd, Ned. If you can enjoy looking at pretty girls, why mayn't we look at the boys?'

'Frank's good-looking, no question, and he's clever enough,' said the Duke.

'Bright as a button,' Connie said quickly, 'but he's not an intellectual like his friend Charles Thayer. I told you, didn't I, Elizabeth, about the poor boy losing his father in that dreadful way? We've rather taken him under our wing. The only person he's got to look after him is an aunt or cousin or something. He's going to spend most of the summer holidays here with us at Mersham.'

Edward saw Elizabeth bite her lip and go quite white. Rather meanly, he thought afterwards, he decided to rub it in that the boy was alone in the world. He was convinced that Elizabeth was the red-headed girl Thayer's butler, Barrington, had seen saying goodbye to him in a taxi and that she had some responsibility for his death. He had no real evidence but he had a theory – a theory he was hoping to prove this very day. He said,

'Charles is Frank's particular friend. I haven't met him since the funeral but Frank says he's taken it very bravely.'

'He says Charles is coxing Monarch,' the Duke informed him.

'Gosh, Gerry, that's an honour,' Edward said in surprise.

'Tell an ignorant woman what "Monarch" is,' Connie commanded.

'Oh, you know, it's the "eight" which is in fact rowed by ten boys in the procession of boats,' the Duke said.

'Clear as mud. I know what the procession of boats is. It's actually quite fun, Elizabeth. Just as it's getting dark, all these eights row past and the boys stand up in the boat with their oars upright in front of them.'

'Do they fall in?'

'Sometimes, but not often,' said the Duke.

'But Monarch's different. In the last century, boats could be rowed by ten or even twelve, not just eight,' Edward lectured Elizabeth, who had regained some of her poise.

'And Monarch is one of them?' she asked politely.

'Yes, and not only is it very awkward to handle but it's also rowed by drybobs as well as wetbobs – I mean boys who usually play cricket as well as those who row.'

'So they are most likely to fall in?'

'That's right, but not when they first process down the river when it's still light. About nine or ten o'clock, when it's dark, they process again and in the dark it really is difficult. Then, just short of the weir, they turn and float back downstream. That's when they stand up.'

'If there's no light, how do we see them?' Elizabeth asked.

'There are flares on the bank. After that are the fireworks, which are the climax of the whole day, but the boys are often rather "lit up" themselves by then.'

'Got at the scrumpy,' Gerald said, knowingly.

'On a wonderful hot day like today,' Connie said, 'the procession really is beautiful. The boys all wear such pretty costumes.'

'Costumes?' said Elizabeth, puzzled.

'Yes,' Edward said. 'For some reason, they dress up in costumes resembling the uniforms which midshipmen wore in Nelson's time. I don't suppose they're very accurate. Prettified Victorian versions, I expect. Anyway, it looks good.'

'But why did they choose Charles to cox Monarch?'

'Can't you guess, Connie?' the Duke said. 'They wanted to cheer him up – make him feel he has a family.'

Elizabeth was very nervous by the time they reached Eton and Fenton drew up outside Frank's house. The tangle of cars made progress very slow, despite much waving and whistle-blowing by white-gloved policemen. From that point, it made sense to walk everywhere and Fenton was told where to park and to meet them on the river bank at eight o'clock with the picnic. They were to have luncheon with Chandler, Frank's housemaster, but the evening picnic was a tradition, however wet the weather and uncomfortably crowded the situation.

Frank greeted them with enthusiasm which he tried unsuccessfully to disguise, no doubt considering it to be childish. For the first minute or two, he assumed an air of sophisticated world-weariness and professed to be bored by the whole occasion but he could not conceal his excitement at his friend's starring role in the procession of boats that evening.

He explained the significance of this to Elizabeth in considerable detail. 'Of course, he's the best fellow in the world but not everyone knew it. Now they will.'

Charles was much quieter than Frank. He talked to Edward and the Duke about the cricket and about his new passion for painting. Edward was relieved to see that the boy did not seem to have been as badly affected by his father's murder as he had feared. As they had time to spare before lunch, he said he would walk over to the art school with him to look at the exhibition which included three of his pictures. The others went off to see Frank's room.

Eton, like most English public schools, did not give the arts a high priority and the art rooms were cramped and badly in need of redecoration. Edward was therefore not expecting to find anything very startling on the walls but, when Charles shyly pointed out his own paintings, they fairly took his breath away. Instead of the insipid watercolours of cricketing scenes or views of College Chapel which he saw all around him, he found himself face to face with three dark and angry portraits all featuring the bloodied carcass of a male figure looking uncannily like butcher's meat. He looked at the boy beside him and his clear, grey eyes met his with chilling calmness. Edward said nothing but looked back at the pictures with a concentration which seemed to please Charles.

'Do you like them, sir?'

'I think "like" is too bland a word, Charles. I think they are magnificent but . . .'

'Yes?' the boy prompted him with polite interest.

'They are very fierce, very savage. Are they in any way portraits of . . . do they symbolise . . .?'

'They don't symbolise anything. They are based on a photograph of my father.'

'I see,' said Edward cautiously. 'Forgive me if I am wrong, but they seem angry. You must tell me if I am being too obvious.'

'Oh no, sir. My art master, Mr Boyd, suggested it might help relieve my feelings if I painted them. He said I shouldn't bottle them up – my feelings, that is.'

'He sounds a sensible man. But the anger . . . is that directed at his . . . his murderer?'

'Yes, sir. Frank says you will find out who he is so he can be punished.'

Edward caught his breath. This calm confidence in his powers of detection might, he feared, be unfounded. 'I hope so,' he said.

'I was so sorry to hear that your friend, Miss Browne, had been attacked. Did that have anything to do with my father's death?'

'I believe it has,' Edward replied gravely, 'but if you don't mind, I won't say anything more just at the moment. And Charles – I'm probably being absurd but I think it's just possible that you might be in some danger. I don't want to alarm you but until all this is cleared up, and that should be no more than a few days I hope, I want you to keep with the others as far as you can. Don't wander off on your own and . . . and don't go anywhere with strangers.' He saw the look in the boy's face and thought he had gone too far. 'Please, I'm sure it's nothing but . . .'

'Oh no, sir, I'm not afraid. I *want* to meet the man who killed my father. I want to ask him why he did it.'

'Well, I hope it won't come to that, my boy. Now, let's go back to the others. They will be wondering where we've got to.'

Chandler was giving a private lunch for selected boys and

their parents. Charles and his aunt had been invited at the Duke's request. Chandler was, in most respects, a sensible man who ran his house with judgement and enthusiasm. If he had a fault, it was that he was something of a snob and enjoyed having a duke's son under his wing. It was all harmless enough and Gerald, rather unexpectedly Connie thought, enjoyed a touch of sycophancy. The other parents included the Home Secretary, a man of considerable stupidity and infinite cunning with a wife who smiled and smiled but said not a word, a bishop and his wife, and a doctor whose wife complained continually about the expense of having a boy at the school. Edward was seated beside Charles Thayer's aunt, Mrs Cooper, who was now his guardian – a woman of about fifty-five, he guessed, who did not seem to fit her clothes. She gave the impression that she found her new responsibilities an almost intolerable burden. Elizabeth had Charles on one side and the bishop on the other.

Edward made a point of being friendly to Mrs Cooper but found her dull and predictable. He became even more determined that he would make Charles his charge as far as it was possible. He felt he owed it to his dead friend to keep an eye on his son and guide him through the crucial years of adolescence. Mrs Cooper, when he hinted that he would like to take an interest in her nephew, seemed gratified but he knew he had to be tactful so she would not resent his patronage.

'I'm afraid I'm too old and stupid to bring up the boy as his father would wish,' she said. Edward demurred politely. 'I know nobody and go nowhere so if you, Lord Edward, really mean to take him under your wing – well, that would be wonderful and a great weight off my shoulders.'

In a gap in the conversation, he said casually to Chandler, 'It was so good of you to put me in touch with my old Dame, Miss Harvey. I had the most interesting talk with her when I was last here. I thought I might call in on her this afternoon, if you think she would not mind.'

'Oh dear, Lord Edward, I am afraid you cannot have heard.'

'Heard what?' he said sharply.

'Miss Harvey fell downstairs only last week. Her sight was not what it was, you know.'

'Was she badly hurt?' inquired Edward, with a sinking feeling in his stomach.

'She's dead, Lord Edward. She died immediately – broke her neck, I'm afraid.'

'How ghastly,' said Connie, a glass of wine half-way to her lips suspended in mid-air.

'Yes, it was a great shock. She was old, of course. Nearly eighty-five, I believe, but we had got into the habit of thinking she was immortal.'

Edward uttered conventional regrets but his mind was racing. Someone had wanted to prevent him getting the whole story out of Miss Harvey – the secret behind the public scandal which she had refused to divulge on his first visit to her. Now he was too late. Damn, damn, damn. Why had he delayed in coming to see her? He had never dreamed that the murderer would move so swiftly and efficiently against a harmless old woman. Though, of course, she was not harmless – not to the killer. It suddenly occurred to him that he had been right to worry about Charles. He must put an end to all this danger, all this anger. His lips thinned and two heavy creases appeared on his brow. Mrs Cooper was saying something to him, but he did not hear a word. He lifted his eyes and met those of Elizabeth across the table. She was staring at him intently and her face was white beneath her suntan. In that instant he knew that Elizabeth knew who had killed Miss Harvey and who might have killed the father of the boy who sat at her side eating over-cooked lamb. He laid down his knife and fork and pushed away his plate. Suddenly, his appetite had vanished.

25

After luncheon they strolled across to School Yard where Absence was called by the headmaster on the steps of the chapel. It was an oddly impressive ritual: the slow toll of names, each boy's shouted response, the occasional silence, the repeated call to confirm that a boy had failed to appear and then a sense of loss – of something being not quite right. Elizabeth was so pale that even the Duke noticed and asked if she was feeling faint.

'It's this heat,' he said. 'Ned, there are deck-chairs in the shade on Agar's Plough. Why not take Elizabeth over there and sit her down so she can rest. There's nothing to do now except watch the cricket until the first procession of boats at six.'

'Yes, do that,' said Connie, solicitously passing Elizabeth a handkerchief soaked in eau-de-cologne. 'This will make you feel better. I never come to something like this without eau-de-cologne.'

'And we'll disappear too,' Frank said. 'I've got to help get Charles ready for the procession.'

The party broke up and Gerald and Connie went over to talk to friends. Edward, taking Elizabeth by the arm, led her across School Yard, over the ancient cobbles and past the bronze statue of Henry VI. Without either saying a word, they walked under Lupton's Tower, through the cloisters and on to the playing fields. Elizabeth's arm was limp under his and neither had eyes for the ancient beauty around them. They found two canvas chairs in the shade of a great oak. In the distance, they could see a cricket match in progress. The white-flannelled figures were too far away to be recognisable as individuals, but the occasional cheer or groan reached them on the breeze. Even the sharp crack of leather on willow could be heard above the rustle of the leaves which shaded them.

At last, Edward said, '"Regardless of their fate the little victims play." Do you know that when a boy leaves Eton he is presented with a specially bound copy of Gray's poem? It certainly touches the spot. I mean,' he said, twisting in his deck-chair to look at Elizabeth, 'in a rather sentimental way, it does remind us of the fleeting nature of happiness. One day we are children playing happily with ball and bat on a green field and the next – where are we? Old, wrinkled, disappointed, disillusioned? Is that worse than the fate of my eldest brother, Franklyn, after whom young Frank is named?'

'Playing happily, did you say?' Elizabeth said in a low voice. 'Are you so sure?'

'You mean, we are privileged here and many children have nowhere to play in safety?' Edward was by now so used to the sort of comment Verity would make that he thought he knew what Elizabeth was saying, but he was wrong.

'That too, but it's not what I mean. I know of at least one boy – a boy I think you may have heard of – who was here and who was not happy. Indeed, his unhappiness ended in his suicide.'

'Suicide! Elizabeth, you must tell me. Is it this . . . this suicide which lies behind the deaths – the four deaths we now know of? If so, someone is exacting a high price.'

She did not answer but stared unseeing toward the white specks in the distance.

'Please, Elizabeth, tell me who is playing judge and jury.'

'You know who it is,' she said, turning towards him for the first time. 'Don't you?'

'I believe I do. It's . . .' Before he could utter the name, Elizabeth held her finger against his lips and he did not finish the sentence. 'It's over now, isn't it?' he said at last. 'So why not tell me about it? I'm not a policeman. I just want to understand.'

'Oh, Edward, I wish it *was* all over,' she said bitterly. 'God knows, I want it to be. I tried to stop it. You must believe me, I tried to stop it.' Her face was wet with tears and the expression of pain on her face made her almost ugly.

'The boy . . . that was Federstein . . . Oliver Federstein, wasn't it?'

'Yes, I wasn't sure you knew. But did you know his father entered him at Eton as Featherstone?'

'Why, for God's sake?'

'Because he didn't want him to be a Jew at Eton. He thought it would help if Oliver was enrolled under the name of Featherstone. It was a fatal mistake because, of course, it was a secret that could never be kept. Whether it was the housemaster or someone else, the truth got out – that Oliver Featherstone was really a tradesman's son and a Jew.'

'But there have always been Jews at Eton.'

'Jews called Rothschild, Samuel or Seligman – a dozen or so families. I'm talking about an ordinary Jew. Rich, maybe; successful, certainly, but not one of those names. However, the bad times for Oliver began not because he was a Jew but because his father owned department stores. They called him "grocer". He tried to laugh it off but he was only thirteen and it really hurt.'

'But Max Federstein's wealth was based on oil, wasn't it?'

'Yes, but that cut no ice with certain young Etonians. He had come to England as a refugee from the pogroms. He was Russian and learnt the language of his adopted country slowly, but he loved all things English. He knew he could never be an English gentleman but he wanted . . . he wanted so badly for his son to be one.'

'And he thought he could buy it? He thought if he sent his son to Eton . . .?'

'Yes, but it didn't work. You don't remember anything about it?'

'No, I . . . I don't. It was a big school and I . . .'

'But, Edward, it was your friend Stephen Thayer who made his life a misery even if it wasn't his intention.'

'I can hardly believe it. Thayer? He didn't have any reason to. He was a success . . . he was in Pop . . . he was a hero.'

'Maybe, but he and Hoden and Tilney – those two were in Oliver's house – were in the . . . you know . . . the room?'

'The library?'

'Yes, they were in the library. They ran the house and the housemaster . . . he had no interest in it and left everything to the older boys.'

'And they bullied him?'

'They bullied him, but it was more than that. You see, Oliver wasn't good at games and he wasn't too bright but he did have two things going for him: he was rich – his father gave him all the money he asked for – and he was pretty.'

' "Pretty"?' said Edward with distaste.

'Yes, damn you, pretty. He was their fag – their servant . . .'

'But that's normal!'

'Is it normal for there to be a "beauty parade" of new boys? Is it normal to make the "winner" . . . do things with the older boys?'

'Do things?' said Edward faintly. 'You mean . . .'

'Yes, I do,' she said, measuring out the words as though they were links in a chain.

'Why didn't he tell someone?'

'Who could he tell? The housemaster? He was never there.'

'His father?'

'How could he tell his father who was so proud of him . . . was so proud he was at Eton with lords and dukes . . .' she said with withering scorn.

'He didn't have any friends?' Edward asked, shocked to the core by what he was hearing.

'He had no friends . . . he was isolated. A small boy alone and abused by people who should have cared for him. But that was not all. Your friend Stephen Thayer . . . your hero . . . he found out . . . it wasn't difficult . . . that Oliver's mother was not an ordinary woman but a film star.'

'Dora Pale,' Edward said flatly.

'Yes, Dora Pale, as you discovered. It changed everything. Dora Pale was famous . . . glamorous . . . shocking. Thayer was entranced. He said everything would be different for Oliver if he invited his mother down to the school, and for a time it was. He was popular . . . he was even happy.' Again, Elizabeth's voice was drenched with bitterness.

'Until . . .?'

'Until he found out that his mother was . . . was "entertaining" Thayer and his friends in the hotel at Bray.'

'She must have been mad!'

'She was mad by all accounts. She was a dope fiend and she liked . . . and she liked sex.' She spat out the word. 'She was a nymphomaniac.'

292

'Oh God! And Oliver found out?'

'No, he did not find out. He was told. Hoden, who preferred little boys to vamps, wanted to do something horrible with him and he refused. So Hoden taunted him; told him he was . . . he was a whore and his mother was a whore. Told him everything.'

'Oh no!'

'Oh yes! . . . oh yes! But he didn't believe what had been said about his mother so he ran to the hotel where she was staying and found . . . and found her in bed with Stephen.'

'And what did he do?' Edward almost whispered.

'You know what he did. He went out and drowned himself. He died because the two people he loved best in the world betrayed him. Can you understand *that*?'

'Yes,' he said miserably. 'I can.'

'Dora Pale died of her . . . of her vices quite soon after her son committed suicide. Of course, Oliver's death was hushed up. They said it was an accident. They took the stones out of his pockets and threw them back into the river so no one would know.'

'But *you* know. How do you know so much about him? Did you know him?'

'He was my stepbrother.'

'Your stepbrother! Then . . .'

'Yes, Max Federstein married my mother. Max – I always called him Max – you can imagine, was distraught when he heard of Oliver's death and he didn't believe it had been an accident. Oliver wasn't much good at games but he could swim. So Max set a private detective on it and eventually he got the whole story.'

'But the detail – how could you know about Hoden and . . .?'

'Because my darling husband *told* me – just before he died. That's how.'

'What did Federstein do when he had the private detective's report?'

'He did nothing. He couldn't bring himself to do anything. Eton was everything he believed in. He didn't believe in any god but he did believe – poor fool – in the idea of the English gentleman.'

'He remarried?'

'Yes, he married his nurse, would you believe it?' she said

sarcastically. 'After Oliver died he had some sort of nervous breakdown and was ill for about a year.'

'And you were her daughter?'

'Yes. My father was a clergyman and, when he died, he left my mother badly off so she went back to nursing.'

'And she became Max Federstein's nurse?'

'They fell in love. Max was utterly dependent on her and my mother loved him for his gentleness and, I imagine, because he had suffered so much. My mother was deeply Christian and compassionate.'

'And how did you feel about it?'

'I was suspicious at first, I suppose, but then I came to love Max. He was the most lovely man. He may have been a shrewd businessman but in ordinary life he was . . . oh, hopeless. He was so trusting . . . It was his good fortune to meet my mother and not some gold-digging hussy who would have stripped him of everything and made him miserable.'

'When did you hear about Oliver?'

'I think he told my mother almost the first time they met. He was so devastated he couldn't have kept it to himself. I heard a bit about it from her but not the whole story . . . not until he died.'

'He died quite soon after he married your mother?'

'Yes, just a couple of years. He never properly recovered but there was time enough for me to get to know him . . . to get to love him.'

'And when he died . . .?' Edward gently prompted her.

'When he died, he left me a huge amount of money . . .'

'But I thought you had no money . . . that was why you were nursing.'

'I never said so! I was brought up to value work. I didn't have any desire to lead the life of your rich friends. Anyway, there was something else my stepfather left me . . . a letter.'

'A letter?'

'It was a long letter about how he loved me and how he wished we could have known each other for longer . . .' Elizabeth took out a handkerchief and blew her nose. Edward kept silent. 'He also told me the whole story of Oliver and he included the report written by the private detective. He said that, when I was older, I was to use some of the money to take revenge on my stepbrother's murderers.'

Edward was deeply shocked. 'That was a terrible thing for him to have done.'

'To have left me such a legacy?'

'To have laid such a burden on you. You ought to have torn up the letter.'

'And done nothing?'

'Yes, done nothing. I don't understand why you felt you had to do what he asked. Surely you knew that violence resolves nothing.'

Elizabeth looked at him in amazement. 'You don't understand anything, do you? I loved my stepfather. He was a good man. He had been cheated by his first wife and by the "English gentlemen" he trusted. He had lost his only son – the boy he lived for. Love . . . it's the most powerful thing in the world. It makes you do things you could never imagine doing in cold blood.'

'I do know what you mean. I feel about Frank in that way . . .'

'And Verity . . .?' she said wryly.

Edward did not answer. He sighed. 'So what happened?'

'When my mother died five years ago, I thought I ought to do something about my stepfather's letter. I decided to find Make-peace Hoden.'

'How did you do that?'

'Oh, that was no problem. I wrote to the school.'

'To Eton?'

'Yes, and they couldn't have been more helpful. I said I was a friend of his but we had lost touch and I wanted to see him again. They sent me his address by return.'

'Did you intend to kill him?'

'I intended to make his life a misery.'

'But instead he made *your* life a misery.'

'Yes. I was a fool. I saw he was looking for a wife. I didn't ask myself why. I thought that if I could marry him I would have him in my power. You can see how husbands and wives make each other suffer, even when they don't intend to. Look at my stepfather and Dora Pale.'

'And he married you just like that?'

'It turned out he had his own reasons. I thought I was clever but he was cleverer. I discovered much later, when he was doing his best to humiliate me, that before he decided to marry me he had hired a private detective to find out all about me. That was the sort of man he was.'

'So he knew you were Oliver's stepsister before he married you?'

'Yes. There I was thinking I was in control but he had me checkmate all along.'

'How long after your marriage did you discover he . . . liked boys?'

'After just a few months he told me he had only married to protect himself.'

'To protect himself . . .?'

'Yes. No one could accuse him of being . . . perverted if he had a wife. That was when I started to hate him. Up till then I wanted revenge for my stepfather's sake and for Oliver's. It was . . . theoretical . . . abstract.'

'But now it was flesh and blood?'

'Yes, now I saw he was using me. I could see with my own eyes what it meant to be a child in that man's clutches. This was the reality. I didn't need to use my imagination. I tell you, Edward, I could not bear to let him touch my hand.'

'Did he mind that you were disgusted by him?'

'When I discovered what sort of pervert he was – that was when I told him who I was – do you know how he reacted? He laughed. He laughed and laughed and then he sat me down and told me that he had known all about me before we were married.'

'So you decided to kill him?'

'Yes . . . no. I fell in love. This man . . . he was on that safari. He was helping Johnny, our "white hunter". He was everything my husband wasn't. We loved each other the first moment we met. I know it sounds ridiculous but we did. I told him every-thing. Perhaps I shouldn't have. He said he . . . don't laugh, Edward . . . he said he was my knight in shining armour and would kill for my honour . . . to win me.'

Edward had never felt less like laughing. 'You got your lover to kill for you?'

Elizabeth shivered, despite the heat. 'It wasn't like that. I told you . . .' Her voice tailed off.

'And your lover . . . did he kill Stephen Thayer and Tilney, and poor old Miss Harvey?'

'I don't know! Truly, I don't know. He said . . . he said he was going to go away . . . after my husband . . . after he died . . . to "cleanse himself". He said it wasn't safe for us to be together until everyone had forgotten he had been on the safari when Makepeace was killed. He told me that knights of old, having pledged their troth, would go on a long journey to earn their lady's hand. I know it sounds like . . . like tosh . . . it is tosh . . . but it didn't seem like that at the time.'

'It doesn't sound like the man I knew.'

Elizabeth laughed. 'You've been in Africa. Love under the stars . . .? It didn't make you feel romantic?'

'Sounds like bosh to me,' he said spitefully. 'Did you give him your stepfather's letter and the detective's report?'

'Yes,' she said in a low voice. 'And the ring.'

'The ring?'

'Yes, my mother's wedding ring . . . Max's ring. I gave it to him as a kind of pledge.'

Edward looked up at the canopy of green leaves and then across the grass to where the cricketers played, blessedly ignorant of the pain and suffering of one small boy who had also been an Etonian and had been driven to end his life before it had properly begun.

'What makes you tell me all this now? You didn't tell me before. You told me lies then.'

'Not lies – but not the whole truth. But I had to tell you – you see he came to me yesterday while you were in London . . . to claim his reward.'

'Reward?'

'He asked me to marry him . . . he gave me my ring back.'

'The ring he had beaten Verity unconscious to retrieve?'

'I'm afraid so. And I . . . I didn't like him any more. He frightened me. He was no longer my saviour as I had thought in Kenya. I now saw him as a ruthless killer. It didn't seem to be about me any more.'

'What do you mean?'

'I don't know. I suppose I felt that he wanted to take revenge . . . to kill . . . not for my sake but his own. I was just the excuse.'

'So what did you do?'

'I said I couldn't marry him.'

'And he was angry?'

'No, he was deadly calm. He asked why and I said you had . . . you had changed me. I said I didn't want any more killing . . . any more revenge. I said . . . Well, it doesn't matter what I said.'

'And he left you?'

'He left saying he had been betrayed and that . . . he would kill you. He said you were an interfering bastard and that you had come between him and his happiness.'

'He knew you were coming here today with me?'

'Yes, I had told him. He said he would see you here – whatever that means – and if I warned you . . . I too would . . . be in danger.'

'You've been very brave, Elizabeth, and you did the right thing. He's a murderer – he might think he's a knight in armour but he's just a murderer. Hoden may have deserved to die but the others . . . By the way, how did he kill him?'

'He didn't tell me how he arranged it . . . we never discussed it. I think he thought it would sully me to know the details.'

' "Sully" you! That's good . . . that's very good.'

'Edward, try and remember the hell I was in. He seemed to be the key in the prison door. I truly believed he was sincere.'

Edward felt the anger rising inside him. 'I'm sorry, Elizabeth, but all that . . . chivalrous stuff – it sticks in my throat. Getting to know me – was that part of it? Did you think I had something to do with Oliver's death?'

'I didn't know. The detective my stepfather hired said that Makepeace, Godfrey Tilney and Stephen Thayer were his chief tormentors but there were probably others . . . friends.'

'So did you find Stephen's address in the same way as you discovered Hoden's – through the school?'

'I didn't need to. It was in my husband's address book. I found it when I was going through his things . . . after he was killed. I arranged to bump into him at a party. We liked each other immediately. We were both lonely people. We saw each

other a few times. We were never lovers. I still thought then that
I *had* a lover.'

'So what happened?'

'I told him who I was. I told him about how I had married
Makepeace Hoden . . .'

'But not that he had been murdered?'

'No. I couldn't tell him that. I wrote to him . . . my lover . . .
and told him Stephen was not to blame for Oliver's death . . .
that he regretted his foolishness with Dora Pale . . . and that I
believed him.'

'So you wrote to your Sir Galahad and told him he was not
to harm Stephen?'

'Yes. I told him that the killing had to stop.'

'And did you get a reply?'

'No,' she said in a low voice.

'And how did you find out I was a friend of Stephen
Thayer's? You were lying when you said it was Hoden who
wanted you to talk to me?'

'No! He did talk about you. So did Stephen.'

'I was the reason you got a job nursing at the hospital here?'

'Yes,' she said in a low voice. 'I thought I'd get to know you
and find out what sort of person you were. I thought you would
probably be horrible, like my husband, but . . . but I liked you
from the start . . . from the first time I saw you kneeling at your
brother's bed in the hospital and that confused me.'

Edward blushed. 'I didn't realise I was being observed.'

'I wasn't spying on you.'

'Look, Elizabeth, I'm desperately sorry about what happened
to your stepbrother and I promise you I knew nothing about it.
Perhaps I ought to have known, but I was in a different house
and our paths never crossed. I wish they had. Perhaps I might
have helped him. Do you believe me?'

'I do but . . .'

'You told me you thought Hoden was being blackmailed?'

'He never said he was but he may well have been. What he
was doing was not only wicked but illegal and, as I told you, he
was getting reckless. He didn't seem to mind who knew . . .'

Edward rubbed his forehead vigorously. 'Miss Harvey!' he
said aloud. He was responsible for her death. Somehow, the

man who was here today to kill him – Elizabeth's lover and her husband's murderer – must have found out that he had talked to her and been frightened he was getting too close to the truth. He rose, unable to keep still any longer, and began pacing up and down, dragging on his cigarette. He had a growing feeling that he had made a terrible mistake asking Thoroughgood what he knew about the Dora Pale scandal.

Elizabeth watched him sadly. If only they had met in different circumstances. It was all over between them. She knew that. All over, even before it had begun. 'You don't think she could have fallen down the stairs by accident?' she faltered, reading his thoughts.

'Well, do you?' he said roughly. 'I've got to find your para-mour before he finds us or rather me – and you're going to help. Come on!'

Looking for a murderer at an Eton festival was rather easier said than done. The boys might be wearing colourful waistcoats but their fathers and uncles were dressed in a uniform from which no deviation was permitted. The black coats, the stiff white collars, the faces of the men half-hidden by top hats – only the presence or absence of facial hair differentiated them.

They marched across the acres of green playing fields until Elizabeth complained that she was about to drop with exhaustion. 'Can't we go and get a cup of tea?'

'I don't want to attach ourselves to Connie and Gerald just in case your friend takes a pot shot at me and damages someone else by mistake.'

'But surely he's not going to do anything like that here?'

'Maybe, maybe not. I just don't want to run any risks. It occurs to me that he might want to end his "quest" with something of a flourish.'

'Stop tugging at me!'

'I want you near me. I think it might needle him a little if he thinks you and I are . . . close.'

'Oh, so you want him to kill you? Is that it?'

'I want him to try. I can't imagine it will be possible to find enough evidence to charge him with the murders in Spain or Africa, but he left a clue when he murdered Stephen Thayer and I think he knows he did. You see, he killed him on an impulse. He must have confronted him and they talked and, when Thayer turned his back, he killed him with a heavy ornament. He hadn't come prepared to kill, I'm almost sure of it. In his hurry, he dropped something – something he knows I noticed and which associates him with the killing. I want him to try to kill me though I'd rather he didn't succeed,' he added grimly. 'If I can get him to attack me, I think even Chief Inspector Pride would have to take me seriously.'

'The police? They're here?'

'Yes, I alerted Pride to what I thought might happen today and most grudgingly, I have to say, he agreed to place a few men in the grounds.'

'And they know who they're looking for?'

'They do, Elizabeth. What you told me today only confirms what I already suspected.'

26

At six o'clock, a good-natured but weary throng of parents and boys congregated on the river bank to watch the boats process from the railway bridge down river. As each boat passed the crowd of spectators, the rowers stood up one by one holding their oars upright beside them. Finally the cox rose, still clutching his rudder lines and desperately trying to stop his boat colliding with the one in front, or the river bank.

The Duke, applauding enthusiastically, leant over to Elizabeth. 'I always remember as a boy how we hoped one of the boats would capsize, but it never happened. All the more surprising because so many of them are not wetbobs but are cricketers like Charles Thayer there. Oh! Well done,' he cried as, with a final wobble, the boys successfully lowered themselves back on to their seats and rowed off. 'Didn't you once do this, Ned?' he added, glancing at his brother. Even he had wondered if his brother was feeling well; he was so absent-minded and unlike his usual loquacious self.

'Yes, once, when I was captain of the eleven,' said Edward, hardly noticing the question. Connie glanced at him and at Elizabeth, white and strained-looking, balanced on a shooting stick beside him. She could only assume they had quarrelled but she could not imagine about what.

Despite the heat of the day it was beginning to feel a little damp so the whole party strolled in the direction of Masters' Boathouse to look for Frank. They found him without difficulty and, rather at a loose end, went back to his house to rest for an hour before returning, as dusk descended, to picnic on smoked salmon and strawberries while the midges picnicked on them.

Fortified, they could enjoy the final spectacle of the day – the second procession of boats followed by the fireworks display. The Duke was tiring visibly and Connie was beginning to wish they had brought two cars so she could have taken him home.

Edward, on the other hand, had begun to relax. He had seen nothing of either Tom Sutton or Basil Thoroughgood and it seemed as though his forebodings had been unwarranted. He smiled wryly when he thought how Pride would lambast him tomorrow for wasting police time and resources. He sighed. As he had walked back through the school, the light soft and milky, Eton had never looked more beautiful: the dome of School Hall, up which he had shinned long ago to place a chamber-pot on its peak, gleamed like some creation of Brunelleschi's. Frank had begun to complain his stomach was rumbling from hunger and insisted on dashing into Rowlands, where he gobbled down a sausage wrapped in bread followed by bananas smashed in cream and ice-cream.

Edward had watched him indulgently as he gorged, recalling the savage hunger of adolescence and the supreme pleasure of satisfying it. At what age, he asked himself, did one cease to crave food and was it then one also began to lose that other hunger – for life itself? He was not one of those who believed that his schooldays had been the best years of his life – far from it. The years which followed – Cambridge and then adventuring in South America and Africa – had been in many respects richer and more rewarding but, somehow, seeing Frank at Eton – earnest but eager, his expectations untarnished by disillusion – he began to feel a twinge of nostalgia for the world he had lost.

He suddenly became aware that the rest of the party were looking at him. He had been asked a question but had no idea what or by whom.

'I say, Uncle Ned,' said Frank, 'you are all right, aren't you? You seem very far away.'

'Oh yes, I'm afraid I was,' Edward said, lighting a cigarette. 'I was thinking of my own schooldays and lamenting that I hadn't lived up to the hopes m'tutor had of me – or *said* he had of me – when I left. Anyway, considering he had ignored me for four years, I don't suppose he knew what he was talking about. Why do we old folk talk such tommy rot to the young? What do you say, Frank?'

'You're not old and you've never talked rot to me, so stop feeling sorry for yourself, Uncle Ned.'

'Come now, Ned,' said Connie, 'everyone agrees you will reach the very top, if you bother to apply yourself.'

'The top of what?' he replied drily.

'The FO, politics – anything you like,' the Duke said crossly. 'Damn it all, I can't do anything because of Mersham and so on, but you ... well, you only need the love of a good woman, what?'

Connie, seeing her brother-in-law visibly pale, broke in hurriedly. 'Well, Frank, I think it's time we walked back to the river. We must be sure of our places for the procession of boats.'

It was delightful to be beside the river once again. True, the midges were making everyone scratch but the water glimmering in the near darkness, the feel of so many people gathered together for one purpose, the growing excitement ... it was a special occasion.

'I do believe if we were in Italy, or anywhere but pagan England, we would expect the procession to be religious: an effigy of the Virgin carried aloft by churchmen with boys singing psalms,' Connie said, 'but we English dress our schoolchildren in the clothes of a past century and make them perform acrobatics! It's wonderful, but quite absurd.'

'And the boys watching here on the river bank are dressed in mourning for King George III who died – I don't know – over a hundred years ago,' added the Duke.

In the darkness, Edward leaned his head against Elizabeth's and squeezed her hand. 'Don't worry,' he whispered, 'nothing will happen.'

'Oh, but it has, it has,' she murmured. In an effort to show he was enjoying himself, Edward regaled the company with an account of how in Chile, the May Christ is paraded about Santiago on the shoulders of the faithful and worshipped as a protector against the dreaded earthquakes. 'The queer thing is, if they try and take the crown from round Christ's neck – the result of an earthquake a century ago – something dreadful happens.'

As he talked, he thought he caught a glimpse of the man he had been waiting for, and his heart missed a beat. Calmly, he concluded his story, while considering what was the best thing to do. He had no wish to evade him – it was a meeting he had been anticipating all day – but he had to avoid bringing danger to anyone but himself. This was a private matter. He whispered to Connie that he was going to stroll up towards the weir where the boats turned before floating downriver. Sensing that there was something more to this than the need to stretch his legs, she said anxiously, 'Oh but Ned, do you have to?'

'I won't be long, I promise,' he replied, removing her hand from his arm. Frank and Elizabeth were a few feet away peering at the river, so he was able to escape without anyone else noticing. The Duke, whose sight was not very good at the best of times, could see nothing much in the gloom.

As he walked towards the edge of the crowd where he thought he had spotted his quarry, he began to feel rather a fool. Stepping over parents and boys sprawled on rugs waiting for the entertainment, he found he had quite lost sight of him. Then, close to a wicket gate through which the spectators had passed to reach the river, he suddenly felt, rather than heard, a harsh whisper from behind him.

'You're not afraid, Corinth? You really ought to be.'

Without turning his head, he replied, 'No, why should I be afraid? I know what you have done and why you did it, but it's finished now.'

'Is it finished?' said the shadow who now came up beside him. 'I don't think so – not quite yet.'

'What can you mean? Elizabeth said . . .'

'Oh Elizabeth! I see you charmed your way into her *beaux yeux*. She told you I was earning my right to take her as my wife, I suppose?'

Edward risked half-turning. If he was going to die, he would prefer to face his enemy. In the darkness, it was difficult to see more than the outline of a face, but he had no difficulty identifying Tom Sutton.

'Yes, it is me,' he said, 'just as you thought.'

'Isn't murder too high a price to win a woman's love? Could you ever keep such a love based on so much hatred?'

'Hatred?' Sutton mused. 'Not really. Although I despised them – despised the lot of you – public school types – thinking you can do what you want in the world without caring – without imagining . . .' He seemed suddenly lost for words. Edward remained silent, curious as to precisely how he would justify the killings. 'You see, Corinth, I'm a communist and, if I could reduce this place to rubble, I would feel my life had not been wasted.'

'But, instead, you pushed an old woman downstairs and broke her neck. Very brave.'

'I didn't, as a matter of fact. She fell. I went to ask her what she had told you. Thoroughgood said you knew some of the story. But the stupid old woman wouldn't talk to me. She pushed past me to go upstairs. I called to her and she looked round . . . and fell.' His voice trailed off, but then he roused himself: 'But what does it matter – one old woman. The battle we're fighting is a class war. There must be casualties. The proletariat has to destroy people like you. The dictatorship of the proletariat . . .'

His voice died away again as if he had lost the thread of what he was saying.

'So you killed Hoden as an act of class warfare, not "for love"?'

'You can mock all you want, blast you.'

'I was just curious,' Edward said mildly. 'From what I've heard, he was a nasty piece of work but Stephen Thayer – he was my friend.'

'If you want to know, Corinth, I didn't kill Thayer. Elizabeth begged me not to. She said she had got to know him . . . to like him. She wrote to me saying that he was not the man to have bullied Oliver Federstein to death. She said maybe he had been less than perfect as a boy but . . . Anyway, if that was what she wanted, I wasn't going to argue. And I didn't kill Godfrey Tilney either. I made him sweat – told him I knew about his murky past – told him I had been sent to take revenge for what he did to the boy – but I didn't kill him. I would have done but I didn't need to. Griffiths-Jones had already been ordered to liquidate him because of his indiscipline. He said he was going to tell the world's press that the Communist Party was in league with the Nazis and bought arms off them. Well, that couldn't be allowed, could it?'

'I don't believe you! How could Griffiths-Jones have killed Tilney? He was in gaol.'

'He said you were naive, Corinth, but I had no idea just how naive. It was he who thought up the plan of getting Verity to send for you to "find" the body. You never thought it was all a bit too easy?'

'Yes, but . . . he was in gaol.'

'The prison governor, Ramón, is one of us. He gave David the perfect alibi. Let him out of gaol to kill Tilney just before you got to him. Tilney was in hiding, knowing he was in danger, but he foolishly underestimated Rosalía Salas. She was his minder – the Party never trusted him, you see. He told her where he was hiding. He needed someone to bring him supplies and news.'

'Rosalía? But she loved him! I'm certain of it.'

'She was an accomplished actress.'

'I still don't believe you.'

'Perhaps she did love him. What of it? The Party comes first. Orders have to be obeyed.'

'But if what you're saying is true, what about the ring – your ring?'

'Yes, that was stupid of me – stupid and sentimental. You know, when Elizabeth gave it to me I bought a gold chain for it so I could hang it round my neck, out of sight next to my skin. It was too small for me to wear on my finger but it meant a great deal to me. When I thought all the police had gone I went to the cave and left it there as a sign, as it were, that Max Federstein and his son had been avenged. I never thought that interfering bitch would find it. I know what it is to be an outcast – a victim of the sort of scum who drove the boy to his death. But I shouldn't have done it. I am punished for being sentimental. I thought Elizabeth loved me but . . . that's all over now. There's no place for love in this world. There are more important things . . . the Party . . .' His voice trailed off.

'So you weren't really trying to avenge Oliver Federstein. That was just "a hobby", to be pursued when Party duties allowed?'

'No, Corinth. It was Federstein who led me to the Party. It was the injustice done to him – and to me – which made me want to throw over all the corrupt bourgeois institutions . . . I might as well tell you, as we're talking for the last time. I was brought up in a children's home. Home! My God, what a travesty. If that was home, it was a home from hell. The head of the place – a clergyman no less – got the prettiest boys to sleep with him and, if we protested, we were locked up without food or water for as long as it took.'

Edward hesitated. 'So that is why you identified yourself so closely with Oliver? It wasn't love which made you hate.'

'We were both victims. Oliver died. I lived to change the world and, if possible, to take revenge for what we both suffered.'

'Was there no one to complain to . . . at the home?'

'I did complain – to the doctor who came to examine us once a month for head lice.'

'And nothing happened?'

'Oh yes, something happened all right. I was told I was ungrateful. I was told I was wicked to tell such lies about a man of the cloth. They beat me and I . . .'

'Look, Sutton, if what you say is true, I'm sorry for you but . . .'

'You're sorry? Sorry! Do you think I care if you – any of you – are sorry that my life was . . . was twisted?'

Edward said gently, 'An evil man did you a terrible wrong, Sutton, but does that justify murder?'

'Execution not murder. I fell for Elizabeth as soon as I saw her. When she told me Hoden, that dung beetle, was . . . was one of those, I knew it was my duty to kill him – for Elizabeth, for her dead stepbrother's sake, for *my* sake, curse you. God, how I hated you when you swanned into my office with all that self-righteous arrogance, demanding my help to discover who had killed Godfrey Tilney. When you had gone – oh, how I laughed!'

The two men were walking beside the river along a path narrow enough to force them to press against each other like lovers. The path was one used for coaching fours and eights – the coach bicycling dangerously, one hand on the handlebars, the other clasping a speaking trumpet through which he could urge on his crews. Edward remembered that the path ended by the weir, a long way from the crowd watching the procession of boats. He had no idea where Pride's men might be, if indeed they had not already gone home, and in any case, the likelihood of anyone having seen him meet Sutton was remote. But he was strong and, as far as he could see, Sutton had no weapon. He must keep the man talking until an opportunity arose to . . . to what? Take him into custody? He supposed so but, unless Sutton was prepared to repeat his story in the presence of witnesses, he couldn't see how anything could be proved against him to a jury's satisfaction.

'Edward, are you all right?'

The question, from the darkness behind them, startled both men.

'Elizabeth!' Edward exclaimed. 'What are you doing? Why are you here?'

'Frank and I saw you slope off and we followed you.'

'Frank? He's not with you.'

'Yes, I am,' the boy replied indignantly from the blackness. 'I couldn't let Elizabeth come alone, could I?'

'I'm glad you're here,' Sutton said. 'I was going to come and find you after . . . after I had dealt with your friend here. I've done what you asked of me but it's over between us. I've got duties . . .'

He spoke with a kind of hopeless gravity, as though he were reporting for duty knowing that he was to be sent on some impossible mission.

'Oh, Tom, Tom. I wish I'd never shown you that letter from my stepfather . . . never involved you.'

They had all stopped in a small clearing beside the river. The moon had risen from behind the trees and illuminated the scene. They could hear a dull roar, which Edward at first thought was the crowd they had left watching the festivities but then he realised that what he was hearing was the water sliding like a silk sheet over the weir to crash down on the other side. They had reached the stretch – almost a pool – in which the boats turned before floating back past the waiting crowds. He heard the splash of oars and clear, high voices from the boat coming towards them. At any moment, they would be in sight of each other. He wondered if he should call out and ask the boys for help, but that was ridiculous. They would think he was some practical joker and, even if they did take him seriously, there was nowhere they could land. Three or four feet of weed and rushes formed a treacherous fringe along the bank.

Edward cursed silently. Elizabeth, Frank! He had tried his best to remove himself, and the danger he might be in, from those he cared about. Instead, he had brought them all together in a place where no one could come to their rescue. He must hurl himself on Sutton and pin him to the ground. It shouldn't be difficult. He looked at Sutton and saw his eyes staring towards him – glittering in the moonlight – as if they read his every thought. Something else shined silver in the moonlight. He saw a small revolver in his hand – so small it would be useless except at close quarters. But that was precisely where he was – at close quarters – no more than two feet away from Sutton and with no chance of running.

Elizabeth said, 'Oh God, Tom, why was I ever so wicked as to turn you into a . . . a murderer? It's true. The sorrows of one generation become the sorrows of the next.'

Sutton turned on her furiously. 'I'm not guilty of murder. I'm a warrior . . . an executioner. I loved you, Elizabeth – but now it's over. It was *you* who betrayed . . . the cause.'

'But my friend's father?' Frank's cool, clear voice cut between them like a knife. 'Why did you have to kill him? Why did you? He wants to know.'

Edward saw Sutton's eyes swivel towards the boy lurking in the darkness. He tensed himself to jump but Sutton saw him move and pressed the gun against his stomach. 'No!' he shouted, meaning, Edward thought, that he must not think of trying to wrestle the gun off him. Or was he denying any responsibility for Stephen Thayer's death? Whatever he meant, Edward did not have time to discover. Frank, brave but foolish boy, hurled himself on to the back of the man he believed had killed his friend's father, tugging him backwards. Unfortunately, he was not strong enough to pull Sutton to the ground and merely unbalanced him. To steady himself, Sutton raised the arm holding the pistol and, as he did so, it went off. Edward felt a sharp stab of pain in his shoulder. With a cry, he lunged at Sutton as though attempting a rugger tackle and managed to pull him to the ground.

The sound of the gun going off, Edward's cry and Elizabeth's screams reached the eight struggling to turn their boat before floating back downstream. Only it wasn't an eight; it was Monarch, the ten-oared boat which Charles Thayer was coxing. Charles, in mid-turn, relinquished his hold on the rudder and half-stood to see if he could identify the source of the noise from

310

the bank. In doing so, he managed to upset the clumsy old boat and, with a mighty splash, it turned turtle. No doubt, this disaster would have been merely farcical in daylight or if the boys had not drunk so much strong cider but in the darkness, with the current dragging them towards the weir, there was real danger that they could become caught up in the oars still attached to the upturned boat or trapped under it.

Edward, hearing the boat capsize, released his hold on Sutton who threw off Frank and got to his feet. He had no pistol now – it was somewhere in the undergrowth – and he looked about him for a way of escape. Elizabeth, who had been watching the water, cried out, 'Charles, I can't see Charles.'

For a moment, the two men and Frank hesitated, staring across to the water which foamed white where the crew was thrashing about. Some were even laughing. Charles was nowhere to be seen.

Edward said, 'I can't see the boy. I think he might be trapped under the boat. I'm going to swim out there.'

He started to peel off his coat and cried out in pain. There was no question of his being able to swim anywhere. Frank had already taken off his coat and shoes and now leapt into the water but, as he thrashed about in the weed and rushes, Edward had a terrible feeling that the whole ridiculous business would end in tragedy. Time had gone into slow motion. Charles was going to drown and he was standing on the river bank unable to do anything about it. Then, beside him, he saw Sutton, coatless and shoeless, dive clean as a knife over the rushes into the dark water. It was quite deep, even at the edge of the pool, and Edward saw him cleaving through the water using a power-ful Australian crawl. For several minutes, nothing could be seen from the bank. Elizabeth helped Frank back on to the bank and then two or three boys from the capsized boat arrived and also had to be helped through the reeds on to dry land.

'Look!' Frank cried. He was dripping, covered in evil-smelling mud, his hair plastered across his face. He was pointing out into the pool.

'I see him!' Edward shouted. 'Quick, Frank, I think he needs help.'

Sutton was swimming with one arm, using the other to

support Charles. It was obvious the boy was unconscious because he made no effort to help himself. With a splash, Frank jumped back into the water.

'The weir makes the current treacherous,' Edward shouted above the cries and splashes of the boys making for the bank. 'You, lad,' he called to one of those swimming towards them from the boat and who, miraculously, still wore his straw boater, 'you over there, help that man!'

With considerable effort, covering themselves in mud and weed, they dragged the half-drowned boy on to the bank.

'Stand back,' Elizabeth said, once again the competent nurse. She turned Charles on to his front, squeezing and pumping the water out of his lungs until the boy's reflexes took over and he vomited.

By this time, other boats turning to join the procession had appeared. Soon there were chaotic scenes as the coxes tried to avoid the capsized Monarch, while their crews twisted and turned to see what had happened.

'Are you bleeding?' Elizabeth asked Edward distractedly. 'I can't see in this light. We've got to get Charles somewhere warm and dry. Oh, who's that?'

It was Fenton. Connie had become increasingly alarmed at the length of time Edward, Frank and Elizabeth had been absent and she had gone off to where the cars were parked to seek reinforcements. There she found Fenton smoking Craven A and had urged him to go and find out where they had got to. He had been only a few hundred yards away when he had heard the shot and Edward's involuntary yelp of pain. As he ran into the little clearing beside the weir, he saw Elizabeth kneeling beside Charles who was wrapped in her cloak. Taking her words as an instruction, he caught the boy up in his arms and – with surprising strength and gentleness – carried him back towards the car. Edward followed with Elizabeth and Frank, the latter soaked to the skin but otherwise unharmed. Sutton, to Edward's relief, had disappeared.

As the little party walked through the trees back to the car they bumped into Connie and Gerald.

'It's all right,' Edward reassured them. 'Nothing to be alarmed about. Charles has had a wetting, that's all. Monarch capsized.'

'Goodness me!' Connie cried in alarm. 'He's not hurt, is he?'

'He's rather water-logged but he'll survive.'

'And Frank dived in to save him,' Elizabeth added.

'Frank, come over here. I can't see in this light. You're wet through. And Edward – what's wrong with your shoulder?'

'Let's get back to the car and drop the boys at their houses. Charles has had a bit of a fright and his Dame will probably want to see he's all right. And Frank . . . you're all right, aren't you?'

'Yes, but . . .'

'Another time, old lad. I've just got one or two things to clear up and then I'll come down and give you and Charles a full report. Until then, the less said the better, eh Frank? Connie, I've managed to catch a bullet in my shoulder. Nothing to worry about. Elizabeth's patched me up for now but we might call in on the doctor if he's still awake when we get back.'

'A bullet! What on earth . . .?' Connie caught Elizabeth's eye and stopped. The bullet was obviously not something to discuss in front of Gerald. The Duke seemed unable to take in what had happened and Connie and Edward tacitly agreed that he should not be enlightened. He was half-asleep and showing signs of exteme fatigue. It was enough that he knew the boys had fallen in the river but were otherwise unhurt.

'Shouldn't we go to the hospital?' Connie said in a low voice.

'No. I don't want a lot of questions and hospitals have to report gunshot wounds to the police.'

Further conversation was made impossible as, with a crack and several bangs, the firework display began. The sky was lit up with coloured stars, showers of gold and silver, and a rocket pierced the black-velvet sky to break above their heads in a glorious umbrella of fire. Everyone except the boy in Fenton's arms involuntarily raised their heads to watch the night sky transformed into light and colour. Then, at Edward's urging, they continued their trek. He put his good arm round his nephew's shoulders and whispered in his ear, 'Frank, you're a brave boy and I probably owe my life to you. And Charles . . . you did what I couldn't do and tried to get him out of the water.'

Frank raised his head and a smile lit up his face as brightly as one of the brilliant flares illuminating the sky.

'Did I really, Uncle Ned? I thought perhaps I had made things worse.'

313

'Not at all,' Edward assured him. 'But say nothing to anyone about what happened tonight between that man and me. We saw Charles fall into the water and, when he didn't surface, you went in after him.'

'But who was the man?'

'Someone I know – someone who had a grudge against Charles's father but he wasn't his killer, I think. I promise I'll tell you about it but, for the moment, I'd like to keep it all quiet. Do you understand?'

'Yes, but . . . your shoulder?'

'I'll get that seen to as soon as we've dropped you two off. It hurts like hell but I don't think it's very serious.'

The boy said nothing but squeezed his uncle's undamaged arm. As they reached the car, he said, 'Uncle Ned, is it all over?'

Edward looked at his nephew gravely. 'Not quite over for me perhaps, but over for you and Charles.'

Then, for the first time since Frank was a small child, he kissed him – on the forehead. 'Over for you,' he repeated.

27

'How's it feeling . . . your head?'

'I'm perfectly well, thank you, Edward.'

'Well enough for me to take you out tonight after the play?'

'Certainly . . . of course.'

'Why do I get the feeling you're cross with me?'

'Why should I be cross with you?'

'That's what I wanted to know. Is it because I had to do without you . . . I mean, in England? It was you finding the ring which was the clue connecting Tilney's death with Sutton.'

'I know. It's not that.'

'What is it then?'

'Oh, do stop asking me questions.'

'Sorry.'

They were silent. Edward had come back to Madrid eager to tell her about Tom Sutton – how he had saved Charles Thayer from drowning and then disappeared. 'Vanished off the face of the earth,' he would have said, but she had not questioned him. She had not been suitably interested in how he came to have a bullet wound. He had been all prepared to shrug off his bravery under fire – well, not literally of course. That would have been too painful. She had not even congratulated him on almost managing to catch a murderer. In a way, he was relieved. There were still some 'aspects of the case' – that was the phrase he found himself using to himself, as though he were a proper detective – which he would have enjoyed puzzling out with her. On the other hand, there was all Sutton had told him about Griffiths-Jones, how he had alleged David had got to Tilney and shot him so that all he had

315

to do was celebrate the event. He didn't want to have to tell her that, even if it were all lies. So, maybe, it was a relief to find Verity in a deep sulk.

After a moment or two, she put out her hand and touched his. 'I'm sorry, Edward. How's your poor shoulder? I didn't mean to be irritable. It's just that ... I feel I'm missing everything.'

'How do you mean?'

'Well, you've been rushing around chasing murderers and all I've been doing is waiting ...'

'I didn't catch Sutton. No one did. You should have seen Pride's face when I reported on the night's events. He didn't want to believe me but, of course, I had witnesses to most of it – Frank and Elizabeth. He's not really interested in Makepeace Hoden's death – I can understand that. That's not his problem and he as much as told me it wasn't mine either. However, to find there was a spy at the Madrid embassy and then let him escape! He had the cheek to blame me; said I ought to have – how did he phrase it? Oh yes, apparently I ought to have "apprehended him". As if I hadn't had other things to worry about – like whether little Charles was still alive.'

Edward found he was burbling on to try to lighten the atmosphere. 'Pride thought I was fantasising at first, but when the embassy confirmed that Sutton had cleared his desk and, he hinted, other people's too ...'

'Stolen things?'

'Not money, but files ... secret documents ... about British intentions in Spain ... that sort of thing ...'

Verity shivered. 'I don't know what to think. His motives were good ... The Party has to act if Britain and France won't ...' She hesitated. 'But he definitely killed Hoden?'

'Hoden was the worst sort of ... Don't feel you have to mourn him, Verity. Anyway, I feel grateful to Sutton. He saved Charles when no one else could have done. If he took a life, he also gave one back.'

'So that would suggest he didn't kill Charles's father?'

'Yes, although we still can't quite say QED. Saving Charles from drowning might just have been spontaneous – something anyone would do without considering who it was. In any case, he had no quarrel with the boy. That's the most likely thing, though it *might* have been an act of contrition to save the son of the man he had killed but . . .'

'But you don't think so.'

'No, the boat capsizing . . . the boy in the water . . . it all happened so fast. I doubt whether anybody would have had time to analyse why they acted as they did.'

'So, did he kill Stephen Thayer?'

'Hard to say for sure. We don't have enough evidence but, on balance, I would say he didn't. He said Elizabeth had written to him saying she had come to like Stephen and she didn't want him killed, and she confirmed it.'

'That was big of her,' Verity said sourly.

Edward ignored her. 'Elizabeth had heard Stephen say how sorry he was that he had contributed to Oliver's anguish, that he had been bored and selfish as a young man and regretted he had been seduced by Dora Pale. He had a conscience.'

'Hmf! Very cosy. I suppose they all wept and forgave each other . . . ugh!'

'I think he wanted to talk to me about it and about Mike Nadall's amateurish attempt to blackmail him. Elizabeth thinks Pride is right and the bank was finished and Stephen was all but bankrupt . . . and that he was desperately trying to find ways of paying the investors back. Even if it meant dealing with the Nazis, and even though his conscience told him it was wrong.'

Verity snorted. 'I don't believe a word of that. He was just a capitalist exploiter who was about to get his come-uppance.'

Edward was silent. He thought Verity was, consciously or unconsciously, trying to lead him away from accusing David of . . . anything. She had decided that Tom Sutton, whom she had never liked, was to be the villain of the piece. After a moment he said, 'One thing I can't forgive him for is banging you over the head.'

'Oh, that was my fault. I shouldn't have waved my hand around. You're sure that was Tom?'

'Yes, whether he killed Godfrey Tilney or not – and whatever he says, he's still our prime suspect. He left the ring – Elizabeth's ring – the ring with which Max had married her mother – in the cave as a sign that Oliver had been avenged.'

'Ugh! How macabre.' Verity shivered. 'Whatever you say in his defence, Tom was a twisted, unhappy man.'

Like David, Edward was tempted to add but restrained himself. Instead he said, 'I don't defend him. Don't forget that he got someone to put something unpleasant in Harry Bragg's food hoping to kill the both of us.'

'How is Harry, by the way?'

'He's quite recovered. He has the nerve to pretend he wasn't *that* ill and that I got the wind up and nearly crashed his "old gel".'

He saw he was failing to amuse her so he became serious. 'You really think there's going to be an uprising? A civil war?'

'I know so. David's never wrong about that sort of thing . . . politics.'

'Well then, aren't you pleased? It will be your chance to make your name.'

'Yes, and that's what I hate about myself. I feel like a hyena or a jackal, whichever it is, waiting to feed off someone else's misery.'

'You shouldn't feel that, V,' he said gently. 'You've spent months trying to alert the world – Britain in particular – to what's happening over here – that something should be done to prevent civil war. In article after article, you've argued that if the democracies do nothing it will send out the wrong message – that there is no will to fight Fascism.'

'Yes,' Verity agreed, looking a little less miserable, 'and I'm right. I know I am. If only France and Britain had given their whole-hearted support to the government . . .'

'You think it's too late?'

'David says it is.'

'You've seen a lot of him?' he asked causally.

'No. He blows in when I least expect it and then he's off again for weeks at a time. He's terribly important in the Party here, you know. The President relies on him.'

Verity looked at him with naive pride in the man she still clearly loved. Edward hadn't the heart to be angry, or even jealous, but he was sad and apprehensive. He didn't know if it was prejudice or instinct, but he believed what Sutton had told him. He believed David Griffiths-Jones had killed Tilney – because he needed to, because the Party thought it necessary. One thing was certain: he could never *tell* Verity that he believed her lover to be a murderer. She had to arrive at that conclusion herself. If Edward accused David, she would see it – however unreasonably – as an attack upon herself. He had to let her find out for herself what kind of man it was she loved. And that meant – it made him sick at heart to admit it – allowing her to go off with this man into God-only-knew-what danger. It wasn't that he thought Griffiths-Jones might hurt her. He wasn't that sort of a brute. He was a cold-blooded killer of anyone who came between him and what he was trying to achieve. 'The ends justify the means' – that was what he would say. In any case, reluctantly, he had to admit that, as far as Griffiths-Jones was capable of loving anyone, he probably loved Verity and, more importantly, she was useful to him and to the Party.

He took a deep breath. 'Do you want to know the rest? About Tilney?'

'Yes . . . yes, of course I do. Tell me – you knew the ring I was waving around was something to do with Sutton before your Eton shindig?'

'I *guessed* because, of course, I hadn't seen it.'

'Then what?'

'Well, when we found Tilney in the cave, I could see the body wasn't yet stiff – rigor mortis hadn't fully set in.'

'How could you have been so . . . so objective?' Verity said, shuddering. She was silent as she thought back to that day. Finding him like that had saved David's life but it was still a horrible sight – Tilney dead in his chair with the flies buzzing in and out of the hole in his head like bees round a hive. 'What else?' she said at last.

'Well, we had been with Belasco quite a lot of the time when he might have otherwise been up in the mountains. Anyway, I can't see what possible motive he could have for killing Tilney.'

'I remember you saying he had been shot with a small gun – a woman's pistol – like the one Sutton used on you.'

'Yes, and he had been shot at such close range. It must have been someone he knew quite well, or was even expecting.'

'Perhaps the murderer stole up on him while he was asleep – you know, like Claudius in *Hamlet*.'

'Possibly, but you may remember that Tilney's pipe was close by his body. You don't fall asleep when you're smoking a pipe – at least I doubt it.'

'The murderer could have been a woman – at least in theory.'

'Yes, I wondered if Rosalía had done away with him but her grief was real enough.'

'But why did she agree to take us to his hideout?'

Edward paused. 'Sutton says she is – and was – a member of the Party and under orders.'

'Orders?'

'Orders to take us to him and so provide David with his alibi.' He looked anxiously at Verity to see if she realised what this meant.

'I don't believe anything Tom Sutton says . . . not any more . . . not without evidence. Rosalía has been a good friend and I don't believe she would ever have put us in danger.' She paused, and then said firmly, 'Who are our other suspects?'

'Maurice Tate for one. We know he hated Tilney. He had tried to blackmail him about his homosexuality. But I found out that Maurice was rehearsing the play when he ought to have been in the mountains killing Tilney. There were plenty of witnesses.'

'What about Hester? You've ruled her out?' Verity said brutally.

Edward tried to answer her as objectively as he could. 'Yes, I did. I thought for a moment that she might have had a motive.'

'What motive?'

'Well, not a motive exactly, but she is Jewish and I had it in mind that a Jew might want to avenge the destruction of a Jewish family but I became convinced she knew nothing about Max or Oliver Federstein. That was a burden Elizabeth had to carry.'

'Revenge for a death so many years ago? It does seem . . . I was going to say "unbelievable".'

'Suicide's not an accident, V, and you know that Elizabeth felt bound to carry out her stepfather's last wish. And you also know why Tom Sutton identified so closely with Oliver. There are always reasons behind a suicide. A suicide which, in this case, led to a father's despair . . . bitter wounds, bitter guilt! I guessed it must be something like that when the horrible little man – Mike Nadall – told us the rest of the story of which Miss Harvey had told me the first part.'

'Revenge is a dish best taken cold,' Verity mused. 'It's a strange story but then English public schools are such strange

320

institutions. I mean . . . does any boy come out at the end of his schooling at one of these places undamaged? I only ask out of curiosity.'

'We learn to run the empire,' Edward said in mock seriousness.

'Pooh! You can't even run the country let alone the empire and, when we come to power, you know what will be the first thing to go?'

'The public schools?'

'Yes, of course, but I really meant the empire. It's an anachronism. The masses are kept down by . . .'

'Quite,' said Edward hurriedly.

'It's lucky, isn't it, that David was in gaol when Tilney was murdered?'

'Very fortunate,' said Edward solemnly. It's certainly where he ought to be, he added, but not aloud.

'He had a motive after all. Tilney didn't approve of him buying arms for the government from . . . wherever he could.'

'From Fascists,' said Edward, rubbing it in.

'The corrupt may be corrupted,' she responded sententiously.

'That's what David says, is it?' Verity scowled at him. 'Please don't tell me the ends justify the means,' he said. She scowled even harder.

'As I understand it – and this is David's story as far as he's prepared to tell it to me – Tilney needed to "disappear". He wanted his enemies to think he was dead while he did what he had to do for the Party. Afterwards, he was supposed to come back to Madrid, explain breezily that he had been away visiting friends and hadn't heard all the hoo-ha and David would use his "get-out-of-gaol-free" card.'

'Right, but he didn't come back because he wanted David dead at the hands of the Republic?' Edward suggested provocatively.

'He didn't because he had been killed by Sutton,' Verity corrected him.

'It's odd that, isn't it? Why did Sutton leave it so long before killing Tilney?'

'That's easy! He didn't know Tilney was still alive until he heard that David had asked you to go up the mountain and find him. As a spy, he must have known where Tilney had his base camp – and he went there to kill him before you could find him alive – to fulfil his "quest".'

'Yes, that must be it,' Edward agreed. 'He thought Tilney was dead so it must have been a nasty shock to discover he had tricked him and was just pretending.'

'Do you think Tilney was aware that Sutton was after him?'

'Probably. Sutton said he had hinted that he knew Oliver Federstein's story. He wanted to see Tilney sweat.'

Verity brooded for a minute and then said, 'Let's talk about Stephen Thayer. It's queer Tom was so easily persuaded by Elizabeth not to kill him, isn't it? It doesn't ring true to me.'

'Well, it's hard to say. He may have wanted to concentrate on politics and the impending revolution. He had orders from the Party which probably didn't include taking time off to go back to London and murder someone. After all, he didn't have a particularly strong motive. I mean, no one has accused Stephen of . . . of liking boys. In fact, it looks as if he did everything he could to protect Oliver from Hoden.'

'He might have had a motive. What if he was jealous of Elizabeth's friendship with Stephen? Perhaps he thought it was something more than that? Maybe he thought she had betrayed him.'

Edward considered this. Then he said, 'It's just as likely Sutton had got sick of the "quest". Absence doesn't always make the heart grow fonder. Maybe he didn't feel as intensely about Elizabeth as he had in Kenya. We don't know.'

'Maybe Elizabeth did ask him to give it up and stop the killing . . .'

'And he refused? If he did kill Stephen, I don't think he meant to. The fact that the killer didn't use a gun suggests he – or she – hadn't brought one. I think the killer tried to reason with Stephen – perhaps get an apology out of him. As I imagine it, they talked for some time before something happened which made him – let's call the killer "him" – pick up the nearest heavy object and hit him over the head. Perhaps even then he didn't mean to kill him.'

'Why did Thayer turn his back on him? He must have known he was talking to someone who was a threat – even mad?'

'We can only guess, but Stephen wasn't lacking in courage.

Let's say it was Sutton. Stephen tells him how much he regrets Oliver's death, how he did what he could to protect him from Hoden's bullying. He offers him a cigar and they smoke together – Stephen thinks he can relax. He takes Sutton's glass to "top it up". He turns with the tumbler in his hand and says something which enrages him.'

'Hold on. No drinks. Sergeant Willis said there was no evidence that Thayer had offered anyone a drink.'

'No, you're right. We'll never know exactly what happened but Stephen could be very arrogant.'

'Was he anti-Semitic? I mean, you said that might have been Hester's motive for murdering Tilney, in revenge for his having persecuted Oliver because he was Jewish. Maybe that's also a motive for Stephen's murder. Perhaps, just when he thought he had calmed his visitor, he let on somehow that he was doing deals with the Nazis and that caused . . . the explosion.'

'He wasn't particularly anti-Semitic – just the usual.'

' "Just the usual",' Verity repeated bitterly.

'Sorry?'

'You said, "just the usual" – the usual anti-Semitism.'

'Yes,' Edward said, 'I did, didn't I. I'm afraid it's true, though. I'm not saying anyone approves of the way the Nazis are treating their Jews but . . .'

' "*Their* Jews"! Edward, sometimes I think I hardly know you.'

'I'm sorry,' he said and was silent.

'It's convenient that Sutton's disappeared, isn't it?' she said at last. 'Could we prove anything against him?'

'No. We have to face it: Sutton has nothing to fear from the British police. Pride is only investigating Stephen Thayer's death, not Hoden's, not Tilney's. And unless he has turned up something we don't know about, the only hard evidence we have is that the photographs of Thayer's body show that the killer dropped a fountain pen and a matchbox from Chicote's beside the body. You wouldn't hang a dog on that.'

'They might hold him for spying?' Verity thought for a moment. 'It's a problem for any Communist Party member if they work for the British government. Is it better to try and influence policy from inside or does there come a moment when one has to choose between betraying one's country or one's principles? Thank God, it's not a dilemma David or I face.'

323

'Not yet, anyway,' Edward said grimly.

'You know who else was in London when Thayer was murdered?' Verity said slowly.

'Who?'

'Maurice Tate.'

'Maurice? But the play, he was rehearsing the play!'

'No, his mother was ill, he said, and he dashed back to London. He was away for forty-eight hours. Long enough . . .'

'Oh God, why didn't I know that?'

'Because you left me to do the questioning and I got knocked on the head before I could report back.'

'So Maurice could have knocked you on the head to prevent you telling me . . . in which case you may still be in danger.'

'Not just me. He'll assume that I've already told you.'

'Oh God, I'm so confused and yet, just a few hours ago, it all seemed so clear!' Edward cried in frustration. 'Well, I'll wire Pride and get him to investigate Maurice's mother and see if she is ill or well or not even alive. Tell me, Verity, could any of our other Madrid friends have been in London when Stephen was murdered?'

'No, everyone else was definitely here . . . except David, of course. I don't know where he was.' She laughed. 'He said he was on Party business somewhere and I assumed that meant here in Spain, but it could have been Germany, England or anywhere else. He's learning to fly, you know. He thinks it might be useful if there's a war . . .'

She stopped chattering and looked at Edward, seeing his face, suddenly serious. 'You don't really think . . .'

'Verity, I'm just so . . . I don't know what to think. Look, I'm going to leave you in peace while I go for a walk and send that wire to Pride. If you'll let me, I'll come and fetch you at eight and we'll go to the Institute together.'

'Oh, I'll be all right . . .'

'I think it would be safer,' he insisted.

'Very well, but it's not necessary. Off you go then,' she said, struggling to sound cheerful. 'By the way, Edward, there was something I've been meaning to ask you and keep forgetting. Before you went back to London, you said you had two questions to ask: one for Sutton and one for Hester. What were they?'

'I asked Sutton if he was Jewish and he said he wasn't. And I asked Hester what was her maiden name.'

'Hester? What do you mean?'

'Hester's been a little mischievous. She confirmed what I had already guessed: before she was Baroness Lengstrum, she was Hester Belasco. She's Ben's sister.'

'But I ... I don't understand. Why didn't she tell me? What was she hiding?'

'Nothing sinister though for a moment I thought it might have been. It began as a sort of joke. She and Ben have always been very close. Their parents were divorced when they were children and they were tossed about from pillar to post. They found they could only rely on each other. As you know, they both tried marriage but for whatever reason – perhaps because of their own childhood experiences – neither marriage had a chance of success. So, when they teamed up after Hester's fiasco with that poor blighter Lengstrum, they decided not to advertise their relationship. Much as she loved him, Hester didn't approve of the way Ben behaved, particularly with women ...' Verity blushed but Edward pretended not to notice. 'Ben, for his part, thought it was a good prank. He knew everyone would think Hester was or had been his lover.'

'Damn him! Damn them both!'

'Oh, don't be sore, V. They told you no lies. It was just that it never occurred to you to ask. Hester's been a good friend to you. Ah, talk of the devil! Here she is!'

Hester put her head round the door and said, 'Honey, are you mad at me? I guess you've every right to be ... '

Edward slipped out of the room and left the two women to it. The other side of the door he paused and smiled to himself. Verity did not like being made to feel ridiculous. He was sure she would forgive Hester for the trick she had played on her but Ben Belasco ... Was it too much to hope he wouldn't be forgiven?

28

It was odd, Edward thought, when Madrid was awash with rumour and counter-rumour that so many Spanish had decided to spend the early evening in the stifling heat of the British Institute watching a performance of *Love's Labour's Lost*. But Madrid was always agog with gossip, political and social, and the Institute was as convenient a place as any to carry on this activity. Verity had insisted they sit in the front row – 'in order to give Maurice our full support' – alongside Hester and Ben Belasco. Edward would have preferred to be at the back where he could make a discreet exit if he so wished. He thought he might very well so wish. He normally avoided amateur dramatics; they were at best charming – particularly if one had a child of one's own on stage – and at worst boring and embarrassing. And *Love's Labour's* . . . it was such an abstruse play. He still could not see why Maurice had chosen it. The wordplay was difficult for the English to make head or tail of, let alone the Spanish. He tried to think what he would feel like being made to sit through a play by Lope de Vega – in Spanish – and he shivered.

'Surely you're not cold?' Verity said irritably. 'The temperature must be over a hundred already.'

The first scene was quickly over and Edward was surprised to find that he was actually enjoying himself. The plot was absurd, of course – as if a group of men could remain celibate for three years! Could he, he wondered, if at the end of it he won . . . love? He smiled grimly. He very much doubted it.

At least the young lords in the play were acting out their charade in the open air! How perverse of Maurice to trap them in this hothouse instead of staging the play outside as he had originally proposed. 'Our court you know is haunted by a refined traveller of Spain . . .' That was good! The Spanish in the audience chuckled. The clowning ought to have been teeth-scraping, but somehow he found himself laughing. 'Tender juvenal . . .' Oliver Featherstone – he had been a tender juvenile. Wait, what was this? 'How mean you, sir? I pretty?' Hoden had called Oliver pretty. 'Love is familiar. Love is a devil. There is no evil angel but love . . .'

Edward's brain spun and twisted as the voices on the stage duelled, thrust and parried. He had been quite wrong. He had wanted to believe that the deaths of three Eton contemporaries – all within a few months – had been in some way linked and that he had found the connection! But it had all been too neat. He had wanted ends to tie up as they would in a novel, but Shakespeare had known better. Reality is rarely neat and men's actions reverberate in succeeding years through new generations.

In the interval, they drifted out into the street where a soft breeze refreshed them. Edward was so silent that Verity asked him what he was thinking about.

'Just what a fool I am,' he said with a half-smile. Verity snorted and went off to talk to a Spanish journalist she knew. She came back with sparkling eyes and flushed cheeks. 'He says something's happening,' she whispered.

'What sort of thing?'

'He thinks there may be some sort of uprising.'

'People have been saying that for weeks,' Edward yawned.

'As soon as this is over, I must make some telephone calls.'

'But after that, can we have supper? I've got something to ask you.'

'Maybe, if there's time,' was all she would say.

'Isn't that David?' Hester whispered in Edward's ear when they returned to their seats.

'Yes, you're right. I wonder if there's something wrong. Look, he's seen us. He's waving.'

He was about to tell Verity that her . . . her what? he wondered, her Svengali? her ex-lover? had materialised when the auditorium lights were lowered.

Edward continued to listen to the play with one ear while he puzzled things out. David: he was certain he had killed Tilney. Tom Sutton had been telling the truth when he said he only got to the cave after the body had been removed. Otherwise the ring would have been found earlier. The Spanish police weren't fools. David had denied it but the prison governor – what was his name? Captain Ramón – was his friend. What could have been easier but to give his prisoner parole? How would anyone know? Edward wondered who could tell him about Ramón's politics. He didn't doubt that he would discover he was a committed communist. If he were a member of the Party . . . What an alibi! Anyway, what did it matter? No Spanish court would, in these days of political turmoil, order one of its most important foreign workers to be rearrested in order to charge him with a murder of which he had already been cleared. It was a preposterous idea.

Makepeace Hoden; now his death he *had* finally cleared up. He had been killed by Tom Sutton at Elizabeth's urging. He had probably deserved to die. That was Edward's only comfort because, once again, he could never hope to bring Sutton to justice. He was not sure he wanted to now. At one time he had thought he had also murdered Stephen Thayer and for that murder he might have been convicted. But now? Now, he did not believe Sutton had killed him.

What was that in the play? 'Beat not the bones of the buried.' What did that mean? Don't speak ill of the dead? No, 'let the dead rest in peace.' That was it, but could he do that? His accursed conscience would not let him. 'To move wild laughter in the throat of death.' That was all he could do.

It was over: enthusiasm for the actors – for Agustín in particular – applause for the show's director, Maurice Tate, then a surge into the street. David came up to them.

'Verity, I must speak to you. I have had confirmation. The Army of Africa has mutinied in Morocco and Franco – the traitorous bastard – has taken command. General Goded has taken the Balearic Islands.'

'What is the government doing?' Verity demanded.

'What do you think?' David said bitterly, 'Nothing at all – dithering. Azaña is suicidal and the Prime Minister is in hysterics.'

'We must get down there,' Verity said decisively.

'Where? Not to Morocco, I won't allow it,' Edward broke in. 'If you two were captured, you would be shot.' Verity looked at him with interest. She had rarely seen him so vehement. The English gentleman, for whom good manners were the highest virtue, had suddenly shown steel.

David said grudgingly, 'He's right. In any case, we've got things to do here in Madrid first. The government are procrastinating about arming the trade unions and so we must do it for them.'

'The police?' Edward asked.

'They look like joining the rebellion,' David said gloomily. 'Verity, the first thing you must do is file a report for the English papers – a call to arms – the Republic in danger – that sort of thing. You know what to do. It must be done at once in case the telegraph goes down. I'm going to the armoury. Join me there when you can.'

'What shall I do?' Edward asked.

'You?' David said contemptuously. 'What's it got to do with you?'

'It certainly is to do with me. Communists are not the only anti-Fascists.'

David stared at him. 'Well, if you mean it, come with me.'

The next few days were chaotic, frightening and – Edward had to admit it – exhilarating. Here, at last, was something to do – something worth doing. He helped break open the armouries and distribute weapons to the workers. These latter were men – and some women – of a type unknown to Edward. They spoke a patois he could not understand. They were clad in coarse cloth and many wore caps. Few had shirts and fewer still boots. They stank of garlic, sweat and the earth out of which they had sprung. When they smiled, which they did often, they revealed bad teeth, and few of them, but they showed no fear. This, Edward imagined, was what it must have been like in those first glorious days of the French Revolution before the hard men took control.

The Prime Minister, Casares Quiroga, resigned and his successor, Martínez Barrio, was hooted out of office by the crowd before he had even chosen a cabinet. As the government lost authority, power passed to self-appointed 'Anti-Fascist Militia Committees' who set up road blocks and began house-to-house searches through the better neighbourhoods hunting out traitors and 'class-enemies'. Hangings and lynchings became commonplace and, by the third day, Edward began to feel that he was no longer helping protect the Republic but involving himself in class warfare. David Griffiths-Jones was in his element commanding one of the most effective 'Committees' and Verity stood alongside him in a state of ecstasy. This was what she had been waiting for. This made all the hanging about in cafés worthwhile. This was the head-to-head war with Fascism she had dreamed of.

David's greatest achievement was to secure the airport and save for the Republic the aeroplanes he had bought from, among others, Nazi Germany. With a rifle in one hand and a pistol in the other, he dismissed the airport commander and replaced him with one of his own men. Hester had difficulty in saving Ferdy's life. Apparently the little man had made enemies in the Party. In a moment of madness, Edward volunteered to 'bomb up' a small de Havilland Leopard Moth which was standing on the tarmac. This consisted of laying three bombs on the empty seats for his passenger – one of David's militant unionists – to throw out of the door. This he did over the nearby Sania Ramel airfield which was supposed to be in the hands of the rebels. As far as Edward knew, his bombing raid had no effect whatsoever but thereafter he always claimed to have carried out the first aerial combat mission of the Spanish Civil War.

By the fourth day, Madrid was firmly in the hands of the Republic which meant, in fact, under the control of the Communist Party. Edward became uncomfortably aware that the Republic had fallen into the hands of faceless men trained in the Soviet Union who, whatever was said in public, had no interest in restoring the Republic. On one occasion, he was questioned – as though he were a Fascist spy – by a man from the Servicio de Investigación Militar and had to call on David to get himself released from the interrogation.

Later on the same day, as they rested briefly after their Herculean efforts to secure Madrid for the Republic, Edward expressed his misgivings to David. As he might have expected, he was treated to a lecture which confirmed his detestation of everything the Party stood for. David was quite frank, perhaps hoping to shock him.

'The Party welcomes the revolution. You think this is a fight for freedom, but it's not. It is a manifestation of the class struggle. The revolution will be ruthless in its class-based discrimination until the upper and middle classes cease to be a threat. Violence is the midwife to change.'

'Is that why you had to get rid of Tilney?' Edward broke in.

David, who was leaning against a packing case in what had been the Ministry of Defence, looked puzzled for a moment and Edward realised that Tilney's death had been forgotten. It had been merely a necessary act of cleansing.

'Tilney? Surely you're not still thinking about that? I thought you had decided Tom Sutton had done the deed.' He smiled wolfishly.

'I had, David, but I was wrong – as I have been wrong about most things.'

'Yes, you are rather absurd, aren't you? So easy to use. When I sent Verity over to get you, I never thought you would come. But there we are, "a gentil parfait knight".'

The contempt in his voice was palpable.

'Did Verity know it was just a ruse?'

'No, I thought she might not be convincing if she had to pretend to be concerned about me. Do you think I was right?'

'David, you are the most utter bastard.'

'I don't know what you mean,' he said, stubbing out his cigarette on a metal filing cabinet, and Edward thought he probably didn't. 'Tilney was a typical product of the corrupt British class system. He pretended he wanted the revolution but he had "reservations", as he quaintly put it, about the Party's methods. He didn't understand why it was necessary to bring down the Popular Front and incite a Fascist rebellion . . .'

'You admit you wanted . . . this?' Edward waved his hand towards the chaos outside.

'Of course. Revolution is a necessary first step. Don't you ever listen to what I say? Tilney didn't understand either and he didn't understand why the Party had no qualms about buying arms from the Nazis. He was a fool and, what is more important, a danger to the Party. If he had started sounding off to the press

. . . well, it couldn't be allowed. I had my orders from the highest quarters.'

'Can't you achieve your ends without . . . without murder and mayhem?'

'My ends? What do I matter? It's the Party. My wishes, my desires, my "conscience" are immaterial . . . of no importance in the scheme of things. Party workers are just agents of change – inevitable change – history working through us.'

He punched his chest and his voice carried a messianic note of hysteria which turned Edward's blood cold. Tired though he was, David lit another cigarette, smiled wryly at Edward and went out into the streets once more. The 'dictatorship of the proletariat'! Edward's heart pounded. What was that but an invitation to people like David to indulge in licensed terror? Capitalism might be all the socialists said of it – the landlords, the bankers, the politicians – he had no illusions, they were no doubt greedy and corrupt – but what did this state terrorism promise but hatred and misery continuing from generation to generation? What was that proverb Rosalía had taught him? *Por la calle de luego, se va a la casa de ahora.* By the street of *then*, the house of *now* is reached. It was at that moment he knew he must get out of Spain. He was proud to have taken up arms for the Republic but now the Republic he had fought to preserve was gone for ever, regardless of who won the war.

'Well, you go then, Edward,' Verity said that evening. She was exhausted but there was a light in her eye which made her look more beautiful than he had ever seen her. She had been transformed from an innocent, middle-class, English girl into a revolutionary – a soldier in the fight against Fascism. She could now look any Party member in the face and say with pride that she had made her mark. David had refused to give her any official position: she had to remain nominally independent. Her job was to excite the conscience of the French, American and English proletariat through her reports of the Republic's struggle for survival. Already her stories filed for the *New Gazette* had been reprinted in the *Washington Post*, the *New York Times* and in the Canadian newspapers owned by Lord Weaver.

She had another role too. There had been very few foreign journalists in Madrid when the rebellion had been proclaimed by the generals. Now, dozens were arriving from all over Europe but, for the most part, they did not speak Spanish and had no idea how to report the conflict. David ordered Verity to make sure they had their stories – stories of course dictated by the Party, telling the tale the Party wanted the world to hear: Fascist atrocities – and there was no shortage of them to report – but, more importantly, reports on the small band of almost unarmed freedom fighters dying for the Republic – angels of light at war with the forces of darkness.

'Don't you feel used?' Edward had dared to ask her.

'Used?' she spat the word back at him. 'Can't you understand? We are fighting for our life, for liberty, and we have to use every weapon at our disposal.'

He knew that men like David Griffiths-Jones did not understand the meaning of the word 'liberty' but it was more than his life was worth – perhaps literally – to say so.

'But V, should truth be twisted into a weapon? Can you touch pitch and not be defiled? You seem to have no compunction about replacing truth with propaganda.' He was suddenly very angry and, not for the first time, wondered if he really knew Verity Browne.

'Look, Edward,' she said, suddenly gentle. 'Go back home, go back to England. You mean well, I understand that. Your heart's in the right place; I admired the way you volunteered to help us . . .'

'"Us"? What do you mean "us"? You're not one of these people. You're not Spanish, you're not working class . . . And I certainly hope by "us" you don't mean the Party.'

'You know I do.'

'You are proud to identify yourself with those who kill without reason, without hesitation, like that SIM thug who interrogated me yesterday? Believe me, Verity, these are not the people you think they are, and they are not fighting for freedom or liberty . . . they just want naked power.'

They looked at each other – full of anger and sadness – and there was nothing left to say. They were in the flat Verity shared with Hester. Verity was packing a small bag. She was to go to Barcelona to report the struggle from there. At last she said, 'Edward, don't let's quarrel. We have different ways of looking at things, that's all. You go with Hester in the car tonight. You'll be in France tomorrow. Ben and I are going to Barcelona.' She saw his look. 'As comrades – nothing more.'

'On David's orders? When will I see you again?'

'Oh, I don't know. Not for a year perhaps. Who knows.'

'But I love . . .'

'Shh!' she said, putting a finger on his lips. 'This isn't the time for love. Surely you can see that? There are things I've got to do before . . . before I can think of love.'

He took her hand in his and squeezed it and suddenly she was in his arms and he was kissing her. After a moment she pulled herself away. 'Bourgeois self-indulgence,' she said with an effort at a joke. 'For a class enemy you have your attractions,' she said with an effort to smile. 'Maybe you're too nice for this world.'

'Too nice! Oh God, what a damning thing to say. You mean too weak, or too stupid.'

'No I don't,' she said, 'and don't fish for compliments. I have to go now. Please Edward, don't make a scene. Let's remember this as a good parting.'

Edward pursed his lips. 'Go then, Verity, but . . . but . . .'

He wanted to say that she was going at the behest of a murderer – a murderer whom at one moment she had been enthusiastically pursuing to bring to justice . . . but what would be the point? She would not believe him – or worse, she would believe him and it wouldn't make any difference. He couldn't risk finding that out.

Verity blew him a kiss and opened the door of the flat. Without turning, she lifted her hand in a gesture of leave-taking. It was a wave of dismissal with which he was achingly familiar.

At that moment, Hester appeared as if on cue and, for a second, he wondered if Verity had asked her to come to ease their parting – to give him comfort of a sort.

'You're off, honey?'

'Yep. Look after that booby there for me.'

'I will.'

When the door had closed behind Verity, Hester, without apology or permission, took Edward in her arms and said, 'Ben's going too. I guess we can comfort ourselves the only way we know how?'

They had dinner at Chicote's that night. It was another leave-taking – this time of the city itself. For probably the last time, they sat at their usual table and saw themselves reflected in the wall of mirrors. Despite the chaos in the city, Chicote's remained very much as it had always been: a news exchange, a meeting place in which one could gossip for hours over a beer or a small cup of black and bitter coffee. Perhaps if anything the gossip was more intense, more feverish. Rumour was elaborate, absurd, extravagant and all-pervading. This atrocity had been carried out by General Mola, this by Franco's Moorish troops – 'little better than savages', it was said again and again.

The only other people at their table were Maurice and one of his boys – a dark-faced youth Edward had not seen before. Agustín was no longer playing the piano but fighting 'somewhere down south' as Maurice put it. They had just ordered their food when, to Edward's amazement, Tom Sutton arrived.

'Surprised?' he said to Edward, sitting down. 'I don't know why you should be. Did you think I would be "behind bars"? If so, you were optimistic. I went to see Chief Inspector Pride. I had no trouble convincing him I was nowhere near Stephen Thayer when he was murdered. By the way, why does that man Pride dislike you so much? I tried to stick up for you – I really did. Perhaps he felt you had led him up the garden path. I did tell you I had never even met Thayer but you wouldn't believe me. In fact, I had what I believe is called in detective novels "an unbreakable alibi". I was with General Mola on the night Thayer died. He was good enough to offer me a bed ... Not one of my favourite men I have to say but as an alibi ... well, as I say, "unbreakable". You really should do your research, Edward, if you want to be a real detective.' He smiled annoyingly.

'Oh,' said Edward, 'I'm not a real detective. I just wanted to get justice for my friend and for his son. Absurd, I know. As it happens, though, I did know where you were when Stephen died. I asked Basil if you were in London that night and he told me you were in Spain. I got him to check exactly where you were with the ambassador. Still, I thought the FO might not like your loyalties being so obviously with the Communist Party.'

'Oh, the old dears don't want any publicity. No "show trials" for them. In any case, when it came down to it, there was no proof of anything. They knew I was a member of the Communist Party, but that's not a crime – at least not yet.'

'But you're not still working for. . .?'

'No, no – amicable parting and all that. I've got other fish to fry. I'm recruiting a "foreign legion" – volunteers from all over the world to fight for the Republic.'

Hester, who had been listening, said, 'Why did you think Tom murdered Thayer? I thought everyone knew who . . .'

Edward looked at her and her voice died away. Maurice, who had been whispering to his boyfriend, now joined the conversation. 'If we are all in the confessional mood, I suppose I had better come clean – but why do I get the feeling you already know?'

Edward said slowly, 'I did suspect Tom, but when I knew it couldn't have been him, then of course it had to be you. You were the only one of our little party who was in London on the night Thayer was murdered. You managed to leave your pen at the scene and one of these.' He picked up a matchbox from the table. 'But I haven't really discovered why. Money, I suppose?'

'Yes, money. I have . . . I've not been fair with you. I know Thayer was your friend but . . . but he was a crook. Even so, it was all a mistake. I didn't mean to kill him. I'm not a *man* – not like David or Ben – I mean, what they call "a real man". I don't kill and yet . . . and yet I did.' He looked momentarily puzzled, as if he did not quite believe it himself. 'It was my mother. She went quite senile and I had to put her in a home – a wretched place, near Godalming. But I had a bit of money. I'd saved a few hundred pounds – though not from the pittance the British Council pay me. Or rather paid me – I've been sacked, did you know? The cheek of it! No, you can't make any money working for the British Council. I did a bit of smuggling. I was quite good at it.'

He sounded surprised and rather proud of himself. 'I got together enough to pay Maggie's school fees, which were – are – frightening, but I wanted to move my mother into a better place. When I was back in England on leave two years ago, I looked for a way of investing the money so I could make enough to get

Mother into a good home I had my eye on. Of course, I couldn't invest it in anything the income tax people might notice because they would wonder where the money came from. Anyway, banks don't provide the income I needed unless you rob them. Someone – I won't say who – introduced me to Thayer. I knew it was all a bit dodgy. You may say it was all my own fault for being dishonest, but lots of people are dishonest and get made peers of the realm or Prime Minister. Well, I gave the whole thing – my little nest egg, to him – to Thayer. Then, when I was in London a few months ago to see my mother – they said she was dying – I found out it was all gone – the money – vanished – into thin air. I went wild.

'Thayer tried to tell me it was all right. He said there was some big deal brewing. I didn't believe him. As he was sitting in a leather chair in his beautiful Belgravia house – a house I could never have afforded in my wildest dreams – giving me rhubarb about what a financial genius he was – smoking Havanas, talking about his Nazi banker friends – I don't know, I suddenly snapped. It was a madness, I know it now, but I'm still not sure I regret it. As he turned his back on me, I got up from my chair, picked up a heavy-looking ornament and smashed him on the head. It wasn't me who did it – not the real me. I'm not violent. I don't do that sort of thing. I deserved to lose my money because of the way I had got it and for then giving it to a man like Thayer. I didn't know about the son – Charles – he's at Eton, isn't he? Of course, I'm sorry for him but I expect his rich friends will look after him, won't they? Somehow these people always seem to have rich friends.'

'And your mother?' Edward asked, feeling sick in the stomach.

'My mother? I went down to Godalming. I think I was still mad. I went into her room where she was sitting in her chair, in a filthy dressing-gown, dribbling. She didn't recognise me, of course. She hadn't recognised me for years. I stood her up and held her in my arms and I saw she had wet the chair she had been sitting on. So I wiped her dry, laid her on the bed and set her free.'

There was a silence, broken only by the chatter from nearby tables and the clink of glass. Edward saw the absolute hopelessness of Maurice's position and dared not say a word. How could he, with all his money, his servants, his grand houses, say a word against a man living on the edge of penury who had just lost the little money he had so dangerously accumulated? How could he criticise him?

'You "liberated" your mother?' Hester said doubtfully.

'I put a pillow over her face. She didn't struggle. I honestly think she was grateful.'

'Oh no! Maurice, I would never have believed you could kill your own . . . Didn't the nurses see you?'

'No, Hester, my dear,' he said gently. 'The place in which I had to leave my mother did not have many nurses. It didn't have much of anything, except misery. It had a lot of misery.'

'But if you go back to England . . .?' Edward began.

'Oh, I'm never going back to England. I'm staying here with my friend Francisco.' He put an arm round his shoulders and the boy smiled shyly, not understanding the conversation except that they were talking about him. 'He has a little money and we're going to open a bar on the Gran Vía – for the journalists and the foreigners, you know. They'll like having someone who speaks English. We'll make our fortune.'

They left the restaurant in a group. On the pavement, Edward turned to Sutton and said, 'It was you who hit Verity on the head, wasn't it?'

Sutton grinned. 'Sorry about that, old man. I'm afraid I just saw red when I spotted Elizabeth's ring on her finger. Naughty of me, I know.'

Edward stepped back a pace and punched him hard in the mouth. The blow sent him staggering into the gutter, blood dribbling from the corner of his mouth. The light from the restaurant windows illuminated the scene like some Victorian melodrama. Sutton smiled crookedly at Edward but made no sign of retaliating. 'So you care about the little cow, do you? Pity she doesn't care about you. She has *otros novios*.'

Edward punched him again, and this time, Sutton lay in the gutter too dazed to move. The wound in his shoulder ached pleasurably. One or two other people had come out of the restaurant and were gazing at the scene with interest. Maurice went to help Sutton get to his feet. Hester took Edward's arm and said softly, 'That's enough, now. He's not worth it.'

Edward hesitated and then turned his back on Chicote's and on two men who had got away with murder.

29

Edward and Hester spent two weeks driving across France. They stayed in small hotels, ate like princes and made love with the passionate energy of those who know they are soon to part. The Alfonso attracted a succession of admirers and only broke down three times – not including punctures, of course.

'To be honest, Hester,' Edward said on the night before they parted – he to cross the Channel, she the Atlantic – 'I'm rather dreading getting back to London.'

They were sipping cognac in the empty dining-room of the Hôtel Meurice in Calais. The waiters had finished clearing the other tables and were looking at their watches.

'Well then, don't go back. Come with me to New York. I guess from what you've told me you've been happy there.'

'Yes, but one shouldn't go back to places where one has been happy. In any case, I can't run away. I have to tell Charles Thayer who killed his father. I promised him and I promised my nephew I would.'

'Then, do it. Tell the truth. Children are much tougher than you think. They can deal with the truth better than we can sometimes. If, in a few years the boy discovers you didn't tell him the truth – for whatever reason – he may not forgive you.'

'You're right, Hester. You're a wise woman.'

'I am and, after *that* dinner, I think there's only one thing we can possibly do which will be better.'

The next morning, Hester drove him to the dock. She was not leaving until the following day. When it was time to say good-bye, Edward held her and kissed her. 'What will you do with the Alfonso?' he said at last.

'Sell it, before I go back to the States.'

'That'll be sad.'

'Yes, but the past still remains with us. And I'm now your past.'

'You won't change your mind and come with me to London?'

'No, honey. We've had a great time and I'll think better of English lords after this, but it's best we call it evens, don't you think?'

'Call it "quits", Hester,' he said with a grin. 'I suppose so, but you saved my life – if not my life, my sanity.'

'What did I do?'

'Gave me faith in myself to start with. I mean, I made a mess of it all didn't I? I thought I was looking for one murderer but really there were three and have I brought any of them to justice? No! And, what's more, I've seen the girl I love – you don't mind me saying that? – go off with a man I detest and despise – a killer – to do a job she shouldn't be doing.'

'Holy herrings, as you English say – that is what you say, isn't it?'

'Near enough!'

'I didn't figure on you turning out to be so passionate. I thought English lords were cold as . . .'

'Marble?'

'Ice – cold as ice!'

'What do you mean? Of course I have feelings. I feel as strongly as the next man. I feel such sadness that Spain is drowning in violence and hatred. I thought for a moment there was a "good" side to fight for, but I'm cured of that now. I feel for Charles Thayer and for his father who was once my friend. I feel for Maurice and Tilney and for little Oliver – perhaps for him most of all. And I feel for myself – I thought I loved Elizabeth but that was just spring madness. And I love . . . oh well, enough of that.'

'You poor boy,' Hester said, stroking his face. They were standing on the dockside and the rain had begun to fall. She opened her umbrella and held it over them. It was scarcely big enough and made it necessary for him to hold her more tightly. 'And do you feel sorry for me?'

'No, Hester! How could I dare to feel sorry for a woman as

340

strong and generous as you. I just hope we meet again in happier times.'

'The rain's easing. You'd better be going or you'll miss the boat.'

'I'm good at that,' he replied.

'I'm glad you don't feel sorry for me and you are to promise you won't feel sorry for yourself. I'm certain there is a job out here – a job only you can do. You have to keep faith and recognise it when it presents itself.'

A ship's siren sounded the call to arms. He kissed her once again, picked up his suitcase and walked towards the gangway. He looked back and saw her, very much as he had first seen her, a tall woman, standing immobile beside a car. When he was aboard he looked for her again but she was gone.

'So there it is, Charles. I'm afraid I didn't do very well, but I did discover the truth. I'm sorry you had to hear it but I knew you would have the courage to face up to it.'

'Yes, thank you, sir. It was very good of you to have taken so much trouble.' The boy spoke formally, as if it mattered a lot to him not to cry. Frank went over to him and reached out and took his friend's hand in his but said nothing.

They were in Charles's room in his house at Eton. The summer half was all but over. Around them was all the paraphernalia of boyhood: a photograph of his father on the mantelpiece, a cricket bat in a corner, a few textbooks on a shelf, a chess set on the three-legged table. Edward stared out of the window but saw nothing. There was no easy way of telling a child so cruel a tale.

Frank broke the silence. 'Uncle Ned, it was a good thing you decided to tell us what really happened. I mean it was *right* of you. We can face up to the truth, however horrible, but not knowing, that was what we couldn't bear. Was it Verity's idea to be honest with Charles? She seemed to me to have that sort of courage herself.'

'No, Verity's away fighting Fascists and trying to report the truth but it's all such a muddle. It's hard to know what the truth is.'

341

'I don't understand, Uncle. It seems quite clear to me.'

'Yes, but . . .' Edward began but then gave it up. 'Oh, never mind.'

'Verity's not your girlfriend yet?' his nephew said with a cheerful lack of tact.

'No, she's got other . . . other fish to fry.'

'And Elizabeth? I liked her too . . . but not as much as Verity.'

'She's gone away as well . . . to Spain. She thinks they'll need nurses there soon.'

'Oh dear,' said Frank, looking at Edward with mock dismay. 'Everyone seems to be going to Spain except you. You've gone in the opposite direction.'

'I don't know which direction I'm going in. That's the problem!'

'Love's labour's lost?'

'Cheeky monkey! Let's go down to the Cockpit and gorge ourselves on scones and jam. Do you feel up to that, Charles?'

'Poor Dad. I do miss him so much . . . but yes, I do feel hungry.'